1

For my mother, Brandy; my father, Terry; and my little

sister, Emily

You always knew this day would come,

even when I couldn't see it

Thank you for believing in me

Table of Contents

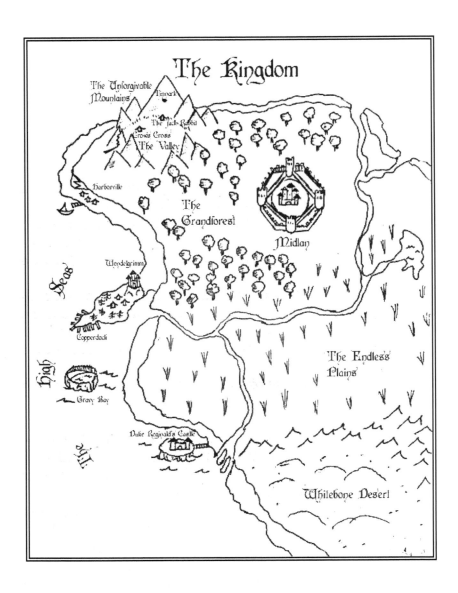

The Kingdom

The Unforgivable Mountains

Timark

The Jack Rabbit

Crows Cross

The Valley

Harborville

The Grandforest

Seas'

Wendelgrimm

High

Copperdash

Gravy Bay

The

Duke Reginald's Castle

Midlan

The Endless Plains

Whilebone Desert

Prologue
The Dragongirl

Earl Hubert pressed a delicate silver goblet against his fat lips. He sucked down three mouthfuls of wine without even taking a breath. The sound of his slurping reverberated obnoxiously off the dining room ceiling, but the servants, ringed around the walls, kept their eyes trained carefully on the floor.

A hunk of venison sat on the plate between Hubert's fleshy arms, still warm in its own juices. Steam rose from the pink grain against the chilly mountain air. He inhaled the seasoned tendrils and smacked his lips. Then he reached for his knife.

The first steaming bite was almost to his mouth when the door slammed open.

"Your Earlship!"

Hubert twisted around as far as his sizable belly would let him. He glared at the sweaty, panting guard who stumbled through the doorway. "What is it? You'd better have a good reason to interrupt my din —"

"Your Earlship, we've found her," the guard said quickly. His eyes were wild, he dashed the wet lengths of hair from across his forehead and took ragged breaths. "She's wounded — we've got her in chains. Come quickly!"

He was speaking nonsense: gasping, heaving nonsense. And in the meantime, Hubert's dinner was getting cold. "Her *who?*" he said.

The guard looked at him incredulously. His eyes grew wider; blood throbbed at the vein in his neck. His chest heaved in time with the throbbing. None of the blood seemed to be reaching his face. Not a word left his open mouth.

But he didn't have to speak. Hubert read his terror as

clearly as the panicked, hurried words of a castle scribe. All the feeling left his body and dropped straight into his gut. The knife slipped out from between his fingers and clattered to the floor. "*Her*?"

The guard nodded.

Hubert jumped to his feet. His backside toppled his chair and his belly sent the plate of venison flying. "Where?"

"The courtyard," the guard said, jumping out of the way as Hubert barreled past him.

Tapestries and flickering torches blurred out the side of his eyes as Hubert rushed down the hallway. Two sturdy wood doors loomed ahead of him, and he shoved them open with a thrust of his pudgy hands.

Evening was settling, taking the warmth of the sun down with it. Hubert pulled his fur cloak tighter around his shoulders and his labored breath came out in puffs. Summer in the mountains was just as miserable as the winter — the only real difference was the lack of snow.

As he waddled to the far corner of the courtyard, he saw that the entire guard stood clumped together. Every sword was drawn and gripped firmly in trembling hands. Along the walls above them, archers stood at the ready. Their bows were arched back and their arrows tucked under their chins. Each of their unblinking eyes was locked on the beating heart of a single target.

The guards were so busy watching their captive that they didn't hear Hubert approach. "Move!" he said, shoving through the first line. "Get out of my way!"

They scrambled to obey him — and the ones who didn't move quickly enough were bounced aside by Hubert's girth. When the guards finally parted and he could see, Hubert stopped. His legs stiffened as all the warmth left his face.

Three strides away, a young woman knelt in the dirt. Though she looked no older than seventeen, her body was propped up against the castle walls — held there by several lengths of chain that wrapped around her every limb. Locks hung from the chains in a mad tangle, holding her bonds tight.

She kept her head bent, and the dark waves of her hair hid her eyes. A steady stream of blood dripped off the end of her nose and pooled in the dirt beneath her. Every drop that struck the ground sizzled and popped — like water striking fire.

Hubert let out an astonished gasp of air. He realized that he never really expected to find her. For years, he'd seen nothing — not a charred rock or a toppled tree. Not even so much as a clear trail. All the patrols he sent to track her down never returned. He didn't know if it was the perils of the mountains that claimed them ... or her.

"What should we do, Your Earlship?"

The question brought Hubert back to the moment. The guard who spoke watched him through a swollen eye. His lip was split and blood stained the collar of his gray tunic. The gold wolf's head on his torso was covered in dirt. Several of the others had cuts and bruises. One man had his bloodied arm wrapped against his chest.

Apparently, their prisoner had put up a fight.

"We'll send word to the King," Hubert finally said. "He'll want to punish the traitor in person. But we have to be sure it's really her." He nodded to the guard with the wounded arm. "You there — pull her hair back."

The guard's face crumpled. "Your Earlship, please —"

"Do it, you whimpering lout! Or I'll have you run through." A one-armed soldier wasn't any good to him. At least if the girl managed to escape her bonds, Hubert wouldn't lose an able-bodied man.

The guard bit his lip and inched forward. He kept his body as far away from the girl as possible, and stretched his good arm towards her. His fingers barely touched her hair when her head suddenly jerked up.

The guard yelped and fell on his rump. He scrambled hand over knees to get away from her and dove into the safety of his companions, who lowered their swords and took a collective step backwards. Above them, wood creaked as the archers tightened their grips.

When he saw her eyes, Hubert's gut twisted in a knot. Now there was no mistaking who she was.

Bright green and blazing, they went straight through him. They locked onto his and burned their way into his soul. He knew she could sense his every feeling — his every fear. She must have heard how his heart raced, because she lurched towards him. Hot blood poured from her wound as she quelled the instinct to attack. She could crush him in a second — Hubert knew this well. And even though he knew the danger … he couldn't help but admire her.

It was human weakness that brought him a step closer. Beneath the dried blood that caked her face she was achingly beautiful. With the shadow of her hair and the blaze of her eyes, with the bend of her full lips set against her pale skin … she had a face that men would die for.

"Is it her, Your Earlship?" one of the guards asked.

Hubert collected himself quickly, shaking his head in an attempt to free himself from her spell: "Yes. It's the Dragongirl."

At the sound of his words, her eyes flickered. They slipped out of focus. "I cannot stay," she said. "I'm searching for something. It's very important."

The flatness in her voice caught him off-guard. There was something wrong with her. "What, no insults? No oaths of a gruesome — albeit creative — death to all who stand in your way? You're not the bloodthirsty criminal His Majesty makes you out to be."

She didn't seem to hear him. "Release me. I must leave this instant, it's very important," she said again.

The blow to her head must have knocked something loose. Yes, that was it. And with so much blood gone she couldn't possibly have any strength left to fight. Hubert might have skipped with excitement, if he thought he could actually get himself off the ground. For once, he had the upper hand.

"I'm afraid release is simply out of the question," he said, his confidence growing with every second she remained bound. "You'll stay in the dungeon for the night, and in the morning we'll turn you over to the King. I'm sure he'll want to string your traitorous carcass up with the others."

She was quiet for a breath. Then her request came again — this time as a growl. "Release me."

Hubert smirked. "No. Guards! Take her to the dungeon."

Two men hauled her up roughly by her arms and began dragging her away. Hubert smirked at her for a final time before he made his way back towards the castle. He was thinking about how he would spend the bounty gold when he heard a noise that made his heart shudder to a stop: it was the shriek of breaking iron, of chains splitting in two and locks falling away. He spun around and watched in horror as the fire in the Dragongirl's eyes swelled to a blaze.

Hubert's legs had never moved faster. He hauled himself across the courtyard, screaming for the guards to open the gate. He fell through the doors just as a monstrous roar shook the ground.

"Close them, you fools!" he said, kicking the nearest men with his boot heels as he tried to roll off his back.

One guard looked shocked. "But Your Earlship, what about the others? They'll be killed —!"

"We'll all be killed if you don't bolt that door!" Hubert bellowed over the top of him.

Fear won out over bravery. The guards slammed the doors and slid the gigantic iron bolt in place. Outside, Hubert could hear the panicked charge of men trying to make it into the castle. He covered his ears to keep from hearing their screams.

"She's going to kill us all," a man close to Hubert moaned. "We have to write to the King —"

"And tell him what? That we had the Kingdom's most wanted outlaw *in our grasp* — and we let her escape? No!" Hubert shouted. "The King can never hear about this."

They cringed as something heavy slammed into the door with a sickening crunch. Moments later, dark liquid slid underneath it, trickling along the path of the mortar. Hubert tucked his legs tighter beneath him to keep it from touching his boots.

"She wanted freedom. She'll leave when the courtyard is clear," he said, mostly to reassure himself. "But wounded as she is, she won't get far. The Unforgivable Mountains will finish her ... and the King never has to know."

Chapter 1
The Last Arrow

Kael took a deep breath. He let it out slowly.

"Today is the day," he said, for about the hundredth time that morning. He hoped that if he said it often enough, he might actually start to believe it.

A gust of wind made the tall pines creak above him. He glanced up at their towering branches and strained to see where their tops met the sky. The trees in the Unforgivable Mountains were the tallest in the Kingdom — they were even taller than the trees in the Grandforest, or so he'd read.

He was convinced he would never know for sure.

The rough surface of the branch he perched on dug mercilessly into his rump. A meager layer of skin was all that separated his bones from bark, and every few minutes he had to change positions to keep from going numb. But if his plan worked, it'd all be worth it.

He tightened his grip on the curved redwood bow clutched in his hand. The weapon was a lot like its owner: plain and thin. Every male in Tinnark had the exact same bow. He'd carry it with him always, and when he grew old and the winter frost set in his joints, he'd retire it proudly above his mantle.

For most, the bow was a symbol of freedom. But for Kael it was a burden — a constant reminder of what his grandfather, Amos, referred to as his cursed pig-headedness. And if things went wrong ...

No, he wouldn't allow himself to think about it. Not now. Not today. Instead, he would do his best to keep his mind focused on something else.

He kept a small book balanced in the crook of his lap. Its worn cover lay open across his knees, the battered pages

13

flipped to the first. Along the spine there used to be gold letters that read *Atlas of the Adventurer*, but after years of being shoved into Kael's pocket they'd faded to nothing.

The *Atlas* began with a brief history of the Kingdom's six regions. He'd read it so many times that he probably could have recited it without looking. But in the solitude of the woods he couldn't help but read it aloud, listening to the patterns of the words as they left his tongue:

"Sit at my table," Fate said to the land,
"Come roll the die and take what you can."

The Forest stepped up, so brazen was she,
And claimed for herself the land of trees.
"I'll call you Grand, the Grandforest you'll be,
Your children will eat of the fruit of the trees."

With a roll of the die the Desert did claim,
A harsh, barren land that could never be tamed.
"Fear not my child, even Whitebone when maimed,
Releases sweet juice of marrow from strain."

When the Seas took his turn, Fate said with a cry:
"You, sweet child, are far from the sky!
May your children glean bounty however they try,
And for this my child, I'll call you the High."

Then the Plains made her throw and took as her boon,
A land whose lover is the white-shining moon.
"Crops and strong children will come from your womb.
Your name will be Endless, your braids never hewn."

Then Midlan marched in, his heart all alight,
And took for himself what he thought was right.
"Your children will be of power and might,
May Kings grace your halls and war fill your sight."

But the Mountains came late; all the good land was had.

"Spurned of my brood, most Unforgivable and mad,
Your children forever in red shall be clad.
And yet unto them great strength will I add."

Though she promised them strength, as far as Kael knew Fate had only given the children of the mountains one thing. He ran a hand through the wild curls of his hair and the deep red tones winked back against the faint sunlight. The elders called it Fate's crown, but Kael thought it was more like rotten bad luck.

The other five regions all had a trade, and all were prosperous — except for the mountains. They had stone, yes, and lumber and game and perhaps if a man dug long enough, he might strike ore. But the perils were too great for any reasonable merchant to see profit in setting up shop. So while the rest of the Kingdom grew, villages like Tinnark were forgotten.

Forgotten, but not lost. For while it was common knowledge that nothing good ever came out of the Unforgivable Mountains, it was less-commonly known that plenty came into them.

Thieves, murderers, traitors and whole bands of outlaws flocked to hide themselves among the cliffs. All the worst sorts of criminals knew that not even the army of Midlan would risk chasing them through the mountains, so there they fled. The small, battered villages scattered along the rocks were the last refuge of desperate men. They may have come as thief lords or banished knights, but if they stayed, the weather warped them and the dangers changed them. Their hands grew rough from work; their skin withered in the cold.

And in exchange for sanctuary, the land erased their heritage. It didn't matter if his father had the midnight of the Grandforest or the stark white of the plains: any child born in the mountains would have flaming red hair.

The elders thought this was part of Kael's problem. They thought his hair might be the reason he tripped over things so often and why he couldn't pull his bow back all the

15

way. For while his father and grandfather were true sons of the mountains, Kael was not.

He'd been carried into Tinnark by his father — who died shortly thereafter— and grew up knowing absolutely nothing about his past because Amos refused to speak of it. From what he could gather, some feud split them apart long ago, and the wounds had never really healed. Even now, Amos refused to say his son's name aloud, and referred to him only as *That Man*.

All Kael knew for certain was that he'd been born somewhere in the Kingdom, in what the Tinnarkians referred to as the lowlands. He knew this because the red in his hair was mixed with light brown.

The other villagers never let him forget that he was different. They called him a half-breed and sneered whenever he passed. He knew what they said to one another when they thought his back was turned:

"There goes Kael the half-breed, the curse of Tinnark."

He wanted so badly to prove them wrong, to silence their whispering forever. And because of that, he'd been forced to make the worst decision of his life. His heart began to pound just thinking about it, the hand that held his bow sweat freely into the leather grip as the memory rose unbidden.

In Tinnark, a boy's twelfth birthday was a time of celebration: it was the day when he would claim his bow and take his place among the men of the village. But for Kael, that day had been just as miserable as any other.

His birthday fell on the first snow of winter — a day so cursed that families went to great lengths to make sure their children were born nowhere near it. As he'd made his way to the front of the Hall, alone, every eye in Tinnark was upon him. Most people watched him pityingly. The old women shook their wrinkled heads as he passed and whispered:

"You poor, Fate-forsaken child."

Which did nothing to ease his nerves. By the time he'd made it to the elder's table, he could hardly breathe. He stood with his arms pinned to his side and waited.

Brock, the eldest, bent his gray head and addressed him with a parchment-thin voice. "The day has come, boy." His hand shook a little as he rested the knobs of his fingers on the table in front of him. "You've earned your bow and your place in the village. But now you must choose: will you take a full quiver and accept the position we assign you? Or will you endure the Trial of the Five Arrows?"

At the time, Kael thought it was a difficult choice.

Boys who chose the full quiver would learn a trade like smithing or fishing, and they were often assigned to the same trade as their father. For Kael, it would mean being doomed to the life of a healer.

Healing was Amos's trade, and he was exceptionally good at it. But while Amos seemed to enjoy reading thick, dusty tomes with titles like *What to do if You Lose a Limb*, Kael thought he'd rather put an arrow through his foot and find out for himself.

No, healing was simply not for him. He needed to do something a little more adventurous, a little more exciting, and even though he knew it was folly, he couldn't help but dream of becoming a hunter.

The hunters of Tinnark worked throughout the seasons, enduring every peril of the changing land to keep the storehouses full. They were the strongest men, the fastest and the best shots. The elders believed they were Fate's chosen — set apart by trial and tasked with the responsibility of keeping Tinnark alive. And for that, they were treated like Kings.

But the elders never assigned anyone the position of hunter: it had to be earned through the Trial of the Five Arrows.

"What have you decided?" Brock said.

Kael knew what everyone expected him to say, and he knew what he *should* say. But when he opened his mouth, that wasn't what came out. "I want to face the Trial."

Gasps filled the Hall — and Kael thought he could hear Amos groaning among them.

Brock snorted in disbelief, but somehow managed to keep his face serious. "Very well. The rules of the Trial are simple: you have five arrows and five years to slay a deer. Bring the carcass back to Tinnark, and you will earn your place among the hunters. Fail, and the elders will assign you a more ... fitting, trade. May mercy guide your fate."

The years had passed in a blur and now Kael needed mercy more than ever. He was only a breath away from his seventeenth winter, and at this point he had no other option: he *must* succeed. That's why he'd been so careful this time, why he'd scoured the forest for tracks and followed them here.

He was perched high in the bend of a giant oak and a wide-open grove yawned out in front of him. Acorns littered the uneven ground beneath him and their shadows, elongated by the feeble light of the morning, made the earth look pockmarked. Fall was coming fast and the leaves were starting to shrivel on their branches.

There weren't many things Kael's skinny frame was good for, but hiding was one of them. He found there wasn't much difference between the width of his twiggy arms and the nearest limbs.

He'd hung his rucksack where the foliage was the thickest. It was bursting full of small game: rabbits, squirrels, and a few unfortunate geese. He wasn't a steady hand with the bow, but he'd been so intent on learning how to hunt that Roland, Tinnark's oldest hunter, had taken pity on him.

He was an old friend of Amos's, and most believed he was a strange man. But nevertheless, he saw something in Kael that all the others missed: potential. It was Roland who taught him the art of trap making.

Kael was good with his hands, and Roland said his mind worked in a way few did. It only took him a week to master the simple snare, and a few weeks more to understand the more complicated ones. And Roland was so pleased that he'd taken him on as an apprentice of sorts — teaching him everything he knew about the forest.

Though the iron sky did its best to hide it, Kael knew the sun was rising. Soon the carcasses in his rucksack would begin to smell — warning everything within a mile of his gruesome intentions. He wagered he had only a handful of minutes left to wait, and he was thankful for it. He thought he might go mad if he had to sit still any longer.

Roland often scolded him for being impatient. "The prey isn't going to jump into your lap, boy," he would say, throwing his hands up in exasperation. "And it isn't going to stand politely by while you lock an arrow on it. The woods aren't going to give you a perfect shot — you've got to make one."

Kael knew this. Somewhere, deep down, he knew there was a proper way to hunt. He just wished the proper way wasn't so rump-numbingly dull.

When a few moments passed and nothing exciting happened, his eyes wandered back to the *Atlas*. He turned the next page and ran his hand across a map of the Kingdom. He traced the deadly points of the mountains with the tip of his finger. Halfway up the tallest mountain was Tinnark. It wasn't originally marked on the map, but Roland put a tiny dot of ink where he thought it was.

Nestled in the very center of the Unforgivable Mountains was a bowl of green land. It was marked simply as *The Valley*, and Kael found he envied the people who lived there. Green was a rare color in Tinnark: if the ground wasn't frosted over, it was usually cracked and brown.

A flick of movement drew his eyes back to the grove. He glanced over the top of his book, not really expecting to see anything. And then he froze.

A young buck had materialized out of the trees. Now he stood just a stone's throw away, nibbling on acorns, his neck arched and his nose nearly touching the ground. Spring must have been good to him: his ribs were completely hidden beneath his meaty flank.

Even as his heart thrummed with excitement, Kael knew finding a deer was only half of it. Perhaps anywhere else in the Kingdom, the deer were slow and stupid. But in the mountains, they were as cunning as any man. Roland swore they were descendents of shapechangers — the tribes in the Grandforest who could take the form of beasts. He thought the mountains must have cursed them to live forever in their animal forms.

Kael wasn't sure he believed that, but he couldn't argue with the fact that the deer were blasted hard to catch — he'd once scared one off by just the thought of sneezing. So even though he was yards away, he drew his arrow from its quiver a fraction at a time.

It was his last one, his final shot at freedom. The other four had been dashed against rocks or buried in the flow of savage rivers. He couldn't hunt like the rest of his peers, with their sure feet and explosive speed. He could run for miles without having to stop for breath, but he couldn't chase a deer and shoot an arrow at the same time.

So he'd had come up with a way to lure the beasts in and face them when he was at his greatest advantage. It was an elaborate trap: he chose this particular grove for the abundance of acorns, this particular tree for its thick cover of foliage, and this particular branch for the angle of his shot. All he had to do was loose the arrow, and the force of the earth would do the rest.

There was absolutely no way he could botch it up. This deer was *his*.

He nocked the arrow and leaned forward, squinting to see through the tangle of leaves. The buck was giving him his flank: the largest target Kael could've hoped for. He drew the arrow back and his heart pounded furiously against his ribs.

In the thrill of the moment, he forgot about the *Atlas*. As he pulled the string towards his chin, the book slipped out of his lap. It clattered through the branches, its pages flapping loudly as it struck what must have been every single limb on its way down. When it finally tumbled to earth in a heap of twigs and leaves, Kael looked at the deer.

It was too much to hope that the beast hadn't heard.

He stared at the tree, his meal forgotten. His white tipped ears stood like sentries, his wet nostrils flared. His head spun away and Kael knew his body would follow. He'd melt into the trees, taking all hope with him.

He'd searched for weeks and not seen a deer — what if this was the last one he ever saw? If he didn't fire now, he might never get a second chance. This was it.

He leaned forward and fired blindly. He tried to watch his arrow as it left the string and whistled after the deer, but then leaves sprung up in front of him and blocked his view.

That's when he realized that he was falling.

He followed the *Atlas*'s path, striking branch after unforgiving branch and flailing helplessly as the earth pulled him downward. When the leaves finally gave way, there was nothing but the ground left to fall through. The world went black.

****

The first time he blinked, everything was a fuzzy mass of brown. A few blinks later, he could tell what was a tree and what was a bush. Slowly, all the feeling returned to his limbs. He half-wished it hadn't.

His elbows and knees stung. He could feel bruises rising up on his back. His head pounded in protest. He felt like he'd been tied in a sack with an angry mountain lion.

Above him, the shattered branches hung on by thin strips of white sinew. If he could hear them speak, he imagined they'd be swearing. He reached out and found the *Atlas* lying next to him. Remarkably, it was still intact. A little crumpled maybe, but readable. When he tried to roll over, something dug sharply into his rump and the small of his back. He reached under him and tugged it free.

The ache in his skull made it difficult for him to focus on what he held. Three outlines danced around, crossing over one another until his eyes managed to lock them down.

Oh no.

He brought it closer to his face and his mouth dropped open when he realized he wasn't imagining it. He forgot about the deer, he forgot about his arrow, he forgot about how much pain he was in because none of it mattered anymore.

For there, cradled in his hands, was his bow. Only it wasn't a bow anymore: it was two pieces of broken wood held together by a string.

No amount of mercy could save him now.

Chapter 2
An Unfortunate Twist of Fate

This was worse than being an outcast, worse than being teased about his skinny arms and mixed hair — worse, even, than failing the Trial. No man in the history of Tinnark had ever broken his bow. It was unheard of, un-thought of. Fate herself couldn't have devised a more wicked thing to happen to someone.

And yet, it'd happened.

He was no craftsman, but he knew it couldn't be fixed. The weapon was snapped at its grip and large splinters of it littered the ground around him. At that moment he wasn't thinking about how vulnerable he was, sitting in the middle of the forest with naught but the hunting dagger at his belt. He was worried about what he would tell Amos.

A starving mountain lion could rip him to shreds, but Amos could do worse. What he didn't have in claws and teeth he more than made up for in words. He'd never raised a hand to Kael, and yet a tongue-lashing from Amos still made him sore.

Then there was Roland, who wouldn't say a word and still somehow manage to flog him. He'd just let his mouth sag, let his shoulders go slack and let Kael boil alive under the disappointment in his eyes.

Between the three of them, he thought he'd rather tell the mountain lion first.

He turned the bow over in his hands and let his mind whir on through the protests of his aching body. There was only one thing he could do if he wanted to keep his bow a secret: he'd have to go before the elders tonight, tell them that he'd failed the Trial, and then take whatever trade they gave him.

Whatever would happen, it would be better than the truth. At least a healer was still a man.

When his mind was made up, he jumped to his feet. A likely looking patch of briars grew next to where he'd landed. He leaned over them and dropped his poor bow directly down the center, where the thorns were thickest. He circled the patch once, just to be sure, but he was certain that no one could wander by and see it.

No sooner was he finished than a loud voice bellowed from behind him:

"Well, if it isn't the Twiglet."

Two men materialized out of the forest. One was exceptionally tall, the other was exceptionally short. They were both undeniably ugly.

The tall one's name was Marc. His smile looked like a wolf's snarl, and lately he'd been sporting a patch of hair on his chin. He had a deer carcass draped across his massive shoulders, fresh blood caked the wound over its heart. He smirked as Kael's eyes wandered up to it.

"Recognize him? He's the latest deer you shot at and missed. Good thing we happened to be around, or Tinnark might have gone hungry." Marc shook his head and his face became a mask of pity. "What's it like to be a failure, Twiglet? Must be hard, I imagine."

The short one, Laemoth, wore his hair in a long braid down his back. He crossed his stocky arms and jerked his head at Kael. "Eh, he's used to it by now. If he ever did something right, it'd probably kill him."

Kael had grown calloused to their bullying. Marc and Laemoth were only a season older than him and turned twelve the same year he did. But by the time they were thirteen, both had killed deer and joined the hunters — something they never let him forget.

He wasn't surprised to find them in the grove. No matter how he tried to cover his tracks, they always followed him and killed the deer he missed. To them, it was a game. What *did* surprise him was the fact that they weren't already sprinting back to Tinnark, yelling from the tops of their lungs that he'd broken his bow.

Perhaps they hadn't noticed.

He was suddenly aware of the empty quiver on his back and the bare feeling across his shoulders. If he didn't keep them distracted, they might sprout a brain and figure out that his weapon was missing. "Yeah, and I'm sure the elders would be thrilled to hear that you wasted the whole morning tracking me down," he said, as casually as he could with his stomach twisting the way it was. "I wonder what happens to hunters who don't feed the village?"

Marc let the deer drop to the ground. He crossed the space between them in two long strides and grabbed a fistful of Kael's shirt. "Go on and tell them, Twig — and I'll snap you."

Though he thought he could have gone blind from the stench of Marc's breath, Kael stubbornly met his glare.

Marc was seriously considering knocking his teeth out — he could read it in the flint of his eyes. But though he was a stupid oaf, Marc was no fool. After a tense moment of glaring, his lip curled and he shoved Kael away with a growl.

"You know we wouldn't forget our chores, especially with winter so close," Laemoth said. He walked among the debris of Kael's fall, picking through the shattered branches, looking for something. When he found it, he grunted in triumph. "What have we here?" And he held the rucksack full of game high in the air.

Marc snarled in delight. "Well, would you look at that? We've done good today. I'm sure the elders will be pleased."

Kael knew he shouldn't pick a fight he couldn't win, but anger boiled up to the top of his head and blocked out all reasonable thought. He stomped over and grabbed a fistful of the rucksack. "Hand it over."

Laemoth laughed in his face. "Or what, Twiglet? What are you going to — ompf!"

Kael's fist struck his mouth, cutting his sentence short. Laemoth stumbled backwards and pressed his hand to his lips. When he saw the bright red blood staining his fingers, he let out a roar. He dropped his half of the rucksack, drew the hunting knife from his belt, and charged.

It was a good thing Kael thought to hold the pack to his chest: Laemoth's knife went through the surface, wounding rabbit and goose but getting nowhere close to his skin. Marc shoved him aside before he could strike a second time.

"You can't kill him."

"Sure I can! I can rip his heart out and blame it on the wolves! No one'll ever find out —"

"The old man will," Marc said, keeping his voice low. "He'll know we've done it. And he'll get us for it."

The anger in Laemoth's eyes vanished, replaced immediately by fear.

Mountain people were notoriously superstitious. Roland wouldn't step outside if it rained while the sun was shining, because he believed it meant the spirits of the dead were passing through the village. He also wouldn't leave his bow strung overnight and cringed every time he heard an owl screech.

The Tinnarkians also believed that healers could pass through death's door and trade for souls. Everyone went out of their way to respect Amos because if they slighted him, they were afraid he might retrieve their souls when they died and plant them back in their dead bodies.

And while that wasn't entirely true, Kael didn't see the harm in letting Marc and Laemoth believe it.

He made to run off when Marc grabbed him by the shirt and pinned his arms behind his back. "Keep it in the stomach. We don't want anyone to see the bruises."

Laemoth cocked his fist back and Kael knew what was coming. If he'd had any muscles in his stomach, he would have tightened them. But as it was, Laemoth's punch sailed through his feeble defenses and knocked the wind out of him.

"Next time we'll break one of your legs. Now get out of my woods, half-breed." With a hard shove in the back, Marc sent him into the trees.

Every breath felt like a knife between his ribs and the world swam in front of him, but he managed to keep his footing long enough to get away. He knew full well that an unconscious man might as well be a dead one, in the mountains. So he put every ounce of his strength into a run.

His head pounded against his ears, keeping time with the jostling motion of his legs. A strong gust of wind whipped over him, followed by a loud *crack*. The sudden flip of his stomach told him what was coming.

He forced every muscle and sinew into a dive. Not a second after his chest hit the ground, a wave of dirt and pebbles rained down on him, slung by the force of a colossal oak branch as it struck the path. His speed was the only thing that saved him from being crushed beneath it.

There was a reason the mountains were called *unforgivable*: they only allowed one mistake. One trip, one fall, one run-in with an angry bear — that was all a man could expect to get. So great were the dangers that even the King stopped trying to conquer them. The people of Tinnark hadn't been taxed in centuries.

It was several minutes before Kael's heart stopped racing, and his legs shook as he pulled himself from the ground. But for all he'd failed that day, it gave him some satisfaction to know that he thwarted the mountain's gruesome plans once again.

He imagined the trees snapped their twigs and glared as he jogged away.

******

When he broke from the cover of the trees, he slowed to a trot. A large boulder rose out of the ground to the left of the path, and he climbed it expertly.

It was his favorite view of the village. From where he stood, he could see a smatter of tiny wooden houses perched on the slope beneath him. They had the triangular shape of tents, with their roofs falling from a point to touch the rocky ground. People moved between them, scurrying along the roughly cut path like beetles through wood. They carried bundles of sticks across their backs or strings of fish in either hand. Even the smallest villagers walked behind their parents, toting a portion of the work.

Two of the houses were larger than the rest. The hospital sat at the edge of the village, close to the woods. It was the same width as an average house but roughly thrice as long. The largest building was the Hall. It stood directly in the center of Tinnark, and its roof was wide enough to hold the entire village under it for three meals a day.

A good rain might have washed it away, but it was still home. Kael wondered what people from other lands might think of it. How would it compare to the endless blue ocean, or the gentle wave of grain fields? He watched the clouds roll overhead, covering the tiny houses in one shade of gray after the next, and almost smiled.

The sun rarely shined on Tinnark. But when it did, people complained.

He knew he couldn't put it off any longer. He would have to leave the forest eventually: it was too dangerous to travel through the woods without a bow. As he jogged down the slope, he didn't look back. He knew his days among the trees were over, but he refused to let the mountains see how much it hurt him.

Next to the hospital sat the small, one-room cabin he shared with Amos. No one else wanted to put their home nearby because they believed it would invite ghosts across their thresholds. So they had the land mostly to themselves.

He pushed the battered, weatherworn door open, listening to the familiar creak of its hinges. Amos promised that he would talk to the blacksmith about having them fixed ... nearly a decade ago. But they spent so many of their days and nights at the hospital that things like creaky hinges went forgotten.

Now their hearth had more dust than ash, the holes in their roof went un-mended, and it all smelled faintly of mold.

A small family of mice had taken up residence under their floor planks. When he opened the door, they scattered

— making off with the bits of straw they'd been busily nicking out of a hole in his mattress. Their little feet tapped against the floor as they scurried into their den. He could hear them muttering to one another while he tried to find a place to hide his quiver.

In the end, he stuffed it rather unceremoniously under his bed, deep in the shadows. The shafts of light filtering through the roof were too weak to find it. And he figured that the mice would eventually become numerous enough to carry it off on their backs, anyways. So without giving too much worry to it, he left the cabin and made his way down the dirt road to the hospital.

He opened the door and wasn't at all surprised to see that the beds were nearly full. Most of the patients were fishermen— the snow melting off the summit made the rivers swell this time of year, and made fishing all the more perilous. Many nursed broken arms or sprained ankles and groaned as they shifted their weight.

In a shadowed corner of the room, a group of young women sat around one of the cloth-covered tables. They held their noses and grimaced as they sipped from earthen cups, pausing every now and then to scratch at the sickly green splotches on their necks. They must have gotten into last night's blueberry stew.

In the mountains, even the most unassuming berry had to be cooked — raw, their juices had a poison in them that settled in the throat and spread to other victims through coughs. Amos called it thistlethroat, and the remedy was one of the most unpleasant tonics in his cabinet.

Kael knew he'd been right to choose a different pot.

Just beyond the coughing women was a man who looked like he'd tangled with a beehive: the skin on his face was red and taut, stretched across the sharp lumps of his swollen cheeks. He moaned unintelligibly through his puffy lips, and Kael stopped to put more ointment on the stings. He'd read that in other regions, the bees actually lost their barbs. But in the mountains they could go on stinging a man until he crushed them ... or died.

He finally discovered Amos in the back of the room, tending to a boy with a large cut on the top of his arm. Though his hair was gray, Amos's brown eyes were still plenty sharp. Hardly a thing went on in his hospital without him knowing about it.

"Don't pick at those stitches, young man! Do you want it to turn black and rot off?" he snapped.

The boy jerked his hand away from the wound and his eyes filled with tears.

"I didn't think so." Amos wrapped the boy's arm in a clean white bandage and then gave him a serious look. "No more climbing on rotten trees, all right?"

The boy nodded stiffly. And as he left, he held his arm far to the side — as if it might fall off at any moment.

"Don't forget: you're to come see me again in one week. Tell your parents," Amos called after him.

No sooner was the boy gone than a fisherman stumbled over to take his place. He grimaced and leaned heavily on his companions — who supported him on either side.

Amos looked him over. "What happened here? A bruised knee, a twisted ankle?"

"No. Thorns," the fisherman grunted. "I was standing on a rock and when I threw my line, my boots slipped out from under me. Fell flat into a patch of brambles, I did." His friends turned him around, revealing the dozens of thorns that peppered his back. They poked through his shirt and left little rings of blood around each one.

It made Kael's skin itch to look at it, but Amos just rolled his eyes. "Oh for mercy's sake. You look like an oversized hedgepig." He led them to the nearest table and spread a clean sheet over it. "Lay him out here — no, on his *stomach*, boys! I shouldn't have to pull them out through his lungs."

When they had him situated, Amos forced a cup of sharp-smelling tonic down the fisherman's throat. He was soon snoring peacefully.

"This shouldn't take long. I'll send him home when we're done," Amos said, shooing his companions out the door. When they were gone, he walked past Kael and said without looking: "Bring me those tweezers, will you?"

He'd worked with Amos long enough to know exactly which tweezers he meant. They were a pair with grooves cut out of them: perfect for gripping onto the smooth surface of a thorn.

"I'm going to pull these out, and I want you to dab the blood dry as soon as they're free, all right?" Amos said.

Kael got a clean cloth and held it next to the first thorn. Amos's hands shook a little as he latched the tweezers onto it. But he furrowed his brows in stubborn concentration, and his hands became still. "Ready?" he said, and Kael nodded.

With one sharp tug, Amos wrenched the thorn free and Kael pushed the cloth over the wound. He thought there was an awful lot of blood, and he heard Amos mutter a curse under his breath.

"Hooknettle," he grouched, holding the thorn up for Kael to see.

Hooknettle was one of the nastier mountain brambles. Its thorns were shaped like a fisherman's hook: with one barb at the tip and another on the side. The barb at the tip dug into flesh while the other latched on, making it nearly impossible to pull free without taking a sizable chunk of skin with it.

"I don't have time for this." Amos dropped the thorn into a bowl, reached behind him and grabbed another instrument. It was a long, thin rod of metal that he used to pull debris from deep wounds. He latched onto the next thorn and stuck the rod down into the puncture. This time when he pulled, the barb came out cleanly.

It took them hours to remove all the thorns, clean the wounds and bandage them. "Well if that wasn't the biggest waste of my time ..." Amos let his sentence trail into a string of grumbles as he finished the last bandage. While he scrubbed his hands in a bowl of water, he locked his sharp

31

eyes on Kael. "See? If you hadn't been here to help, it would have taken me all blasted week. I wish you'd give up this hunter nonsense and take your place as a healer."

They'd been arguing about his future since the day he turned twelve. Usually, Kael would cross his arms and remind Amos that hunting was his dream, and he had a right to face the Trial of the Five Arrows. But not today.

"Healing is your love, not mine," Kael said. He knew the words sounded hollow the second he spoke them.

Fortunately, Amos didn't seem to notice. "You shouldn't scorn your gifts, boy. You have a knack for healing. And sooner or later you're going to have to face it."

He hated that. He hated hearing it. So what if he had a knack? It didn't change the fact that his heart didn't beat for it. He didn't care about herbs or salves — he wanted adventure! He wanted to fight, to defend the realm. Deep in the pit of his soul, Kael was a warrior.

But Fate told it differently.

"I'm going to dinner," he muttered. He didn't wait for Amos to follow, but went straight out the door.

****

The noise in the Hall was deafening — but then dinner was always the loudest meal of the day. When the sky finally went dark, the Tinnarkians would put their boots up and celebrate. Sure, they may have limps or scrapes or arms in slings, but at least they'd managed to live through the day.

Long tables fanned out from the middle of the Hall like rays from the sun. A huge bed of coals burned in a hole cut out of the floor and a dozen pots hovered above it, their bubbling contents suspended by iron spits.

This was where all the food in Tinnark wound up: the pot. Most days, it was a mushy stew with thick brown broth. But stews with berries in them usually turned a murky gray.

Kael chose the shortest line and grabbed a clean bowl off the serving table. There were few jobs for girls his age. Besides getting married and having children, about the only other thing they could do was cook. When he stepped up to the pot, the girl who ladled his stew plunked it down without a care, splattering it across his boots.

He was used to it. The girls teased him about his skinny limbs just as much as the boys did — though never to his face. At least with a punch, he could stand tall and take it like a man. But the girls waited until his back was turned before they flogged him with their laughter. Which he thought might've hurt worse than a blow to the gut.

The hunters claimed the seats closest to the fire — which meant Kael had to pass them anytime he went to get a meal. He tried to ignore their jeers, but then Laemoth stuck his leg out to trip him. He skipped over it — and Marc shoved him for dodging.

Hot stew sloshed out of his bowl and onto the front of his tunic. They laughed, and normally he would have been ready with a clever retort. But tonight he had worse things to worry about. So instead, he ignored their name-calling and went straight for his table.

Amos and Roland were old men, which meant they didn't have to wait in line for food. By the time Kael made it to the table, they were already arguing between spoonfuls.

"You know what I saw this morning?" Roland said as he leaned over his bowl, his wiry gray beard nearly dipping into the broth.

"I can only imagine," Amos grumped.

"A raven sitting outside my door. I walked out and there he was, staring me down with those beady black eyes. And of course, you know what that means —"

"You'll have to clean the droppings off your doorstep?"

Roland frowned at him. "No. It means we'll have company tonight."

Amos snorted. "Company? You know as well as I do that there hasn't been a traveler in Tinnark since before either of us was born."

"Mayhap there would be, if tales of your crotchety ways hadn't seeped down the mountains and scared them all off."

33

Kael knew there was no point in trying to interrupt them. Roland and Amos had been friends since childhood, and now that they were old widowers, neither had anything better to do than grump at the other — or heckle Kael.

When Roland noticed him trying to sit quietly, he grinned through his beard. "What have you got?" he said, his voice as rough as his calloused hands.

Kael put a spoonful of stew in his mouth and grimaced as the flavors hit him. "Rabbit and blackberries."

Roland laughed. "It's quail and pine nuts for me. Amos?"

"I don't know. Leeks and salmon." He didn't like Roland's game. He'd lost his sense of taste years ago — which was perhaps why his tonics were so notoriously foul.

"Salmon?" Roland dipped his spoon into Amos's bowl. His dark eyes roved while he chewed. "That isn't salmon — it's hog, you crazy old man!"

Half of what the hunters caught was dried and stored for winter; the other half was prepared and tossed into the pot — without a care as to how it all might taste together. Rabbits and blackberries certainly wasn't the worst mix he'd ever had.

"How did it go today?" There was a glint in Roland's eye — a glint he always got when he had the chance to talk about hunting. The joints of his fingers may have been too swollen to draw a bow, but he still had the heart of a young man.

"Not well. I didn't come back with anything," Kael said, keeping his eyes trained on the table. It wasn't a lie, but when he saw the disappointment on Roland's face, it felt like one.

"Aw well, that's all right. Sometimes the forest is mean, and sometimes she's less mean. But at least she weren't mean to everybody: Marc and Laemoth brought home a whole sack of game *and* a deer." He grinned and elbowed Amos, jostling the stew out of his spoon. "A deer, this late in the season. Can you believe it?"

"I'm amazed," Amos grumped as he tried his bite again.

Roland arms crossed over his bony chest. "You ought to be. The elders think it's a good sign for us. They think the winter won't be so harsh this year."

"Do they? Well my joints tell a different story — it's going to be as cold and miserable a winter as ever in these blast forsaken mountains, mark my words."

Roland laughed.

While they argued over the next thing on their list, Kael sat in silence. He was grateful for the noise in the Hall, grateful that they couldn't hear the sounds of rabbits and blackberries waging war in his stomach. Dinner was coming to an end, and at any moment the elders would stand and ask anyone who had business to approach them. That was the moment he was dreading.

"Are you feeling all right?"

Roland's question brought him back to the present. He wiped at the cold sweat on his face and nodded.

Roland gave him a long look, then shrugged. "Well all right. I want you to feel good tonight because I've got a surprise for you." He leaned forward and his face split into a wide smile. "I've been talking to the elders for weeks now — battling, really. Bunch of stubborn old coots. Anyways, I think I've figured out a way to get you in."

"Get me in where?"

Roland looked at him incredulously. "The hunters, of course!"

Kael's stomach sank to his feet. He felt like he was going to be sick. Whatever Roland had planned wouldn't work, not if he didn't have his bow. Why hadn't he been patient and waited one more day to go on the hunt? Why hadn't he let up and allowed the deer to get away?

It was all too gruesome a coincidence, and it made Roland's words sound like cotton in his ears. He only caught a few of them:

"... knew you'd be excited ... perfect timing ... should go join the boys, now ... elders'll want to discuss this with the people!"

By the time he pulled himself out of the daze, it was too late. Roland was already at the hunters' table, laughing and shaking hands with them. Across the fire pit, Brock was standing. He held his arms wide and the Hall suddenly fell silent.

"People of Tinnark," he said, resuming his seat. "The elders will now hear anything you might have to say. Does anyone have anything they'd like the elders to hear?"

And to Kael's horror, Roland was the first to step up. "Elders, people of Tinnark. Winter is almost here," he said.

A few people laughed. In the Unforgivable Mountains, winter was always either here or almost here. In fact, some joked that winter claimed three of the four seasons — leaving spring, summer and fall to share.

Roland smiled and let the laughter die down before he continued. "I'm too old to keep up with the hunters anymore. Trapping is in my blood, but my blood has thinned with age. If we want to make it through another winter, we need to find a younger man to take my place. I've got a man in mind, and he's a man that I've trained myself." He spread his hands wide. "But he hasn't slain a deer."

A chorus of hushed conversations sprung up throughout the Hall. No one joined the hunters without killing a deer.

Brock raised his eyebrows, adding to the many wrinkles on his forehead. "Are there none among the hunters who are fit to take your place?"

Roland shook his head. "None. Trapping is a game that requires talent as well as skill. Even winter isn't long enough for me to train another. But Kael already knows the trade, and he's the best I've ever seen."

More whispers buzzed through the crowd at the mention of his name. He burned as a hundred faces turned to stare at him.

"Really?"

"*Him?*"

"That scrawny one?"

"... like a toothpick."

Brock cleared his throat and the Hall fell silent. "I don't recall ever seeing Kael return with game. Are you certain he has a talent?"

His face reddened as people laughed, but Roland was quick to defend him: "The lion slays, but the vultures do the feasting."

Brock shifted uncomfortably and seemed to stare at Roland in order to avoid looking at the hunter's table — where Laemoth's face was like stone and Marc kept his eyes out of sight.

The elders had their favorites; there was no doubt about that. Half of what they returned with wasn't theirs, but Marc and Laemoth looked the part. The elders would rather believe it was they who provided for the village — not a half-breed runt. And Roland knew it.

After a very tense silence, Brock relented. "We will agree with you. We'll accept Kael as a hunter — but only if the other hunters will agree."

He actually breathed a sigh of relief. There was no way Marc and Laemoth would let him join. They would refuse him, he was certain of it. And then he could step up and ask for a different trade without shame. No one would blame him for choosing another path if the hunters refused him now.

He would have to thank Roland for this someday. He couldn't have planned it better.

It only took a few minutes of heated bickering at the hunters' table for one side to win out over the other. The losers huffed and crossed their arms over their chests as Marc stood to address the elders.

"No one can trap like Kael," he said. "We want our pots to stay full through the winter, and the hunters can think of no man better for the job."

The hair on the back of Kael's neck stood on end. He knew something was coming. He could see the smug look on Marc's face from across the Hall — hear the dark triumph in his voice. Then it dawned on him.

Marc and Laemoth noticed his missing bow — they must have. And they knew he would have to go to the elders eventually and stand before all of Tinnark to ask to be assigned a trade. So they'd waited.

No, he thought desperately. He looked at Marc, searching for any glimpse of mercy in his eyes. But there was none. If anything, his smile widened.

"But a hunter's not a hunter — and a man's not a man — unless he has his bow," Marc said, his mouth twisting in a grin. "So if Kael wants to join the hunters, that's fine with us. All we ask is that he bring us his bow."

Chapter 3
The Traveler

"What are you waiting for? Get your blasted bow," Amos hissed.

For a few moments, Kael had been somewhere else. He found himself trapped in the depths of every curious eye in the room, lost in the thoughts that must be bouncing around in their heads.

What's he doing? Why isn't he moving? their faces said.

His mind went numb and his legs became like lead. Slowly, he managed to turn to Amos. When he saw Kael's face, his frustration melted into disbelief. And he groaned aloud.

"Where is your bow?" Brock said. His voice had more life to it than it'd had in years. He was standing now, his hands planted on the table in front of him. He watched Kael's face grow red, and frowned. "Where is it? Speak, boy!"

"Elders," Marc cut in, "I think I know where it is." He nodded to Laemoth, who pulled a rucksack out from under his bench and opened it. He sneered at Kael through his freshly busted lip before he reached in and pulled out the bow.

The string dangled off the end of Laemoth's finger and the two broken halves clattered together as he waved it around for the whole Hall to see. Gasps rang out, Amos groaned again and dropped his face into his knobby hands. Across the Hall, Roland looked as if someone had kicked him in the gut.

Brock's mouth hung open, but the expression was forced: the O of his lips bent slightly upwards as he fell back in his seat. "What does this mean?"

His question was directed at Marc, who was only too happy to oblige. "I left the village early this morning to track a deer," he said, holding the grin off his face long enough to assume a more serious tone. "Along the way, I stumbled upon Kael. He'd broken his bow and then tried to hide it in the bushes. But I retrieved it. The good people of Tinnark deserve to know the truth, after all. And Kael certainly wasn't going to tell it." He shook his head amid a fresh wave of murmurs. "He lied to us, though it pains me to say it."

Kael leapt from his bench and stepped out into the aisle. He was no liar — and he was going make sure the people of Tinnark knew it. He'd filled his lungs with the first angry words when Roland's voice cut him short.

"Is that true, Kael?"

He wasn't smiling. His shoulders were slumped forward and his mouth sagged into a miserable frown. The defeat in Roland's eyes knocked the fury out of him, and Kael realized, in one heartbreaking moment, that his wasn't the only dream that had died that day. He hadn't only failed himself, but he'd failed Roland as well.

And it was that sorry realization that snuffed his fire out.

"Yes." The word came from his mouth louder than he meant it to. It bounced off the ancient pine beams of the Hall's roof and filled the air with murmurs. "It's all true. And I'm sorry."

He left. Even when Brock yelled at him to turn around and face the elders, he didn't turn back. There was nothing they could do to him that would be worse than the look on Roland's face.

A pair of torches hung outside the Hall's front doors. They were meant to serve as beacons — so that if a fog rolled down from the summit, the villagers could still find their way to food. Tonight, they would serve a different purpose: they would lead Kael as far away from Tinnark as his legs could carry him. He grabbed one of the torches and ran.

The night was cold and still. With every breath the fresh scent of rain filled his nose. In the back of his mind, he knew he shouldn't wander far from the village. He could freeze to death in less than an hour if the rain fell. Part of him knew this, but the part that drove his legs pushed him on. It wasn't long before he found himself in the middle of the woods.

Night made two of everything. The torch bounced from the motion of his jog and the trees danced along with their shadows. Wind raced down from the icy tops of the mountains. It cut through his skin and made the leaves rattle like dry bones. A lonesome wolf howled up the trail — his eerie song rode the wind and sent chills down the back of Kael's neck.

Still, he thought he'd rather risk getting eaten than go back to the village. He could survive in the mountains. He knew how to build a shelter and hunt for food.

Yes, it would be better if he stayed on his own.

A loud *boom* sounded above him and when he looked up, a snake of lightning flexed across the sky. That one glance, that second of distraction, was all the opportunity the mountains needed. Before his mind could grasp it, he was falling.

He smacked his knees against the rocks and heard his trousers rip. His torch flew from his hands and he had to scramble to catch it before it rolled away. Cursing whatever rock or fallen branch had tripped him, he turned to kick it aside — and froze.

The thing jutting onto the path was no root or stone. In fact, it shouldn't have been in the forest at all — not this hour of the night. He had to step closer to be sure, but when the light crossed it, there was no denying what it was: a pair of human legs stuck out from the brambles.

The boots were caked in mud and the pants were so dirty he couldn't tell what color they actually were. He tried to think if the hunters had mentioned anyone getting lost in the woods at dinner. He was sure they hadn't. So if this man wasn't a Tinnarkian, he must be a traveler.

Or he must have *been* a traveler ... the legs were laying very still.

41

"Hello?" Kael said, and he felt foolish saying it. There was almost no question the man was dead. "Are you all right?"

When a long moment passed and the traveler didn't move, he stepped closer. He pushed the brambles aside and held them back with his shoulder. "Don't be alarmed. I'm just going to —"

And he nearly dropped his torch.

He'd been expecting a to see a man — a big fellow with a scraggly beard and leathered skin. Or one of the wild men from the summit perhaps, or at the very least someone who'd been dead for a while. But that wasn't at all what he found.

A girl. A girl lay on the ground in front of him. She looked young — close to his own age. Her hair was the color of a raven's wing. It fell past her shoulders and covered the ground near her head in waves. Twigs and leaves were tangled in it, like she'd been crashing through the forest at full tilt. He followed her red lips up the straight line of her nose — and arrived directly at the fist-sized gash on the side of her head.

Days-old blood covered the wound and matted the hair near it. Brown streaks stained her face: tracks from where drops of blood had rolled down her pale cheeks while the wound was still fresh. Kael knew there was no way she could still be alive. No one lost that much blood and lived.

He'd seen plenty of death, and learned long ago that there was nothing he could do to stop it. Still, he thought it was a shame. The girl's clothes were filthy, but her face was remarkably beautiful. Why had she been in the woods? Where was she headed?

Something about her attire seemed strange. He reached out and touched the material of her leggings with the tip of one finger. It wasn't leather, of that he was certain. It felt more like iron, but it wasn't as cold as iron ought to have been. Then he scraped some of the dirt away and saw her clothes were made of tiny, interlocking pieces — almost like chainmail.

What in Kingdom's name was a girl doing in armor?

Then his heart flipped when he saw the weapon strapped to her leg. It was a sword, curved and sheathed in black. He reached out, prepared to grip the smooth hilt and draw it from its sheath —

Thunder clapped above him, startling his hand away. As much as he wanted to look at the sword, he knew the rain would start falling soon, and he knew he needed to find somewhere dry to spend the night. He thought briefly about taking it with him, but Roland always said that to steal a dead man's weapon would bring no end of bad luck. And that was the last thing he needed.

He turned to leave, but couldn't stop himself from glancing back at the girl one last time. As the light touched the gentle curve of her neck, he thought he saw something. He paused for half a breath, staring. Then it happened again — this time unmistakable: a vein throbbed below her jaw.

She was alive!

He dropped on his knees and drove the torch into the dirt next to him. "Miss? Can you hear me?" He placed his fingers on her neck and felt her pulse. It was weak, just barely thrumming. She needed Amos's help — he had to get her to the hospital.

He looped one of her arms around his shoulder and got his legs beneath him. Great mountains, she was heavy. He pushed and strained until he was out of breath, but there wasn't enough meat on his legs to get her off the ground. Perhaps he could run back to the village, get some of the hunters to help —

Thunder roared over his head, and then rain started to fall. Drops that were more ice than water lashed his skin. They came down in blinding sheets, billowing up as the wind ripped through them.

He tore his shirt off and stretched it over the brambles above them. He couldn't move fast enough to save the torch: it sputtered out, leaving them in darkness. He knew his shirt could only keep them dry for a few minutes before the rain would leak through. When that happened, it would only be a matter of time before the cold took them.

He pulled the brambles tighter overhead and tried to fashion some sort of roof by tying them together. "It's going to be okay," he said to the girl while he worked. "We're probably not going to freeze to death … but we might. I'm not going to lie to you, we might."

Amos was always better at comforting people. Kael had a tendency to read the story the way it was written.

Water started leaking through their roof and he shielded her with his body. He put an arm and a leg around her, forming a sort of lean-to over her wound.
A few minutes later, his lips were in danger of freezing shut. He tried to keep them moving.

"You know, I don't think I've ever really talked to a girl before — especially not one as pretty as you. But I don't suppose this counts, does it? You aren't exactly talking back."

Thunder clapped — he jumped.

"— ael!"

Someone yelled his name, right at the end of the peal. "Here! I'm over here!" he shouted, forcing the words through his chattering teeth. A long moment passed and no one replied. Maybe the ice in his ears was making him hear things.

"Kael!"

Now he was certain he heard it. Someone was looking for him. He crawled out of the shelter and stood in the middle of the path. "Here! Over here!" he said, as loud as his voice would carry.

"I hear him!" someone bellowed.

He shouted until his throat went hoarse. He waved his arms and jumped up and down. His bare chest burned from the cold and he couldn't feel his nose. Just when he thought he might be stuck as a frozen, waving statue forever, a lantern bobbed up the path.

"I found him!" His hood shadowed his worried face, but Kael recognized Roland's stiff gait as he limped forward.

"What were you thinking, boy? We all know Marc is given to tell tales, why didn't you stand for yourself?"

Before the light could touch him, Kael quickly crossed his arms over his chest. He forced himself to meet Roland's eyes. "Because he was right. I broke my bow and I tried to hide it."

Roland's smile was kind, even in the eerie glow of the lantern. "Well, I can't say I wouldn't have done the same myself. The good news is that the elders have agreed to meet with you tomorrow. And don't you worry," he clapped a hand on Kael's shoulder, "we'll think of something. In the meantime, you'd better put this on."

He took the oilskin cloak Roland handed him and immediately tossed it over the brambles. "There's a girl, and she's wounded pretty badly," he said in answer to the question on Roland's face. "We have to get her down to the hospital."

"A girl? Are you sure the cold hasn't got to your head?" He stuck his lantern into the shelter, and his mouth dropped open. "Well my beard, there's a girl under there. Amos! Hurry those old legs along — we've found a wounded woman!"

Now it was Kael's turn to be shocked. What was Amos doing out in a storm? He was going to kill him.

It wasn't long before Amos hobbled up the path, a handful of hunters close behind. "What did you say? Kael's wounded?"

"No, Kael's fine —"

"Not for long, he isn't!" Amos roared as he caught sight of them. "What are you thinking, dancing out in the rain without a shirt on? You aren't a wood sprite —"

"And you aren't young," Kael lashed back. "What were *you* thinking, running out into the forest in the middle of a storm?"

Roland stepped between them. "We all need to stop thinking, and start doing." He nodded to Amos. "There's a girl in the brambles, and she's hurt pretty bad."

Amos shoved past them and held his lantern up. He blanched when he saw her, and Kael knew her wound must have been more serious than he'd thought.

"What do we need to do?" Roland said, but Amos didn't respond. "Amos?"

He tore his eyes away from the girl. "Eh? What was that?"

"I asked what we needed to do."

He squinted through the rain at the hunters. "I'll need a litter — quick as you can. And if one of you boys has an extra oilskin, give it to Kael."

Someone threw a cloak at him and he fastened it around his shoulders, pulling the hood over his head. He made sure the folds of the cloak covered his chest.

They placed the girl gently on their makeshift litter and started the climb back down the mountain. The rain made the rocks even more slippery, the cold even meaner. While the hunters did the brunt of the work, Kael and Amos walked sideways with the litter between them — keeping the spare oilskin stretched over her like a roof. Roland led the way, lantern in hand.

It was slow, dangerous work, but they eventually made it back to the hospital. The beds were empty that night — which meant they would be able to work in peace.

"Stoke the fire," Amos said.

Kael didn't need to be told twice: he was surprised he had any teeth left, after all the chattering.

With the hearth blazing, Amos chased the curious hunters out the door. "I'll let you know how she's doing in the morning," he said, shooing Roland away.

"Fair enough. And Kael," he looked up to see Roland pulling on his hood, his face serious beneath it, "don't run off just yet. The storm comes, but the grass is all the greener for it." His smile was reassuring as he ducked out into the violent night.

With the hunters gone, Amos went straight to work. "Fetch a pail of water, will you?"

In the time it took Kael to get the water, Amos had removed the girl's filthy clothing and placed a thick wool blanket over her body, up to her chin. He handed Kael her clothes and placed the sword on top of the pile. "Set these in my office. I'll clean them later."

"What sort of armor is it?"

"Armor? Why do you think it's armor?" Amos said, rather snappily. "What could a girl want with armor?"

"I don't know —"

"That's right, you don't. So let's just see if we can keep her heart beating through the night."

Kael tossed her clothes in the floor of the office and set the sword on the cluttered table Amos used for a desk. He took off his cloak and fished a patient's shirt out of the pile that had just been cleaned. While he pulled the itchy tunic over his head, he got a strange feeling. He swore someone was watching him.

He spun around, not sure what he expected to see. The only things in the room besides Amos's clutter were the armor ... and that sword. He wondered what the blade looked like. He wanted to draw it and hold it in his hand. He took a step closer.

"A bowl of warm water and a fresh cloth!" Amos barked from the main room.

Kael tore his eyes away from the sword and as he left, shut the door on it. All the while he worked, he tried to shake the odd feeling from his toes. He warmed the pail of water over the fire and stirred in a few herbs for numbing. The dried leaves slowly melted, turning the water a smoky blue. He poured some into a bowl and left the rest over the fire.

Amos dipped a cloth into the mixture and dabbed the girl's wound, his brow bent in concentration. "It's going to take some time to get this mess fixed. She didn't even *try* to staunch the bleeding."

Under the grime, the skin around her wound was red and inflamed. A huge scab had formed over the top of it — mixed with strands of hair and bits of debris from the forest.

But the herb water did its job well: after only a few minutes of scrubbing, the wound was nearly clean.

Amos set the now-filthy cloth to the side and scratched at the top of his head. His eyes flicked from the gash to different corners of the room, and back again. Kael knew he was trying to decide on how to seal it.

"Do you want me to get the needle?"

Amos shook his head, and his eyes went to the door. "I think I may try the other," he finally said, and Kael understood.

As Amos put his hands on either side of the girl's wound, Kael stepped around to block what he was doing from view — because if anyone happened to walk in and catch them, they'd have to run for their lives.

While Amos may not have been able to capture souls, he was certainly no ordinary healer. He was among the last of a dying race — an ancient people with extraordinary powers. They were called the whisperers.

Unlike the mages with their complicated language of spells, a whisperer needed no words — only the power of his mind and the strength of his hands. An ordinary blacksmith required the hammer and heat of the flames, but a whisperer skilled in craft could bend iron with his fist and sharpen a blade with his thumbnail. Most soldiers spent a lifetime honing their strengths, but a whisperer skilled in war never grew tired, and he never missed.

And if a whisperer skilled in healing studied long enough, there was no wound he couldn't mend.

Amos pushed his fingertips against the ragged edges of the gash, and the girl's skin became like clay: molding obediently, softening under his touch. He worked with nimble precision, pinching the corner of each end together and sealing them. It was a remarkable talent, and one that could have saved countless lives ... if only he were allowed to use it.

Not so long ago, the whisperers served the King in Midlan. A child who was born a whisperer was accepted into the house of nobles without question, and given a room in the

King's fortress for as long as he lived. It was the whisperers who raised the impenetrable walls of the fortress, and kept the Kings alive long past their years. It was they who trained the army of Midlan to be undefeatable.

Then two decades ago, a great rebellion changed everything.

They called it the Whispering War, and it began when Banagher — a weak-minded and idle King — tried to turn the whisperers into his slaves. He believed they were property of the crown, his by right, and should be given no more privilege than the stones that paved his floors. Not surprisingly, the whisperers didn't take kindly to this idea, and they rebelled.

But what started out as a show of unrest quickly became something much more sinister. As they won victory after victory over land and sea, the whisperers began to realize what a power they had — and they wanted more. It wasn't long before they marched on Midlan and tried to seize the throne for themselves.

After three long and bloody years, the Kingdom finally won. Banagher perished in battle and because he left no heir to succeed him, his warlord was elected to take the throne.

The warlord's name was Crevan, and he was an evil man. Shortly after the war ended, he summoned all the surviving whisperers to Midlan. He said he wanted to make peace with them, to rebuild the Kingdom with their help. But it was all a trap.

No one knew precisely what happened that day, but Amos said not a whisperer who walked into the fortress was ever heard from again.

A week later came the decree: whispering had been outlawed. Anyone caught in the act would be executed immediately; anyone who turned a whisperer over to the crown would receive a bounty of two hundred gold pieces. In the war-ravaged Kingdom, that was coin enough for a man to live on for three lifetimes — and plenty took him up on the offer.

And any whisperer left alive fled to the mountains.

Though Amos had lived in Tinnark for as long as anyone could remember, he never told a soul of his abilities. "These people are superstitious enough," he'd always say. "What do you think would have happened if I'd gone around snapping bones back together? They would've lopped off my head and buried it."

Not telling had ultimately saved his life.

Kael watched as Amos sealed the gash. His fingers moved surely until he reached the middle, and then he stopped. "Her skull is cracked. I'm going to have to mend it before I can finish the skin," he said with a frown. He slid his index finger gently inside the wound. "Let's see. I think — ouch!"

He let out a string of curses and jerked back, slinging his fingers around like he'd accidently stuck them to a hot cauldron. Kael grabbed the bowl of water, but Amos shook his head.

"No, the cloth!"

"But it's filthy —"

"I don't care! Wipe!"

The shrill in Amos's voice startled him. He grabbed the cloth in one hand and Amos's wrist in another. Fresh red blood covered his fingertips, but it wasn't the normal sort of blood. This blood bubbled, and steam rose up from it. Amos groaned as Kael dragged the rough surface of the cloth over his hand. His stomach flipped when he saw how red and raw Amos's fingers were. The blood soaked into the cloth and cooled, hardening almost immediately.

"What happened?" Kael said.

Amos dunked his hand into the bowl and jerked his head at the girl accusingly. "What does it look like happened? She burned me!"

"But, how —?"

"I don't know," he snapped, which only worried Kael further: very rarely did Amos not have an answer. He walked back to the girl, toting the bowl with him, and bent to look at her wound. "Huh, it's already scabbed over. Well I've never seen anything like this ... it must be magic. Yes, I'll bet she ran afoul of a mage and got herself hexed."

"But how could that be? I thought Crevan had all the mages in chains."

Amos made a frustrated noise. "Well she must've done something to get the King's attention. I can see no other way around it."

Kael's heart leapt excitedly as an idea came to him. "You don't think she's a whisperer, do you?"

"There wasn't a mark," Amos said after a moment, and Kael felt disappointment slide back down in the place of his hope. "No, I think it was a spell." He looked at Kael, and his gray brows shot up in surprise.

When he saw what Amos stared at, he drew in a sharp breath. A drop of blood glistened on the back of his forearm, bubbling wetly. Carefully, he touched a finger to it. The blood felt warm, but not unpleasant.

"Remarkable," Amos breathed. "It isn't hurting you, is it?"

Kael shook his head. He looked back at Amos's fingers, at the angry white blisters rising up on them. Why didn't the magic hurt him?

"We'll have plenty of time to figure this out later," Amos said. He picked up his bowl and situated himself at the table next to where the girl lay. Then he looked at Kael expectantly.

"No."

His voice was hard. He felt the wall rise up in his heart — the one that always rose when Amos tried to get him to use his gift. Healing was the weakest of the three schools of whispering. And in Kael's opinion, Fate gifted him just enough to thoroughly ruin his life. So he vowed to ignore it. He tucked it away and pretended to be normal.

"If you don't help her, she'll die," Amos countered.

Blast it all.

Kael flung the dirty cloth against the wall and stomped over to the girl. Her face was smooth as she slept; her chest rose and fell steadily. For some reason, the peace on her face calmed him.

In the deepest part of her wound, he could see where her skull was cracked. It was an angry, scarlet line no longer than a fingernail. But he knew even a small crack could turn deadly if left un-mended. Blood might leak inside, which would surely kill her.

He took a deep breath and put his finger in the wound. Warmth, wet and the hard, slippery surface of bone — those were all familiar. He knew the textures, he knew how they all fit back together. Slowly, he ran his finger along the line, holding a memory in his head.

It was a memory of his childhood. He used to spend hours playing in the ponds near the village, building Kingdoms out of clay. It was an unsteady material, but clay had its virtues: if one of his castle walls cracked, he could simply push them back together.

With one finger on her skull, he closed his eyes and thought: *You are clay*.

When he opened them, he was no longer looking at a complicated mass of muscle, skin and bone: it was all simple clay.

Now the bone of her skull slid together when he pushed it, sealing under the force of his thought. When the crack was healed, he pushed the folds of skin back towards each other. Blood leaked out and washed over his fingers as he pinched the gash closed. It was much warmer than normal blood, but it didn't scald him.

When he'd sealed the wound, all that remained was a thin white scar. He didn't think the girl would want a scar on her head, so he brushed it with his thumb until it smoothed away.

"Very good," Amos said when he finished.

Kael didn't realize how focused he'd been. Amos's voice sounded like it floated in from miles away. He sat up and let the fog drain from his ears before he frowned at the smug look on Amos's face and said: "Now what?"

His frail shoulders rose and fell. "Now we wait, and hope she wakes up."

Chapter 4
The Sovereign Five

Across the mountains and miles away, the great fortress of Midlan stood undefeated.

Its outer wall was a colossus of stone: a great, gaping jaw that rose from the earth and consumed the land around it, hemming every tree and blade of grass into a giant, fortified circle. High towers stood along this wall like pointed teeth, their heavy shadows draped over the barracks that covered the ground beneath them.

The middle wall was actually an impregnable keep. It leered from behind the cover of its iron towers, its many slit windows stared unblinkingly — watching the four horizons.

At the top of the keep loomed another citadel, one designed to survive any blast or siege. It was out of the archer's reach, too powerful for the catapult and warded against every spell. And it was from this highest, insurmountable point that King Crevan enjoyed the view of a man with ultimate power.

From where he watched, the soldiers of Midlan scurried across the fields like ants, doing whatever he ordered. It was fear — the weight of his eyes on the tops of their little ant heads — that kept them obedient. Yes, let them build his cities, let them fight, die and bleed for him. Then when they grew too old to lift a blade, he would crush their tiny bodies between his fingers ...

A knock at the door brought him back to the present. He turned and saw a steward peeking his head through the slightest of cracks. "Forgive me, Your Majesty, but your guests have arrived."

He waited for the King to nod before he darted behind the door and closed it. After gazing out the window for a while longer, Crevan began his stroll to the throne room — where his guests would be waiting.

The halls of Midlan had a torch for every three stones. Crevan ordered that they remain lit day and night. Shadows were the cloaks of thieves ... and assassins. He wouldn't give them anywhere to hide.

At the end of the hallway, a huge onyx dragon guarded his chambers. It bared its violent teeth and reached out with curved claws. The black dragon had been the symbol of Midlan since the time of the first King — a crest of power, the lord of all beasts.

Nevertheless, Crevan was careful to avoid its stony glare. He pushed the spines at the end of the dragon's tail, and one shifted under the pressure. It sunk down and clicked. A segment of the wall to the left of the statue slid over with a chalky groan, revealing a narrow passageway hidden in darkness. He grabbed a torch from the hall and made his way down a tight spiral of steps.

Tunnels crisscrossed through the fortress like spider webs. They wound behind every door and under every corridor — and he kept them all a secret. Here in the darkness, Crevan moved without fear. The passageway was sturdy and the walls were thick enough to hide the heavy fall of his steps. A man could even scream for hours on end, and no one could hear him.

This, he knew for a fact.

At the end of one tunnel was a small wooden door. He snuffed his torch and opened it slowly, careful not to stir its hinges. Beyond the door was the backside of a tapestry. As he peered through a worn section of thread, his throne room came into focus.

Five people lounged about the long table in the center of the room. They were Crevan's chosen few: the Sovereign Five.

When King Banagher ... perished, several nobles fought to seize the throne, but Crevan outwitted them all. He was strong, yes, and he towered over everyone else in the King's court, but his pride was in his cunning — not his strength. And now he ruled the Kingdom the same way he'd commanded the King's army: mercilessly.

Gone was the tangled mass of lords and ladies that used to rule the realm. Purged were the mumbling, argumentative old men and overzealous young nobles. Squashed were the many noisy opinions and the general stench of democracy. Under Crevan's rule, there was only one voice — his. And when he spoke, the Kingdom listened.

He'd taken Midlan and its vast army for himself, but there were still five other regions to control. For these he assigned a small group of nobles, handpicked for their particular brands of ruthlessness.

A woman's laugh drew his eyes to the hearth behind the table. Time could not touch Countess D'Mere, ruler of the Grandforest. She was as alluring now as she had been seventeen years ago. When the Countess tossed her golden-brown hair and batted her pretty blue eyes, her enemies fell. No man could hold his ground against her charms — or survive the kiss of her dagger.

Duke Reginald of the High Seas smiled like a born swindler. His close-cropped hair rolled in tight waves across his head. He tugged absently on the end of his goatee and lounged against the wall; the firelight glinted off the sharp edge of his smile. Though he feigned indifference, his eyes wandered repeatedly down D'Mere's liberal neckline while they chatted.

Baron Sahar of Whitebone Desert had the dark skin of his people. His mines in the sand filled Midlan's treasury with gems and precious metals. The many jeweled rings on Sahar's fingers sparkled in the torchlight as he inspected the golden goblets on the table. If there was a flaw in any of them, Sahar would find it.

The man to his left was not as concerned with the cups as he was with their contents. Earl Hubert sucked down glass after glass of an array of liquors, his watery red eyes watching greedily for the bottom. Though his vineyards in the shadow of the Unforgivable Mountains produced some of the best wines in the Kingdom, their flavors were wasted between Hubert's gluttonous lips.

The last ruler was Lord Gilderick the Gruesome of the Endless Plains. If someone took a bit of skin, stretched it over a skeleton and topped it with a mop of lank hair, they might end up with something that looked like Gilderick. But it would take some dark magic to make it half as wicked. He lurked in a shadowy corner, watching the room through sunken eyes — and the others pretended not to see him.

Crevan rarely bothered with gathering the Five together: as long as his coffers and storehouses remained full, he didn't care what they did. But today was special. Today, one of them would die.

The steward entered the throne room, and Crevan saw his chance. While their backs were turned he darted out from the tapestry and strode up behind them. "Hello, my friends!"

They all jumped and collectively dropped to one knee. "Your Grace," they mumbled in unison.

Crevan waved them to their feet. "Come now, there's no need for kneeling. And you may leave us," he said to the steward, who scuttled obediently from the room.

He ordered the Five to take a seat at the table and lounged in his own chair at the head. Sahar had to jerk his hands out of the way as Crevan dropped his boots squarely on the tabletop.

Ah, silence. Nothing told more than a bit of silence. He put his hands behind his head and waited, looking at each of them in turn.

It was Reginald who spoke first. "To what, Your Majesty, do we owe this rare privilege?"

Reginald was a gutsy man. After all, one did not come to own every ship on the High Seas by shying away from negotiation. But Crevan wasn't interested in playing business, and he didn't have to. "Surely a man with your connections must know why I've called you."

Reginald blinked. "My Lord — if something troubles you, all of the High Seas are at your disposal. We move at your command."

The others were quick to add their vigorous nods and pledges of allegiance. He let the Five murmur their promises for a moment before he raised his hand.

Silence.

"Now that I think about it, I *am* troubled by something. One thing. And what could that be?" He leaned back in his chair and tapped the side of his face in mock contemplation. It was a common enough gesture, but to the Five it meant something particular. None of them would look at where his finger tapped.

"We've all tried, Your Grace, and we've all been wounded," D'Mere said. She kept her eyes wide and serious. The Countess knew better than to use her powers on the King.

"Yes but to be fair, Hubert's squandered more opportunities than the rest of us combined," Reginald said.

Hubert stopped slurping long enough to gasp. "I'm sure I don't know what you mean."

"Don't know what I mean, eh?" Reginald leaned forward and fixed his sharp eyes on Hubert's. "Every time you take some half-hearted jab at her, she flies off and wreaks havoc on the rest of us. She's sunk three of my vessels. Three! Do you have any idea how expensive it is to replace a ship?"

Hubert shrugged. "Well I don't see how that's my faul —"

"And the last time she was in Whitebone, she dropped a net full of trolls in the middle of my palace," Sahar said, inspecting his rings. "The stupid, slobbering beasts ran wild in the halls for days before we managed to find them. And I'm still trying to air the stench from my silk cushions."

Hubert snorted. "Trolls? Really, I find that hard to —"

"And why do your vineyards never scorch?" D'Mere interjected. "Why have my forests been burned when she hasn't so much as bruised a single one of your grapes?"

Hubert didn't seem to have an answer for that. He opened and closed his mouth like a fish gasping for air. Little indignant sounds escaped from between his lips while the others gutted him.

"An excellent point, Countess," Reginald said. His eyes glinted as he moved in for the kill. "Yes, I do believe I'm beginning to see a pattern: every time Hubert fails, she comes blazing from the mountains, breathing fire down our necks —"

"And on our fields," Gilderick added. He fixed his dark-pitted stare on Hubert, who looked quickly in the other direction.

"Precisely," Reginald agreed. He jabbed a finger at Hubert. "If I didn't know any better, I'd say you made a pact with the barbarian."

"I've done no such thing!" he shrieked.

Reginald smirked through his goatee. "I'd like to see you prove it."

Hubert licked his dry lips as his eyes shifted around the table. "She's — she's dead," he said finally.

The other four sat a little straighter.

"You've killed her?" Sahar made no attempt to mask the skepticism in his voice.

"Yes. Well — good as. What I've started, the mountains will finish," Hubert continued quickly before Reginald could cut in. "My scouts found her, wounded by a blow on the head that no human could have survived. I could've fit my fist in the hole it made. Anyways, she fled into the mountains. There's nothing up there but rocks and trees. I wager the forest took her in a couple of hours."

His news silenced the others. D'Mere pursed her full lips. Reginald tugged on his goatee. Sahar's jeweled fingers tapped furiously on the table. Gilderick stared.

A moment passed and Hubert began to squirm. He turned to Crevan. "I hope, Your Majesty, that this news eases your worries."

He slid his boots off the table and assumed a more Kingly pose. A carefully-practiced expression of concern

59

masked his face. "My friends, it pains me to hear you fight each other. After all, did we not conquer the whisperers side by side?"

They nodded.

"Did we not share in the reward and together bring this Kingdom into glory?"

They nodded again, more cautiously.

"Then remember that our bickering only gives the enemy a foothold." At his command the steward reentered the room, balancing a tray of six silver goblets on one palm. Crevan served the Five himself, pouring them all a generous amount of his finest wine. "Today, my friends, is a day for celebration. Earl Hubert has just informed me of the death of my most hated enemy." He raised his glass. "And he shall be rewarded for it."

Hubert shot a smug look at the other four.

"To the Earl of the Unforgivable Mountains!" Crevan declared. He brought his cup almost to his lips and paused, watching as Hubert slurped down his entire goblet.

The other four never moved. They knew better than to drink when the King didn't.

Crevan watched as Hubert's eyes bugged out and he began to claw at his throat. "Though I hate to admit it, your attack nearly did the trick. She would have died, all alone — only there's more than just rocks and trees where she fled." He had to raise his voice to be heard over the noise of Hubert's choking. "It turns out there's a miserable, nothing of a village halfway up the mountains ... and they found her."

Foam gathered at the corner of Hubert's lips, his watery eyes grew emptier by the second. At Crevan's word, two guards entered the room to take his body away.

"One moment." He stopped the guards and pulled a gold medallion off Hubert's neck — a task made more difficult by his many wobbling chins. He held the medallion before Hubert's fading eyes so that he could see the wolf's head engraved on its surface for a final time. "I relieve you of your rule."

Then the guards dragged his body from the room, squeezing his pudgy legs through the door and closing it shut behind them. The fear they left behind was so potent that Crevan thought he might have smelled it from the other side of the castle. He could hear the question that swarmed in the heads of the other four:

Had everyone's drink been poisoned, or only Hubert's?

Let them wonder. Let them steep in their expendability.

"Well, good riddance to the lazy cod," Reginald finally said. He turned to Crevan. "What the Unforgivable Mountains need is a firm hand. If Your Majesty wishes, I'd be happy to take charge of the territory myself."

His offer set off another squabble amongst the Five. Why should Reginald get more territory than anyone else? How did he expect to tame the mountains? Who got murdered and made *him* the best man for the job?

Their cawing and squawking drove Crevan to grind his teeth. He slammed his fist down, toppling his goblet onto the floor. It clattered loudly as the room went quiet.

"If I wanted another herd of fat, greedy-eyed merchants roaming my Kingdom, I would gladly put the region in your hands," Crevan said to Reginald. "But I have a different vision for the mountains. A much more ... aggressive, vision."

Almost on cue, the door to the throne room swung open. A man clad in full armor marched up to Crevan. His coarse hair fell nearly to his shoulders and a wolfish grin peeked out through his tangled beard. He bowed before he sat in Hubert's empty chair.

Crevan smiled at the stunned looks on the others' faces. "You all remember Titus, my warlord."

It wasn't a question. Titus lounged in his chair, sizing the other four up with predator's eyes, and they stiffened under his gaze.

"I agree with you on one point, Reginald. The Unforgivable Mountains *do* need a firm hand. And I believe

Titus will give its citizens the discipline they lack," Crevan said.

Titus took the gold medallion from him and slid it over his head. He grinned at the other four — and soaked up their scornful looks like sunshine.

Crevan stood and the Five scrambled to their feet. "I trust you will all work a little harder to capture the Dragongirl, now that you've seen the fate of failure." He nodded to Titus. "You'll find her in Tinnark. Go quickly — and remind those mountain rats of their King."

Chapter 5
Bow-Breaker

Kael's meeting with the elders didn't go well.

He'd never been in the Hall when it wasn't packed full of people. As he walked down the endless line of empty tables and chairs, he kept his eyes firmly on the crisscrossing pattern of scratches on the back of Roland's jerkin. Though he knew the chairs were empty, he swore he could feel the weight of eyes upon him.

Perhaps his ancestors were there, shaking their ghostly heads as he shamed them.

When Roland stepped aside, he saw the elders fanned out around their table. They leaned forward, squinting hard with failing eyes and combing their hands pensively through their beards. Brock was even making the effort to stand, though he leaned heavily on the table for support.

Kael's face burned hotter with every second they made him wait. He stared pointedly at the many paper-thin wrinkles between Brock's eyes and tried not to betray his emotions.

"It has long been our belief that you were most doomed of us all. And now it seems we've been proven correct," Brock said, though he didn't seem particularly upset about it. In fact, he sounded rather smug.

"Tell the boy his fate," Roland growled.

Brock actually smirked at him. "It is fortunate that you have so many protectors," he said to Kael. "A man who runs away can hardly deserve them."

"I didn't run." His fists shook as he thought about how badly he'd like to knock the sneer right off Brock's face. "I won't let you call me a coward —"

"Hush, boy. Be like the fox," Roland muttered.

He spoke well out of the elders' range and when Brock asked him to repeat it, he wouldn't. Not that it would have mattered: few understood Roland's words. But Kael had heard them long enough to understand that he was telling him to be cunning. He must know when to fight, and when to yield.

So as much as he didn't want to, Kael apologized and clamped his mouth firmly shut.

Brock was far from appeased. He pursed his lips so tightly that they nearly disappeared in a crevice of wrinkles. "For the shameful act of breaking your bow, the elders ruled to banish you. But out of respect for your grandfather, we've agreed to lessen your sentence." His fist came down with every term, sealing them in Tinnark's law. "You will live out your days as a healer, bound to the hospital. You will not be allowed to venture into the village — and this includes the Hall. Your meals will be brought to you thrice daily. You are stripped of your privileges as a man of Tinnark, forbidden to walk where you aren't wanted and forbidden to speak without permission. The elders have spoken."

When his fist fell that last time and the hollow thud finished bouncing through the rafters, Kael's first thought was that he'd have rather been banished.

"That isn't what's fair, that's torture!" Roland bellowed, shaking his fists.

Brock's arms trembled as he leaned to put his nose in Roland's face. "The elders have spoken!" The others stood in a chorus of creaking joints and took up his chant. "The elders have spoken!"

"I'd like to see every one of you strung up by your beards!" Roland said through their cries. "A colony of miserable old bats, that's what you are —"

Kael grabbed him by the arm. "Enough, it isn't worth it."

"You aren't allowed to speak!" Brock shrilled.

"He has my *permission*!" Roland snapped back.

Kael squeezed his arm hard, fighting his own fury long enough to quell Roland's. It would do them no good if the elders decided to punish them both. In the end, he seemed to realize this. Roland went silent — but did not relinquish his glare.

When the Hall was quiet, Kael nodded once. And then he left.

Roland went to follow, but the elders held him back. "We are troubled over the storehouses," Brock said. "They aren't anywhere near full enough to get us through the winter. And this morning your men brought in less than half the game of the morning before — hardly enough to fill the pots. Do you have an answer for this?"

"I'm no Seer, but perhaps it has something to do with the fact that the best trapper in Tinnark is no longer allowed out in the woods."

The uncomfortable silence that followed made Kael's chin lift a little as he headed for the door, but for the most part he felt like he'd been sentenced to death.

Everything was numb: from the soles of his feet to the top of his head. He didn't feel the air rush past him as he strode out of the Hall, he didn't feel the rude wood of the heavy doors as he shoved them open. When he saw Marc standing bowlegged up the path, some object clutched in his meaty hand, he didn't even break his pace.

"Get out of our village, Bow-Breaker!" he said as he threw.

The rainstorm from the night before left the ground sopping wet. Footprints in the dirt path filled with water, which turned to mud. And mud made for a handy weapon.

A fistful of wet earth struck him in the head, the slapping sound it made stung his ears. The tiny bits of rock stuck into it cut his face. Grit caked his tongue and he staggered backwards as he tried to spit it out. That's when another clump struck his ear.

He heard Laemoth's voice, muffled through the dirt: "Get out, Bow-Breaker!"

Soon mud was striking him on all sides. He could hear the angry cries of the villagers as they cursed him with every throw.

"Half-breed!"

"Bow-Breaker!"

"You're a bad omen!"

"Get *out*!"

The mud hurt worse than their words and, even though he could feel blood welling in the scratches on his arms, he kept walking. He would keep his head down, but he wouldn't give them the satisfaction of seeing him run — even if it meant losing an ear or an eye.

He would never run again.

They stopped following him a few yards from the hospital. The noise of the mob drew Amos out the door and when they saw him, the villagers made a hasty retreat.

"Inbred swine," he cursed after them. "I have half a mind to give every one of them something to think about — what are you doing? You'll track mud all inside my hospital!"

"I just need a few things, and then I promise I'll be out of your hair forever," Kael said as he shoved past him. He grabbed an empty pack off the floor and began filling it with bandages and bottles of herbs. Several patients tilted their bloodied heads and a few more watched him curiously through swollen eyes, but he ignored them.

Amos followed at a hobble. "And what's that supposed to mean?"

"I'm leaving."

Kael didn't have to turn around to know that Amos's mouth was hanging wide open. "But you can't leave — I need you here. *She* needs you."

He said that last bit quietly enough that the patients couldn't overhear. Kael looked up from where he'd been stuffing his hunting knife away and found the closed door of Amos's office.

They decided to keep the wounded girl back there for the time being. Her fever was gone, but she was still trapped in sleep. There was no telling how many Tinnarkians would crowd their way into the hospital, craning their necks for a better view, if she was out on display. They'd decided it was better to keep her under lock and key until she woke.

"What if I can't save her?" Amos pressed. "What if you're the only one who can get around the hex —?"

"Well that's too bad, isn't it? I'm not going to be a prisoner for the rest of my life. Not for anyone," Kael said back, and he half-meant it.

But a tiny voice in the back of his head chose that moment to speak. *If you leave*, it said, *she could die. You're always talking about being brave, so why don't you do the brave thing?*

He didn't see how such a small something had the power to hold back a flood of rage so hot that it practically baked the mud onto his skin. And yet with one utterance, the voice folded his anger on top of itself, wrapping it up again and again until he could've fit it in his pocket. He thought about all the stories he read in the *Atlas*, all the knights and warriors who'd had to do something they never wanted: Sir Gorigan, Scarn, Setheran the Wright ...

They'd all had to make sacrifices — most resulting in their deaths. If it had been Brock or Marc or Laemoth lying sick, he wouldn't have thought twice about turning on his heel and putting Tinnark to his back forever. But it wasn't. It was a traveling girl — a girl who very likely didn't deserve to die.

"Help me bring her back," Amos implored him, latching onto the struggle in his face. "Once she's healed, you can leave. You don't even have to wait for the snows to come."

"Fine." Kael tossed his half-filled pack onto a nearby table and went to go scrub the mud off his clothes. Even though it killed him to stay, he couldn't sentence an innocent girl to her death.

But only until spring, he told himself. As soon as the snows came and cleared, he'd leave Tinnark for good.

****

The next month was nothing short of torture. The elders decreed that Kael wasn't allowed in the Hall, which

67

meant someone had to volunteer to bring him his meals everyday. When he opened the door that first morning, he was surprised to see a hunter carrying his breakfast.

The man tried rather lamely to mask his laughter with a fit of coughs, so when Kael dug his spoon in, he knew to look carefully. Alongside the raspberries and turtle meat was a number of floating black things. They were about the size of pebbles and when he used the edge of his spoon to break one open, his worst suspicions were confirmed: deer droppings.

He went without breakfast.

Marc brought his lunch, and there was almost more droppings than broth. "Eat up," he said, shoving it roughly into his chest.

Kael replied by emptying the bowl on Marc's boots.

"So, the Bow-Breaker is ungrateful," Marc said, his voice splintered with rage. "Well, I'm sure the elders won't mind not feeding you." And his boots made a wet squishing noise as he stomped away.

Kael made no mention of it to Amos. He chewed on herbs as he worked to keep his stomach from growling too loudly, and tried to keep himself busy. Just when he'd resigned himself to a slow death of starvation, Roland showed up with dinner.

"I hope you know the trouble you caused, dumping that stew on Marc," he said as he handed the bowl over.

Kael didn't even mind that it was fish and dandelion — he dug right in.

"Don't worry, I got yours from the clean pot."

The food stuck to the roof of his mouth. "The clean pot?"

"Yeah, your hogshead of a grandfather put blackroot in the others."

Stew nearly came out his nose. Dried and powdered, blackroot was useful for all sorts of stomach ailments. But more than a pinch of it, and a man would likely spend his whole night in the latrine. And knowing Amos, there'd probably been a good deal more than a pinch.

"It'll be extra work for him, but he says everyone'll just blame it on the cooking." Roland slung his pack onto the ground and began digging through it. When he found what he wanted, he glanced over his shoulder before he tugged it free. "Here."

In his hand was a bow. It was a simple short bow, well worn and made of yew. "Roland, you know I can't —"

"Oh, sure you can. What the elders don't know won't kill them. Or better yet, maybe it will." He grinned and thrust it at him again. "Go on, take it. It was my great grandfather's — brought it with him from the lowlands when the King's men chased him up here. I put a new string and grip on it, but the wood ought to bend nicely."

Kael couldn't help himself — he took it. The bow was sturdy and felt good in his hand. Just above the new grip a number of shallow marks cut into the wood like rungs on a ladder. He grinned when he saw them.

Roland's ancestors were bandits: wild men who made their living raiding villages all throughout the Grandforest. Though he refused to talk much about it, Kael figured out the markings from some of the drawings in the *Atlas*. A score that was a single line meant his great grandfather had killed an enemy. The ones cut into an X meant he'd lopped off his head as a souvenir.

It was funny to think a man as kind as Roland had come from such a bloodthirsty family. And Kael was surprised at how well the bow was made: he pulled on the string and marveled when it slid easily back to his chin.

"It's different having one that's broke in, eh?" Roland was watching him, his voice getting gruffer by the second. "I was going to give it to ole Tad, but ..."

But he'd been killed.

Both of Roland's sons had been hunters. Tad was the eldest, and Hammon the youngest. The same bear had slaughtered them both: a seven-foot tall monster with teeth as long as a man's finger. Roland was heartbroken when he discovered their mangled bodies, but he never wept. Instead, he spent five seasons tracking the beast through the woods, waiting for the perfect shot. And when it came, he struck the bear in the heart with an arrow.

Roland later said that he thought it was the animal in him that gave him strength. He believed that men once knew the forests as well as the animals, and a little of that wild spirit was left in every one of them. As the bear lay dying, he said he saw blood before his eyes and felt nothing as he flung himself upon the beast.

He drew his dagger and in pure rage, sawed off the bear's head while it yet lived. Only after the anger faded and he collapsed, did he realize that the beast had slashed his back to ribbons.

Amos healed him, and months later he was able to walk again, but the angry red and white lines never went away. He showed them to Kael once because he begged to see them, and bile rose in his throat when he saw there was more scar than skin.

The bear's head sat on a stake out in Roland's yard. Though the fur was long gone and the bone bleached white, Roland spat on it every time he came home. He said once that he could spit on it every day for a thousand years and the score would never be settled.

"If Tad can't have it, then I think you ought to. A man shouldn't be left alone with no way to defend himself." Roland pulled out a quiver and handed it to Kael. It was so packed full of arrows that he wondered if he'd be able to get one out. "Yeah, you ought to have it," Roland said again, and then he smiled. "Especially since I'm so close to taking the walk —"

"I don't want to think about that," Kael said. He felt a wall go up in his heart at the very thought of it. "Can't you just stay here with us? We'll take good care of you."

Roland laughed from his belly and slapped his knees. "I know you would — and keep me alive a lot longer than I ever should be. No, I want the woodsman's death. I know you don't agree, but that's what I want."

In Tinnark's earliest days, a man who was too old to provide for his village would often choose to die rather than continue eating out of the pot. He'd take his bow and a quiver of arrows and walk out into the woods alone, prepared to accept whatever death the mountains gave him. They called it the woodsman's death.

But those were the old days. Now Tinnark had a healer, now the pots were full. There was no reason that a man shouldn't be allowed to die in the comfort of his own home. But Roland refused to listen.

"Let's find a place to hide that," he said quickly when he saw the set to Kael's chin. "There's probably a loose plank around here that'll do the trick."

They found one under a cot and stuffed the bow and quiver into the hollow space beneath it. "Thank you —"

"No, don't even." Roland pulled the hood of his cloak up and prepared to step outside. "Amos told me you were planning to leave in the spring and I just thought you ought to have a proper bow, is all. Good night."

****

The Day of the Last Leaf came in early morning, when the elders stepped outside and declared that every tree in sight was bare-limbed to the roots. That afternoon, the air froze over and the clouds turned a heavy, ominous gray.

Roland came late with dinner, his cloak tangled about him and his beard stiff with cold. "We're in for it now, boy," he said as he set the stew on the table.

There were two bowls: one for Kael, and one for the girl who refused to wake up. Both were stone cold, so he dumped their murky contents into a pot and hung it over the fire to warm. Since he was bound to the hospital anyways, Amos had tasked him with the responsibility of feeding the girl every evening, coaxing the broth down her throat by the spoonful. It was a tedious duty, and it was beginning to wear on his patience.

"Why are we in for it?" he said as he stirred the broth around.

71

"Well, I left the sacrifice this morning in the same spot as always. But when I checked it just now," Roland's eyes went wide, "it was still there. Not a bite taken out of it. What sort of under-realm omen do you think that is, eh?"

Another reason the people of Tinnark hated him was because the year Kael was born, a monster moved into the woods. It would leave deer carcasses strung around the village — picked clean, and not a bone had been broken. Every skeleton was perfectly intact.

The hunters thought it must have come from the summit. Everybody knew that monsters lived at the top of the mountains — and the great clans of summit people often chased them downwards. The elders wanted to hunt and kill it before it started feasting on people, but Roland didn't think it meant them any harm. So as a sign of good faith, he killed a deer and left it a mile outside of Tinnark.

"If it's a beast of any thought," he reasoned, "it'll understand that we don't want it hunting on our grounds."

The next morning, a whole group of men went out to inspect offering and found it'd been picked clean in the same bizarre way. After that, the carcasses stopped appearing, and it became a tradition for Roland to leave a deer for the monster every year on the Day of the Last Leaf.

"What do you think it means?" Kael asked, trying to keep the lumps of meat from sticking to the bottom of the pot.

Roland shrugged. "Kingdom if I know. It can't be good, I'll tell you that. Maybe our truce with the monster is up."

"Maybe it's gone back to the summit."

"Maybe ..." Roland stared into the flames for a moment, the hot embers reflecting back in the dark of his eyes. "I had a dream last night, Kael. And it was a bad one."

"What was it about?"

"Wolves," his voice was barely a whisper, "wolves with iron teeth. They tore us up, they ate the entire village."

Chills rose unbidden across Kael's arms. Some of Roland's dreams were nothing, but some came true. Kael had long suspected that he had a bit of Seer in his bloodline. "It was probably only a dream," he said, more to convince himself than anybody.

Roland's smile didn't quite reach his troubled eyes. "Yeah, probably." He stood stiffly. "I ought to get back to the Hall. And before I go — do you have a spare oilskin around here? Amos swears the snows aren't coming tonight, but I know they are. I can feel it in the crick of my toes."

Kael fought back a smile as he tossed him a cloak. They always wagered over when the first snows would fall. While the rest of the village wrung their hands, Amos and Roland made a game of it.

When he was gone, Kael stirred the pot a few more times before he went to check on the girl. They were alone in the hospital that night, which meant he could talk all he wanted to without getting in trouble.

They'd wedged her cot between the wall and the front side of Amos's desk. If Kael turned sideways, he could edge his way back to the chair in the corner — which he'd situated right by her head. Amos insisted that lowlanders weren't used to the cold. So even though her skin was warm, they had a mountain of pelts draped over her body.

"The stew should be ready in a few minutes," he said as he sat. He knew she couldn't hear him, but it was still nice to have someone his own age to talk to.

Her face was smooth as she slept, her full lips bent almost into a smile. He wished he knew what she was dreaming about. What sort of dreams did lowlanders have? Most likely they were good ones. He doubted that she dreamt of wolves chasing her, or bears ripping her limb from limb. She'd probably never even had a nightmare.

"Do you want to hear a story while we wait?" He pulled the *Atlas* out of his pocket and flipped it to a random page. "*Scarn Who Wouldn't Die*, this is one of my favorites ..."

He read far too long, and soon the potent scent of burning meat wafted in from the main room. Swearing, he dashed out to save the stew. But it was too late.

About three inches of it was caked completely onto the bottom. He scooped up a spoonful of what was still liquid and grimaced as the horrible flavor burned his nose. Perhaps if he added a little water to it, and maybe some herbs ...

His body knew before he did. The spoon froze halfway to his lips and his teeth stuck together. Every little sound magnified itself in his ears: the low whistle of the wind, the scratching of trees on the roof, the creaks and moans of the walls around him. The noise made his heart beat faster — but what he felt stopped it short:

Someone was standing behind him. Watching him. Waiting.

And he was fairly certain they meant him harm.

Chapter 6
The Singing Sword

He felt a breath of air leave the room as the predator inhaled. If Roland were there, he'd say to listen to the animal part of him. And right now it whispered to remain perfectly and completely still.

But his mind knew it wasn't a monster behind him; nothing that waited to rip his innards out and string them across the floor as his body might have him believe. No, he knew the thing behind him was probably only Marc, perhaps even Laemoth.

While the rest of the village ate supper, they must've snuck out to the hospital to teach him a lesson. They'd made a habit of showing up during the day and tormenting him every chance they got. They tripped him and then laughed as he smashed several bottles of haywart ointment on the ground. But their laughter fizzled out when he cleaned the mess without a word, and their faces went dark. Blows came next: carefully-placed kicks in the shins and elbows to the ribs. They wanted to hear him grunt in pain, cry out or curse — any sound that might give them an excuse to haul him before the elders and have him banished. Kael's shins were swollen and bruised, it hurt to breathe, but thus far he'd not made so much as a moan.

And now he was going to pay for it.

He fought against the instincts that screamed for him to freeze and instead got to his feet. His knees were hardly bent straight before the sharp edge of a knife touched his throat. It pushed against his skin, digging at the vein below his chin but not breaking.

So this was it. They were finally going to kill him. He supposed the elders wouldn't defend the death of a Bow-

Breaker. And whatever fear they had for Amos was dwarfed in comparison to their hatred for Kael.

He would not moan, he would not cry. He'd straighten his shoulders and meet death with honor —

"Where am I?"

He didn't recognize the voice at his ear. Though it wasn't the high-pitch shrill he was used to, it was decidedly female. The voice was rough, low, almost like a growl. And it caught him off guard.

"Where am I?" it said again.

He swallowed and felt his throat slide uncomfortably against the edge of the knife. "Tinnark."

A sharp exhale. "The village in the middle of the mountains?"

"Yes."

His body spun around, forced by a strong hand. He blinked, and the next thing he knew, he was staring into the face of the girl.

He'd gotten so used to the smooth calm of her sleeping features that he wasn't prepared for the dark arches of her brows to be bent so low, or for her full lips to be stuck in a serious frown. The wisps of hair that fell across her face cast shadows over her skin, drawing every gentle line into one heart-stopping picture. But for all her face surprised him, her eyes knocked the wind straight out of his lungs.

They were the color of spring: that blink of time when everything in the mountains turned an astonishing shade of green. They were wild, dangerous. And they snared him.

She caught the look on his face and her frown deepened. "What is your name? Tell me quickly."

She seemed on the verge of releasing him. All he had to do was answer this one question, and she would let him go. She'd disappear into the night and take those deadly eyes with her.

He forced his lips to form the word, forced his lungs to push it out: "Kael."

And the next thing he knew, his feet left the ground.

He felt his back pop and his ribs cry out in protest as she shoved him against the wall. She held him there, using the weight of her body to pin him. He flailed his arms and kicked his legs, but the knife slid back into place: a warning, a promise.

He froze.

With the other hand, she tore at his shirt. He felt the cold air glance his chest as the fibers split open, heard the clatter of his buttons as they struck the ground, and the fight surged back into his limbs.

With a roar, he shoved her back. She stumbled and he tried to dart past her, but he only got two steps in before she had him wrangled by his collar and hurled back into the wall. The arm that held the knife clamped across his chest like an iron bar and he knew there was no escape.

At any second she would see — and then she'd drag that knife across his throat and head to Midlan for her reward.

When a second came and passed and she still hadn't killed him, he cracked an eye. He watched her stare at the patch of chest exposed by his torn shirt. He flinched under the pressure of her fingertips. He felt her trace the mark up and down: the red, raised line that extended from below his collarbone and nearly to his stomach.

Amos told him to hide it at all costs, even from Roland. His powers could be explained away but there was no denying the mark. Once anyone saw it, they would know what he was.

She took him under the chin and he braced himself for the moment when she would snap his neck — but it never came. She turned his head, gently, towards the fire. He looked away as those strange eyes locked onto his.

All at once, the pressure of the knife relented and she took a step backwards. She watched him for a moment with the same wide-eyed shock that he watched her. "You are him," she breathed, so quietly it was almost a whisper.

"I am *who*, exactly?" he said. Now that the knife hung loosely in her hand, his temper came back with a vengeance.

"Kael of the Unforgivable Mountains."

"Yes, I am. Didn't I just say that?"

"Kael the Wright."

He laughed. The nerves, the stress of being very nearly skewered, the sheer ridiculousness of what she'd just said all came bursting out his lungs. "You've got the wrong Kael. I'm no Wright."

Her frown was back. She crossed her arms and the knife stuck menacingly out from the crook of her elbow. "Don't tell me I'm wrong. You know nothing about it."

"I think I do, considering I'm the one living in my skin," he retorted. "I'm a whisperer, yes. But I'm only a healer. Don't worry — I'm sure I'll still fetch some gold."

"I'm not going to turn you in. I just can't believe you've been here the whole time, right under my nose." Her gaze drifted to the fire, as if she had a sudden thought, then her eyes turned back to him. "Do you have any idea how long I've been searching for you?"

"Me?" The fumes from the burning stew made his head stuffy. He ripped the pot off the fire and set it on the ground to cool. "Then you've wasted your time. Do I look like a Wright to you?" He stood and spread his arms wide so she could see how very bony he was, how his skin was so white it was practically transparent. He blushed as her eyes wandered the length of him, but stood firm.

She tapped the hilt of the knife thoughtfully against her chin. "Well, when you put it that way … yes."

Either the blow to her head knocked something loose, or they'd rescued a mule by mistake. He strongly suspected the latter.

He was no Wright — one glance and that would've been obvious to anybody. Wrights were the most powerful of all whisperers: men fated with all three gifts. They were master craftsmen, healers impervious to disease and unbeatable warriors. The last Wright, Setheran, had singlehandedly won the Whispering War. He shattered a cliff side with his bare fist, burying himself and all the rebels in the debris. It was his sacrifice that saved the Kingdom.

And to think that Kael could ever measure up to a warrior like Setheran was ... laughable.

"You're —"

"Please," she held up her hand, "I have no interest in an argument. You mountain people carry on pretty famously over the stupidest things. Let's talk about something else." She looked down and pulled at the skirt of her nightdress. "Like why I'm wearing the Kingdom's ugliest, itchiest piece of fabric."

If he hadn't already been cross with her, the way she snarled at the gown might have made him laugh. "All the female patients wear them."

"Do they?" She let the dress fall back into place. "Well did it ever occur to you that I might not like having winter's vindictive fury blowing up my skirt? My privates aren't any less important than yours."

Kael didn't know a thing about women's privates, and the burn in his cheeks more than proved it.

An amused half-smile took the place of her frown. "Never mind. Just tell me where you've stashed my armor."

He pointed to the office and she walked away, flipping the knife high into the air and catching it deftly every few steps. The moment she was out of sight, he tried to collect his thoughts. What had he been about to do?

His stomach growled, reminding him.

He got what little of the stew was edible divided into separate bowls. He wasn't entirely sure how she was used to eating, but he tried to make the table look presentable. Even after he'd scrubbed it down and settled the spoons just so, it looked more prepared for operation than anything else. Well blast it, she'd just have to manage.

"Is something on fire?"

He'd prepared a scathing retort. But when he saw her, his throat sealed shut.

It'd taken Amos a week to clean all the grime from her armor. Every evening he would close himself up in his office and work late into the night. He borrowed oil from the blacksmith and grumbled about how filthy it was. But he'd done his job well.

Every inch of her attire was black as the darkest hour of night. The high collar of her jerkin nearly brushed her chin, and the hem fell almost to her knees. A wide belt wrapped around her waist, framing her graceful figure. Gauntlets covered the tops of her hands, ridged on their backs for the sole purpose of dealing ending blows. They stretched down to her elbows, where they ended in deadly points.

When she turned to check the hearth, he saw the hood attached to the shoulders of her jerkin. She moved, and the tight material that clung to her arms and legs caught the light. He was certain now that they were made of interlocking pieces of metal — so fine they were almost smooth.

"Who are you?"

She smirked at his question. She had her hair pulled back into a pony's tail, but a few strands fell across her eyes, dulling their brilliance in shadow. "My name is Kyleigh."

He'd been expecting her to say that she was an agent of the Earl, or perhaps even an assassin. But a name made her at once less menacing. His eyes wandered to the boots she had clutched in her hands, past the deadly spurs sticking out from the heels, and down to her bare feet. "Aren't you cold?"

Kyleigh shrugged. "Rarely." She dropped her boots next to the hearth and sat at the table. "This is nice. It's been a while since I've had a proper meal." She looked at him expectantly.

"What?"

She nodded to the chair across from her. "Won't you sit?"

He did, stiffly, and tried to avoid her eyes. When she was dressed in rags and holding a knife to his throat, he didn't think much about the fact that she was a girl. But now he was very aware of it.

"This is yours, by the way." She slid the knife across the table to him.

He grasped at his belt and realized that his hunting dagger was missing. "You stole it."

"If you don't want it nicked, you ought to keep it in your boot," she said with a shrug.

He stuck it back in his belt — just to spite her.

She rolled her eyes and put the first spoonful of stew in her mouth — which she immediately spat back out. "Ugh, what *is* this?"

"Well if you hadn't attacked me, it might not have burned."

"I'm not talking about the broth." She dipped her spoon in and held it well away from her, as if she thought it might be poison. "What's this?"

"It's a leek."

"A what?"

"It's a sort of vegetable."

She glared at it. "Well I don't eat prey food. Here, you can have it."

And before he could stop her, she dropped it into his bowl. "You've just had that in your mouth!"

"What? I didn't chew it."

He managed to grab the leek before it sunk and flicked it into the fire. When he turned back around, five more had mysteriously appeared in its place. "You are most definitely not a lady," he muttered.

He'd been so used to talking to her however he liked that he jumped when she laughed. "Of course I'm not a lady. If I were, I'd find the idea of eating off a bloodstained table disgusting."

He supposed she had a point. "Just what are you, then?"

"Isn't it obvious?" She spread her arms wide. "I'm a knight."

That might have been the most ridiculous thing he'd heard all evening. "No you aren't. There's no such thing as a woman knight."

"I beg to differ," she said, propping her feet up on the table. She balanced the stew in her lap and dug through it, making a face at every leek she found.

"Well I've never heard of any women knights. And I've read all about them."

"Have you?" She raised an eyebrow. "Then surely you know how secretive the knights of Midlan are, how their very names are forged to hide them."

Of course he knew. Only the most elite of the Kingdom's soldiers were recruited into the army of Midlan, and only the most skilled of those became knights. They were the deadliest warriors in all the Kingdom: nobody but the King knew how many there really were, or what exactly it was that they did. But rumor had it that they traveled all across the realm, doing the King's most unsavory bidding in shadow.

He supposed it was possible that one of the knights was a woman. But these days there was a price for joining the army of Midlan. And if Kyleigh was telling the truth, it meant she was a murderer.

He suddenly lost his appetite. "Who'd you kill?"

"Loads of people," she said, around a mouthful of charred squirrel.

"You know what I mean."

She must have caught the serious edge in his voice because she set her bowl down and leaned forward. "Kin or friend?"

He nodded.

"Neither, because I have neither."

"I don't believe you. Everyone has someone."

"Well I don't." She leaned back and crossed her arms defiantly. "The King's goons slaughtered my family, and I've been on my own ever since."

He could tell by the hard lines around her eyes that she was telling the truth. "But why would you serve the King if he murdered your family?"

"I don't anymore. I'm an outlaw — a renegade knight bent on reform."

"Don't you mean *revenge*?"

She smirked. "If I took blood for blood, all I'd have is a mess. No, I want things to change. I want to see Crevan toppled and the Five kicked off their thrones."

He snorted. "And I'd like it if the stew pot were always full."

"It's not a fancy," she said, frowning at him. "It can be done. All I need is —"

The door burst open and Amos rode in on a flurry of curses. "It's snowing!" he spat, brushing the white flakes off his shoulders. "I had to listen to Roland gloat all through dinner. *I told you it would snow. My toes never fail!* Huh, I think he was the only cheerful person in the village. Besides you, of course." Amos jerked his head at Kael without looking. "To the rest of us, snow just means no food and nothing to do."

"Why would Kael be happy about the snow?" Kyleigh asked.

Amos snorted and said without turning around: "Because it's his birthday, of course! I thought everyone in Tinnark knew that."

She leaned back in her chair. "Ah yes. Mountain folk use the weather for birthdays. I'd forgotten about that."

Finally, Amos seemed to catch on. He spun around and his mouth dropped open. "You're awake."

She frowned. "Awake? Have I been asleep?"

He nodded. "For over a month, now. Ever since Kael found you in the woods." He took an instrument off a nearby table and advanced on her. "Let's just see how everything's holding up."

She batted his hand away. "Hold on a moment. Why was I in the woods?"

Amos frowned. "You don't remember? Well, that's not unusual for someone with a head injury. I'll tell you what we know ..."

She stared into the fire as he told the tale, her brows bent low. The more he talked, the more troubled her face became. At first, Amos tried to leave out the part about how they healed her, but then Kael told him that she already knew their secret. He raised his eyebrows, but didn't say a word about it.

When he was finished, Kyleigh slumped forward and put a hand over her face. "Oh yes, now I remember," she muttered. After a moment, she sat up straight. "Well, this complicates things."

"How so?" Amos asked.

She looked at Kael. "You saved my life."

"No I didn't." It was the only thing he could say to keep the heat from springing into his face. "Plenty of other people helped. All I did was seal the wound shut."

"And if you hadn't, she'd most certainly be dead," Amos said rather smugly. "Speaking of — is there a reason your blood cooks hotter than the inside of a forge?" He held up his bandaged fingers. "Are you a cursed woman?"

She smiled wryly. "You might say that."

"Do you remember how you got wounded?" Kael asked.

"Oh, that was just a ... misunderstanding," she said with a wave of her hand. "But the important thing is that you saved my life. And by the laws of my people, I owe you a debt."

"Mmmm, and just who are your people?" Amos interjected.

"Warriors from the Grandforest."

It was a vague reply, but before Kael could ask for details, Amos butted his way back in. "I see. And you say you owe my grandson a debt? What sort of debt?"

"A life debt. I must fight alongside him until I save his life in return. And in the meantime, it seems I'll have to put my personal mission on hold."

Kael wasn't in the market for a companion. He had a long road ahead of him and doubted very seriously if Kyleigh could survive for any length of time in the mountains. "Thanks, but I don't need your help," he said, and glared to prove he meant it.

"I'm afraid you don't have a choice. My sword is yours." Her hand twitched involuntarily for the scabbard at her hip, and she found it wasn't there. "Where's he run off to?"

"He?" Amos said.

"Yes, *he*. Every ship and sword in the Kingdom is a she, so I thought it was high time for a he. His name is Harbinger, if you must ..." She bolted upright and froze. "Harbinger?" She cocked her head, like a fox listening for the scratch of a rabbit beneath the snow. Then she turned on her heel and dashed for the office. "I'm coming, Harbinger!"

"Gah, head patients," Amos muttered.

By the time they caught up with her, it looked as if a whirlwind had blown through the room. Amos's books were tossed every which way, clean and filthy clothes lay in heaps together. The cot was turned on its side and the desk lay on its head, its legs stuck up in surrender.

"Not the floorboards!" Amos said, but it was too late.

Kyleigh's heel came down on one of the planks and it broke with a *crack*! She ripped it free and sent another two sailing to opposite ends of the room. When the hole was large enough, she reached down inside of it. Her arm disappeared to her elbow before she let out a triumphant whoop.

"I've found him!" she said excitedly, pulling the curved sword free.

"Blast it, girl! If you'd kept your breeches on for another minute I could've got him for you — and with a great deal less ruin," Amos said. He'd gone out of his way to hide the sword from prying eyes, and now his entire workspace was destroyed.

"I'm sorry, I didn't know you'd put him away," she said, working the scabbard onto her belt. "He was calling for me, and I couldn't just —"

"Calling for you? Are you mad?" Kael interrupted. He knew very well who was going to have to clean up the mess, and it wasn't going to be Amos.

"I'm not mad," she said, her voice flinty. "And I can prove it."

She drew and swung the sword in one fluid motion. Its blade was a solid, bright-shining white, and curved in the

85

middle for the sole purpose of catching flesh. He'd never seen such a blade — he imagined it could cleave a man's head from his shoulders with hardly any effort at all. But that wasn't the strangest part.

The sword hummed as it cut through the air. It was an eerie sound, almost human. He thought he could hear the delight in its call … and the hunger. For some reason, it made him itch for a fight.

"Where did you find it?" Kael said, not taking his eyes off the blade as she swung it around in dizzying arcs.

"He found me, more like," she said with a smirk.

He'd doubted before, but seeing the way she moved with a sword in hand made him believe: Kyleigh was a warrior. "Have you ever killed anybody?"

"Kael," Amos said sharply, but she wasn't at all offended.

"I already told you I have."

"What's it like?"

She stopped swinging. "Like? Well it isn't pleasant, I'll tell you that." She thrust Harbinger into its sheath and gave him a hard look. "I've met your type before: daydreamers, book-readers and the like. You think battle is something glorious."

"Well isn't it? There's glory in defending your home, surely. And in helping those in need, and fighting for people who can't protect themselves. Or are those sorts of things not important to outlaws?"

Her lips curved into a smile. She started to say something, then shook her head. "Never mind. I see the light in your eyes, and I won't be the one to put it out. Now, where are we off to?"

Amos looked alarmed. "You're leaving? But the snows just started. You'll be frozen before midnight."

"I'm not leaving yet." He turned to Kyleigh. "And you're not coming with me."

She opened her mouth to retort when a loud *boom* interrupted her. It sounded like a thunderclap, but the whole house shook beneath it. Kael grabbed Amos by his frail shoulders to keep him from toppling over while Kyleigh held her arms out for balance.

"What in Kingdom's name was that?" Amos sputtered when it passed. He pushed Kael aside and jerked the door open.

Light poured in from outside — bright, orange light. Angry light. Shouts and the sharp clang of metal drifted in with the snow. Tiny bumps rose up on Kael's arms that had nothing to do with the cold. "What is it?"

After a long moment, Amos finally spoke: "Tinnark is under attack."

Chapter 7
Wolves with Iron Teeth

Shock filled his head like gobs of cotton. He hardly felt it when Kyleigh pushed by to stand next to Amos. She leaned out the door, squinting into the night. "It's the Earl's men," she said after a moment. "Great skies — they've got mages."

The house shook again and a burst of lightning flashed, followed by screams. Kael went for the door, but Amos stopped him. "There's a whole army on our doorstep and no time to play the hero. You've got to leave — now."

"We can't let them burn Tinnark, we have to fight!" He shoved past Amos but couldn't get through Kyleigh. She pushed him back with her elbow and closed the door.

"Tinnark's already burned. The only thing we can do now is make sure you get to safety," Amos said as he opened a chest at the foot of one of the hospital beds. He stuffed a leather cap over Kael's head while Kyleigh forced his arms through the sleeves of a deerskin coat and buttoned it. Amos tossed her a rucksack and she slung it over her shoulders.

Its sides bulged out, as if it was already packed.

Explosions rattled the door, much closer this time. Kael cornered Amos. "What about the other villagers? What about Roland? Who's going to save him?"

Amos planted two knobby hands on his shoulders and looked him hard in the eye. "You are. One day, you'll save them all. But not today."

"What? Grandfather, you don't know what you're —"

"Shut your mouth and listen," he snapped, digging his fingers into Kael's skin for emphasis. "Follow Kyleigh, do as she does."

"I don't want ..." Hold on a moment. He didn't remember Kyleigh ever introducing herself to Amos. "How do you know her name?"

He blanched. "You have to run. It's time for you to run."

But he didn't want to run. He swore he would never run again. When he tried to push this thought to his lips, it jumped from his grasp like a slippery fish. His ears clogged. He suddenly couldn't remember how to breathe.

Run.

The tiny lines in Amos's eyes were all-consuming. He felt his feet leave the ground. He was falling further and further into darkness and he couldn't seem to stop.

Run.

Amos's voice was everywhere. The house was gone. Tinnark was gone. Even the mountains were gone. His voice, his command was the only thing left to hold on to — and Kael grasped for it.

Run!

Snow flew up from under his heels as he followed Kyleigh through a tunnel of blazing streets. She was a shade with a white sword, a shadow made even darker by the walls of fire around her.

His legs moved of their own accord, his arms swung with his legs. Fog filled every crack and crevice of his mind, numbing him. With every blink, the darkness lasted an age. He could only see shreds of the horror around him.

Fire arced across the sky. It hit a house in front of them, blowing the roof off. Smoldering planks rained down from the sky and hissed as they fell around him, thudding into the snow. *Darkness.* He saw Brock leaning against the side of the Hall. He stared with empty eyes as fire consumed the roof; death froze his mouth in shock. *Darkness.* Shadows stood in their path. They raised their swords and roared out through the slits in their iron helmets as they charged. *Darkness.* A flash of gold: a wolf's head emblazoned upon a soldier's tunic. It bared its teeth and seemed to snarl as he lunged. Kyleigh rushed to meet him. *Darkness.* Blood — blood everywhere. It melted the snow and trickled out from the wolf's painted eye. *Darkness.* The snow was slush: dark, sticky slush. Men wearing wolves lay everywhere. Kael had to leap over bodies to keep up. *Darkness.*

And then a cry.

Someone shouted, and the familiar sound blasted through the fog in Kael's ears, tearing the numbness away. He could feel the world again — feel his heart as it beat wildly in his chest. His lungs burned from the cold and his eyes streamed against it. His legs still ran, but now he fought against the power. His neck ground against his shoulder as he forced his head to turn. He blinked, clearing up the darkness long enough to see ...

Roland.

He lay on the ground a stone's throw away. He crawled backwards, clutching at the arm that hung limply at his side. Blood squeezed out between his fingers and his eyes burned defiantly as they met the man standing over him.

"Go on, do it!" he roared. "Do it, bloodtraitor. Kill me in the name of your precious Earl — and may the mountains take you!" He spat a mouthful of blood on the soldier's boots.

Time seemed to turn back on itself as the soldier raised his sword. No — this wasn't how Roland was supposed to die. This wasn't what he wanted. He deserved better than to perish at the hands of a traitor.

Kael's legs kept moving, but he managed to free an arm. His shoulder cracked as he pulled his hand towards his only weapon: the knife at his belt. He held it by its blade and watched as the soldier's head tilted back, as his sword reached its pinnacle and that tiny shred of white skin peeked out from under his helmet.

Then he threw.

The sword began its fall — but never got to Roland. He watched as the soldier stumbled backwards, grasping at his throat, before he finally collapsed.

Kael's body jolted as his knees hit the ground. His head came shortly after. Pain. Impossible, fiery pain glanced his skull. It blinded him. In the back of his mind he knew what had happened. It'd only happened a few times before, but he remembered the pain well.

He'd used too much of his power to break whatever Amos did to him, and now he had a whisperer's headache. His body would go limp and at any moment, sleep would take him. He'd lay in the snow, paralyzed and unconscious, until the cold devoured him or the wolves tore him to shreds.

This was the end, he was certain of it.

****

The ground beneath Titus's feet was still hot. Little bits of grass glowed red all around him in a bald patch of earth that stood out like a hole in a sea of snow. A twisted lump of metal lay in the middle of it. He kicked it over.

Swords.

"She was here," he said to the crowd of soldiers around him. He pointed to the nearest cluster of men. "Scour the woods. Look for any sign of where she might have gone. Move!"

They hurried to obey.

He'd been close, then. So close to catching her. He stalked over to where his guards held the surviving villagers. At the front of the herd, an old man knelt in the snow. They'd found him lying just a few yards from the carnage, clinging to his wounded arm. His face was pale from blood loss and his eyes were glazed in pain.

Titus knew he would be dead in a few hours. "What is your name, subject?"

"Roland," he muttered, his lips swollen through the blood.

"Tell me, Roland — which way did she go?"

His eyes sharpened, then hardened. "I don't know who you're talking about."

Titus fought the urge to knock the beard off Roland's chin. "Tell me where she went, and I promise you'll be rewarded. She's dangerous, subject. She threatens the Kingdom's peace."

"What peace?" Roland spat. He jerked his head in the direction of the smoldering village. "If this is the Kingdom's peace ... then I'm glad someone's fighting it."

"We found a couple more, Your Earlship!" someone shouted, just in time to save Roland's life. "Caught them hiding up in the trees."

Soldiers dragged two men on a lead behind them. They were young, hardly old enough to be men at all. The one with hair on his chin whimpered and clutched a bloody hand. The other one had a long braid — and a lump the size of an egg on his forehead.

In two strides, Titus drew even with them. He smacked the bearded man's face with the back of his hand. "Where is she, maggot? Where's the Dragongirl?" He opened his mouth, and Titus hit him again. "I'll make you bleed, maggot! I'll dress the trees with your innards, beat you to death with your own severed arm. I'll —"

"No, don't! I'll tell you anything," the bearded man gasped, falling on his knees.

Titus wrenched the man's head back by his beard and forced him to look into his eyes. "Tell me where the Dragongirl is."

"I don't know anyone by that name, I swear it!"

Titus could tell by the panic in his sputter that he was telling the truth. He shoved the bearded man down and pointed at the one with the braid. "You. Have you seen her?"

He shook his head.

Titus fought to hide his frustration. He knew it'd been a small chance: these people, stuck high on this miserable pile of rocks, wouldn't have heard of her. They wouldn't have even known to look for her. It was most unfortunate.

"You've deeply disappointed me, both of you," he said. "There's nothing I hate more than feeling disappointed. I should kill you for it."

The bearded man whimpered from his place in the snow while the one with the braid took a defensive step backwards. But Titus had no intention of killing them. He'd lost a good number of men to the perils of the mountains and could use an able-bodied tracker — someone who knew the trails well enough to keep his march alive.

So at his signal, the soldiers forced the two men to kneel. With another wave of his hand, they threw Roland into the snow between them. He gave the cowards a sword each.

"Kill or be killed, gentlemen. That is how I run my army — it's the price of entry. Slay your kinsman and I'll make you a soldier of the Earl. Or you can be brave … and try not to scream when we split you open and leave you for the crows. I believe in choices." Titus raised his hand. "You may begin."

The one with the braid leapt up.

"You don't have to do this, Laemoth," Roland said as he advanced. "I know it's hard, but be brave. Trust it'll work out."

The one called Laemoth sneered through his bruises. "Keep your trust, old man. I make my own fate." He turned to the bearded one. "On your feet, Marc. We've got a chance to live and I'm going to take it."

Marc needed a little encouragement. The soldiers beat him with the flats of their blades until he stood.

"Put it on his chest," Laemoth said, sticking his sword to Roland's back. "We'll gut him at the same time."

Marc stood like a man caught in a bog, as if any sudden move would sink him faster. Time dragged on and Titus grew impatient. "If neither of you are going to accept my offer, then I suppose there's no point in waiting. Archers!"

Having a dozen arrows trained on his chest seemed to help Marc reach a decision. He held his sword to Roland's other side and watched with wide eyes as Laemoth began the count.

"One —"

"I've got to, Roland. I'm sorry, but they'll kill me if I don't. I've got no other choice." Marc's voice was pleading.

"— two —"

Roland held his chin up. "You've always got another choice. It may not be what's easiest, but it's always there."

Marc took a step back. The hand that held the sword

trembled.

"— three!"

With a cry, both men lunged forward. Their swords went straight through Roland and out his tattered jerkin. Laemoth ripped his blade free, but Marc's slipped through his fingers as Roland fell.

He died without a struggle: just a soft breath, and then his body lay still.

Marc fell to his knees. "I'm so sorry," he choked.

"Never apologize for surviving, boy. It makes you look like a whelp," Titus said, and reiterated his point with a kick to Marc's rump that sent him sprawling face-first into the snow. "Do we have tunics for these men?"

The soldier responsible for the armory gave him a smirk. "Sorry, Your Earlship — we've only got one."

"Oh, what a pity. It seems that I won't be able to take the two of you on, after all."

Laemoth snarled. "There's one, isn't there?"

Titus pretended to think about it. "Yes, but two men can't share one tunic. That's the problem."

Laemoth figured it out first.

He charged at Marc, sword raised, and the poor fellow barely had time to dodge before the blade cut the air above his head. Laemoth swung again and in his scramble to get away, Marc tripped over a snow-covered log. He fell hard on his elbow. Laemoth was on him in a second.

Marc rolled to the side and the sword got lodged in the skin of the log. Laemoth tore it free with a roar, stumbling backwards as the blade came loose. He was off balance for half a second, nothing more. But when Marc lashed out and caught Laemoth's knee with the side of his boot, it was enough to send him to the ground.

He fell hard. A mixture of pain and shock creased his face as the sword tore through the front of his shirt and out his back.

Titus never grew tired of the fights. When the King sent him to raise the Five's armies, he'd set friend on friend, kin against kin — it was the only way to ensure absolute loyalty to the crown. He promised the victor life, and the loser death. It was amazing how much blood a man was willing to shed to save his own.

But survival came at a price.

When the fight was over, the victor would stare down at the broken body of his opponent and lose a part of himself. He would lose his fear, his compassion. Every weakness of his soul would be driven out: purged by the work of his own bloodstained hands. And when it came time to fight, he would fight. He would kill without remorse and bathe in the gore of battle. There wouldn't be enough ale in the Kingdom to drown his nightmares, but he would have nowhere else to turn. His people would scorn him as a bloodtraitor.

Battle would be his only relief.

As Laemoth died, Titus kept his eyes on Marc. Those anguished lines around his mouth would eventually harden and freeze in a mask of hate. The many long nights that lay ahead would drive out his mercy. Titus knew he was witnessing the birth of a warrior — and it was a glorious thing.

"Never run with your sword facing up," he said, throwing the spare tunic at Marc's feet. "Or you might end up like this poor fool." He kicked Laemoth's body aside, hauled Marc up by the hood of his coat and shoved him away. "Congratulations, maggot — you've earned your place in the Earl's army."

While his soldiers made camp, Titus walked among the surviving villagers, asking for their skills. Those with valuable talents he added to his forces ... the rest he disposed of.

Most of the villagers fled when his army attacked, melting into the cover of the woods like the mountain rats they were. The only ones left were those too old to run — or too stupid to hide. He was about to give the order to kill them all and be done with it when an old crow caught his attention.

He had tangled gray hair and sharp brown eyes. Maybe it was the stiff set of his jaw or his practiced, concentrated stare. But for whatever reason, Titus liked the look of him. He ordered the man on his feet. "And what's your name?"

"Amos," he said.

There was no fear in his voice. Titus could hardly keep the smirk off his face. "Any skills?"

"I'm a healer."

His instincts were right: at long last, Fate smiled upon Titus. He'd lost his healer to a rockslide several miles back, and knew he would lose a good portion of his men to their wounds without one. But he kept his face stern. "A healer, eh? Well I suggest you get to work, healer. Prove to me that you're worth your meals and I'll let you live."

With a slight bow, Amos left to tend the wounded.

Titus cut his thumb across his chest, signaling his men to begin the slaughter. Screams pierced the air of the snow-silenced night, and he had to raise his voice to be heard over the strangled cries for mercy:

"Rest well, my wolves. For with the dawn comes glory and fresh blood!"

Chapter 8
A Long Climb

"Amos! Amos!"

Fire burst through the cracks in the wall, raced across the floor and swallowed their beds. A corner of the roof caved in, a wave of heat and embers flew out from the rubble and burned Kael's cheeks.

He was standing in the doorway, reaching in as far as he dared. He stretched his hands till his fingers hurt. He could see Amos standing by the hearth.

"Amos!" he said again. "Take my hand!"

But he didn't move. Sparks showered down as the ceiling buckled in the heat. He shouted as loud as he could, he begged Amos to move. The ground shook and the roof sank further. The red-hot end of one plank nearly brushed the top of Amos's head.

Though his throat burned, he shouted with all of his might ... but Amos simply couldn't hear him. Then the roof collapsed in a wave of blistering heat and ash — and Kael went flying backwards.

****

He jerked out of his sleep and the back of his head smacked against the floor. When he opened his eyes, Kael saw he was surrounded by rock: it made up the walls, the ceiling, even the floor he slept on. Gray, uncut stone stained with the black lines from a fire.

Fire. He smelled smoke.

The cold panic left over from his dream welled up and he jumped to his feet. His skull connected with the low ceiling and the pain sent him promptly back to his knees.

"Oh good, you're awake."

He blinked several times before the blurry shape ahead of him turned into Kyleigh. She was sitting cross-legged in front of a large hole in the wall. Behind her, he thought he could see snow and white clouds. He realized they must be in some sort of cave.

"I've got your breakfast ready, and I've cooked it just the way you like it," she said, nodding to the small fire beside her.

Dangling from a spit in the middle of the flames was what might once have been a leg of meat. But now it was so charred beyond recovery that he doubted if even the flies would eat it.

"I'm not hungry," he said, and it was the truth. From the moment he woke he'd been grasping at his foggy memories of the night before, piecing them together. Much of it had been lost in the darkness of sleep, and the rest ...

He grasped at pictures as they swam by, but couldn't get a hold of them. It was as if he stared through a filthy window into his memory: he could see the shapes moving outside, had some wisp of their meaning, but couldn't quite tie them together.

After many long and frustrating attempts, he saw something — a wolf's head, rising out of the darkness. He tied it to the armor, tied the armor to the man, and very suddenly remembered that Tinnark had been under attack. But by whom?

And then he remembered that the wolf's head was the symbol of the Earl of the Unforgivable Mountains.

"Why now?" he said, more to himself than anybody. "Why would Hubert suddenly decide to come after us when he's left us alone all this time?"

"Because it wasn't Hubert — it was Titus," Kyleigh said. She pulled the ruined meat off the spit and chucked it outside. He heard it hiss when it hit the snow.

"Titus ... but I thought he was Midlan's warlord," Kael said. "How do you know it was him?"

"I could smell him from a mile off. That man reeks of death. I also saw him when I went back to retrieve my boots." She pointed to her clad feet. Then she bent and began digging through the rucksack, looking for something.

But he was stuck on what she'd just said. "You went back, and all you got were your boots?"

"Not *all*. I found this as well." She held up his bow, the one Roland had given him. He couldn't think to ask her how she'd found it. He couldn't even be happy to see it. In fact, he knocked it out of her hand.

"Why didn't you save Amos? You went back for boots and a stupid piece of wood, and you couldn't be bothered to save my grandfather?"

"No, I couldn't," she snapped back. "You passed out. And by the time I hauled your sorry carcass to safety, Titus already had them rounded up."

"Who?"

"The villagers!"

His stomach sunk down to his ankles. For a moment, he'd been relieved: Roland always said that a dream of a loved one's death actually meant they were alive and well. But for how long? He knew all too well what Titus did with his captives.

"Were any ...?"

"I don't know." The anger was gone from her voice, but her eyes were still hard. "I couldn't stay. The woods were crawling with soldiers and I had to get back to you."

"Why?"

"Because *you* are my first priority. We're tied together, you and I."

"Not anymore." He grabbed the bow off the ground and dug through the pack until he found his quiver. His hand brushed something familiar, and he pulled out *Atlas of the Adventurer*. He didn't know how it had found its way into the pack, but he crammed it in his pocket nonetheless. What he didn't find was his hunting dagger. It wasn't in the pack and his belt was empty. Where on earth had it gone? "If what you say is true and you really *did* pull me to safety, then your debt is repaid. We can go our separate ways."

She rose when he did, blocking him. "Not so fast — there's no guarantee that you would've died, had I left you."

"Really?" he stepped to the side, but she moved twice as fast.

"Really. Think about it: the fires from the village would've kept you from freezing to death, and the light would've scared off the wolves."

"What about the Earl's men? Wouldn't they have used me for a pin cushion the first chance they got?"

"Not likely. They probably would've just counted you as a body," she said with a smirk. "No, I'm not content to have just saved you from *almost* certain death. When I save you from *certain* death, then we can consider the debt settled. Until then, you're stuck with me."

He couldn't get around her, he couldn't fight her off and even though he very briefly entertained the idea of clubbing her over the head, he couldn't bring himself to knock out any more of her sense. He supposed he really *was* stuck with her. "Fine. You can come along, just stay quiet."

"Fair enough. Where are we headed?"

"Where do you think? To get the Earl — or Titus, or whoever."

"*Earl* Titus. I believe he's been promoted," she said as she slung the pack over her shoulders.

"Well whoever he is, he can't be far ahead of us. I was only out for the day, right? And the two of us can move faster than an army. As soon as we find their trail, I wager it'll be less than a week before we've caught up."

She started to reply, but he ignored her. He strode out of the cave and looked around for something to climb — he had to get his bearings. There wasn't much nearby, but as it happened a large boulder sat on the hill above the cave. He climbed its unfamiliar side and took in the land around him.

Just a few yards away, the snow ended. It stopped in a perfect line and brown grass extended beyond it — jaunting down the slope and into a thick forest of pines. Beyond that ... no, it couldn't be.

He scrambled down the side of the boulder and onto the nearest ledge, where he could clearly see what lay beneath him. He didn't have to open the *Atlas* to know that what he stared at was the Valley.

Cradled on a sea of green, little dots of trees and winding streams coursed the length of it. Tall grass flowed in waves, teased by the wind that cascaded down from the mountains surrounding it. Here, quiet houses rested far from their neighbors and sleepy tendrils of smoke rose from their chimneys. Off in the distance, he thought he could make out the gray tops of the western mountains.

He realized they weren't anywhere near Tinnark, or Earl Titus. Somehow, they were already at the bottom.

"It's beautiful, isn't it?" Kyleigh called up to him. She was standing at the cave entrance, watching him. "Nothing at all like those Miserable Mountains of yours."

"*Unforgivable* Mountains," he said testily. "And why are we at the bottom? How long have I been asleep?"

"A night and half a day. We've made good time."

Good time? *Good* time? No, *extraordinary* time, impossible time! He gripped a handful of hair and fought the urge to yell at her. "How have we managed to make it all the way down the mountains in a day and a half?"

"I can't tell you that. As a former knight, I've sworn to protect my secrets."

It took him approximately ten seconds to reach her. "Take me back," he said, as dangerously as he could.

She looked him hard in the eyes. "No. If I take you back now, you'll only get yourself killed —"

"No I won't, because unlike you I actually know how to survive in the mountains. *I've* never cracked my head on a rock and had to be rescued —"

"Oh, it was no rock."

"What was it, then?"

She clamped her mouth shut and her face turned slightly pink. "It doesn't matter what it was. All that matters now is that you stay alive."

"Why?" he countered. "Why do you need me alive? And why did Amos seem to think that I had something important to do?"

"I've already told you."

He thought back for a moment. "You still think I'm a Wright, don't you?" he guessed. "Well that's completely ridiculous. I've already told you I'm not —"

"And I'm not interested in arguing over it," she said, throwing her hands up. "So tell me what you plan to do, Kael Not-A-Wright. Where are we headed?"

Behind him, there was nothing but a wall of solid rock — a treacherous climb that pierced the clouds and jutted upwards. It would take weeks to reach Tinnark in fair weather, and the clouds that covered the mountains now were far from fair: they were the color of iron and unmoving. They'd found their perch for the winter and were prepared to squat till the sun came to burn them away.

Which wouldn't happen until spring.

In the meantime, the snow would cover the army's tracks. Any abandoned camps they found would be months old instead of days. Their trail would be long gone. It was like Roland always said: even the best tracker still needed tracks.

He felt his heart twinge when he thought of Roland, and he hoped to mercy he was safe. "Was there any food in the pack?"

Kyleigh shook her head. "Not to speak of. Though I found a pair of ratty old gloves we might be able to chew on, should things get desperate."

He frowned at her. "One of the houses at the bottom must have some supplies we can trade for ... um, have we got anything to trade?"

She dug around for a moment and pulled out a tattered purse. A number of copper and silver coins sat in the bottom of it, but he had no idea what they meant.

"All right, well you can be in charge of that," he said, thrusting them back at her. "Come on. If we move quickly, we can reach the bottom by nightfall —"

"And then what?"

"I just said it — we'll get supplies."

"No, I mean after all that. Where will we go, once our packs are full?"

"Back up the mountains to find my grandfather." He had to wonder if she was so dense *before* she cracked her skull. He'd made it almost to the trees when he realized she wasn't following. "*What?*" he snapped.

"Might I make a suggestion?"

"No."

"Regardless, I can't help but think that you've got us on a doomed quest."

"Oh? And how do you figure that?" he said, making no attempt to hide the annoyance in his voice.

She sidled up to him, hands clamped behind her back. "Well, say we *do* make it back to Tinnark. Say we avoid freezing, falling and getting eaten long enough to make the climb. And what if, against all foreseeable odds, we manage to find Titus ... what then? How do you hope to defeat him?"

Did she expect him to have some detailed plan stashed in his breeches? "I don't know. I'll cross that river when I come to it."

She snorted. "You won't be crossing that river at all, not without some help. Believe me — I've seen Titus on the battlefield. There's a reason Crevan made him warlord. No," she looked off into the distance, "we'll need help ... friends with fighting skills."

"Well, I haven't got any friends. Much less friends with fighting skills."

"You've got me," she reminded him. "And I just happen to know some men who're mad enough to help us. But it'll be a hike to reach them."

"How far?"

She took a deep breath. "The High Seas."

Now it was his turn to shake his head. The quickest way to the seas was through the Valley, but he knew from the stories in the *Atlas* that the land was far more dangerous than it looked.

Bandits thrived in this corner of the Kingdom, where they could attack unsuspecting travelers and escape quickly into the shelter of the mountains. Thieves cut purses freely, slipping a few coins to the town guard here or there to keep from getting pinned. The general lawlessness also attracted patrols from Midlan — which would arrive with every intention of restoring order. But then the soldiers would drink far too much of the heady mountain wine and, in a drunken stupor, end up pillaging everyone in the name of the King.

And that was before Earl Hubert came into power. Kael imagined things had only gotten worse.

"It's not as far as you think," Kyleigh said when she saw the look on his face. "We'll travel during the day and at night, we'll sleep well off the road. We should reach the seas in a fortnight, if we're careful."

He knew he didn't really have a choice. Kyleigh was right. He would've died rather than admit it, but the two of them didn't stand a chance against Titus's army. They needed numbers on their side. At times like this was when Amos used to roll his eyes and say: "You can't leap to the top of a tree, boy. You've got to climb it!"

And what a long climb it would be. "Can't you just use whatever power brought us down the mountains to take us across the Valley?" he said.

She pursed her lips. "And risk being spotted by every eye in the Kingdom? I think not. Look — we've got a small enough chance of succeeding as it is. Everything depends on how long we can stay unnoticed. And the Valley isn't as empty as the mountains — the King trusted Hubert least of all. More soldiers roam this land than the towers of Midlan. No, we'll have to take the long route."

"All right," he said after a moment, finally resigned to his fate. "We'll do this your way."

Which seemed to please her to no end.

They traveled hard for the rest of the day. Kyleigh skipped over rocks and rotted logs while he followed the safer route at a trot. Occasionally, she'd disappear for several minutes before he'd see her running along a ledge above him, or skirting across a river on the mossy back of a toppled tree.

Well, it was no wonder she'd nearly lost her head, if she always sprinted through the mountains like she owned them.

At long last, they broke from the woods. There was only one slope left to climb down — and it was steep enough to be mistaken for a wall. If they lost their footing, they wouldn't stop until they hit the bottom — or impaled themselves on one of the many jagged rocks that lunged out from the gravel like spears.

The sun was setting, but he thought if they moved quickly that they might be able to make it down before the light disappeared all together.

"Ladies first," he said, waving at it.

She must not have realized that he was joking. "Here goes," she said with a grin. And before he could stop her, she leapt off.

She sprinted down the slope like it was no more trouble than an open field. She slid between rocks in places where the gravel was thickest, kicking her legs up wildly behind her. It took her less than a minute to skate her way to the bottom.

When she made it to safety, she turned and waved to him. "Don't just stand there, come on!"

She was completely mad, no doubt about it. "I'm not going to throw myself off and wind up in a bloody heap," he shouted back. He began his descent slowly, going only a few feet at a time and stopping to rest between rocks.

"Sometime this decade, please," she called.

"If you're bored, why don't you make camp?" he snapped back. Sweat trickled into his eyes, blinding him as he stretched for a foothold that was just barely within his reach.

"Why don't I build us a house? I think I'll have plenty

of time."

"I don't care what you do — just don't distract me."

"Fine. Shall I make it one story, or two?"

He looked up to retort, and promptly lost his footing.

Chapter 9
The Jackrabbit

"Hold still," Kyleigh said, grabbing him under the chin. He grimaced while she dragged a wet cloth down his cheek. It felt about as pleasant as a bee's barb, and when she went to dip it back in the bowl, he saw it was covered in a wet mix of dirt and dried blood.

His climb down the mountain hadn't gone quite like he planned — and he blamed it entirely on Kyleigh. If she hadn't been heckling him, he might've noticed the rock he stood on was a bit loose. Then he might not have gone tumbling down head over heels, striking every stone and upraised root on his way.

Fortunately, a large nettle bush saved him from falling to his death. Though when he tried to get up, it clung very stubbornly onto his clothes. He'd been stuck for several minutes before Kyleigh stopped laughing long enough to pull him free. She'd helped him limp down the road for another mile or so before they came to a small inn called *The Jackrabbit*.

The innkeeper was a jumpy man. When they knocked on the door, he'd peered out at them through a crack before he swung it open. He had short hair and a wild mess of a beard. In his hand, he'd clutched a woodcutter's axe.

"It was one of them monsters again, wasn't it?" he said, his eyes on Kael's wounds. "I've seen them out in the paddock late at night — horrible wolves the height of men! The goats start bleating and I run out there to try and scare them off, but ..." He shook his head. "I haven't ever been fast enough. Took my Nancy last night, they did."

Kael couldn't be sure, but he thought he saw the innkeeper's eyes well up a bit.

"No monsters," Kyleigh assured him. "Just a rather nasty fall. Might we come in?"

"Of course you can, miss. We don't call it an inn for nothing," he said as he let them by. After he found them a table, he'd gotten a fresh bowl of warm water and several rags for them to clean up with.

Now Kael scrubbed his limbs while Kyleigh worked on his face and neck — and she was being far from gentle. "Would you stop that?" he said, jerking his head out of her reach. "I'd like to keep some of my skin, if you don't mind."

"Oh, don't be such a fawn about it — I haven't even got down to the skin." She twisted the cloth over the bowl and a large amount of murky brown water came out of it. "See?"

He tugged a thorn from his elbow and pressed a cloth over the dot of fresh blood. "This is just for show, anyhow. I'll fix it myself later," he muttered.

She looked over his shoulder at the kitchen door, where they could hear the innkeeper cursing and clanging pots together. "Just keep it subtle, will you? We don't want anyone to start asking questions."

"I'm not a child. I've managed to keep it a secret this far. I know what I'm doing." He threw his cloth down on the table, where it stuck.

"Dinner's served!" The innkeeper pushed through the doors and made his way to their table, balancing a plate in either hand. "We've got roasted turkey legs, bread and cheese. And if you don't mind, I think I'll sit with you for a bit. Business is a little, ah, slow tonight."

It was indeed. Of the dozen or so tables before the hearth, theirs was the only one with anyone in it. They had the whole inn to themselves.

The innkeeper lit up a pipe and took several quick puffs. "I tell you, I think I've got the only grass-eating cat in the whole Kingdom. Those rats will skip right past him, so fat that their little bellies drag on the ground. But he just watches them go by. You ever heard of anything worse?"

"Worse than a cat? I don't think so," Kyleigh said with a grin. "Tell me — do you feed it off the table?"

"I don't, but my wife sure might ..."

While they worked to solve the mystery of the cat, Kael dug in. He tore off a huge chunk of the turkey leg and swallowed it without chewing. Then he turned on the bread and cheese.

He'd never had them before: there were no farms in Tinnark and even if there had been, he suspected the villagers couldn't have stopped eating their animals long enough to let them make cheese. All he knew was that anytime the heroes in the *Atlas* sat down for a great feast, there was always bread and cheese.

He tore off a chunk of the roll, topped it with a pinch of cheese and stuffed the whole thing into his mouth. The bread was thick and rich, like stew broth, and the cheese melted into it. He was sure he'd never tasted anything so delicious.

His turkey leg was down to the bone when a chorus of howls interrupted their dinner. Three scruffy dogs bounded in from outside, cornering them at the table. Their barks pierced the sensitive parts of Kael's ears, and he thought very seriously about giving the nearest one a sharp kick.

"Oh hush now, you mutts!" the innkeeper bellowed over their protests. "Can't you see we've got company?"

An ear-splitting whistle from Kyleigh finally silenced them all. They cocked their furry heads at her and their tails stood straight. "Come here, you lot," she said, slapping her knees.

"I'd be careful, miss," the innkeeper warned, but it was clear by the way the dogs covered her face in wet kisses that they meant her no harm.

She led them to the hearth and got them to sit quietly while she scratched their ears. She spoke sweetly to them, and their tongues lolled out between their pointed teeth as they hung on her every word.

"Those mongrels nearly took the hand off of one of my guests last week. Now look at them." The innkeeper shook his head and chuckled. "Where'd you find that girl, anyhow?"

Kael realized that he would now have to be the one to answer the innkeeper's many nosy questions. So he took a leaf out of Kyleigh's book: "She found me, more like."

"She just found you, eh?" the innkeeper said with a grin. "Well that don't surprise me. That's the way it always happens ... when you meet that special lady."

Kael nearly choked on his bread.

"I know *exactly* what you mean, boy," he continued, a knowing twinkle in his eye. "You're just going about your business one day and," he clapped his hands together, "it's like a slap around the ears, like the first time you ever felt something. Leastways, that's how it was when I found my darling." He glanced at the hearth, where Kyleigh and the dogs had settled down for a nap, and lowered his voice. "Do you know how to catch a woman's heart?"

No, he didn't have the slightest clue. And he certainly didn't want to hear the innkeeper's advice. But he could only manage an "Uh —" before he pounded his rough hand on the table and declared:

"You tell her. You get off your rump and you let her know that she's the prettiest, most wonderful —"

"Sir —"

"— amazing woman you ever laid eyes on! Then you just scoop her up in your arms and give her a kiss, real passionate-like."

"I don't think —"

"Well of *course* you can, boy! Sure it takes a bit of courage. But it's worth it, ain't it? And," he dropped his voice again, "a girl as pretty as yours isn't going to wait around forever. There's plenty of boys out there — handsome boys — who'd be happy to take her off your hands. Men like you and me, well, we've got to work a little faster than the rest."

At this point Kael wasn't sure which was burning hotter: his face or the hearth fire. But at that moment the innkeeper's wife appeared, saving him.

She was a small, dainty woman, and when the innkeeper saw her, he smiled. "Well, speaking of lovely ladies."

110

She blushed under his look. "I've drawn up the baths, whenever our guests are ready."

Kael practically jumped to his feet.

She frowned at Kyleigh's empty chair. "And where has the lady wandered off to?"

"Ah, she's somewhere under there, love." The innkeeper gestured to the snoring pile of fur next to the fire. "I'll wake her and send her up."

"All right. But you be careful not to disturb those dogs," she called as she led Kael to his room. "Remember what happened last time."

He grumbled in reply. Apparently, the memory was still very fresh.

The rooms at *The Jack Rabbit* were small and tidy. But all Kael really cared about was the bed. "Your bath is over here, sir," the innkeeper's wife said quickly, before he could dirty up her sheets.

She pointed to what looked like an oversized barrel that had been turned on its side and cut in half. Steam rose from the water and when he dipped his fingers into it, he thought it felt like a warm bowl of stew. Because she seemed to think that he knew how to work a bath, the innkeeper's wife bowed out the door and left him to his own devices.

He'd had only a few past experiences with bathing. Usually, they involved a simple bucket-full of cold river water. But the night air was chilly, and he was filthy enough to strip off his clothes and give the bath a try.

The water was surprisingly pleasant — the problem was that it only reached halfway up his thighs. A shelf that held all sorts of odd things covered one half of the bath, leaving him with only a small portion to bathe in.

At first he tried to sit down, but his legs were far too long and he ended up feeling like a turkey that wouldn't quite fit in the pot. Then he accidentally lost his footing and discovered that the space beneath the shelf was hollow. His rump was sore and a good bit of the water sloshed out on the ground, but the warmth felt fantastic.

He grabbed a knife off the shelf and scraped at the bit of stubble that'd grown on his face over the past few days. He never could grow a full beard. And the few times he'd tried, the Tinnarkians hailed him as *Patches* for weeks after.

Though he couldn't see the wounds on his face, there were plenty more he could see well enough to heal. But he only managed to get a few sealed before a headache started to build up in the back of his skull. He didn't want to pass out again, so he decided to clean his wounds the long way.

One of the items on the shelf looked like it might be helpful: it was a yellow lump that smelled a bit like flowers. But when he went to scrub with it, the lump shot out of his hand and escaped into the depths of the bath water. Every time he grabbed it, it leapt away.

He was in the middle of a very intense wrestling match when Kyleigh's voice stopped him short: "Is everything all right in there?"

What in Kingdom's name was she doing in his room? He spun around and tried to cover himself, but only managed to slam his knee into the side of the bath — which knocked several things off the shelf. He grimaced as a painted dish hit the ground and shattered neatly to pieces.

"I'd appreciate it if you kept the damage to a minimum, seeing as how I'm the one paying for all this," she said dryly.

He realized that her voice was not coming from in his room, but from behind the wall next to him. "Sorry, but I can't get a hold of this yellow stuff," he said as he coaxed the lump towards him with his toe.

There was a long pause. "Surely you've used soap before."

He didn't know why she sounded so incredulous. "No, we didn't have the luxury of *soap* in Tinnark."

Her laughter rang out clearly, burning him. "Well that certainly explains a lot. And to think — I've been blaming the smell on rotting animals."

"Very funny. Are you going to tell me how to use soap or not?"

"You can start by picking it up gently. Don't strangle it, or it'll just fly out of your hand."

Once again, she was right. If he held it loosely, he found he could wield it without losing it. He scrubbed until the soap was reduced to hardly the size of a pebble, and couldn't believe the amount of dirt that came off of him. It was like magic.

When the innkeeper's wife came by to pick up his dirty clothes, he couldn't help but notice that she held them as far away as possible — like she thought his tunic might very well bite her if she got too close. Maybe he really *did* smell horrible.

As soon as he climbed into bed, he found he didn't care if he stunk or not: his eyes slammed shut and the world went quiet.

Chapter 10
Garron the Shrewd

Even after she paid for the broken dish, Kyleigh had enough coin left to buy some salted meat for their rucksacks. The round bits of copper she traded for it had no value to Kael, but the innkeeper seemed pleased.

"You're always welcome at *The Jackrabbit*," he said cheerfully. "You stop by here anytime."

After she bid the dogs farewell, they were off. When he looked back to wave goodbye, the innkeeper gave him a gesture that clearly meant he approved of Kyleigh's physique, and Kael should get on with it, already.

"Why does your face look like it's ripe to be picked?" Kyleigh asked when he spun back around.

"Nothing. It's warm out here, is all," he said, just as his boot crunched some frost-covered weeds.

The further into the Valley they walked, the more beautiful it became. Green grass waved playfully around their boots and the breeze was heavy with the scent of flowers. Here, the trees reclined like lazy men after dinner, their gentle curves the opposite of the mountain pine's rigid stand.

When the afternoon sun bordered on becoming hot, they stopped under a large tree for lunch. Kael rolled up his sleeves and sat in the thickest patch of shade he could find, while Kyleigh sprawled out in the sunlight. He didn't see how she could stand the heat, covered in black armor. But she seemed to thoroughly enjoy herself.

While she napped, he flipped through the *Atlas*. He thought he might find some useful information on bandits — like how to avoid them. But there was only a basic outline of their history, which was something he'd already read. He tossed the book on the ground and let out a frustrated sigh.

"Trouble, my book-loving friend?" Kyleigh said. She had an arm draped over her head and watched him through one eye.

He frowned at her. "It's nothing."

She turned her face back to the sun and grinned. "Sure it's not. I imagine it's not frustrating at all to be able to remember every word you've ever read."

"I don't remember every word."

"They say a Wright can read something once, and remember for the rest of his life."

So they were back to this, then? Well it was too blasted hot for an argument: he'd end this nonsense once and for all. "I'm not a Wright, and I'll prove it." He threw the book and it landed next to her elbow. "Read a few sentences — if you can read, that is — and if I'm a Wright, I'll be able to tell you what sentence comes next."

She sat up and opened the *Atlas* across her lap. "Oh, *Sir Gorigan the Dragonslayer*. Well, if this isn't the biggest crock of —"

"Just read it," he said through gritted teeth. He liked this story, and didn't want to hear her talk badly about it.

She seemed to be fighting back a smile as she began. "*Of all the terrible creatures, none was greater than the mighty dragon. With his serpent body clad in iron scales, his teeth the length of swords, and fiery breath with enough heat to singe your knickers off —*"

"No, it's *enough heat to melt armor*," Kael interjected. "Stop fooling around. It's not going to work if you don't read it correctly."

She looked at him from over the top of the book, but didn't say anything. "*The dragons, in their lust for the realm, swarmed upon the holds of men and invited them to dinner —*"

"*And destroyed all they held dear.*" He glared when she grinned. He couldn't believe she wasn't taking the story seriously.

"*The knights of the realm rose to fight, but then they got bored —*"

"*But the dragon's scales broke their swords*. You aren't telling it right!"

"So sorry. Ahem … *only Sir Gorigan, ferret among men —*"

"*Fairest.*"

"*Wore spectacles for his sight —*"

He wrenched the book from her hands and stuffed it back in his pocket. "*Didn't give up the fight*, he *didn't give up the fight*! I know you don't believe the stories, but you don't have to butcher them. They could be true — Sir Gorigan could have chased the dragons away. Have *you* seen a dragon lately? Because I know I haven't."

He stomped down the path, determined to put as much distance between them as possible. But it wasn't long before he heard her footsteps coming up behind him.

"I don't want to talk to you."

"I'm sorry, truly I am," she said. He didn't look at her, but she sounded sincere. "I was just having a bit of fun. I had no idea the stories meant so much to you. Next time I'll tell it right."

He shrugged because he didn't want her to think he cared. But the truth was that he cared very much.

It would have sounded ridiculous if he said it aloud, but in his head he thought of Sir Gorigan as a close friend. When the other children wouldn't play with him, he'd found refuge in the world of stories. He would escape between the pages and imagine himself fighting alongside warriors like Sir Gorigan, slaying dragons and saving the realm. In many ways, the heroes he read about were the only friends he'd ever had.

But he would die before he admitted it to Kyleigh.

They walked for another hour in silence. It didn't take long for his anger to fade, and soon he was back to thinking darkly about the weather. Sweat gathered around the collar of his shirt, making it itch more than usual. Or perhaps it was because his head swiveled to the left and right so often that it tickled.

Every bush, every crop of trees was a potential threat. He strained his eyes and watched for any sign of movement. He gripped his bow so tightly it made his fingers hurt. But he wasn't going to let the bandits take them by surprise. If he let his guard down for half a second, they might spring out, rob them blind, slit their throats and leave them for the crows.

But a while later it began to feel like he worried over nothing: they hadn't come across another soul all afternoon. Then they climbed a gentle hill, and what they saw below shattered their peace.

A large caravan sprawled out on the flat ground beneath them. Six covered wagons made a circle around the smoldering remnants of campfires, each stamped with the great twisting oak of the Grandforest. Dark-haired forest men swarmed all around them, calling to each other as they rushed to pack their camp.

"I wonder if they'd let us follow along for a bit?" Kyleigh said.

He thought that was a horrible plan. "You can't be serious. For all we know they could be bandits disguised as merchants. Or rogue mages, or assassins, or slave traders, or —"

"Terrible, bone-crunching rabbits! Oh, come now," she said when he glared at her. "They're only merchants. Besides, traveling with a caravan will keep us safe from the *real* bandits — and whatever other nonsense you're worried about." And before he could stop her, she strode purposefully down the path.

"I still think we should be careful," he grumbled as he followed. "Rogue mages are a real concern, you know. I've read all about them."

He wasn't sure, but he thought he saw the side of her face crease in a grin.

The forest men were so busy packing that no one noticed them approach. When they were within shouting distance, a man on a black horse finally spotted them. He galloped up the hill and reined in his horse an arm's reach from Kael, barring them from the path. He didn't say anything for a moment. His stern blue eyes flicked over the pair of them while he stroked impatiently at his regal, gray-tinged beard.

"You're nearly a day late," he finally said, his voice every bit as serious as the slick crop of his hair. "I sent word to the Earl over a week ago, requesting an escort. What if we'd been attacked by bandits? Would His Earlship have compensated me for my stolen goods? He probably just sent the two of you to search our bodies. Kingdom knows he's already swindled me. For all the gold I paid, I should have gotten a small army, not a pair of children —"

"We aren't children — sir." Kael added that last bit quickly, when the man raised his brows in dangerous arcs.

"Not children? Well a full-grown man would know how to tell time," he huffed. The horse snorted in agreement, blowing its hot breath through Kael's hair. "You've put my whole caravan behind, and now we're in danger of missing the market. How do you propose we make up the difference? Gold doesn't fall from the sky, you know."

Kael didn't know where gold came from, but he was fed up with this pompous man and his smelly horse. He was about to tell him exactly where he could put his difference when Kyleigh stepped in.

"You're right. And if we miss the market, you can take the difference from our wages," she said.

The anger left the man's face immediately. "Well, I'll agree to that." He crossed his arms over his slightly protruding belly. "I'm rather impressed — your sort usually doesn't admit wrong, much less remedy it. And what do I call you?"

"I'm Kyleigh, and this," she nudged him, "is Kael."

He nodded to each of them in turn, then swept a hand to his chest. "I'm Garron the Shrewd, a merchant of the Grandforest. Don't call me Mr. Shrewd — it gives me indigestion. Stick with Garron, for now." He jerked the horse towards the caravan. "Take your packs and fall in the with the rest of the men. Quickly, now — we haven't got time for dawdling!"

Kael waited until he galloped out of earshot — then he swore. "Perfect. Now he thinks we work for the Earl. And what happens when the *real* escorts show up? Do you think *Mr. Shrewd* is just going to let us get away with it?" He turned towards the caravan, where he could hear Garron laying into some poor man who wasn't moving fast enough. "He'll probably tie us to the back of that devil horse and drag us till our skin comes off."

Kyleigh raised her eyebrows. "That's quite inventive, actually. But I don't think we have to worry about the escorts showing up. Earl Titus is dragging the better part of his army through the mountains, remember? And he'll have left the rest behind to defend the castle."

He immediately felt foolish. He should have thought of that. "I suppose we *would* be doing Garron a favor, if we went along ..."

"Exactly. He needs escorts, and we need safe passage through the Valley. See?" She clapped him on the shoulder. "We haven't been with them five minutes and you're already learning something about trade."

"It still doesn't seem entirely honest."

She shrugged. "It never is. Now, are you coming or not?"

"Okay. But if we get caught —"

She grabbed him by the arm and pulled him forward. "Then you can say *I told you so* — right before they hang us by our own entrails."

Garron the Shrewd had tied up his horse and was marching among the carts, barking orders, when they arrived. The air around him must have been charged with a shock: everywhere he went, men leapt off their rumps and scrambled to find a task. They secured fastenings, loaded equipment, and doused fires — anything to avoid the sharp edge of his tongue.

He was in the middle of inspecting a cartwheel when a pretty young woman flitted to his side. His stern expression melted away as he caught her in his arms and kissed the top

119

of her head. They talked for a moment, and then he turned and pointed.

The young woman spun around and caught Kael watching her. He tried to dart behind one of the carts, but ran into Kyleigh instead. It was like running into the side of a house.

"Are you all right?" she asked, grinning, as she helped him off the ground. She read the panic on his face and her hand went immediately to her sword. "What is it?" Her eyes shot up the path ... and found the girl.

She burst out laughing.

Before Kael could stop her, she waved. The girl waved back, and all too soon she was running towards them.

Her powder blue dress made the clothes the Tinnark women wore look like rucksacks with holes cut out the top. It fell lightly to her feet and flowed out as she ran. When the breeze caught her skirts, they curved more tightly to her body, revealing her figure.

Kael turned red before she even reached them.

"Papa told me you've just arrived. Welcome to our caravan! You may call me Aerilyn," she said, her clear blue eyes lighting up with her smile.

Kyleigh took the hand she offered and introduced them.

"It's so refreshing to have new faces among us. Shall I give you a tour of the caravan?" Aerilyn looked at him, and he pretended to be very interested in watching the merchants latch a team of horses together.

"Of course. I'm sure we'd find a tour very helpful," Kyleigh answered.

"Excellent." She looped her arm through Kyleigh's and waved for Kael to follow.

Except for Aerilyn and Garron, the rest of the caravan was full of dark-haired, dark-eyed forest men. Kael had a difficult time telling one man apart from the rest, but Aerilyn knew them all by name.

The men would smile when she approached, as if they knew she was about to brighten their day. At first, Kael thought she was a silly girl. But the more she talked, the more he realized that she was surprisingly clever. Nothing any of the men said could catch her off guard. If they teased her about her dress, she would toss her golden brown hair and pipe back with something about their trousers. Kael thought some of her banter bordered on insulting, but the smiles couldn't have been any wider.

The men shook Kael's hand when she introduced them, but their eyes stayed on Kyleigh. Even the most talkative man could only sputter when she smiled. In fact, there were so many open mouths in the caravan that Kael actually began to worry for the fly population.

Perhaps if they'd known how thoroughly annoying she could be, they wouldn't have gaped at her so.

Aerilyn's tour lasted longer than was probably necessary. Even after Garron bellowed the order to move out and the carts began to roll, they pressed on. She'd just shown them around the tannery cart when a roguish-looking fellow came out of nowhere and wedged himself in between them. He seemed older than Kael by a few years, but his lopsided grin made him look more childish.

Aerilyn groaned when she saw him, an involuntary smile bent her lips. "This is Jonathan," she said, waving to the rogue. "He's our resident fiddler and mischief-maker. He'll be in trouble at every stop from here to Midlan, I guarantee it."

Jonathan's laugh carried like a thunderclap. Several people ahead of them turned to look in annoyance. "I'd stay at home if they didn't toss me out every year to go merchanting with the likes of you," he said.

"I don't think the village could survive without these six months to clean up your mess," Aerilyn retorted.

Jonathan shrugged at Kael, as if the two of them shared a common problem. "I get bored trying to keep myself out of trouble. A man without a hobby is just a crow without a scarf — that's what I always say. Anyways," his gaze turned to Kyleigh, "aren't you going to introduce me?"

Aerilyn rolled her eyes at him. "This is Kael." Jonathan grabbed his hand and shook it vigorously, grinning like a madman. "And this is Kyleigh."

When Jonathan brought her hand to his lips, Kael thought he was as good as dead. But even after he winked, she did nothing but laugh. "I'd act offended, but I don't think that would put you off any."

Jonathan shook his head gravely. "No miss, 'twould only encourage me. Now then," he narrowed his eyes at her, "you have a gift for music, don't you? I know a fellow musician when I see one."

Her face was about as telling as a mute. But that didn't curb his enthusiasm.

"Aha! I knew it. Are you going to tell me what instrument you play, or do I have to guess?"

Kael almost laughed at the thought of her playing anything, but she seemed surprisingly ruffled. "Can't we just leave it?"

"Not an option. If you won't tell me outright, then you leave me no choice — and I shall need her other hand, if you please," he said to Aerilyn, who still had her arm firmly wrapped around Kyleigh's.

She reluctantly let go.

"Thank you," he said, taking both of her hands in his. He studied her palms for a moment. "Hmmm, oh you're a tricky one. Look here." He pointed to a row of calluses under her fingers. "These are from years of swinging swords around. Usually you just see them on one hand or the other. But I once knew a fellow who could wield swords in both hands. He was a one-eyed thief with a taste for the theatrical! Blighter still owes me money —"

"None of your tales, Jonathan," Aerilyn said before his story could take off. "We don't want their ears to start burning before they've even had a chance to settle in."

He waved her off. "All right, keep your bloomers on. You must have quite a bit of practice at swordplay, Miss Kyleigh." He wagged his eyebrows at her. "You're a dangerous one, aren't you?"

She smiled sweetly. "Keep dragging this out, and you'll see for yourself."

He laughed. "Pressing right along, then. And what have we here?" He traced a long, thin scar on her other palm. It was white and slightly raised. "You weren't trying to stop a blade with naught but your hand, were you?"

"You tell me."

He scratched at the generous amount of scruff on his cheek. "Well my dear dangerous lady, I'm not sure I can tell you much of anything. You don't have any marks on your string fingers, so that rules out a fair few instruments. I don't think you play the drums ..."

She smirked. "I suppose that means you've lost. I'll just take my hand back —"

"Not yet." Jonathan's dark eyes twinkled mischievously. "I hear it now, the way you carry your words — it's like the old ear was made to hear them." He dropped her hands. "You can sing."

Aerilyn's squeal of delight cut over the top of anything Kyleigh might have said. "Oh, you simply *must* sing for us! Jonathan is all we've had to listen to for weeks. And he only sings very rude songs." She shot him a look.

"I'm afraid the right mood has to take me," Kyleigh said hastily.

Jonathan puffed up his chest. "Spoken like a true artist! I shall make it my personal duty to play a song you can't help but sing to. No, no," he said when she started to protest, "it would be my honor. But first, I've got to find my fiddle."

Then with a very exaggerated bow, he sprinted away — and nearly collided with the back of a rolling cart.

"He's a bit strange, but completely harmless," Aerilyn said as she looped her arm through Kyleigh's once again.

Kael was still taken aback by the strangeness of it all. "Can you really sing?"

Kyleigh looked up from where she'd been tracing the scar on her palm. "Only when there's nothing better to do."

He wouldn't have guessed that, not for all the copper in the Kingdom. "What else don't I know about you?"

She smiled. "Loads of things."

Before he could press her, Garron found them. "Have you gotten our escorts acquainted with the caravan?" he said to Aerilyn.

"Yes, Papa."

"Thank you, my dear. And judging by the red in your hair," his eyes flicked to the top of Kael's head, "would I be right to assume you're from the mountains?"

"Yes, sir."

"So you're a hunter."

It wasn't a question. He wanted to say he was, but he felt guilty about lying again. "Actually, sir, I never earned my spot as a hunter, sir."

"One sir per sentence is quite enough," Garron quipped. "And you should hold your chin up when you speak. It gives you a look of confidence." He waited until Kael tilted his chin before he continued. "I don't know what you mean, but as far as I'm concerned anyone who comes off of those mountains is an accomplished woodsman."

"Thank you, sir."

"None of that." Garron swatted his thanks away like bothersome flies. "I said that only to say this: in addition to keeping a lookout for bandits, I'd like you to join the men who hunt for our food. I'll pay you extra to teach them your skills."

This time, Kael's chin lifted without a problem. "Sure, I'd be honored to help."

"Well, I don't know that I'd call it an honor, but it's certainly a help," Garron said, a hint of amusement in his otherwise serious voice. Then he turned his attention to Kyleigh. "I'd originally planned for you to be our scout, but under the circumstances," he glanced at the way Aerilyn's arm was latched to hers, "I think it might be best if you stayed with my daughter — as her personal guard."

Aerilyn clapped excitedly. "Oh thank you, Papa!" Then she turned to Kyleigh. "You have no idea how absolutely *dreary* it's been without another woman around. Men are very limited conversationalists, and I've found they know nothing of fashion or face paint — or anything else worth chatting about, for that matter!"

Kyleigh killed things with more poise than most people ate supper, but at the prospect of chatting about anything, a look of such horror crossed her face that Kael nearly laughed. Aerilyn led her away, talking animatedly about one thing or another, and Kyleigh followed with the stiff legs of someone about to be severely punished.

Chapter 11
A Mistake

Crevan did not take the news of Titus's failure well.

He kicked the hapless servant who brought him the letter and stormed out of his chambers. Corridors flew by as he thumped across the castle. Not a single curious servant peeked out from door or hallway — they knew by the thunder of his steps that heads were going to roll.

So they kept theirs bent firmly on their business.

In the southernmost corner of the castle, a guard stood watch over a small door. When he didn't move fast enough, Crevan grabbed the front of his breastplate and threw him aside. He fell on his back, and his limbs flailed out like overturned beetle as he tried to right himself.

Crevan wrenched the door open and took the climb of twisting, narrow stairs two at a time. His angry breathing became more like panting the higher he went. At the top of the stairs was another door. He shoved through it and nearly collided with someone on the other side. "Out of my — oh, it's you," was all he could think to say to the hideous man standing before him.

The royal beastkeeper grunted in reply. His skin was a patchwork of white, crisscrossing scars, his hair sprouted from his head in patches. He peered down at Crevan through a swollen lump over his one good eye — the other was milky white and unseeing.

"Where's Argon?" Crevan said, trying not to stare at a greenish, festering cut that raked down the beastkeeper's chest.

He grunted again, turned his huge frame and pointed to a room behind him. The tip of his finger was missing.

Crevan edged past him and ducked into the room, nearly tripping over the many trinkets scattered across the floor in the process. Books lay opened on every surface, their pages covered in foreign scribbles. He kicked them out of the way.

In the very center of the room stood a large stone basin, supported by an iron table. The water at its bottom was still as a mirror. It was so clear that when Crevan bent his head over it, he could see himself glaring angrily in the reflection. His flinty gray eyes found the jagged scar that cut across the right side of his face — the one his beard couldn't hide. It was a scar the beastkeeper might have been proud of.

He dashed the water with the back of his hand.

"You called?"

Argon's voice was about as startling as crumpled parchment, but Crevan still jumped when he saw the old Seer standing across from him. He hated mages' tricks. "You know why I'm here," he growled.

Argon watched him with eyes like deep pools. His blue robe stretched down to the floor and his gray beard stretched down to his stomach. "I can only assume that your prey eludes you still," he said. He reached out and passed his hand over the basin. The mad ripples caused by Crevan's tantrum melted back into the water, turning it smooth once again.

"I'm here because you made a mistake. You told us she would be on the south end of the village. You were wrong, and because of your *incompetence* she escaped!"

Argon shrugged. "The future is a fickle thing —"

"Don't," Crevan hurled a book at his head, "lie to me!"

Argon didn't blink as the book skimmed the top of his silver hair and struck a table behind him, scattering all of its instruments.

The miss only made Crevan more furious. He was an inch from grabbing Argon by his beard and slinging him off the tower. "If you saw the girl's future change —"

"I couldn't."

"What do you mean you couldn't see it?"

Argon sighed. He reached into his robes and pulled out a ball of smooth black marble. It was about the size of a spearhead. "Look into the water, Your Majesty, and I'll show you what I mean."

He dropped the marble into the very center of the basin. As Crevan watched, the ball began to roll around the earthen bottom, spinning faster with each turn until it became a solid ring of motion. The water swirled into a whirlpool that rocked the basin so violently that it threatened to fall off the table.

With both of his hands on the basin, Argon whispered her name. Colors leaked out from the sides of the bowl and the whirlpool spun them until they could see her face: her dark hair, her green eyes ... she was smiling about something.

Looking at her was like being stabbed in the stomach by a poisoned knife. "Get on with it," Crevan growled.

The image scaled back, as if they were watching from the eyes of a bird taking flight. Her whole body came into focus. She was holding her hand out to someone.

Just as they were about to get a look at her companion, the image broke. An entire shield, dented and battle-worn, rose out of the water and startled Crevan backwards. It stood on its bottom for a moment and the water foamed around it. An eye was engraved in its middle, but where the color and the pupil should have been there was a symbol: a series of lines forming three triangles on top, facing each other, three interlocking triangles on the bottom, and one black triangle in the very center.

Slowly, the shield sunk back into the water and disappeared, taking Crevan's gut with it. "Impossible," he hissed.

Argon waved his hand and the ball stopped spinning. It popped out of the water of its own accord and dropped neatly into his palm. "Your Majesty knows that emblem?"

It took Crevan a moment to hear him. "What I know isn't any of your concern. And if you'd like to keep your head on your shoulders, I suggest you find a way to fix this."

"Your Highness, this is like nothing I've ever witnessed," he said, spreading his arms wide. "No talisman, no spell can prevent me from Seeing. Nothing the others did could save them. But this time, things are different." He looked back at the basin, studying it. "I don't understand this magic."

Crevan clenched his fists to keep from swearing. Argon's visions were the only thing keeping him safe. Not knowing where she was meant doubling the guard outside his room — and long, sleepless nights of worry.

She was the only one left. When the Whispering War ended, he knew he'd have to kill them all, every last one. To leave any of those troublemakers alive would have destroyed everything he worked for. The pirate was no trouble — he'd gotten what he deserved. Catching the whisperers had been more of a challenge, but outside every wall was a rat waiting to show the way in. Once he'd discovered their secret, disposing of them hadn't been a problem. And then there was the Seer.

Argon didn't want to join his side, but he had little choice. Powerful as he was, he was still no match for an army. Once the other palace mages had him cursed and bound, he'd become Crevan's slave — and he'd proven himself invaluable. When his scouts couldn't find her, when his armies disappeared in the mist of the mountains, he turned to Argon. Even if his bungling forces failed to bring her in, at least the Seer had been able to keep an eye on her. Crevan knew very well that for every moment she drew breath, his life was still in danger.

"Perhaps if I were allowed to study with the others, we might discover a way around the shield," Argon said, turning from where he'd been gazing thoughtfully out the window.

Crevan frowned. He preferred to keep the palace mages apart. He knew for a fact that a roomful of thinking men was more dangerous to a King than any army, and a week ago he wouldn't have even considered it. But now the

129

circumstances had changed. Now Argon was no longer his only weapon.

"Very well," Crevan said distractedly. He slammed the door on Argon's thanks and went to look for the beastkeeper. He couldn't believe the old fool hadn't noticed her form — it was almost to good to be true.

He found the beastkeeper exactly where he left him, only now he was busily rooting through his ear with his smallest finger.

"I have a task for you."

He removed his hand and used it to scratch at a set of angry red claw marks that ribboned across his arm while he listened.

"It's finally happened — the Dragongirl is wearing her other form," Crevan hissed, and the swollen lumps above the beastkeeper's eyes raised in interest. "If we move quickly, we may have a chance to deal the ending blow. Go to the atrium and send the birds — all of them. And when they find her ... release the dogs."

The beastkeeper's mouth split open like a crack, revealing a tangled mass of yellow teeth. On another man, the gesture might have been recognized as a grin.

But on the beastkeeper, it was just horrifying.

Chapter 12
Luck and Skill

Traveling with the caravan turned out to be like living in a small, moving village. Each one of the covered wagons was its own shop: there was a tanner, a blacksmith, a cook, a tailor, a jeweler and a carpenter. After Garron spelled out the details of his chores, he gave Kael permission to trade with the carts for whatever he needed.

But he refused to use what coin Amos had packed for them. Kael was determined to figure out how to trade on his own — which made things much more difficult.

He learned quickly that if he asked for something and didn't have anything to trade for it, he got the cart door slammed in his face. He tried to explain to the blacksmith that he needed a hunting dagger, because he couldn't skin his game without it — and he couldn't turn them into the cook until they were skinned. But the smith just shrugged.

"And if I give it to you for free, I lose coin. And if I lose coin, Garron comes after me. We all got problems, lad. And they're all ours to solve." Then he'd slammed the door.

Kael spent all day long trying to find someone to loan him a dagger, but no one was willing to give one up without some sort of payment. He grumbled to Kyleigh about it all through dinner.

"I'd be happy to give you some coin," she said.

He shook his head. "No, I'm going to figure this out for myself."

"You could always use Harbinger."

He watched as she polished the sword's dangerous, curving edge with a rough bit of cloth. The white blade glowed in the firelight and hummed while she stroked it. The song wasn't unpleasant. "Thanks, but I think I'd just end up cutting my finger off."

"Hmmm, well there's an idea."

"You think someone would buy my severed finger?"

She laughed. "No, that's not what I meant. Didn't Garron say you'd be hunting with someone?"

"Sort of. He said he wanted me to teach my skills to his men. But what does that have to do with anything?"

"Something for something — that's the rule of trade."

He hated riddles. "But I haven't got any coin, that's the point."

She looked up, and her eyes caught with the sparks from the fire. "It isn't only about coin. You've got skills, and Garron's men need them. In fact, we all need them."

Ah ... now he understood. Hunting was just as important in the caravan as it was in Tinnark: if Garron's men didn't find food, they wouldn't eat. And Kael was the key to making sure they stayed fed. He would help them hunt, they would help him skin, and then they'd split the coin. It was a perfect plan.

Little did he know just how much help Garron's *men* would need.

His hunting companions turned out to be a pair of brothers — a matched set of noise and mischief. Claude, the youngest, was hardly twelve and was far more interested in collecting rocks than tracking game. And Chaney, the eldest, couldn't have been a day older than fifteen — yet he carried on like he knew everything worth knowing. They admitted outright that they weren't very successful hunters, and it only took him a few minutes to figure out why.

"Oi Kael! Look at this plant. What do you think it is?" Claude shouted from across the grove, startling a turkey from its roost just as Kael locked an arrow on it.

Chaney turned around and squinted at the flower in Claude's hand. "That's bandit's beard, you dolt! No don't eat it. You'll spend all day in the latrine if you do."

Claude took the plant out of his mouth. "Oh. Hey, Kael! Do you think if I ground it up real small, and maybe put a little water with it, that I could get Jonathan to think it was soup?"

"Even Jonathan isn't that dim-witted," Chaney said. And he knocked the plant out of Claude's hand for emphasis.

The resulting brawl was loud enough to scatter every animal that hadn't already run away.

There was no shutting them up, and there was no losing them. No matter how early he woke or how quietly he tried to sneak away, it wasn't long before they'd materialize at his side — squawking about whatever dragon-shaped leaf or green acorn they happened to find. Kael realized that the grass might turn blue before the brothers quit talking, so he decided to try something different.

The next day, he woke them long before the sun and taught them how to trap. He showed them how to turn briars into snares, how to bend tree limbs in neck breaking arcs and use food for bait. It didn't matter how loudly they cackled while they worked: by the time they turned around and followed their route back to camp, the traps were full. At midmorning they caught up with the caravan — toting a rucksack and a half of small game.

Claude turned out to be better at skinning than he was at making traps, so he volunteered to clean the kills. Chaney, on the other hand, had a real talent for trapping. He could find a likely looking patch of briars and turn them into a snare no rabbit could escape.

When Kael mentioned how well he was doing, his face lit up with excitement. "Do you really think so?" Then he looked at the ground and scuffed the toe of his boot absently against a rock. "But I'm not as good as you, of course. Your traps always have something in them."

Kael didn't think that was anything special. As long as he made the trap correctly, he didn't see why he shouldn't catch something every time. But Chaney and Claude spread the word around the caravan, telling anyone who would listen that his traps never failed. And it wasn't long before he was flooded with all sorts of odd requests.

The smith needed goose plumage for his arrows, and only a certain breed would do. He gladly traded his best hunting dagger for three pounds of feathers. Garron mentioned that he was fond of wild turkey, and there was a new suit of clothes in it for Kael if he could catch a dozen — which he did. Then the tanner needed more wolf pelts and the jeweler needed lions' teeth, for which they paid in silver.

Tales spread like colds in the caravan, and soon the word was out: that scrawny boy from the mountains could catch anything.

"I don't understand what all the fuss is about," he said to Kyleigh. A group of merchants hailed him as they walked by, and he gave them a quick nod. "Plenty of people can trap."

"It's a fuss because most people who trap usually come back empty-handed," she said, as if it should be obvious. "And they certainly don't come back with exactly what they were sent for. But with you, it's like *oh, I think I'll go out and trap three white squirrels today*. And you do."

He thought her impression of him was a bit ridiculous. He didn't sound like that at all. "The white squirrels were just luck."

She arched an eyebrow. "Was it?" She put a finger on his chest. "Or was it skill?"

He knocked her hand away. "It was luck," he said shortly. Perhaps if he'd had the gift of craft, everything he built might do what he wanted it to. But he wasn't a craftsman, he reminded himself, he was a healer.

A few days later he had more copper than he could count, but absolutely no peace. Everywhere he went, people hounded him with their requests, wagering their earnings on whether or not he'd be able to find this or that. And he began to think very seriously about packing his rucksack and running away. He might have done just that had it not been for Horatio, the caravan's cook.

He was a chubby man with ruddy cheeks and a tuft of brown hair that sat on his head like a rooster's comb. He watched over his food with the protective eye of a mother hen — and attacked anyone who lingered in his cart without mercy.

On more than one occasion, Jonathan would burst out the cart door with an armful of whatever food he managed to pilfer. And Horatio would tumble out behind him, brandishing the large wooden spoon he wielded like a sword and crowing for Garron to *stop that stringy snake of a fiddler*!

One day, Horatio caught Kael taking refuge behind a barrel of apples, and he thought he was as good as dead. But instead of flattening him with his spoon, Horatio took pity on him.

"How would you like a job?" he said.

Kael wanted a job badly. He finished his trapping early in the day and after that, there was nothing else to do but try to avoid his companions. Besides, he thought it might be fun to learn how to cook.

Horatio knew almost as much about cooking as he did about eating. He liked to keep his recipes crammed into odd nooks — away from the eyes of anyone who might wander in.

"Make yourself a pie and there's always a dozen crows waiting to snatch it up," he'd rant as he tugged a clove of garlic from its braid. "I'll not have my hard work ruined by halfwits and copy-cooks."

After he pledged his life to protect them, Kael got to read the recipes. It was tough to see the words through the many brownish spatter stains, and a great deal of the ink had been ravaged by spills. The words bled nearly to the point of being illegible in some places. But he eventually managed to figure them out.

The cook's cart had a shallow iron bowl set into the floor and a hole cut out of its roof. Every morning, Horatio shoveled the bowl full of hot coals and used them to cook.

"Hold on a moment. I think the carrots go in first and *then* the onions," Kael said.

Horatio looked up when he spoke, his hand hovering over a pot of boiling water, and frowned. "Kael m'boy, this is my dear mother's recipe. I'm quite positive I know how it's made."

He shrugged. "The recipe said the carrots go in first because they'll take longer to cook. Drop the onions early, and you'll end up with a soggy mash."

Horatio's cheeks puffed out in a frown. "How could you possibly remember that? You barely glanced at mother's recipe last week, and here you are spouting it off like it was in your hand." He shook his head and crammed the onions back in his apron. "Young people have such a gift for being right — at the most annoying of times."

As he passed Horatio a handful of carrots, an odd feeling twisted in the pit of his stomach. He didn't know how he remembered the recipe. The words came to him as clearly as the light of day, rising up in his mind the moment he needed them.

Maybe ... no, it was probably nothing.

Chapter 13
Women's Undergarments

From sunup to sundown, Kael stayed on his feet. It took all day to keep the caravan fed, and sometimes the hours between breakfast and dinner passed so quickly that he didn't even remember having lunch. But occasionally, they would get their work done early.

Those were the days that Kael enjoyed the least — because the extra hours gave Horatio the time he needed to try out one of his new recipes. They were bizarre things: like apple pie with mushroom sauce, or mice tail soup. Horatio called them experiments. Kael thought they were more like poisons.

"What shall we try today, m'boy? It's got to be something really fantastic — something to warm the heart," Horatio said. He sat on a small stool in the back of the cart, his elbow propped on his sizable belly and his chin balanced pensively in his hand. "The fried turkey liver wasn't exactly a hit," he mused.

It certainly wasn't. Half the people who tried it spent the night out in the woods, voiding everything but their innards. The recipe became so infamous that Garron had it outlawed. Jonathan even wrote a song about it — but the lyrics were not repeatable.

"You know, I think we ought to try the tortoise and almond crumble —"

"Or not," Kael said quickly.

"Why?" Horatio said, narrowing his eyes. "A good cook *must* experiment if he ever wants a chance at becoming great. The distance between the mouth and hand is short, and hand to pocket even shorter. There's a mine to be had for the meal that makes the mouth water — and I intend to discover it."

Kael had to think quickly. He felt like someone ought to save the caravan from tortoise and almond crumble. "I was just ... uh, I have an idea. And I wanted to give it a go, if that's all right."

To his surprise, Horatio looked delighted. "Now there's a thought. Yes, what this kitchen needs is a pair of fresh hands. So," he clapped his palms together, "where do we start?"

Kael gave him a list of supplies, making it all up as he went. They killed some of the chickens and plucked them. While Horatio cut the meat into strips, Kael worked on making a sauce. He only put things he liked in it: apples, garlic ... and a few other seasonings he thought went with them. He'd pop the cork out of one of the spice bottles and if he liked the way it smelled, in it went. And while the chicken roasted over the fire, he smothered it in a good portion of the sauce.

The meat was still cooking when the carts rolled to a halt, but Horatio offered to serve dinner on his own while Kael finished up. By the time it was ready, the sauce had formed a crunchy layer around the chicken. He took a bite — just to make sure it wasn't horrible.

When Horatio returned, he tasted it for himself. While he chewed, his eyebrows climbed. They were in danger of disappearing into the tuft of his hair when he finally declared:

"Brilliant! An absolute triumph!" He shook Kael's hand so hard he thought it might come off, then scooped the chicken into a bowl and waved him to the door. "Come along, m'boy. We can't keep our customers waiting!"

The first few people who reached into the bowl did so with no small amount of reluctance. They grimaced when they took a bite and chewed lightly, like they thought it might be the last thing they ever ate. But when the flavor hit, their eyes lit up. And word spread like wildfire.

A large crowd swarmed Horatio, clamoring for seconds. He disappeared in the crush and held the bowl high above the many grasping hands. "One apiece! I said *one*, Claude. Not twelve!"

Kael couldn't stop himself from grinning, and so he didn't try. In the dark, no one could see how happy he was. He could smile all he wanted to and no one would ever know.

It wasn't long before his growling stomach sent him away from the crowd and in search of some dinner. Everyone in the caravan was assigned a fire for meals and sleeping. He shared his with the youngest group at the edge of camp. Tonight, they were pitched under the branches of a wide oak tree — which would be good if it rained, but also meant that he was likely to find a small family of spiders living in the foot of his bedroll.

Kyleigh was sitting alone by the fire, scratching at a piece of beech wood with a dagger. He checked his belt and discovered that she'd nicked it from him again.

"You shouldn't take things that don't belong to you," he said as he glanced in the pot hanging over the fire. It was empty.

"You shouldn't keep your knife in your belt," she retorted. She picked up a small burlap sack and held it out to him. "This didn't belong to me either, but I thought you might be hungry. Of course I can always put it back, if your conscience won't allow you to eat it."

He took the sack out of her hand and ignored her smirk as he sat next to her. "How did you get into the food cart without Horatio spotting you?"

"I waited until he left, of course. I was just going to pop in and say hello, but you seemed so ... focused, and I didn't want to disturb you."

He'd been chomping on a piece of dried meat and wasn't sure he'd heard her correctly. "Wait, you were in there while I was working?"

She nodded.

Well that was disturbing. There wasn't a lot of room in the cook's cart and, short of turning invisible, he didn't see how she could have snuck past him.

"I swear I can hear your wheels turning," she said, and he realized she was watching him, an amused smile on her lips. "Give up, mountain man — you'll never guess it."

He had no intention of giving up, and her taunts only made him want to learn her secret more. But he pretended to surrender long enough to finish his meat. At the bottom of the sack was an apple, a slice of bread and a wedge of cheese.

He made sure no one was within earshot before he scolded her. "You shouldn't have done this," he said, holding up the cheese. "Horatio says it's hard to get in the Valley, and our supplies are running low."

"Oh please," she muttered as she dug at a knot in the wood, her brows bent in concentration. "He'll just get more tomorrow. And besides: they're swindling you senseless. You've earned a cart full of cheese."

Kael knew the merchants were cheating him. Chaney told him to never take the first offer, but he didn't care enough to bargain for more. The coin just made his pack heavy, anyways. "What's tomorrow?"

"Market. We'll be in Crow's Cross by evening, which means you and I will get our wages," she said with a grin.

His cheese caught in his throat. He was excited about market, but he'd also read that towns attracted Midlan patrols. Large collections of people meant more taxes for the crown, after all. "Did Garron say what he expects us to do in Crow's Cross?"

She shrugged. "He'll just want us to look out for thieves. But I doubt we'll have anything to do. We haven't found so much as a bandit the whole time we've been here."

She was right about that. During a few trapping excursions, he'd come across what looked to be a bandit camp. The coals from their fires would still be hot and their weapons would be leaning up against their tents, but there wasn't a soul to be found. It was strange ... almost like they'd disappeared.

It made him wonder if there wasn't something in the Valley worse than a gang of bandits. Perhaps that innkeeper had been right about the monsters.

"So besides trapping and cooking, what else have you gotten yourself into today?"

He tore his eyes away from the fire long enough to answer her. "Nothing, really. What about you?"

She sighed. "Let's see ... well, when I'm not fighting off Jonathan, I'm hiding from Aerilyn."

Poor Kyleigh. Her duties had turned out to be less like a personal guard and more like a personal canvas. Aerilyn cornered her nearly every evening and forced her to sit still while she applied large amounts of paint to her face. It was meant to darken her eyes or to brighten them, redden her lips or flush her cheeks. Whatever the paint was meant to do it usually did, but he didn't like the way she looked with it. And he knew she loathed it.

"What has Jonathan gotten himself into?" he asked, hoping the change in subject would brighten her mood.

She returned his dagger and leaned back, propping herself up on her elbows. "Oh, the usual foolishness. Today he mostly followed me around, abusing that horrible fiddle."

Jonathan kept his instrument notoriously off key. He claimed the screeching notes added an artistic element to his many bawdy ballads. But most people could agree that the only thing it added was swelling on top of an already enormous headache.

"The kick of it all is that I think he can really sing," she continued. "Just this afternoon I heard him humming when he thought no one else was around, and you know something? It sounded really lovely."

"Oh? And where were you hiding that he didn't see you?"

"On top of the jewelry cart," she admitted. "Though in my defense, Aerilyn was trying to get me to read some poetry."

"What's poetry?"

"Just rhythmic nonsense people write about trees — and about each other. The stuff Aerilyn likes is romantic to the point of being revolting." She tossed a twig into the fire, probably imagining that it had some offending line about love etched on it.

"If she can read, then why does she want you to read it?"

Kyleigh looked up at the sky, as if she was imploring the stars for patience. "She says — and I quote — that *there is a particular subtlety that comes out in the words when one reads poetry aloud.*"

She said that last part in a very over exaggerated, high-pitched voice. It did sound a bit like Aerilyn. He couldn't help himself — he laughed.

She raised her eyebrows. "I thought I'd die before I heard you giggle."

He turned his smile into a frown as quickly as he could. "Well you aren't likely to hear it again, so just ... don't go on about it."

"I think I'll have Aerilyn sew the date on my handkerchief. Or maybe I'll write a book about it. You like to read —" She stopped abruptly and peered across the fire. A look of such horror crossed her face that Kael expected a two-headed corpse to rise out of the ground at any moment. "No. Absolutely not," she said, leaping to her feet.

"What is it?" He squinted, but couldn't see anything in the darkness.

"It's too horrible to mention." She grabbed a low-hanging branch and with one graceful swing, pulled herself up into the limbs.

Kael wondered if he should follow her. On the other side of the camp, he could hear Jonathan playing his fiddle while the men laughed and carried on. They obviously couldn't sense any danger.

Kyleigh's whisper came from high in the tree: "Just act as if I'm not here."

He sat on edge for a moment, wondering if his life was about to end. But then he saw the creature that stalked them, and breathed a sigh of relief: it was only Aerilyn. She skipped towards the fire, a frilly, emerald green dress clutched in her arms.

"You should have picked a better hiding spot. She's bound to find you up there," he said out the side of his mouth.

"The only people who think to look in trees are the people who climb them," was her tart reply.

He was about to say something else when Aerilyn spotted him.

"Good evening, Kael!"

She wore a pale pink dress and had the long waves of her hair curled into neat rings. When she smiled, he was glad the light was too dim to show his blush.

"Yes, evening and ... all that," he said rather lamely.

She was gracious enough to ignore it. "You haven't seen Kyleigh anywhere, have you? I've found the most *ravishing* dress and she simply must try it on."

He fixed his eyes on the fire to avoid accidentally glancing at the tree. "You know, I haven't seen her around," he raised his voice a little, "but I wouldn't mind seeing her in a dress."

An acorn plummeted from the tree and conked him on the head.

"Ouch!" He glared up at the branches. When he turned back, Aerilyn was watching him curiously. "Um, it's just one of the hazards of sitting under an oak."

She sighed heavily as she plopped down next to him, her skirts poofing out beside her. "I'm afraid I've run out of ideas. I thought that if I found you, then I'd find her. But if she isn't with you, then I don't know where she is."

"Er, well, I just — I don't know what to tell you. Why did you think she'd be with me?"

She snorted. "The two of you are tight as a sailor's knot. Everyone can see it." She plucked a blade of grass and began weaving it onto another.

He didn't know when *everyone* had found time to make such wild assumptions. "Well, they're wrong. We've only just met — I mean, it just so happens that we've ended up in the same place, is all," he said defensively.

She giggled, knotting another blade of grass onto the next. "Alright, I do apologize. I suppose being away from

143

home bonds you with another person. Speaking of, are you really from the Unforgivable Mountains?"

He nodded.

"Oh, I'm so jealous! I've never been to the mountains, but I've heard such terrifying stories." She leaned forward. "Is it very dangerous? Do people really freeze together if they sit too close?"

"No, I've never heard of anyone freezing together. But we do have a river we call Hundred Bones."

She raised her brows. "And why's it called that?"

"Because it's said to hold the bones of one hundred of the King's bravest knights — all drowned at once."

She clapped a hand to her mouth and gasped excitedly.

"It's true," he said, slightly encouraged by her reaction. "The story goes that old King Fergus wanted his castle built at the very top of the Unforgivable Mountains. He ordered one hundred of his noblest knights to climb ahead of his masons and clear the way ..."

Aerilyn was the perfect audience for his tales. When a monster leapt out from the mist, she gasped. If the story got suspenseful, she would lean forward and listen with wide eyes until his heroes made it out of danger. She even laughed at the funny bits. One tale became two, and two became three. Soon there was very little life left in the campfire.

"And that's why the tops of the mountains are always capped in ice," he finished.

"Because they quarreled with the sun?"

He nodded, and she clapped.

"Bravo! That was wonderful. You're quite the storyteller."

He glanced away from her admiring eyes and scratched his head. "I don't know about that. Amos was always better than me."

The words slipped out before he could think to stop them, and Aerilyn latched on. "Amos? Was Amos your father?"

"No — I never knew my father," he said quickly. He was trying to think of a way to change the subject when she gasped.

"Oh Kael, that's awful! But I know how you feel: I never knew my mother. Well, perhaps I knew her at one point or another but I was far too young to recall. It's just been Papa and me for as long as I can remember. We travel across the realm, trying to keep our village fed —"

"Ahoy there! And what are you two little lambs baaing about?" Jonathan said as he sauntered out of the darkness. He had his fiddle propped up on one shoulder and swung his free arm in an exaggerated arc.

Aerilyn scowled at him. "We were just having a lovely conversation. Until you showed up and ruined it all, that is."

Jonathan ignored her scathing look. "Garron says it's your bed time, mot. You should get tucked in."

Aerilyn wasn't allowed to sleep outside with everybody else. Though she begged and pleaded, Garron insisted that the wilderness was no place for a young lady. He made her set up her bedroll in the garment cart, instead. And Jonathan never passed up an opportunity to tease her for it.

Tonight, she seemed entirely fed up. Her face flushed red as she stood and whipped her skirts about her. "I'll thank you not to talk to me like a child. I'm a grown woman by anybody's standards!"

She made to stomp off when Jonathan scooped the frilly green dress off the ground and waved it at her. "Aren't you forgetting your rather large handkerchief?" He turned it over in his hand. "Oops, looks like I was wrong. It's a tent, isn't it?"

She snatched it out of his hand so quickly that it was a wonder it didn't rip. "It's a *dress*, you buffoon! Not a tent, not a wagon cover — a dress!" Then she hiked her skirts up to her knees and stormed away.

"Good night my delicate, dew-covered rose!" Jonathan called after her. Then he muttered: "I think they must make women's undergarments with a bunch already in them."

Kael thought he was lucky she wasn't armed. "You shouldn't badger her like that."

"Eh, it's good for her," he said, scratching his chin. "A woman who doesn't get badgered enough just becomes one, that's what my mum always says — and she should know. You ought to see the way my pap lights out anytime she walks into a room. Now that's love." He tossed his fiddle on the ground and the strings twanged in protest. Then he collapsed on his bedroll, his long limbs splayed out in every direction, and immediately started to snore.

Chaney and Claude were next to wander up. They congratulated him through the thick rings of sauce around their lips and begged him to cook more chicken tomorrow. Only after their chattering turned into snores did Kyleigh drop down from her hiding place.

"Well, I thought *that* would never end," she said as she brushed bits of bark off her sleeves.

"It was your idea to hide up there," he reminded her.

"Well, it was *your* idea to drag those stories out for ages."

She wasn't smiling. In fact, she was standing with her hands propped dangerously on her hips. He quickly got to his feet. "It's not like I meant for them to go on," he said, raising his voice over the noise of Jonathan's snores. "She kept asking for another story. What was I supposed to do?"

Kyleigh crossed her arms. "You might have just told her you didn't want to."

"I never said I didn't want to." He spoke slowly, as clearly as he possibly could. "I don't mind talking to her. And if you didn't want to listen then you should have just come down and tried on the dress."

Fire blazed behind her eyes. She stepped up to him, but he stood his ground. "Oh? And I bet you would've enjoyed that, wouldn't you? You'd like to see me put in my place. You'd prefer me to prance around like a wind-brained ninny —"

"I don't *care*." It took all of his not-so-considerable patience to keep from shoving her back. "I don't care what

146

you do. I don't care what you wear. A dress, breeches, nothing at all — I don't care."

The fire in her eyes died to embers. She seemed on the verge of saying something else, but instead she turned and walked away.

"Where are you going?" he called after her.

"I thought you didn't care."

When he followed, she broke into a run, and he found himself sprinting just to keep up. It wasn't long before she outdistanced him. Soon the darkness swallowed her black armor and muffled her footsteps, leaving him with only the noise of his own labored breath.

"Fine! Go on, then!" he shouted into the trees. It felt good to yell at her, even if she couldn't hear him. He kicked a hapless branch out of his way and headed back to camp — thinking that perhaps Jonathan had been right about women's undergarments, after all.

Chapter 14
Crow's Cross

The next day dragged by at the pace of a one-legged turtle. It began extra early, when Garron shook them awake to inform them that they were not to go trapping.

"The bandits are thickest in the woods around the city," he said, his voice far too loud and commanding for the hour. "I don't like to have my men spread out all over the place. It makes us an easy target. Stay close, and keep your bows at the ready. Understood?"

"Yes sir!" Chaney and Claude shouted in unison.

Kael mumbled something unintelligible and as soon as Garron was gone, he tried to go back to sleep.

He'd stayed up most of the night, waiting for Kyleigh. At first, he was angry: he wanted her to come back so he could give her a piece of his mind. She shouldn't have been so snappy, she shouldn't treat him like her enemy and she certainly shouldn't go wandering off by herself at night.

Then as the hours changed, so did his feelings. At midnight, he began to worry: what if she was lost? What if she'd been taken by bandits, or eaten by wolves? He got up several times to put more wood on the fire. He circled the entire camp twice; he even walked to the edge of the forest and shouted her name.

Only the crickets answered him.

The first morning hours brought new worries. He began to fear that she'd left him. She didn't need him, after all, and he *had* told her to go away several times. So that was it, then. She was gone.

With that horrible realization, a new feeling struck him. The air around him felt empty, like he could reach his hand back for miles and never touch anyone he cared about.

The merchants were kind enough, but they didn't really know him. He couldn't trust them with his secret. And even if he could, they would still never know him like Roland, or Amos ... or Kyleigh.

And he realized quite suddenly that he was completely, incurably on his own. That he was alone.

More time passed: slow, empty time. Then at the darkest hour of the night, just before the sun was set to rise, he felt something. It was a shift in the sky — a fullness that despair convinced him he'd never feel again. He reached behind him and his fingers touched the strange, interlocking material of Kyleigh's armor. He was too relieved to be angry with her. And when she put her hand on his, he found he was too tired to pull away.

But that had been hours ago. Now the sun was blaring its insufferable light over the treetops, and all he wanted to do was sleep. Horatio had other ideas.

"Wake up, m'boy!" he said as he ripped the blanket off of him. "It's a long travel day so we've got to get lunch packed by breakfast, and dinner packed by lunch."

"When's breakfast?" Kael grumbled as he pulled himself to his feet.

Horatio stuffed a roll of bread and a cup of water in his hands. "Breakfast is now!" he bellowed, steering him towards the food cart.

Garron woke the camp with an order that the caravan was to leave in half an hour. Men scrambled out of bed and lined up behind the cook's cart, squinting out through heavy eyes. Some were still in the process of pulling on their trousers or buttoning their shirts. Some didn't bother getting dressed past their undergarments. They took the bread and fruit Kael gave them, and muttered curses when Horatio hollered not to forget their lunch sacks.

When breakfast was doled out, they climbed into the wagon and packed sacks for dinner while it rolled. At noon, Horatio arranged a mountain of rations on a large wooden tray and sent Kael to pass them out. It was a dull task, and the only one who gave him any trouble was Jonathan. He would sprint by and grab another sack when he thought Kael wasn't looking. The third time he did it, Kyleigh stuck out her boot and sent him flying into the side of the jewelry cart.

He didn't come back for fourths.

When Kael passed the last dinner out, Horatio told him he was through for the day and sent him outside. Having nothing to do forced him to realize just how tired he was, which made the second half of the afternoon all the more torturous.

He was hoping to get a few minutes to himself when Kyleigh found him. She seemed to sense that he was in no mood to talk, and so she walked beside him in silence. He didn't mind having her around, really. If he didn't turn to look at her, he never would have known she was there. But then Aerilyn found Kyleigh and the two of them started chatting about market. And then Jonathan had to butt himself into their conversation and add a good deal of rudeness to every topic they covered. Kael's quiet afternoon went out with the breeze.

"That isn't true," Aerilyn said, her brows snapped low. "No one in the Endless Plains dances naked for the harvest."

Jonathan shrugged. "There's got to be a reason why the crops grow so tall, that's all I'm saying."

"Yes, but it has nothing to do with nudity," Aerilyn huffed. Then she turned back to Kyleigh. "Have you ever tried desert spice rice?"

"Once, but I haven't been to Whitebone for years — and I doubt I'll be getting an invitation anytime soon."

"I love the desert," Aerilyn said, her eyes shining. "The culture is so fascinating. And the spice rice is practically to die for —"

"You'll feel like you died, all right," Jonathan piped in. "First time I had that stuff, it turned me inside out. I'm beginning to get a little burn now, just thinking about it."

Aerilyn swatted him with the back of her hand. "You are so *rude!*"

"Is it really that spicy?" Kael wondered.

"Not really," Kyleigh said with a shrug.

Jonathan whistled. "Well, you must have a stronger stomach than me. I'll tell you what, I was burning so bad I thought my —"

"That's quite enough!" Aerilyn said, smacking him again. "I refuse to be privy to every disgusting detail of your — *experiences.*"

"*Privy* is definitely the word I'd use," Jonathan muttered to Kael.

"Anyways," Aerilyn said over the top of him, "I was so hoping that we'd get to visit some of the island villages along the coast — they sell the most beautiful jewelry. But," she sighed, "Papa says it's still too dangerous."

"Wait, why is it so dangerous?" Kael said.

She looked at him incredulously. "Because of the pirates, of course! Haven't you heard?"

He shook his head.

"Well, I'm surprised you haven't: it's quite the scandal. Apparently, the pirate attacks have really picked up over the last few years. There's a rumor going around that Duke Reginald is beginning to suspect his managers have something to do with it — that his men are in cahoots with the pirates. It's causing all sorts of turmoil and sudden beheadings."

Kael knew a little about the Duke's rule from what he'd heard around the caravan. It wasn't long after he became Duke that Reginald bought up all of the boats in the High Seas. Then he set shipping prices so high that none of the merchants could afford to pay them. When a shopkeeper lost his business, Reginald gobbled it up — slowly turning the seas into the King's personal highway. And instead of keeping a class of nobles, Reginald assigned managers to his different shops and ships. He paid them a set wage and in return, they made sure the Sovereign Five's shipments made it safely across the Kingdom.

All he knew about pirates was what he'd read in the *Atlas*: they were greedy men who would gladly spill blood for treasure. But as long as they were attacking Duke Reginald, he didn't think he minded. "What's so odd about that? The

151

Duke is the only one who's got any coin on the High Seas. He should expect to get plundered."

Aerilyn rolled her eyes. "It's not about the fact that he's getting plundered, it's *how* he's getting plundered."

For once, Jonathan nodded in agreement. "I've heard all kinds of rumors from the chaps I throw cards with. Odd things have been happening on the seas, eerie coincidences and the like. Things that would make any salty sailor curl up and cry for his mum."

"Oh? What sorts of things?" Kyleigh said, looking slightly amused.

"Storms." Aerilyn's eyes were serious. "People say clouds billow up from the waves and turn into squalls violent enough to flip a vessel. And then," she waved her hand, "the storm gets sucked back down into the sea. It disappears ... and so does the ship."

"There's mist, too," Jonathan added. "White fogs too thick to find your rump in. Ships sail into them, and they never sail out."

"Sounds to me like they're just being careless," Kyleigh said.

Aerliyn frowned at her. "They're not. The managers think it's the work of a witch — that the pirates are being helped by magic. And of course Reginald thinks they're making it all up."

"Speaking of pirates," Jonathan cut in, "I hear they've got a knife-throwing game that's completely legendary. If you lose, they feed you to the sharks ..."

Time slowly changed the Valley. It started as a warm, lively oasis — then the sun began to slide behind the mountains. Purplish shadows crept down from the summit and wrapped it up, silencing the song of life for moment at dusk. Soon the crickets' chirping replaced the hum of bees, and strange new life began again. When the stars came out, Garron ordered that torches be lit, and the wagons rolled on in the ghoulish orange light. Most shadows melted away as they passed, but there was a great shade in the distance that never moved.

As they got closer, Kael saw the giant shadow was actually a wall of trees. Their tops had been chopped into points and they were crammed so close together that he doubted if a breeze could fit between them. The wall was thrice the height of one of Garron's carts. High towers jutted out from the corners, warmth glowing in their windows.

The caravan rolled to a stop at a massive pair of wooden doors set into the wall. Garron signaled for them to stay back and approached alone. "Hail, Crow's Cross! A caravan seeking entrance, if you please."

A torch bobbed into view as he spoke. It came out from one of the towers and floated along the top of the wall, bouncing until it was even with the caravan. "Hail!" a rough voice shouted back. "And who's this I'm speaking to?"

"Garron the Shrewd," he replied, holding his torch up so that the watchman could see his face.

"Well why didn't you say so? I'll lower the gate." And the light bobbed away.

A minute later, the large doors creaked open. Armored men stood guard as the caravan passed through, their mouths stuck firmly as their eyes scanned over every detail of the carts.

The second they were inside, the watchman signaled again and the doors slammed shut. He propped his fingers to his head in salute. "Nice to see you back for another season," he said to Garron. The light from his torch made his grin look slightly monstrous. "Sorry for all the extra swords. We've had bandits try to break in, recently."

"Really?" Garron said as they followed him through a series of winding streets. "I don't think we've come across a single outlaw."

The watchman snorted. "That's probably because they're all busy going after Crow's Cross. They've been disguising themselves as merchants, you know. Just yesterday a whole lot of them put black paint on their faces and tried to pass as desert folk. It nearly worked, too — except one of them wiped the sweat off his brow and gave himself away. Hard to explain your skin coming off, isn't it?"

They parked their carts in a large, open square in the center of Crow's Cross. Several other carts and stands were gathered in a ring, illuminated by the fires of the men guarding them. Kael noticed every one of the guards was wearing a tunic with a seal on it. He recognized the sun of Whitebone and the crossed sickles of the Endless Plains. There were a few men with wolf heads on their tunics, and he tried to stay out of their sight.

"I think you're all settled, here," the watchman said cheerfully, and Kael noticed his armor was simple leather: there was no emblem on his chest. "Now, do you have rooms for the night?"

Garron nodded. "I wrote the inn a week ago."

"Good, good. A few years back it would have taken a month in advance to get rooms. Ah, well, the markets just aren't as full as they used to be." He held out his hand. "Got to be getting back to my post, I'm afraid. Safe journey to you."

"Yes." Garron shook his hand. "And do stop by tomorrow. Get something pretty for your wife."

The watchman grinned again. "Will do. Thank you, sir!" He touched his fist to his chest and marched away.

While a few men stayed behind to watch the carts, everybody else followed Garron to the inn. The air was cool and smelled faintly of smoke, in places. Their boots echoed loudly as their heels struck the cobblestone and bounced off the houses. Kael marveled at how many people managed to fit in one place: their homes were crammed so close together that they shared a wall with their neighbors.

Hidden among the darkened windows and sleepy streets was an extra large, extra tall two-story house. It sat by itself at the end of a filthy alleyway. The nearby homes had their windows shuttered tightly against the light that spilled from its dirty windows, and their doors bolted against the people who staggered from it.

For, while the rest of Crow's Cross was sleeping peacefully, the *Rat's Whiskers Inn* seemed to have just woken up.

The front door was painted red and hung slightly crooked — as if it had been ripped from its hinges on more than one occasion, and nailed back by someone who was already several rounds into his ale. The second Garron pulled it open, a blast of noise whooshed out. People laughed, shouted, pounded their fists on the table, cheated each other at cards and sloshed the contents of their tankards all over the floor. The air smelled of roasted meat and warm bread — along with a few less-inviting odors. Kael got separated from the group when a rather fat man bounced into him and knocked him off his feet. He landed in a suspicious-smelling puddle that immediately soaked into his trousers.

The innkeeper led them expertly through the noisy crush of people to their quarters. Kael shared one dingy room with Jonathan, Chaney, and Claude. The only furniture in it were the four small beds that had been stuffed in the only way they would fit. Jonathan's bed kept their door from opening all the way, while Kael's was so close to the window that he thought if he rolled over he might tumble out into the street.

He tried not to think about the brownish stains on the pillows as he tossed his rucksack down and followed the others out the door. Back in the main room, Horatio had managed to grab a large table close to the fire. They fought through the crowd and squeezed in on the bench across from him.

He waved over a frazzled-looking girl who balanced a tray packed with tankards. "Five mince pies, four ales, and I'll have a wine!" he shouted above the din.

She nodded and rushed away. When she came back, both of her hands were full. She sat down a tray of steaming pies — which they emptied immediately — and handed each of them a tankard. Horatio gave her some coin and she disappeared again, swallowed up by the crowd.

The inn might've seen cleaner days, but the pies were fantastic. Kael hardly breathed between forkfuls. When the dough began to dry out his mouth, he reached for his tankard. Two gulps in, he realized that his throat was on fire.

155

"Haven't been drinking long, have you?" Jonathan said with a grin while Kael tried not to cough up his lungs.

"No," he wheezed. "It's — *horrible*."

Jonathan shrugged. "Nah, you get used to it. I grew up on the stuff. When my mum ran out of milk, she hitched me to a flagon!" He threw back the rest of his drink and stood. "I'm going to find some blokes drunker than me to cheat at cards. Any of you gentlemen want to tag along?"

Chaney and Claude couldn't have gotten up faster.

"We have some business to attend to," Horatio said, nodding to Kael. "But you boys go along. And Jonathan! Garron refuses to bail you out again, so see to it that you behave."

When the boys were gone, he turned to Kael. "I want to buy your recipe for the chicken, m'boy. Will you sell it to me?"

Kael, convinced that he *could* learn to like ale, had just swallowed another mouthful of the fiery liquid. He had to cough a few times before he could answer. "Sure, yeah. It's all yours."

"No, I won't take it for free. I've talked with Garron and we've decided that *this*," he plunked a purse down upon the table, "is a fair price."

The sack was practically bursting with silver. He didn't think he'd ever seen so much coin in one place. "That's far too much," he said, pushing it back. "It's only chicken."

Horatio sputtered on his wine. "It's not *only* chicken — it's a product! The very beginning of a culinary empire." He swiveled on his sizable bottom and glanced around. "Kyleigh! Come here and talk some sense into this boy."

She'd been leaning against the bar, chatting with the frazzled serving girl about something. But when she heard Horatio, she made her way towards them.

Kyleigh didn't have to push or throw elbows to get through the crowd: people bent out of her way. The shouting died down and laughter caught in throats. Men stared at her through drunken eyes and ran into things because they weren't watching where they were going. One man backed up too far and tripped on an overturned chair. His tankard went flying and he swore, but everyone was too busy gaping to notice.

Then someone on the other side of the inn shouted that one of his mates was going to try to eat three mince pies in under a minute, and the noise billowed up again as people trampled over to watch.

Kyleigh seemed completely unaware of the spectacle she'd caused. "It's quite a lively place, isn't it?" she said as she sat next to Kael. "Now, what are the two of you arguing about?"

As Horatio explained the chicken business to her, she weighed the purse in her hand. "This is a fair price," she said.

Kael didn't think she understood. "How can it possibly be fair? It only takes three coppers to buy a chicken."

She inclined her head. "True. But if Horatio sells a single strip of chicken meat for three coppers, and he gets twenty strips out of every chicken —"

"Then I'll be a very rich man," he said.

She nodded. "He'll make more than this at tomorrow's market, I can promise you that."

Horatio sipped loudly on his wine, his cheeks much redder than they'd been before. "If you had the means to run your own shop, I'd tell you to keep it for yourself. But since you don't, there's no reason why we can't share in the profit. So ... will you agree to my price?"

He really didn't have to think about it. "All right, we have a deal." And they shook hands.

"Wonderful!" Horatio produced a dirty bit of parchment, a quill and a well of ink from the folds of his apron. "Now, all you need to do is jot the recipe down — be specific. You *can* write, can't you? Good. I wondered how educated you mountain folk were. And while you're doing that, I'll order us a celebratory round of ale!"

The frazzled serving girl brought more tankards to the table. Horatio offered Kyleigh a drink, but she politely refused.

"I rarely touch the stuff. I prefer to keep my wits about

me. Here." She took a coin out of Kael's bag and set it on the table. "I'll keep the rest of your earnings in my room for the night. We wouldn't want some light-fingered thief to take advantage of you."

Normally, he would have argued that he could take care of himself, but tonight he didn't feel like arguing. He didn't know why he was suddenly being so agreeable. He also didn't know why he felt so unusually light and happy. He took another swig of ale and figured it must have been the general excitement of the inn wearing off on him.

****

Eveningwing hated being trapped indoors. The odor of bodies and men's filth was so thick that his lungs almost drowned in it. Noise clawed at his ears and the roof above his head was far too close.

Why did humans always have to travel in flocks? They were much quieter — and easier to find — when they were alone.

He watched from a corner of the rowdy room, hiding in the shadows. The tankard in his hand was only a prop — something to help him blend in. He never once brought it to his lips.

Had anyone been sober enough to look, they might have noticed something strange about the boy who watched them. His trousers were on backwards, for one, and the rest of his tattered outfit was far too big. His feet were bare and dirty. Above his left ankle, an iron shackle rubbed a raw, red line into his skin. But odd as his attire was, it wasn't the oddest thing about him.

He kept the front of his hair long to try and shadow them, but there was still no denying the fact that his eyes weren't human. Bottomless black pupils ringed by solid yellow-brown irises stared relentlessly. He captured every movement of the humans' teetering bodies, every expression on their swollen faces. Not a single mole, freckle or scar escaped his notice.

Every face he saw, he ran against a memory. It wasn't his memory, but one that had been entrusted to him. All across the Kingdom, his brothers and sisters waited in towns just like this one, stalking the inns and meeting places — looking for *her*.

A loud noise drew his eyes to the opposite side of the inn. Someone knocked over a table and the racket hushed the roar of human revelry for a moment. Then cheers rang out as the crowd made way for someone to walk through.

A thin young man with bothered reddish hair was the first to appear. Eveningwing didn't recognize his straight nose, brown eyes, or the crooked mouth he wore — but quickly memorized his face, taking note of his flushed cheeks and the way he slurred his words. The young man had an arm draped around the shoulders of the person carrying him — a young woman. When she showed her teeth in a way the humans used to show happiness, Eveningwing stood straighter. He could hardly believe his luck.

While he didn't recognize the man, he certainly recognized the woman carrying him: stark green eyes, hair like night, her mouth as she nodded to the clapping humans — it mirrored the one in his memory.

The Dragongirl!

No sooner did he think it, than the shackle around his ankle grew hot and began to hum.

He dropped his tankard. The untouched drink splattered on the floor as it hit the ground and onto the boots of some nearby revelers. They looked up in annoyance, but Eveningwing was already gone.

He burst through the back door of the inn. He pushed past a bunch of slobbering, singing humans and made a dash for the stables. The horses watched him with curious black eyes as he fell to the floor. He groaned and bit his lip as the change began, clinging to a single thought:

He must not scream.

Every bone in his body cracked at once, as if a giant's foot stomped him flat. He felt the broken, jagged edges glance across his muscles, raking fiery lines down his back and limbs

159

as they slid into place. Needles stabbed into every pore as thousands of feathers sprouted from his skin, tearing him where they ripped through.

Bloodfang said it wouldn't be much longer — and he comforted himself with this thought. Soon, Eveningwing's two bodies would become one. Then the change wouldn't hurt so badly. Until then, he must be strong.

When the change ended, the boy was gone. A hawk lay on the mound of tattered clothes in his place. His wings were the color of storm clouds, the dark flecks on his chest looked like interlocking scales of armor. All that remained of the boy were the yellow-brown eyes beneath the hawk's feathery brow.

He raised his wings and, with one powerful beat, shot into the air. Crow's Cross became nothing but a smudge as Eveningwing rose. Every few wing beats, he would let out a screech: a call that only his brothers and sisters would know the meaning of. He told them of his find, he told them to warn the swordbearers.

He got closer to Midlan with each stroke, and the King's orders echoed louder in his head: *Find the Dragongirl, return to me. Find the Dragongirl, return to me.*

Chapter 15
A Hasty Escape

Kael had actually been having a decent dream: it involved green meadows and a cool summer breeze. He'd been lying on his back, just enjoying the world around him, when he saw a man approaching from the distance. He recognized him and sat up to wave —

Then an icy cascade of water fell from the sky and knocked him from his sleep. He coughed and spat out a mouthful of water, gasping for a clean breath. When he realized he wasn't in any real danger of drowning, he shoved the wet hair from his face and found Jonathan — who was standing beside his bed with an empty bucket in his hands.

Kael could have hit him. "What in Kingdom's —"

But the sound of his own voice was like a dagger in the head. He collapsed back on his pillow and suddenly felt like he was going to be sick.

"It's the bane of every bloke about town, I'm afraid." Jonathan's words slapped against his skull. "It's the ale that always gets the last laugh. And I believe you set a new record last night, mate — twenty-four tankards! Now that's nothing to sneeze at. Would've probably killed a lesser man."

Kael wanted to tell him to shut up. But he was afraid to even open his eyes, let alone his mouth.

"Here, have a swig of this and you'll be on your feet in no time."

He cracked his eyes open enough to take the cup from Jonathan's hand. He threw the whole thing back at once, because he thought that if he dragged it out he'd be violently ill. It tasted like something Jonathan scraped out of the inside of his boot. His stomach balked as the slimy liquid oozed down his throat, and he fought the urge to gag.

"Just like mum used to make, eh?" His booming laugh made Kael contemplate murder. "Sorry for the abrupt wake up, but there's trouble in town. Garron's given the order to move out immediately." Jonathan was leaning next to the window, peering down into the streets. Kael found the strength to sit up and look.

Gray fingers of dawn were barely scratching at the window, yet the square was already alive with movement. Soldiers in gold-tinged armor marched through the streets, pounding on house doors and demanding entry. When the doors opened, they shoved through. If the doors didn't open, they kicked them in.

A desert merchant tried to hurry past unnoticed, but a guard caught him roughly by the back of his shirt. He asked a question and when the merchant shook his head, the guard threw him to the ground. Then he turned his glare in the direction of the inn.

Kael blanched when he saw the twisting black dragon stamped on his breastplate. "Midlan," he said, and Jonathan nodded.

"I heard them push through the gates this morning. I was out, ah, lightening the purses of some of the local gamblers, when I saw them marching in. 'Course I ran to tell Garron right away."

So his worst fears had come to pass — the King's soldiers were raiding the town, looking for something. And he thought he might be able to guess what they were after. Downing twenty-four tankards of mountain ale would have certainly gotten him noticed. He pulled his shirt over his head, cursing. As he tugged on his boots he thought to glance at the brothers' beds. They were empty.

"Don't worry — we got them out with the first cart," Jonathan said when he saw the panic on his face. He threw his rucksack over his shoulder and tossed Kael his. "It's just me, you and Horatio left. All the others are out — escaped through the back gate, they did. I forgot you were up here or I'd have snagged you sooner. Once those guards move on, we'll make a dash for it."

They stood on either side of the window, watching the guard who'd thrown the merchant. He still had his eyes on the inn. He scanned the bottom floor, then moved to the second. His eyes flicked across the windows and Kael froze when they stopped at his. The guard's eyes narrowed and he started marching towards the inn. He turned and shouted something to a gang of soldiers — who broke from the main group to follow.

"On second thought, now's as good a time to dash as any," Jonathan said, and Kael agreed.

Most of the inn's customers were still sleeping off their ale, so the hallways were quiet. They hurried down the stairs and weaved their way through the first floor corridor. Just before they reached the main room, Jonathan stopped at the corner and crouched.

"All right," he whispered after a moment. "Looks like it's all cle —"

The crooked front door flew open, causing a shower of dust to rain down from the ceiling as it slammed against the wall. In marched the throwing guard and his posse of soldiers.

"Search everywhere!" he barked. "She's been here, I can feel it."

They kicked tables over and toppled chairs, smashing the bottles and dishes piled on top of them. A few people were passed out near the hearth, and they beat them awake with the flats of their swords.

The noise must have roused the innkeeper. He stumbled in from the room behind the bar, red-faced and trembling, with the frazzled serving girl close behind. "Just what do you think you're doing —?"

"I'm looking for a dangerous outlaw, subject. An enemy of the King." The guard stepped up and planted his hands on the bar. "She calls herself the Dragongirl, and there's a mountain of gold waiting for the man who turns her in. Have you seen her?"

The innkeeper snorted. He ducked behind the counter and returned with an enormous book that he plopped down on the bar. A cloud of dust puffed out from between the pages and made the guard cough.

"I can't remember everyone, but you're welcome to look through my ledger," he said, quite sarcastically.

The guard's face hardened. "You're under arrest."

"For what?"

"For hiding an enemy of the King!" At his signal, two soldiers grabbed the innkeeper and drug him, screaming, from the room.

The serving girl made to follow them, but the guard grabbed her by her frazzled hair and held her back. "Please sir, I don't know anybody by that name, I swear it," she said, clutching her nightgown tighter to her chest.

"Her face, then. Tell me if you saw a woman with dark hair and green eyes. She will have been about your age, and likely dressed in armor."

Before Kael could clamp a hand over his mouth, Jonathan let out a gasp — and the serving girl heard. Her eyes flicked in their direction for half a second before they went back to the guard.

He knew they were done for. He knew the girl had seen Kyleigh — they'd been chatting just last night. How could she possibly forget? She would know that Kyleigh traveled with Garron. She'd tell the soldiers, and they would hunt the caravan down. The only way he could stop it from happening was if the guard never heard. Kael reached behind him and started to draw an arrow when the serving girl spoke:

"No sir, I don't recall seeing anyone like that."

The guard frowned. Apparently, he could tell by the defiant line of her mouth that she was lying. He growled and threw her to the nearest soldier. "Lock her up with the other one." Then he turned and barked: "Search every floor, every room from top to bottom. Move!"

They started towards the hallway, and Jonathan swore. He went to back up, but Kael put out a hand to stop him. His eyes were on the serving girl, and her eyes on his.

A soldier had a hold of one of her arms, but the other was free. As he watched, she stretched out her hand, reaching for a bowl balanced on the edge of the bar ... and knocked it over.

It smashed on the ground and every head turned to look, giving Kael the second he needed to grab Jonathan and sprint behind the counter. They went through the kitchen and out the back door; trudging through whatever rotten food the inn couldn't sell until they managed to dash into the cover of the nearest alleyway.

"Well, bludgeon me like a cricket!" Jonathan said, his eyes wild. "Did you know that about Kyleigh?"

"She told me she was an outlaw," he admitted.

Jonathan stopped cursing for a moment when a horde of soldiers tromped by. But as soon as they were gone, he started up again. "You aren't from the Earl at all, are you?" His eyes flicked to the top of Kael's head. "I bet that isn't even your real hair."

"No, we're not from the Earl. And yes," he tugged on his hair, "it's real."

Jonathan shook his head. "Well, we have to tell Garron. This is serious as a knife to the neck."

Garron was the last person who needed to know, in Kael's opinion. He would be angry about missing market — maybe even angry enough to make up the difference by turning Kyleigh in. Especially if what the guard said about a reward was true. He had to wonder what she could've possibly done to stir up so much trouble.

"You can't tell Garron," he said. He grabbed Jonathan by his collar. "Look at me — you can't tell him. I'm serious."

His eyes went wide before he finally nodded. "You're right, mate. I know you're right. Even if she is an outlaw, she's still my friend. And I may be a lot of things but I'm no traitor. Pox Midlan," he spat on the cobblestone, "her secret's safe with me. Besides, I know she's your girl and all. I wouldn't want to be the one to end your conquest."

Kael shoved him. "She's *not* my girl."

Jonathan pointed to his burning cheeks and cackled. Before Kael could punch him, he galloped away.

****

They found Horatio waiting near the back gate. His eyes were red and his cheeks were tinged with green. He took small sips from a flask and grimaced as he swallowed.

"It's about time," he grumbled when he saw them. "You dragged your feet, and now they've posted a guard."

There were two gates in the back. The first one was large enough for a cart to fit through, and was being blocked off by a score of mounted soldiers. They had their pikes lowered and pointed in the direction of the merchants lined up before them. Their horses snorted in the chill morning air and pawed eagerly at the ground. Though they cursed and spat, none of the merchants seemed interested in trying to drive their carts through the pikes.

A few yards down the wall, a flight of stairs led up to the second gate — which was actually just a door no larger than the entrance to a house. A lone Midlan soldier stood with his arms crossed in front of it, glaring down at the crowd of merchants beneath him. His stony glare seemed to be the only thing keeping them at bay. No one wanted to be the first to challenge him.

"We should light out while there's only one," Jonathan said, and Horatio agreed.

He led the way through the crowd — people bounced helplessly off his girth and Jonathan and Kael followed in his wake. They climbed the stairs and stood on the landing, directly in front of the guard. Kael took the spot on the left and tried to ignore the curious tittering from the crowd behind him.

"Merchants requesting passage, if you please," Horatio said.

The guard smirked. "Denied."

He crossed his arms and lowered his brows. "Denied? On whose authority? You have no right to keep us prisoner."

"On His Majesty's authority, so I've got every right," the guard replied with a sneer. "You ain't allowed to leave. So why don't you just march your fat rump back down the stairs —"

"Don't call me fat, you worthless tin-head."

Behind him, Kael could hear the rattle of armor heading their way. He turned and saw a dozen Midlan soldiers reach the crowd. They bellowed for passage, but the merchants refused to let them through. Swears and threats poured in from both sides, making a dangerous mix.

The guard, emboldened by his reinforcements, slunk forward. "Tin-head, am I?" He rapped a knuckle on the side of his helmet. "Well how'd you like it if I used my tin head to crack your skull, eh?"

He was too busy threatening Horatio to see the door open behind him. A hooded figure stepped out from the arch, grabbed him by the shoulder and drove a sword into his back — so swiftly that he didn't have time to cry out. It wasn't until the white blade ripped through the dragon on his breastplate that they realized who their rescuer was.

"Kyleigh —"

"*Shhhh!* Go quickly," she said. She had her hood pulled up, and if he hadn't seen Harbinger, Kael didn't think he would have recognized her.

The guard tried to call for help, but ended up choking on a mouthful of blood, instead. His body grew limper by the second, sagging more of his weight onto Harbinger's blade. Jonathan stared, open-mouthed, at the dying man until Horatio shoved him through the gate. Then Kyleigh stepped to the front of the platform.

She held the guard up by his chainmail, still skewered on her sword. Beneath them, a scuffle had broken out between the merchants and Midlan's soldiers. They exchanged shoves and spittle, but so far all weapons had remained in their belts. Then Kyleigh leaned forward and dropped the body right in the middle of them.

It was amazing how quickly the swords came hissing out of their sheaths.

Before Kael could see what happened, she grabbed him and pulled him through the gate, kicking the door shut behind them. They sprinted for the forest as the angry shouts in the courtyard grew to a roar. When they made it to the cover of the trees, the sounds of fighting erupted.

"What were you thinking, killing a soldier of Midlan?" Horatio gasped as they slowed their pace to a trot. "They're going to hunt us down and slay us all!"

"No one saw me do it," she said, not even out of breath. "We just needed to make sure those soldiers stay busy for a few hours. Nothing slows an army like a riot," she grinned, "and nothing starts a riot like a corpse."

They moved at a trot until Horatio was near to passing out, then they slowed to a walk. Kael glanced down the path several times, expecting to see all of Midlan barreling down upon them. But they never followed.

He realized it could have all gone terribly wrong: if they'd been spotted, if Kyleigh hadn't shown up, if the serving girl hadn't caused that distraction — well, they might be hanging from the town walls instead of joking about it. But even though he knew they could have easily met their ends, his heart still pounded with excitement.

He was having an adventure. A *real* adventure!

At midday, his stomach began to rumble, and the glory of it all wore off. He doubted if they would ever catch up to the caravan, traveling at Horatio's pace. Just when he'd resigned himself to this thought, they crossed over the next hill and saw a welcome sight.

A large grove spread out beneath them, hundreds of trees sat heavy with orange fruit and leaked the perfume of citrus into the air. The dirt road wound directly through it and there, right in the middle of the grove, was the caravan.

Jonathan whooped as they approached and several of the men looked up from their lunches to cheer. They met them on the road, clapped them on the back and shoved rations into their hands. Kael was surprised at how many of them seemed happy to see him. He didn't think he'd be missed. Chaney and Claude kept saying that they'd been so afraid for him; that they thought he'd been captured. But they assured him that if he were ever *really* captured, they'd come to his rescue. Then Garron shook his hand and thanked him profusely for bringing Jonathan and Horatio back alive. He was sorry that he'd ever doubted in his skill.

And then there was Aerilyn. She didn't bother with patting him on the back: she tackled him. "I was so worried I'd never see you again!" she said. When she peeled her head off his chest, he saw her eyes were shining with tears. "We waited so long and you never came out. Then Papa said the guards were coming and we had to leave and, oh, will you ever forgive me?"

"Of course I forgive you," he managed to say, even though she was practically strangling him.

When she had all the air squeezed out of him, she pounced on Kyleigh. "And *you*, how dare you! How dare you just run off like a madwoman without so much as telling me where you were going."

She laughed and tried to pull away. "I told you *exactly* where I was going."

"Um, *to save Kael* isn't a place, in case no one's told you."

Jonathan elbowed him in the side and winked, but Kael tried his best to ignore him. Having Kyleigh show up made things easier — but he thought he still could have escaped without her help.

When she finished scolding them, Aerilyn threw her arms around Horatio. Even Jonathan got a hug — until he did something that earned him a slap across the face instead.

After they'd been welcomed back, Garron gave them an extra few minutes for lunch. They settled under a large tree to eat and Aerilyn left to pick them some oranges. Kael volunteered to help.

"Papa bought three barrels full — plus we get to have one each for lunch," she said, plucking a large piece of fruit off its branch and handing it to him. "He traded the farmer a silk blouse for them. Can you believe it?"

Kael didn't know what a silk blouse was, but he wouldn't be surprised if Garron cheated the poor farmer senseless. "I hope he was pleased with the trade," he said carefully.

She smiled. "I think he was. He lost money, but it makes him ever so happy to help the working class."

Kael nearly dropped his armful of oranges. "Wait a moment — he *lost* money?"

She looked at him curiously. "Silk is the clothing of Kings, not farmers. Of course, the farmer didn't know that: he just wanted to get something lovely for his wife." He must have still looked shocked, because she glanced around her and lowered her voice. "Can you keep a secret, my friend?"

He nodded warily, wondering what sort of secret a girl like Aerilyn could possibly keep.

"Well," she took a deep breath, "Papa and I aren't actually from the Grandforest."

Anyone with half an eye could have seen that, but he tried to act surprised. "Really? I had no idea …"

She nodded. "It's true. My family is from the High Seas, originally. But my grandfather moved our business to the forest when Papa was a child. And do you know why?"

"No. Why?"

"Because he owed the people of the village a great debt — a life debt. You see, one day, while Grandfather and Papa were on the merchant's journey, Papa became deathly ill. They stopped at a small village in the Grandforest, where an old man gave Papa medicine to break his fever. But even after the fever left, he was still too weak to travel. Though Grandfather didn't have enough coin to pay him, the old man swore he would care for Papa while he finished their route.

"Grandfather was so grateful for his help that he moved his business to the forest and gave the villagers work in the caravan. Papa has never forgotten the kindness shown to him by that old man. He says he learned that some of the wealthiest people in the Kingdom are those who have little but kindness to give to others."

Kael hadn't been expecting to hear that about Garron. He cleared his throat roughly. "Well, that was nice of him." And then, because he didn't know what else to say: "Come on, the others will be waiting."

They passed out the oranges and dug into their lunch. Claude was the only one who struggled to get his peel started. After watching his first unsuccessful attempts, Kyleigh took the orange out of his hand and bit directly through the skin. He had no trouble finishing up from there. Kael ate his a slice at a time, savoring the flavor that burst out from the tiny pouches of juice. Chaney amused himself by spitting the seeds at Jonathan's head. It took him a few moments to realize who was pelting him, but when he caught on, Jonathan fired back. A full-fledged war ensued — during which nearly everyone got hit by a stray seed.

They finished lunch in a whirl and still had a few minutes to relax. Kael was thinking very seriously about taking a nap when an ear-grating note came off Jonathan's fiddle.

"How about a little afternoon entertainment, eh? All right, you've twisted my arm. Prepare yourselves, gents and ladies," he glanced at Kyleigh, "and those of us whose outfits suggest that we're on the fence."

She gave him what Kael imagined was a very rude gesture, judging by Aerilyn's offended gasp and Chaney's snickers.

"There's no need to be so coarse," Jonathan said with mock severity. "That having been told, t'would now be my delight to entertain you all with a dirty little ditty I call *The Pirate's Perilous Pantaloons* —"

"Oh, Jonathan *please* — none of your horrid songs today! We were all having such a wonderful lunch," Aerilyn begged.

"Yes, if you're going to sing something, it needs to be appropriate," Kyleigh said.

"Oh, and look who's lecturing on appropriateness! What was it you were saying just moments ago?" Jonathan

171

countered, cupping his hand behind his ear in dramatic anticipation.

"Well technically I didn't *say* anything —"

"Well *technically* it was vile!" Aerilyn cut in. "A lady should never engage in such profanity. Kael's manners are better than yours, and he's a *boy*."

"Thanks for that," he muttered.

Kyleigh gave her a wicked grin. "You're right, I wasn't exactly being ladylike. Why don't you let me make it up to you?"

She crossed her arms. "You can't take back what's already been said."

"For the last time — I didn't say anything. Now," she nodded to Jonathan, "feel free to jump in whenever you like. I know you know this one."

She crossed her legs and stretched her interlaced fingers — like they should all be expecting something extraordinary. Then quite unexpectedly, Kyleigh started to sing.

Her voice filled the air and stunned them all into silence. Jonathan was so taken aback that he nearly forgot to join in. But when he did, his song danced along with hers: lifting in places where her voice fell, and fading back as she carried notes to heights he could not.

Kael lost himself in the story they told.

The pretty blue violets were blooming,
Their blossoms abound in the field.
But Sir Gorigan's eyes were so gloomy,
For he only had but a shield!

The dragons laid waste to the Valley,
The fiery beasts in great horde.
Sir Gorigan cried, "I could slay them,
If only I had but a sword!"

Then the sun called, "I see you, Gorry.
Take the blade from my burning forge.

Hold it aloft and fall on the dragons,
Their fire's no match for my sword!"

When the last line trailed away, he could hardly believe it: he thought she didn't care a whit about Sir Gorigan. But before her audience could erupt in applause, she glanced at him. He saw her smirk and he dropped his head.

All right, but he refused to let her think he was impressed.

"That was absolutely beautiful!" Aerilyn said. "I don't know why you've kept quiet all this time. And *you!*" She pelted Jonathan with a handful of orange peel. "How could you? You've been torturing us for all these years — and you can really sing! How *dare* you!"

Peel flew at Jonathan from all directions. He laughed and tried to block their shots with the back of his fiddle. "How was I to know that you'd like that boring sort of thing? I've considered it my personal duty to educate you lot of heathens, teach you a little something about art, and all that — ow! Well that's gratitude for you!"

He sprang up and ran into the cover of the trees. Chaney and Claude charged in after him, hurling peel.

Chapter 16
Bartholomew's Pass

Beneath the fortress of Midlan, well below the warm hearths and comfortable beds, was a world of darkness: a honeycomb of dank stone rooms that lurked, forgotten. It was a gloomy tangle of crypts, a chapter that should have been struck from the Kingdom's history long ago. And the King had promised to seal them, to judge in death or freedom but never to condemn a man to rot.

Only, he'd lied.

Water dripped from the ceiling in maddening drops. It pooled in filthy puddles and reflected the monstrous faces of Midlan's most dangerous prisoners. The slime on the floors did little to muffle their howling. Some threw themselves against the walls of their cell. Some clawed at stone or whimpered. But try or cry none of them would ever see daylight again, not until the King allowed them to.

Bloodfang listened to their hopeless pounding. The ones who struggled were only pups: they had yet to learn that escape was impossible. Even if they squeezed through the iron bars or dug under the floor, the collars around their necks would burn and force their bodies back into their cages.

His pack was used to their collars. After years of having their bodies twisted and pulled at the King's command, their two shapes had become one.

Now the pack was curled up, sleeping on a mound of straw. But Bloodfang couldn't sleep. He sat against the wall with an arm propped on one furry knee and kept watch. His body looked like a man's, but it was covered in thick black hair. His head and face was entirely that of a wolf. The only thing truly left of his human self were the eyes beneath his furry brow.

The King could have his body, but he'd fought to keep his mind. He ignored the voices that swam in and out of his ears, the scattered thoughts of all those trapped by the mages' spell. He knew if he listened to them that his eyes would go empty and dark. He'd become entirely animal ... like the rest of his pack.

Somewhere down the hall, a door creaked open. Bloodfang's pointed ears twitched as heavy footsteps dragged across the cold floor, moving towards their cell. He stood, listened, then woke his pack with a low whine. They stretched and grumbled that their naps had been ruined, but couldn't ignore the call of their alpha. One by one, they sat up. Their long limbs splayed out over their knees as they squatted, their deadly claws twitched in anticipation.

When the mangled face of the beastkeeper came into view, Bloodfang's tail thumped against the floor in greeting. He yapped at the gray hawk perched on the beastkeeper's shoulder, who flapped his wings in reply.

Bloodfang liked Eveningwing: he was only a pup, but he was clever. He knew to fight against the voices.

It wasn't feeding time, so if the beastkeeper was visiting them, Bloodfang knew he must have a message from the King. The iron gauntlet on the beastkeeper's scarred arm glowed when he touched it. Bloodfang felt his collar get warm. He sat up a little straighter. Suddenly, the King's voice was in his head:

Follow Eveningwing — he will lead you to the prey. When you find her ... kill her. Bring me her head, and you will be rewarded.

The pack joined Bloodfang's excited growl. They were ready for a new hunt and waited impatiently for the King's memory.

Bloodfang recognized the town they were to start at: a village the humans called Crow's Cross. There was a bed at the inn that would have her scent. Then the memory

175

changed, and he saw her face. That's when he realized he wouldn't need her scent, for he already knew it well.

He let out an involuntary howl as his legs bent under the weight of his collar. He fought against it for the first time in years. But it didn't matter how much he struggled: the spell binding him to the word of the King was powerful magic. It controlled his shape, stole his thoughts, and moved his legs. There was nothing he could do to stop himself once the King had spoken.

When the beastkeeper opened the door, Bloodfang leapt out. He dropped down on all fours and his legs galloped beneath him. He followed Eveningwing through the murky tunnels, the excited barks of his pack bouncing off the walls around him.

They didn't remember her face. How could they? Magic took their minds years ago. They were like pups once again: so blinded by their lust for the hunt that they couldn't see the certain death that awaited them. For she would surely kill them all.

When the tunnel sloped upward, they dug their claws into the slippery moss and climbed. They escaped through a small hole in the castle wall and the fresh scent of night air filled Bloodfang's nose.

The great walls of Midlan disappeared behind them as they ran. He followed Eveningwing, a small dot high above them, concentrating on the sound of his claws as they beat the earth. All the while they traveled, he tried to keep his mind away from the prey … he didn't want the King to find out what he knew.

****

For days on end, Kael woke and immediately peered back the way they'd come. He scanned the hills, watched for the cloud of dust that meant the army of Midlan was on their heels, but it never came.

Ahead of them, the western range of the Unforgivable Mountains loomed ever closer. They were no longer purplish shadows in the distance, but the very large, very craggy image of their eastern brothers.

He didn't see how Garron planned to drag six carts over the top of them. Most of the trails would be carved by deer and not even close to wide enough for a wagon. Yet no one else seemed worried. The caravan plodded on like the mountains were no more treacherous than the gentle green hills of the Valley. He didn't think they realized just how impossible the weeks-long journey ahead of them was. In fact, he thought they were all thoroughly mad.

It wasn't until they were nearly at the base of the first mountain that he realized — with no small amount of horror — how they planned to cross it.

The smallest peak did not stand like its brothers: it was split directly in half, like some great axe in the sky had mistaken it for a log and chopped it precisely down the middle. Between the two halves was a narrow crack. It bent into the center of the mountain and disappeared through the towering shadow cast by the peak.

"It's Bartholomew's Pass," Aerilyn said when he pointed it out. "A hundred years ago, Bartholomew the Inventor set up shop in that very mountain. But one of his experiments went horribly wrong, and he blew the whole thing clean in half! Poor man — one just doesn't come back from a blast like that."

Bartholomew's *Pass*? Did the merchants have their heads so full of coin that they'd forgotten to pack their common sense? He left Aerilyn and went for Kyleigh at a jog. "Did you see this?" he said when he reached her.

She looked in the direction he pointed, and shrugged. "Sure, I'd have to be blind to miss it."

"We aren't going through there, are we?"

"Of course we're going through it. The Pass is the quickest way to the coast." She put an arm around his shoulder, like he was a panicked child who needed comforting. "Don't worry — I doubt we'll be crushed to death."

He jerked out from under her arm. "You *doubt* it?"

177

"Very seriously."

"Well I don't doubt it, not for a second," he hissed, keeping his voice low enough that the people around them couldn't hear. "I've seen rockslides in the mountains. I know how quickly they happen. And I tell you, if so much as a *pebble* shifts while we're in there, they won't find us for at least another hundred years — when the next Bartholomew comes along and decides it's a fantastic idea to blow things up. *Why* are you laughing?"

But she was too doubled over to answer him. Her face was red and her breath came out in gasps. A few times she seemed to collect herself enough to say something, but when she looked at him, the laughter started all over again.

He was sick of her giggling, of all her nonsense in general. He turned on his heel and marched away, ignoring her pleas for him to come back. When the mountain caved in on them, he'd turn around and ask her if she still thought it was funny — provided he had the time.

At least Garron partly made up for his foolishness by announcing that they wouldn't stop to make camp: they'd march straight through the Pass and only rest when they were safely on the other side. He led the way in, the feather on his grass-green cap bouncing with the trot of his horse.

As the caravan entered the Pass, their chatter slowly fizzled out. The pressure of being trapped in the middle of a mountain was not unlike having a hand clamped around their throats. With every step, the grip got tighter: the air was too thick to breathe and the silence nearly crushed them. Slowly, the towering walls of rock and dirt strangled the sun and finally snuffed it out, forcing them to travel by torchlight.

Having nothing to do but walk and worry sent Kael's imagination running wild. Darkness made every sound more sinister. A horse whinnied, and he stopped. He held his breath and listened. Pebbles skittered down the walls — the first ominous drops of a deadly storm, he was certain of it. He strained his ears for the deep rumble that meant the mountain was crumbling down … but it never came.

Roots of ancient trees snaked out from the walls, reaching for him, elongated in the shadows. They clawed at his face, warning him: *Turn back now*, they said. *Turn back, or we'll devour you. Your flesh will make us strong, your blood will grow us tall.*

Though his heart railed against his chest, Kyleigh seemed completely untroubled. She walked confidently ahead of him; the light from her torch made her more a shadow than darkness ever could, etching the straight lines of her shoulders against the flames.

An eternity passed before someone finally shouted that they could see the end. He looked up and breathed a sigh of relief. The small pinpoint of gray light in the distance grew larger with every step. Soon, they would be able to put this miserable, dark place behind them.

Just when he thought he might survive Bartholomew's Pass, Kyleigh stopped. Her arm shot out across his chest and when he tried to get by, she pushed him back. "What are you doing? Keep moving, we're almost —"

"Shut up."

Her words were so abrupt, so sharp that they stunned him into silence. She had her head cocked to the side with her dark brows bent low as her eyes scanned the walls above them, looking for something he couldn't see.

Finally, she dropped her arm. "Maybe it was nothing. But I thought I heard —"

Then a hawk's screech ripped through the air, followed by a cry so horrible that it made his blood run cold.

It sounded like the shrieks of a man having a limb cut off. It was anguish, the call of a tortured soul who was helpless to stop the pain — a man trapped in some cycle of agony with no beginning, and no end. He covered his ears and ground his teeth against it.

Then a creature burst from the cliff side, following its cry, and lunged for Kyleigh.

It was a monster — one of the monsters the innkeeper had warned them about. He never would have believed it if he hadn't seen it for himself, but its body looked exactly how

179

he'd described it: like a man who'd swallowed a wolf. Only now it seemed that wolf was fighting its way out.

Patches of coarse gray fur burst through the gaps in human skin, nearly covering its long snout and sunken cheeks. Black, deranged eyes gaped out from their sockets and locked onto Kyleigh. Its pointed claws stretched for her throat.

Kael didn't even have time to be properly terrified before she knocked him to the ground. She stood over him and, as the monster sailed by, she ducked under its claws. There was a flash of white and then a *thud* as its lifeless body struck the wall. She turned, and he saw Harbinger gripped in her hand. Its blade glistened wetly in the torchlight.

More howling tore through the Pass, more monsters erupted from the cliff side and fell upon the merchants. Garron bellowed above the shouts of his men, trying to bring some order to the chaos. Aerilyn's screams cut over the top of everything, piercing their ears.

The creatures must have been stalking them all night, lurking in the shadows, watching with their unfeeling eyes as worry and fatigue took their toll. They'd been waiting for this moment to attack, and they attacked like wolves — with the full force of their pack and with their minds consumed by a single goal:

To kill.

Another monster came after Kyleigh. It snapped for her neck and its deadly pointed teeth crunched shut on themselves as she leapt away. She cracked it over the head with her torch and ran it through. Grabbing Kael by the arm, she yanked him onto his feet. "Follow me!"

And because she seemed to know what she was doing, he didn't argue.

Garron had the merchants rallied together in less than a minute. He organized them into circles and ordered them to stand back to back. They swung their blades and fired arrows, defending their manmade keeps while Garron and his mount charged through the fray. He hewed the monsters with his sword and bellowed: "Hold fast, men! With all that you are — hold fast!"

They found Aerilyn crouched on the ground next to the jewelry cart. The hem of her skirt was filthy and her eyes were red with tears. All the curl in her hair had gone limp. Kyleigh grabbed her and tossed her — skirts and all — over her shoulder. She kicked the jewelry cart's door open and flung her inside.

Kael had an arrow nocked and was ready to step out into battle when she grabbed him by the belt and tossed him in next to Aerilyn. He flipped himself on his feet and made a dash for the door, but she shoved him back.

"You're to stay right here, understood? Don't move!" she growled, green eyes blazing as she slammed the door in his face.

He was furious. He may not have been the strongest man in the Kingdom, but he was no coward: he wouldn't hide while the other men fought. Grunting, he drew his bow and pushed the door open with his foot.

A group of merchants were fighting a losing battle. They managed to bring down two wolf monsters before a third dropped right in the middle of them, breaking their circle. It batted one man down with the back of its claw and sent the second flying with a kick in the gut. The third man countered, swinging his sword until he got the monster back against a wall — and then lunged for its chest.

The monster's claw swooped under his jab, cuffing him in the chin. He went flying and landed hard on his ankle. It crunched as he collapsed.

The monster advanced, sensing its prey was cornered. Its nostrils flared when the man tried to back away, like it could smell his fear. Drool spilled from its snout as the monster leapt for the kill. Its long claws were nearly at the man's throat when Kael's arrow hit it directly in the side.

It flew off course and landed hard on the ground, but didn't stay down long. No sooner did it fall than the monster rolled back on its feet. Its head swiveled on its furry neck; its black eyes found Kael.

While he watched, it wrapped its claw around the arrow and yanked it free. Hot blood poured out of the wound. Then with a snarl, it charged.

He dove out of the way and slammed the door behind him. The monster crashed into the cart and bounced backwards, giving him enough time to fire another arrow. It let out a furious howl as the shot buried itself in its shoulder. Then the monster lunged again, and this time Kael didn't move fast enough.

Its claw clamped down on his leg and dragged him backwards, tearing through his boot, pants leg, and a layer of skin. He gasped as it pulled him in by his hooked flesh. Pain seized his whole leg, throbbing and stabbing and burning all at once. He groaned and the monster inhaled, feeding on his torment.

Then it arched its back and yelped in pain. It twisted around, claws scrabbling madly for the arrow lodged in its back. That's when Kael saw Chaney over its shoulder, lowering his bow.

"No!"

But it was too late.

The monster forgot about him and barreled towards Chaney — whose eyes widened as he fumbled with his quiver. His hands shook too badly to nock an arrow. He couldn't seem to get it locked. The monster leapt.

Kael bit his lip and forced his wounded leg to bend beneath him. Those dagger claws strained for Chaney at the creeping pace of a slug. The monster's jaw opened like a chasm in the center of the earth — a chasm ringed by skull-crushing teeth. He felt nothing but the arrow under his chin as he found his target. Then his fingers slipped from the string.

He blinked, and the monster was dead.

The arrow stuck out from the base of its skull, having cleaved through layers of fur and skin and finally found its mark. It was an impossible shot. He would've marveled over it all day, if he hadn't been so worried about Chaney. He hobbled closer, fearing the worse, and Chaney's head popped out from beneath the monster's torso. He looked shocked to be alive.

"I'm stuck," he muttered, trying to haul the monster's body off of him. Kael pulled while Chaney pushed. Together, they got absolutely nowhere.

"I'll have to find help."

Chaney's face went white. "You can't leave me here! What if another one tries to eat me?"

It was a very real concern. One of the carts was on fire — the tannery cart, by the smell of it. He could see Kyleigh fighting on the edge of the flames. "I won't let you out of my sight, I promise. Just try to play dead."

"Hurry!"

He sprinted for Kyleigh and stopped when he saw the creature she was fighting. Judging by its size alone, it looked to be the King of all wolf monsters. It stood on its hind legs and towered head and shoulders above her; its body was completely covered in slick black hair. It swung one massive claw but Kyleigh batted it away with the flat of her sword. It lunged for her, and she danced out of its reach.

Was she *playing* with it?

He didn't have time to wait for her to finish her game. As soon as he got within range, he aimed an arrow at the monster's head. He was just about to release when she spotted him.

"Don't shoot!" she yelled.

The panic in her voice distracted him and his shot left the string wrong. The arrow grazed the tip of the monster's pointed ear, clipping off the top. It swung its wolfish face in Kael's direction and he got another arrow ready to fire. But when he saw the monster's eyes, he froze.

Its eyes were not like the others: they were not black and mad, but brown, intelligent. For a moment he thought he was looking into the eyes of a human. And that thought made him hesitate.

Kyleigh waved Harbinger and the sword let out an eerie cry. "Kael, get out of here!"

Her voice agitated the beast. It turned around and swung at her head, but Harbinger flashed twice as fast. The monster fell on its knees, one of its great claws gripped the hairline cut across its torso and dark blood trickled out, matting its fur. It looked up at Kyleigh and whined, but she made no move to strike.

Why wouldn't she kill it?

"There's another one!"

Forest men charged at the monster from all directions, swords drawn. But it leapt out of their reach and scrambled up the side of the cliff on all fours. They threw rocks, but it was already gone.

No sooner did its tail disappear over the cliff than Kyleigh was upon him. She grabbed a fistful of his shirt and yanked him down to meet her eyes. "Just *what* were you thinking? How could you possibly —?"

"Chaney's trapped," he said quickly, before she could dismember him.

When they arrived, three men were struggling to pull the dead wolf monster off of Chaney. She stepped through the middle of them, grabbed the scruff of the monster's neck and tossed it aside. She ignored the many open-mouthed stares as she pulled Chaney to his feet.

With the battle over, merchants appeared from all sides of the caravan. Several of them nursed head wounds or held cloths to ragged gashes. But so far, the only bodies Kael could see were of the wolf monsters.

"Where's Aerilyn?" Kyleigh said.

The question made his heart jump into his throat. He'd completely forgotten about Aerilyn. She must have read it on his face, because they both turned at the same moment and sprinted for the jewelry cart.

The door was busted and swinging loosely on one hinge. Jewels winked from the dirt around it, and necklaces and rings were scattered across the floor. But Aerilyn was nowhere to be found.

Kyleigh turned on him. "How could you leave her?"

"It wasn't my fault," he snapped back. "You should've known better than to ask me to cringe and suck my thumb while the rest of the men were fighting."

Her eyebrows slipped low. "I asked you to protect her. I asked you guard her with your life — to defend someone who was completely defenseless! I didn't ask you to *cringe*," her voice dropped to fit her glare, "I asked you to do the brave thing. And you couldn't do it."

Her final words lingered in the air — hot ash that singed a hole clear through his heart. If Aerilyn was dead, it would be all his fault. And he knew it. He dashed outside, determined to find her, but a scream from the front of the caravan stopped him short.

He recognized Aerilyn's voice as she wailed: "Papa!"

Chapter 17
Iden and Quicklegs

Garron lay on the ground and looked past them all, staring at something they couldn't see. His tunic was covered in smudges of dirt, his grass-green cap was torn and half the feather was missing. His gray hair, usually combed back and tidy, stuck out at odd angles. But he didn't seem to care.

There was something in the distance that kept him staring. Perhaps he saw the gate to another realm — a doorway to a Hall where brave men reclined at a never-ending feast, untouched by the harsh edge of winter. Or perhaps his story simply ended. Perhaps he read the final sentence and smiled to know an infinite secret that the living were not yet a part of.

Kael didn't know what he saw, he could only guess: because Garron's eyes were the eyes of a dead man.

Here, the world was real. In this realm, Aerilyn wailed and collapsed in the dirt beside Garron. She threw the broken half of her spear aside and buried her face in his chest. Her hands shook and she gripped fistfuls of his tunic, as if she thought she could pull him back into the light.

A monster's body lay next to Garron. Its wolfish head had been bludgeoned by Aerilyn's spear and its back was peppered with arrows. The deep claw marks around Garron's heart were the work of that monster. The dark stains around the wound stopped their advance, but the damage had already been done.

Aerilyn's sobs were the only sound in the Pass. The rest of them stood in a circle around her, not knowing what to do. A few of them stared through reddened eyes, but all Kael felt was anger. The storm in his chest swelled to the point that his heart could barely hold it. Blood trickled into his boot from the wound on his leg as fury climbed to the top of his head.

When an animal took a man's life in the mountains, there was only one way the family could get revenge. Kael spat in the wolf monster's face, watched as his spittle struck the dry tip of his snout and rolled down. He proved to the mountains that Garron was not afraid to meet his death: he still had comrades who would stand for him.

He could feel it in the breeze when the mountains heard him. Cold air glanced the back of his neck and he knew how they glared. The mountains couldn't have Garron now — he'd live on in Kael.

Others spat behind him. Jonathan was next to contribute, followed by Chaney and Claude. Soon a line of merchants followed: spitting on the wolf monster and kneeling to touch Garron's face.

They couldn't have known what they did, they couldn't have possibly understood the pact they made — but Kael didn't stop them. Garron deserved every honor and more.

Kyleigh had Aerilyn in her arms throughout the whole procession. She held her tightly and whispered the comforting words that only women seemed to know. Aerilyn sobbed into her shoulder, choking out strings of nonsense between tearful gasps. But in time, her wails faded to quiet sniffles.

Horatio knelt to touch Garron's face, then his brow creased in anguish as he closed his vacant eyes with the tips of his fingers. Next to Garron's head lay his grass-green cap. Horatio picked it up from the ground and brushed the dirt off of it. He tucked it into his pocket.

"We shouldn't stay here," he said roughly. "There might be more of them, and in the Pass we've got no where to run."

"What were those things?" one of the men asked, and the others murmured in agreement.

"I'm not sure," Horatio admitted.

Jonathan stepped over to the thoroughly mangled body of the wolf monster and inspected the iron collar around its neck. "They've got His Majesty's kiss on them," he said, and Kael blanched when he saw the twisting black dragon stamped into the collar.

His announcement set off a furious buzz of whispers. "But what could the King possibly want with merchants?" someone asked.

Jonathan glanced at Kyleigh, but then dropped his eyes. Horatio seemed to be trying to keep his gaze purposefully in another direction.

Chaney finally piped up. "He's a greedy piece of horse dung, so he probably wanted our gold."

The men seemed to accept his answer. They clenched their fists, and veins popped out of their necks as they demanded a march on Midlan. It took Horatio several tries to calm them down. "Stop this! Stop this at *once!*" he barked. "Don't let your hearts make off with your heads. The King may be a murderous scab," and the men roared in agreement, "but we haven't got the numbers to face him. March in looking for answers, and he'll hang every one of you. Think of your children, think of your wives."

The cold truth of what Horatio said took the battle out of their cries. Reluctantly, swords went back into sheaths and arrows returned to quivers.

"But what'll we do?" Claude asked, his voice small compared to the others.

Horatio sighed. "We'll go home. We'll go back to the village and to the protection of Countess D'Mere. The Kingdom isn't safe for merchants anymore."

And with that, he gave the order to move out. Only three of the six carts were fit to roll on: two had their wheels smashed and the tannery cart was burned beyond recognition. To make matters worse, Garron's horse stood stubbornly beside his master and refused to budge — which made Aerilyn break down in a fresh wave of tears.

"Someone take care of that beast," Horatio muttered. He took Aerilyn under his arm and led her away. Chaney grabbed the horse's reins and pulled him forward.

The rest of the caravan moved out without a backwards glance, leaving Kyleigh and Kael behind. He really couldn't blame them: Jonathan kept his promise and Horatio returned Kyleigh's favor by not outing her to the men. Beyond that, they owed them nothing.

When they were gone, he watched Kyleigh place rocks over Garron's body, sheltering it from the jaws of scavengers. She arranged them into a makeshift grave and then knelt beside it. He couldn't hear what she murmured, and he was in too much pain to move closer.

At least with no one else around, he could heal his leg the fast way. He rolled up his pants and pulled off his boot, grimacing when the dried blood cracked and flowed anew. He pushed the gashes closed but didn't heal it all the way: he left the scars. He didn't want this to be a day he simply forgot.

When he looked up, he noticed that Kyleigh was building a second grave — and a monster's curled claw stuck out from under it. He leapt up and stomped over to her without putting on his boot.

"What are you doing?"

"What does it look like I'm doing?" She sat a slab of rock down and went to get another, but he blocked her way.

"I can't believe you, I honestly can't. You're going to give those things the same respect you gave Garron?"

"Every man deserves a grave." She tried to push past him, but he stepped in her way.

She'd have to kill him — or at least beat him senseless — before he let her by. "Are you blind? Those things aren't men — they're monsters!"

She made a disgusted noise. "You don't know what you're talking about. Get out of my way."

"No."

The next thing he knew, his feet were off the ground and the sharp edges of the Pass wall were digging into his back.

"They were men once, whisperer," she said, her voice shaking as she growled. "An ancient race of men with the power to take the shape of animals. They roamed the forests peacefully, long before the time of your *Kings*." She spat the word. "And now Crevan has them pinned up like animals. He's enslaved them by the magic in their blood, driven them mad with his own hate. He's stolen their royalty and twisted their bodies into what you see here," she grabbed him under the chin, forcing him to look at the nearest wolf, "into what you call *monsters*."

It took him a few moments to wrap his mind around what she said. Then it struck him. "Wait — are you saying these things were ... shapechangers?"

"Or barbarians, as your kind likes to call them," she snapped, letting him drop back to the ground.

She knew nothing about his kind: shapechagers were revered in the Unforgivable Mountains. The elders believed they were the most blessed of all of Fate's children. How many times had he heard Roland bemoan the fact that he was doomed forever to wander the woods on two legs? That his clumsy human form kept him from running wild, from knowing all the secrets of the forest?

Kael's mind flicked back to the moment when he locked eyes with that final monster, the one he thought was the King of them all. He remembered its eyes, how they seemed to connect with his in intelligence and understanding. Impossible as it was, it all made sense.

"I had no idea, I swear I didn't," he said.

The fire in Kyleigh's eyes died to embers, but her mouth remained curled in a snarl. "No, it's my fault. I shouldn't have expected you to care."

"But I do care. I've always liked the stories about shapechangers."

She went back to burying the wolf without a reply. He helped her move the rocks from the wall to the grave, but she still wouldn't look at him. Her lips stuck in a frown and her eyes were unusually hard. How could he convince her that he was truly sorry?

"When I was younger, I used to imagine that I was one." His face burned when he felt her eyes on him, but he pressed on. "I used to pretend that I could hear the animals talking, or that my senses were really sharp. I know it sounds foolish, but I always kind of wished that I was one."

She was quiet for a moment. "And what animal did you pretend to be?"

"A deer."

"Really?" She was smiling now, and he didn't know whether to be relieved or offended. "I always thought of you as more of a badger."

"Why's that?"

"Well, you're stronger than you look — and famously cranky."

He thought about that for a moment and decided he wouldn't mind being a badger. Those long claws might come in handy. Then he looked down at the next wolf and his stomach twisted a little when he saw how misshapen its body was. "Do they all look like that?"

"After the King gets done with them, yes," she said scornfully. "The curse the mages put on them forces their bodies to change shape against their will. It isn't natural. And after a few years of that, they get stuck somewhere in between."

He saw the iron collar around its neck and the black dragon stamped into it. "It's a shackle."

She nodded. "A cursed one."

Anger swelled in his chest. He'd never met a shapechanger, but like Sir Gorigan, he'd read enough about them to feel close to them. And in his opinion, the Kingdom owed them a great debt.

He remembered Iden the Hale — the only knight brave enough to face the leviathan of the High Seas. The first time they met, the monster smashed his boat and sent him plummeting into the depths of the violent waves. He washed up on shore three days later, barely alive. Had it not been for Quicklegs the sandpiper, he would have died. She pulled him from the surf and brought him to her flock — where she nursed him back to health.

Iden fell in love with her, but Quicklegs knew his love was doomed. So as soon as he was healed, she flew away — over the ocean and into the strange lands beyond the sea.

Though Iden lived, his heart was broken. He took to the waves once again and called up the leviathan. This time, he had nothing to lose: he dove into the monster's mouth and down its throat. When he reached its heart, he cut it from its ties and sent it down into the fiery depths of the leviathan's gut — where it was burned to nothing.

Had it not been for Quicklegs, Iden would never have killed the leviathan. The High Seas were safe for trade because he'd sacrificed himself so long ago.

"Do you think there might be a way to save them?" The words came out of his mouth without a thought.

Kyleigh shrugged. "Perhaps … though I've tried before and it didn't quite turn out the way I'd planned."

"Is that why you're in so much trouble with the crown?"

"Part of it," she said with a nod. She sat on her haunches and propped an elbow on her knee. "Listen — freeing the shapechangers will be a tricky patch of work. Marching on the Unforgivable Mountains is one thing, but Midlan is quite another. We'll have to pace ourselves, all right?"

He nodded, reluctantly. In the back of his mind, he wondered how many years it would take to avenge Tinnark *and* free the shapechangers. At the pace things were moving now, he thought he might be Amos's age before he ever had a chance to live happily.

Kyleigh clapped him on the shoulders, grinning at the heaviness behind his eyes. "Don't worry — it's perfectly normal to pick up a few tasks along the way. A quest is rarely as simple as doing the thing you set out to do."

******

He helped her bury the remaining shapechangers — the halfwolves, as Kyleigh called them — and then they left the Pass.

Thick gray clouds curtained the sky above them and the breeze was a little cooler. The gentle curves of the Valley were far behind: ahead were sharp rocks and thin tufts of brown grass. The pines glared down like underpaid guards as he followed Kyleigh along the path that wound between them.

He never thought he'd miss the noise of the caravan: Chaney and Claude's shouting, Aerilyn's endless chatter and the unpalatable notes of Jonathan's poor fiddle. Yet the longer they walked, the more he found he missed it.

He knew he shouldn't. It was their fault that Garron was dead, and he didn't expect to ever see the caravan again.

They ducked out from under the cover of the trees and stepped into a wide clearing. A shallow stream trickled through it, and all along its bank he recognized the familiar green tunics of the forest men as they scrubbed their wounds in the water.

He saw Aerilyn standing out in the middle of the road, away from the others. Her eyes were red and her arms defiantly crossed. The second she saw them, she started to run. Someone must have told her the truth. He could tell by her glare that they were in trouble, and he braced himself.

She went for Kyleigh first. "I know," she said, lifting her chin to keep the tears from spilling out. "Horatio's told me that you're dangerous. But I don't care. The King set those monsters on *all* of us — he didn't care who perished. But the fact of the matter is that you're my friend, and friends don't let things like bounties get between them." She hugged Kyleigh tightly, quickly, then stepped over to Kael.

She fell directly into the middle of his chest, and he didn't know what to do. So he sort of put his arms around her and tried not to rumple her dress. "I'm sorry," he began, but she clamped a hand over his mouth.

"Don't be. I've already had my cry, and I know Papa wouldn't want me to cry anymore." She smiled weakly. "You know what he'd say, if he were here? *Time is precious, my darling — so don't you drown it in tears.*"

Then she took them both by the hand and led them back to the caravan, where their friends were waiting for them.

Chapter 18
Pirates?

They didn't have to endure the cramped forest path for long: a few hours later, the woods disappeared and an open field yawned out to meet them. The sun was beginning its descent, trailing golden light through a break in the clouds as it fell. Wind made the long strands of grass dance as the caravan moved through them.

Beyond the field, the world suddenly dropped away. Kael broke from the rest of the group and sprinted to the very edge of a cliff, drawn in helplessly by the far-off crash of waves. He stood with his toes hanging over the edge and gaped at the wonder before him.

The ocean.

Not since the sky had he seen anything so unending. Water stretched eternally, waves sparkled in the sunlight as they chased the clouds above them. Gulls rode the cool gusts of wind, squawking to one another, and he found that he envied them. From where they flew, he thought the view must be spectacular.

He could've stood there all day, just gaping at the way the water kissed the sky. But the caravan was moving on. They were all ragged from the lack of sleep and the village at the base of the cliffs tempted them with its promise of a hot meal.

The only way down was along a road that appeared to have been cut right out of the cliff side. The path was steep, folding over itself at the angle of a pinch. It created a punishing, zigzag slope that had the horses neighing with fright and digging in their hooves. At the bottom, a woefully chipped wooden sign greeted them: *Harborville*, it read.

The blue letters were faded and peeling. One of the chains had rusted through. Now the sign hung on only by its remaining chain and the wind beat it mercilessly against its post.

Along the rocks, planks of warped, rotted wood were stacked in mounds the height of a man. They smelled heavily of must and what he could only describe as old ocean: like the water had dried up and all that remained of it was the stench of fish.

After they passed the first few mounds, he began to get the feeling they were not alone: someone watched them from the shadows. He lit a torch and stepped closer, staying on the balls of his feet in case whatever it was decided to attack. The light burned the shadows away and revealed their stalker. The blurred edges of darkness became spindly arms and legs, the round smudge on top turned out to be the startled face of a boy.

He was young, younger than Claude, even. Yet he looked like an old man: his blue eyes had bags under them and his clothes were tattered and filthy. Several of his shirt buttons were missing and his stomach poked out between them, swollen and unhappy.

When the boy saw Kael watching him, he ducked behind the nearest rotting pile. Kael moved his torch to follow and the light illuminated it. He took a startled step back when he saw the many corpses curled up beneath it. Their skin was wrinkled and hanging off their bones, their eyes rimmed red and shut against the light. He was about to turn away when one of them raised its skeletal head and squinted up at him.

Sweet mercy, these people were alive.

Someone — Jonathan, by the smell of it — grabbed him by the shoulder and led him away. He held his torch up as they passed and found more miserable, shrunken people curled up under the mounds of trash. The lucky ones crouched around small fires, their gaunt faces locked on the bubbling pots between them. Others sat with their knees tucked to their chins and watched with sunken eyes as the caravan rolled by.

This wasn't what the High Seas was supposed to look like. All of the pictures in the *Atlas* showed quaint, prosperous fishing villages and an ocean packed full of brightly-colored vessels. There were supposed to be miles of white sand and children who walked the length of it, their arms laden with shells. There should have been sun, not clouds. There should have been a village — not Harborville.

If Jonathan hadn't shoved him along, he doubted if he could have moved his legs at all. He knew Duke Reginald kept his people poor, but he had no idea that he starved them. Horatio's chickens were better fed — and they were destined for the pot.

"Keep moving, mate," Jonathan said quietly, when he stopped again.

But Kael didn't want to keep moving: he wanted to find Duke Reginald and club him over the head. "We have to do something," he growled.

"We can't, it's against the law." Jonathan turned him towards a freshly painted sign sticking out of the rocks ahead of them. He could read the letters clearly, even from a distance.

This colonie of thieves has been found guiltie of stealing from the Crown and is under the just punishment levied upon them by His Excellencie, Duke Reginald. Anyone caught aiding these thieves is also a thief, and will be punished accordinglie.

Beyond that sign, a few large fires burned near the water. Guards stood around them, talking and taking long gulps from their tankards. On the front of their tunics was the symbol of the High Seas: a coiling serpent being pierced in the tail by a harpoon.

He could smell fish roasting over the guards' fires, so he knew the people huddling under the lean-tos could smell it as well. He wondered why they hadn't tried to catch their own food. Then he read the signs at the water's edge and suddenly understood:

The Seas are the propertie of His Excellencie, Duke Reginald. Anyone caught fishing without the Duke's permission will be guiltie of stealing from the Crown and punished accordinglie.

The people of Harborville were not beggars, but honest men who weren't being allowed to work. Just the thought of it put such a horrible taste in Kael's mouth that he had to spit to keep from throwing up. Why wasn't anyone doing anything?

Aerilyn walked with her head down, shedding silent tears that he was sure had nothing to do with the horror before them. Horatio looked angry, but kept his balled fists safely inside his pockets. He couldn't tell what Kyleigh was thinking: she had her hood drawn up again, shadowing her face. Jonathan picked nervously at his fiddle and kept his eyes on the guards.

Maybe none of them knew what it was like to be hungry, but Kael did.

In his eighth winter, the storehouses were so low that all of Tinnark had to survive on nettle and pine bark stew. He remembered tromping to the Hall with Amos, fighting through enormous drifts of snow for his one meal of the day. By the time they arrived, they were exhausted. And by the time they left, he was hungry again. All winter long, he'd held his stomach and cried because it hurt.

He'd worked so hard to become good at trapping so Tinnark would never have to starve again. He didn't know the people of Harborville, he didn't know if they were really thieves or not. But law or no law, he wasn't going to stand for it a moment longer. No man deserved to starve.

The boy he found in the shadows watched from a distance, jogging along the rocks in some places to keep up. His tiny limbs swung out beside him and his legs shook when he landed. Kael could feel those blue eyes on him, begging him, boring into his soul.

A few of the guards watched them pass, but as soon as their dinner was ready, they looked away. While they tore white flesh from the bone and licked the grease off their fingers, it gave Kael the second he needed. He slung off his rucksack and dug into it, grabbing his last orange.

Jonathan saw what he was doing and blanched. "You can't, mate. I'm serious. If the guards see you —"

"Well here's what I think about the guards." He gave Jonathan the gesture he learned from Kyleigh. "And here's one for the Duke."

His mouth fell open in shock. Then he laughed. "All right, I can't argue with that." He reached into his pack and pulled out a loaf of bread. He watched the guards until they slipped under the cover of a lean-to. "Now," he said, and they tossed their food to the children.

The boy caught Kael's orange and a girl next to him caught Jonathan's bread. They looked at each other, mouths hanging open liked they wanted to scream in delight. But instead they tucked the food under their shirts and, with grateful nods, disappeared into the shadows.

They made a game of it. The children would crowd around, using their bodies to shield each other from the guards while Kael and Jonathan tossed them rations. Kyleigh was next to join their game, then Aerilyn. Soon the whole caravan was passing out food. Horatio emptied every barrel and basket he had. Chaney cut dried meat into chunks and dropped them down to Claude, who tossed them into the crowd.

The children tucked their spoils under their shirts and ran back to their families, glee showing clearly on their faces. The bright red of apples and orange of carrots and green of cabbage — all the color stood out brilliantly in the gray world around them.

When they crossed some invisible line in the street, the children stopped following them. They waved excitedly and Kael waved back, smiling as broadly as he could until the caravan disappeared around the corner.

The deeper they went into Harborville, the more the houses improved. Rotten lean-tos became rotten houses, and then decent houses. It wasn't long before they came to the nicest part of town — and the part that was truly revolting.

In the center of Harborville, men and women in gold-stitched clothes ambled through the streets. They browsed at the windows of neat little shops and occasionally opened the overflowing purses at their overflowing bellies to buy something. The men who ran the shops all bore the symbol of the High Seas on their tunics. They sold goods at Duke Reginald's prices: no bargaining, and no exceptions. If a man couldn't afford the price of bread, then he had to do without.

A short walk away, children were starving to death, yet these people in their fine clothes were too worried about their latest wolf skin cape or glass bauble to bother themselves with it. One man strolled by, swinging a gold-capped cane, and Kael tripped him.

"Good heavens, are you all right?" another man said as he helped him off the ground.

"Yes, quite all right," he grumbled. He glanced about him, brushing the dirt off his shoulders. But Kael had already taken refuge behind Horatio. "Must've tripped myself on a bit of cobblestone ..."

The caravan stopped at a sprawling inn called *The Jolly Duke*. Just beneath its title was the painted image of Duke Reginald. He flashed his white teeth and seemed to be enjoying his view of the village.

Kael tried to spit on him, but the sign hung too high for his range.

Several long tables filled the common area of *The Jolly Duke*. They sat down and Horatio went to order their meals. When the innkeeper named his price, he snorted in disbelief — but paid it anyways. Several guards lurked in the back corner of the room, testing their blades maliciously against their callused thumbs. And Horatio seemed to think that arguing over a price wasn't worth the maiming.

Dinner turned out to be a bowl of watery, lukewarm stew. Flaky bits of fish and pieces of shell floated aimlessly through it. Kael poked it a bit, but he was still too angry to eat. Across from him, Aerilyn stared through grief-reddened eyes. She'd scoop up some broth, then tilt her spoon and watch it trickle back into the bowl.

"Listen up, gentlemen," Horatio said, though not a soul was talking. "I've been able to secure us passage on a boat to the Grandforest. We leave at first light."

The men murmured that they understood, then went back to their solemn meals.

Kyleigh had disappeared almost the second they walked through the door. But shortly after the announcement, she returned. "I've got us a boat," she said as she sat her bowl next to Aerilyn's. "We leave at midnight."

Kael's heart sank. He knew this moment would come eventually — he just wasn't ready for it.

Aerilyn's spoon clattered onto the table. "But — but you *can't* leave. What will I do without the two of you? No, you must stay and winter with us in the Grandforest." She wiped her eyes and sat up a little straighter. "Please. Surely your journey can wait until spring."

Kyleigh shook her head. "I assure you, it can't. We've got a long ways to go and the longer we stay with the caravan, the more trouble we'll cause."

"I don't *care* about the trouble!" she said desperately. "Please stay with us for one more season."

"No," Kyleigh said firmly, perhaps a little too firmly.

Aerilyn's eyes got perilously wet. "So that's it, then? Now that we've taken you across the Valley you're just — just done with us? You're going to fling us aside like so — much — filth? How — dare you!" She took a great, shuddering breath, then fled the room as she burst into tears.

No sooner was she gone than Jonathan crammed himself into her spot, sitting as close to Kyleigh as humanly possible. "I've heard the tittering of adventure coming from over here," he said in her ear.

She elbowed him away. "Don't make me kill you with my spoon."

"All right, I won't." He leaned away from her and for once, his face went serious. "I want to come with you."

"Absolutely not."

"Why?"

"Because where we're going is dangerous, and I've already got one life I'm responsible for. I don't need another."

He glared at her. "If you don't take me with you, I'll go anyways. There's nothing left for me back home. I may not have a sword as a third arm, but I still like to think I've got a bit of value."

"Oh? How so?" Kyleigh said, her annoyance muddled by her amusement.

He flashed his lopsided grin. "My charm and general good looks. Besides that, I'm no stranger to the filthier side of society — if you're going to deal with rats, then you've got to know how they squeak."

"And I suppose you're an expert in squeaking?"

"All three dialects," he said with a nod. Then he fell off the bench and onto one knee. "Take me with you, and I swear I won't lay a hand to my fiddle for three hours."

"Twelve."

"Done." He shook her hand, grinning to either ear, and Kael could hardly believe it.

"You should know that we'll likely all end up dead — or rotting in a dungeon somewhere, at the very least," she said.

"I'm all for that. Maybe I'll even get a few scars out of the deal. Ladies really go for blokes with battle wounds. Now," he rubbed his hands together, "where're we off to first?"

She smirked. "South. We leave tonight."

"Oh, a bit of mystery? I like that. Well, better get the old carpet bag dusted off." And with that, he rushed away.

"Are you sure that was a good idea?" Kael said the second he was gone.

She shrugged. "Only time will tell. Though I've found that having a rogue on your side can often be useful. He's friendly, at least — which is something you and I aren't very good at."

Well, he supposed she was right about that. He'd just mustered up the courage to take a bite of his stew when Aerilyn returned.

She stomped up to the table with her chin firmly in the air. Her nose was red, but her eyes had a dangerous glint in them. "I've made a decision," she declared. "There's no point in returning home right away — I'll not spend the winter alone with my tears. So, since you refuse to come with me, I'm coming with you. When do we leave?"

****

At just before midnight, Kyleigh led them out the door of *The Jolly Duke*. Chaney and Claude caught wind of their adventure and begged for hours to come along. But Jonathan finally convinced them to stay with the caravan.

"What'll your pap do come winter, when he hasn't got anyone to help him in the shop?" he said, and the brothers very reluctantly admitted that he was right.

When Kael stepped out into the street, he heard the crash of a window slamming open. Claude popped his head out first, followed closely by Chaney.

"We'll miss you!"

"Bring us back something from your adventure!"

After swearing he would, they waved and went back to their beds.

Horatio came down to see them off. He'd been upset when Kyleigh said they were leaving, but couldn't deny the fact that their contract was up. "At least take your wages," he said, but Kael pushed the silver back into his hands.

"I've got no room in my pack. Use it to take care of the villagers."

Horatio nodded stiffly, and then pulled him in for a bone-crushing hug. "You've always got a place with us, if the mountains don't suit you." He nodded to Kyleigh. "And make sure that girl stays out of trouble."

He promised he'd try.

Horatio seemed prepared to let them go — that is, until Aerilyn came skipping out, a full-to-the-seams rucksack hanging off one shoulder of her pale blue traveling cloak. Then his face went purple.

"Absolutely not!" he roared, snatching her by the pack. "You aren't going anywhere but home."

"I'll go where I please!" she shouted back. "I'm a grown woman, it's high time that I make my own way."

Horatio stepped in front of her, using his belly to herd her back inside. "*Men* make their own way, ladies do not. The realm isn't safe for a woman anymore, and I swore to keep you safe! I'm not going to pack you off to Kingdom knows where, to do Kingdom knows what — that's the *opposite* of safe!"

She shoved back on Horatio's stomach, trying to use her shoulder to wedge herself out the door. "But Kyleigh travels all the time — and she's a woman!"

"A woman with all of Midlan on her trail!"

Horatio yelled until he was out of breath. Aerilyn huffed and stomped her foot at everything he said. It wasn't long before furious tears sprang into her eyes and she started wailing about how unfair he was. Then someone leaned out the window above them and said that if they didn't shut it, he'd called the guards. And Horatio was in the middle of telling the man exactly where to put his guards when Kyleigh grabbed his arm and pulled him aside.

There was a great deal of hissing and spitting on Horatio's end and a lot of calm, even whispering from Kyleigh. Eventually, she got him to speak at a normal volume. Then came the arm-crossing and head-nodding. A few minutes later, they seemed to reach an agreement.

"So we have a deal?"

Horatio glared at her hand for a moment before he finally took it. "Very well. But not a hair on her head, do you understand?"

Kyleigh's face was serious. "For as long as I draw breath."

When Horatio turned and said, very reluctantly, that Aerilyn could go, she shrieked in delight. She threw her arms around his shoulders and told him what a wonderful, generous man he was. The two of them likely would have sobbed about how much they would miss each other all night if Kyleigh hadn't cleared her throat and reminded them that they had a ship to catch. So they said goodbye to Horatio one last time, and then they followed her down to the docks.

Kael couldn't believe how monstrous the ships were. Lanterns hung all along the path, spaced a few feet apart. They were intended to warn travelers of the water's edge, but the light gave him a better view of the boats. He pulled the *Atlas* out of his pocket and made a game of checking off the ones he saw.

Some he knew were sailing boats: they were smaller than the rest and built for speed. The Duke probably used them to pass around his ridiculous laws the second he thought of them. All he had to do was breathe in to know that most were wide-bottomed fishing boats: the stench of dead sea life hung in the air like a rotten cloud. Even if he held his nose, he could still taste it in his throat. Jonathan pulled his shirt collar over his nose and Aerilyn gagged quietly into her handkerchief. Kyleigh had her hood pulled up, so he couldn't tell if she was making a face or not.

He'd be surprised if she wasn't.

Gruff shouts and a chorus of laughter drew his eyes to the tallest ship. A group of bearded men leaned over the high rails and beat their tankards against their breastplates, trying to get Aerilyn's attention. When she looked up, they whistled.

Jonathan pulled her behind him before she could retort and clamped a hand over her mouth. "Sorry, gents — she's spoken for!" he said with a wink.

The soldiers laughed and raised their tankards to him, and he saluted smartly.

"I'll be sure and give her a kiss for you!" he called. Then, out the side of his mouth to Aerilyn: "They aren't worth it, lass. They're drunker than a full moon and hanging over the ocean in armor. I'd bet my favorite toe that at least half of them won't live to see the morning."

They weren't three steps away when they heard a loud *splash* and round of guffaws.

"See? What did I tell you?" he said with a grin.

The ship Kyleigh led them to was a merchant's vessel, judging by the many large crates stacked over its every surface. As they walked down the long bridge to the boarding ramp, Kael felt an odd twist in his stomach. His legs shook a little and he found that if he looked down at the water, the feeling got worse.

He was probably just excited.

Most of the men aboard the vessel were the Duke's soldiers, all clad in full armor. A very few were normal sailors — and yet they seemed to be the ones doing all the work. They weaved around, loading crates, tying them down, getting the ship ready to set sail while the Duke's men leaned against the rails and watched.

Kyleigh led them up the ramp to a soldier who greeted them with a glare. "The coin you gave me was for two, miss," he said to Kyleigh. Fortunately, he didn't seem to recognize her face from under the shadow of her hood. "I'm not allowed to have four passengers, and I haven't got the room for them."

"You aren't allowed to have one passenger," she retorted. "And for the price I'm willing to pay, I think you'll find the room."

He looked at the heavy purse at her belt and shifted his weight uncomfortably. "You don't understand, miss. If the Duke finds out, I'll lose my place. And in these times that might as well be a death sentence. I'm sorry, but you'll have to find passage elsewhere."

Kyleigh's hand went to her sword, but Aerilyn stepped in before she could get them all killed. "Please, sir. Our business is very important and we haven't got much time. Couldn't you see it in your heart to help us? At least until the next port?"

Under the spell of Aerilyn's eyes, it was amazing how quickly the soldier softened. "All right," he grumbled. He took the purse Kyleigh handed him and tucked it quickly into his pocket. "This way."

They followed him to the back of the boat, where a small canopy had been stretched over the space between two stacks of crates. "You're to stay here at all times. If you need to relieve yourself, tell one of the guards. They'll escort you to the railings. Otherwise, stay put and don't make a ruckus." He lowered his voice. "The seas aren't safe anymore, especially for our sort of boat." With that, he marched away — leaving them to get settled for the night.

Their space under the canopy was a far cry from an inn. Even when they camped in the Valley, Kael could sprawl out in every direction. But now he had Aerilyn's shoulder pressed against his side, squishing him into the solid wood of the nearest crate. Jonathan was laying lengthways and already asleep, judging by the heavy breath he kept blowing into the top of Kael's head.

After a bit of squirming, he found that if he rolled over on his side, he could get some space. He turned towards the crate and noticed that it had the sun of Whitebone branded into the side of it. He was tracing the burnt edges with his finger when he heard Aerilyn hiss:

"Kyleigh, are you mad?"

"Last time I checked, no," was her cool reply.

"Well the last time *I* checked, we were stuck on a ship carrying goods from the desert. And do you know what they make in the desert?"

"Sand?"

"Jewelry!" Aerilyn said, with no small amount of exasperation. "Gold, silver, diamonds — these crates are probably spilling over with treasure. Did it ever occur to you that treasure practically makes us a beacon for," she lowered her voice, "pirates?"

Kyleigh snorted. "Pirates are just an old fisherman's tale."

"No they aren't! Didn't you hear what that guard said, about how the seas aren't safe anymore? *Gold* was hardly enough to get him to bring us along. And I'm telling you, it's because of the pirates. We should get off this very instant. I'm sure we can find another ship to travel on —"

"Have you ever met a pirate?"

An indignant gasp. "Of *course* I haven't! They're not exactly the company one invites to tea. Besides, merchants are the sworn enemies of pirates. We actually work for our coin, thank you very much. Pirates are naught but drunken thieves — and they'll kill you and hang your body from the mast of their ship."

Kyleigh laughed. "Oh, please. Why would they do something like that? Just think of the mess. We aren't getting off," she added, "so you might as well get some sleep. I promise things will look much less deadly in the morning."

Chapter 19
Anchorgloam

Part of agreeing not to cause a ruckus meant that Jonathan was absolutely banned from playing his fiddle. When the captain threatened to throw it overboard, he stuffed the instrument hastily into his rucksack and sat on it. Not long after that, he found a pack of cards — and made it his personal duty to teach Kael how to play.

On the front of each card was a painted image of a person or a beast. The highest card in the deck was the King. He glared out from under his crown and clutched a vicious-looking dagger in his right hand. There were four Kings and each ruled over a different color suit: black was the strongest, followed by red, then blue, and finally green.

It took Kael a few hands to figure it out, but soon he could hold his own at the table — much to Jonathan's dismay.

"And here I thought you'd be a purse," he grumbled as Kael collected his winnings: two bread slices and a slightly wrinkled plum.

"What's a purse?" Aerilyn asked.

"A bloke who can't really play and just winds up paying the rest of the table," Jonathan explained. He tossed a black knight out in the middle. "You might as well hand over your cheese, gents! There's not a card left among you that can trump him."

Then Kael played the black dragon and his mouth dropped open in shock. "You're a villain," he said accusingly. "A cold-stomached killer!" He threw his cards down and rolled over on his back, clutching his heart.

And Aerilyn took the opportunity to punch him in the gut.

They passed the long days at sea playing whatever games Jonathan could think of: Madman's Crumble, Scalawaggle, Ditch the Witch, and Burnt Pecan were just a few. Though Kael strongly suspected that Burnt Pecan wasn't a real game: Aerilyn had never heard of it, and the rules kept changing in Jonathan's favor.

As long as he had something to occupy him, Kael didn't think the journey was all that bad. But the moment he ran out of things to do, he began to notice how miserable he was.

Never, in all of his life, had he been forced to live in such cramped quarters. He'd always had the wilderness to escape to, the wide-open land to run across and plenty of trees to hide in. But on the merchant ship there was no escape, and it wasn't long before he began to feel like a rabbit caught in a snare. If Jonathan had a tune stuck in his head, he hummed it until it got stuck in Kael's. If Aerilyn asked him a ridiculous question, he couldn't pretend like he hadn't heard her — because she was always sitting right at his elbow. The soldiers would sneer at him, call him a mountain rat or a redheaded stork, and there was nothing he could do about it.

"If there's one thing I've learned, it's that you never want to clock a man in the middle of the sea," Jonathan warned when he'd muttered darkly about their heckling. "If his mates decide to toss you, it's a long, cold swim to shore."

"I don't know how to swim," Kael admitted.

He shrugged. "So it'd be a short one, then."

For once, the only person who didn't annoy him on an hourly basis was Kyleigh. The boat was small, and the further out to sea they went the larger the waves became. So the vessel rocked back and forth in unreliable patterns, sloshing them around like the last sip of ale in the bottom of a tankard. And Kyleigh's stomach didn't take well to the movement.

Her face was always tinged some shade of green. She had a difficult time keeping her rations down and spent most of her days laying on her side with her hood pulled up, trying to sleep. He actually felt sorry for her, and he got her a cup of water anytime he could.

210

Eventually, the long days would fade away and then the nights were mostly pleasant. He'd had no idea just how big the sky was, but out in the middle of the sea, the stars were magnificent. They danced the length and breadth of the sky, winking back at them knowingly. He wished he could see the world all at once as they did. He imagined his troubles must look ridiculously small from up there. But from where he stood, they were monstrous.

Aerilyn put on a brave face during the day, but darkness left them with little light and nothing to do — except brood. So when night fell, her thoughts must have turned to Garron. Her bravery would melt away and be replaced by tears. Kael often woke to the sounds of her quiet sobbing.

He knew how she felt. When the sky went dark, thoughts of Tinnark would swim before his eyes. He would toss and turn, worrying over Amos, wondering if Roland was safe … and regretting that he wasn't with them. Sometimes he worried that he would never see them again. Sometimes he thought about jumping overboard and swimming back the way he came, giving up this mad quest for the wolf he knew.

So even though Aerilyn kept him awake, he couldn't begrudge her tears. If anything ever happened to Amos, he knew he would cry — death was the only thing a boy from the mountains was allowed to mourn.

****

On the fourth day, Kael woke up and immediately thought he was going blind. He rubbed his eyes, turned his head this way and that, but no matter how he strained all he could see was a cloud of white. The air smelled strange, too — like moldy stockings.

He waved his hand across his face, and the white moved. It felt … slimy, and it made his palm itch. For a split second he could see his feet, then white crept over them again. That's when he realized he wasn't going blind: the ship was sailing through impossibly thick fog.

211

He remembered very clearly what Jonathan said about the fog on the seas: *Ships sail into them, and they never sail out.*

He could tell by the many worried shouts coming from the deck that the Duke's soldiers felt the same way. Armor rattled as several pairs of feet rushed from rail to rail, almost as if they were expecting an attack. Above him, he could hear one of the guards snapping at the man who steered the ship.

"Are you blind, you great, stupid gull? Don't tell me you didn't see it — you couldn't miss a fog like this from seven horizons!"

"I swear I went around it," the man said, an edge of panic in his voice. "I set me course and put it to the rudder. But it kept creeping up on us, even moving against the wind." His voice was shaking now. "I tell you, I've not seen fog move like that in all my years. It ain't natural."

Kael decided it was time for Kyleigh to wake up. He reached blindly, feeling in her direction. When he brushed her armor, her hand shot up and clamped on his arm.

"It's me," he hissed, before she could twist it off.

"Oh." She loosened her grip but didn't let go. After a moment, she seemed to realize their predicament. "What in blazes ...?"

"It's fog," he said as she sat up. "Look." He waved his arm, ignoring how it made him itch, and the white retreated enough for them to glimpse the deck.

"Wait a moment — do that again," she said.

When he obliged, enough cleared that he could see her face. For some reason, she was grinning.

"Help me wake the others, and make sure they stay quiet."

In the time it took them to get everyone up, the fog cleared a little. They could now make out the shadows of men as they ran back and forth across the deck. Several times a loud *clang* would make them jump, followed by a body striking the floor and the muttered apologies of the man who managed to stay on his feet.

The soldier who'd taken their coin was barking for his men to fall in line. Kael thought his voice was coming from the ship's wheel at first, but then it sounded again from the bow. It was the blasted fog, blocking their view and throwing every sound in the wrong direction.

Then all at once, the ship went silent. It was like someone had gone and dropped a wet blanket over their heads. The running and the shouting ceased, the men lined up at the railings froze. Not a whisper passed among them.

He was about to get an arrow ready when Kyleigh stopped him. "I wouldn't do that."

Every instinct in his body was screaming for him to get ready for a fight. His heart was thumping so vigorously against his ribs that it made his hair stand on end.

"Listen to me." The shadow of her hood dulled the color of her eyes, but made them no less serious. "This isn't our fight — but if you draw your bow, it will become ours. And I promise we won't win. Whatever happens, you must stay back with the others. You must protect them. Will you swear it?"

He'd already failed once, and he wouldn't do it again. So against all reasoning, he ignored his instincts and dropped the arrow back in its quiver. "I swear it."

She smiled. "Good man. Now get behind me."

They waited several long moments before someone on deck cried out: "I hear it! It's on the port side!" And a whole company of soldiers abandoned their posts to run to across.

"I don't hear anything," someone said after a moment.

"I swear I heard it," the man insisted. "It was a strange, creaking sort of noise."

"Seas help us," another man gasped. "It's the ghost of the leviathan, I know it is! The great, bloody monster is opening his jaws to swallow us!"

Someone smacked him, and he yelped.

Then a hollow, groaning sound, almost like the final gasp of a rotted tree tipping over, came unmistakably from the starboard side. Swords hissed as they flew out of their scabbards and a horde of feet pounded for it.

They stopped their charge just as the whole boat began to shake. There was a clap of thunder — ear splitting and sharp. The world turned on its side as the deck rocked violently. Bodies tumbled overboard; screams were cut short as the waves sucked hapless men to their deaths.

Aerilyn rolled into Kael with a squeal, pinning him against a crate. While he fought to right himself, the boat groaned and stayed tilted at a dangerous angle. The ropes the sailors used to tie down the cargo trembled as the weight of gold and silver pushed them to their limits. One rope finally gave out.

It snapped, and the large crate it held broke free. It flew towards them, urged on by the slant of the boat. Panic gave him the strength to put his hands under Aerilyn and shove her out of the way, but he was too late to save himself.

He'd prepared to be crushed when Kyleigh slid into him. She knocked him aside and caught the crate under her boots, using her legs as a wedge to hold it at bay. When the boat finally rocked back with a shudder, the crate slid forward.

She ignored his astonished look and glanced behind him. "Is everyone all right back there?"

Aerilyn's hair was piled up in a knot and her skirt was ripped down the side, but other than that she seemed fine. Jonathan was stuck in a tangle at the back of the canopy. A crate full of silk had fallen on him and he was trying to dig himself out from under a mountain of brightly-colored scarves.

Panicked shouts rang out across the deck, and Kael nearly jumped out of his skin when a roar of voices answered them. Shadows slid in and out of the fog, grappling with one another. The shriek of metal striking metal cut over the top of everything, it stabbed at them from all sides.

"What's happening?" Jonathan said as he crawled towards them, kicking free of the last scarf.

"I *told* you this would happen!" Aerilyn wailed. "I told you we should have gotten off this boat. But you didn't listen, and now we're being attacked by pirates!"

Kael's mouth went dry. The sounds of battle were growing steadily weaker, trailing away as one side won out over the other. He hoped the soldiers held their ground. At least the Duke had laws: there was no telling what pirates did with their prisoners. But it probably involved sharks and a good amount of flogging.

"How will we know if they're pirates or not?" Kael said.

Jonathan snorted. "You'll know. They'll be the ones with gold teeth and bones weaved into their beards!"

"Who cares what they look like? We're all going to be murdered —!"

"*Shhh!*" Kael clamped a hand over Aerilyn's mouth. They were talking too loudly on a ship that had suddenly gone deathly quiet. If there was anyone still onboard, they would've heard.

He had an arrow nocked and ready. Blast what Kyleigh said — if man or beast came charging out of that fog, he'd bring it down. He watched the fog, searching desperately for any signs of movement. For a long moment, all he could hear were the quick breaths of his companions and the thudding of his own heart. Then, something creaked.

It was a careful sound, a practiced one. A noise caused by a man who was used to hushing his footsteps. He probably cursed when he stepped on that plank, because it might as well have been a battle horn: now Kael knew he was coming.

A shadow moved behind the wall of white, and then a dozen others joined it. They began to take shape, swaying slowly back and forth as they inched closer. The first man stepped out of the fog and blinked, as if he hadn't been expecting to see them so clearly.

He wore a long black cloak that fell to his knees and had a red, upside down V painted on the front of his white tunic — a mark that stood out even in the fog. In one hand, he held a slender cutlass. His face was clean-shaven, his jaw set

215

tight. He had the eyes of a man who'd lived for a thousand years.

And the mouth of a man who hadn't learned to smile in any of them.

He waited until his cloaked companions formed a half circle around him before he spoke. "A pox on the Duke," he said, and the others leaned forward and collectively spat. "You're under the rule of pirates, now. And you'll answer our questions." He pointed his sword at them. "Which of you is the mage?"

"None of us practice magic. We're simple travelers," Kyleigh said.

The serious pirate frowned. "You don't work for the Duke?"

She spread her arms wide. "Do you see an emblem on my chest?"

"A tunic is easy to change," he countered, his voice every bit as flinty as his stare. "You could be a liar."

"True. Or I could be on my way to help your captain."

His face hardened, his eyes narrowed. "You know nothing of my captain, landscab. And if you aren't careful, I'll gut the lot of you."

Kyleigh stepped out from the shelter, watching him from under her hood. "I know all about your captain. I know about his trouble with the Witch," she said quietly, and the pirates stiffened. "I know that he's at his wit's end — that he's poured over every tome in his ridiculous library and still hasn't found an answer. And I happen to know what he needs."

The other pirates shifted, their hooded heads turned in the direction of their leader, waiting for his answer. He finally sheathed his sword and mirrored her, crossing his arms. "What's this information going to cost me?"

She shrugged. "Our lives, for now. I'll discuss the rest of my terms with Captain Lysander."

A round of anxious whispering broke out among the pirates. The serious one took an involuntary step forward. "Where did you hear that name, landscab?" he growled.

"I have my sources," she replied coolly.

He looked on the verge of hitting her, but instead his mouth bent in a smirk. "Well, I hope your sources weren't wrong — for your sake. Come with me." He marched back into the fog, and Kyleigh followed.

Kael didn't know if they were allowed to come or not, but he certainly wasn't going to stay: the pirates were trying to roast him alive with their glares.

He slung his pack over his shoulder and hurried past them. Aerilyn latched onto his shirt and he could hear Jonathan stumbling along behind her. Once again, he found that if he swung his arms the fog cleared enough for him to see where he was going — which came in handy on a ship littered with crates and bodies.

The first soldier they came across was the one who'd taken their coin. There was a bloody hole in the middle of his chest. His face was frozen in shock. Kyleigh knelt beside him to retrieve the purse from his belt.

"And that's the cheapest way to travel on the High Seas," the serious pirate said approvingly. He looked over her shoulder and his eyes found Kael. "I know you're not a mage, but since flapping your wings is magically clearing out this fog, how about you get up to the front?"

There was a large dose of sarcasm in his voice, and absolutely no nonsense on his face. So Kael dragged his line of followers up even with him. He felt stupid waving his arms, now. And he thought that might have been the pirate's point. But it was too dangerous to worry about feeling stupid.

More than once, he had to tell Aerilyn not to look down because the scene at their boots was beyond gruesome. Several times they had to walk over bodies and through dark, sticky puddles. At one point, he heard Jonathan gag and lose his breakfast — which made the pirate chuckle.

When they reached the far side of the boat, he saw immediately what had caused them to nearly tip over. The noise he'd heard wasn't a thunderclap, but the sound of their boat being struck by another. Now the starboard side was all splinters, its railings were cracked and fallen over on the floor.

A large ramp dropped out into the middle of the wreckage and led directly upwards, to the deck of a monstrous ship.

It perched on the ocean like it had every right to be there — easily thrice the height of the merchant vessel. There were four levels, and whoever built it must have used the tallest tree in the Grandforest for its mast. Waves slapped against it, but couldn't so much as shift the massive planks of deep red wood that made up its side.

"Welcome aboard *Anchorgloam*," the pirate said as they reached to top of the ramp. "She's the toughest vessel to ever sail the High Seas. No tempest can take her."

Kael seriously doubted that. He'd seen drawings of tempests in the *Atlas*, of waves the height of castle towers and swirling pits of water with no bottom. The meetings rarely turned out well for the ships.

The fog was, if possible, even thicker aboard *Anchorgloam*. He had to swing his arms twice as much and they still managed to run into people. "Sorry about that, miss," a pirate said after he nearly knocked Aerilyn flat. "It's hard for a fellow to see in this blasted stuff."

They followed the serious pirate to the back of the ship, where a small cabin sat on top of the deck. The pirate went to rap on the door and cursed when it swung open. "Steady, lad!" he barked.

A sandy-haired boy looked sheepishly out from behind it. "Sorry, Thelred. I was just coming to get you."

"Why? Is there something wrong with the captain?" Thelred asked, a surprising amount of concern in his voice.

"Not yet, but we've run out of wine and now he's turning sour."

"Perfect," Kael heard Aerilyn grumble. "We wouldn't want a sober man deciding our fate."

A rumble of thunder trailed her words, and Thelred glared up at the sky. "Get in, all of you. Pick your feet up," he snapped as he pushed them through the door. "You follow at the rear, Noah."

The sandy-haired boy nodded and took the place behind Jonathan.

When they stepped through the door, it was like they fell through a portal and wound up in the middle of some wealthy man's hallway. The walls were made of dark red wood and every square inch was polished to a shine. Glass-covered cases were built into the walls, each one holding a different treasure or trinket.

There were coins dating back to the time of the first King, tarnished and green with age. One case was full of gold-spined books, opened to pages written in strange, curling symbols. A pearl the size of Kael's fist sat on top of that case, and it was so polished that he could actually see his reflection on its ivory surface. The plaque beneath it read *Seeing Eye of Argus Yar*.

Kael nearly gasped. No one knew what happened to the eye of Argus Yar — a Seer so powerful that legend told he could travel into the future. Though Kael thought he'd believe in the legend before he believed the eye had wound up in the hands of pirates.

He came to the next case, one that held a simple broadsword — badly chinked and rusted from use. He read the plaque that claimed it was the Arm of Vindicus the Broken, and he snorted.

Thelred turned around. "Is something funny?"

He wanted to say that something *was* funny; that he thought Thelred's face looked as if he had a barnacle stuck somewhere highly uncomfortable. But since he probably could've drawn his cutlass faster than Kael could draw his bow, he didn't.

"This isn't the *real* Arm of Vindicus," Kael explained. "Everyone knows that the King keeps the real one locked in a case over the door of his armory."

Thelred smirked, and the gesture didn't quite reach his eyes. "Everyone *does* think that — which is why no one comes looking for this one. And if you'd like to keep them, I suggest you put them away," he added, without taking his eyes off Kael.

Behind him, Jonathan had been reaching out to touch the pearl. But after Thelred's warning, he stuffed his hands hastily back into his pockets.

At the end of the hallway was a solid wooden door. Two twisting sea serpents were carved into it. Their mouths were open — revealing two rows of needle teeth. The one coiled around the handle seemed to snarl at Thelred as he turned it.

The door opened up to a large room. Two of its walls were covered in shelves of books, stretching from the ceiling, over the doorway, and down to the floor. It only took Kael a second to realize they were all arranged alphabetically. He scanned their titles and itched to read through them. One in particular caught his eye: *Travels with Shapechangers*.

It was a thin volume, but exciting nonetheless. He didn't know there were any books at all devoted entirely to shapechangers.

A small bed folded out of the third wall, neatly made up with cream-colored sheets and fluffy white pillows. The space was decorated, inexplicably, with a pair of striped knickers framed like a painting.

In the very center of the room, a large desk squatted on stubby legs. There was a quill and parchment tucked neatly to one side of its shiny top, and a rolled map on the other. Behind the desk were three clear, floor-length windows that overlooked the foggy sea.

There was only one thing in the room that didn't quite fit, and that was the man sitting at the desk. Well, perhaps *slouching* was a better word for it.

While Thelred and Noah had been a bit of a disappointment, this man looked exactly the way a pirate ought to. His shoulders sloped downward and his head lolled from side to side, as if they were making him seasick just standing there. His mouth gaped open through a ratty tangle of a beard that stretched down past his collarbone. His brown hair stuck out like the frayed edges of a rug.

He blinked his bloodshot eyes. "'Ow man' we loss, Red?" he mumbled.

Thelred clamped his hands behind his back and frowned. "None, Captain."

"Goo'," the captain said. An empty decanter sat by his elbow. He slung his arm out and knocked it onto the floor, where it shattered. "Don' een usa glass do I?" He let out a scornful laugh, then dropped his hairy head. "Can' do 'is no more, Red. Is jus too 'ard."

A quiet, tinkling noise drew Kael's attention to the windows. Soft drops of rain pattered against them, sliding down in uneven lines while the captain shook his head and moaned. Kael thought he could have done with a slap around the ears.

Thelred deepened his frown. "I know. But I've brought some people who might be able to help us." He took Kyleigh by the arm and led her up to the desk. "This one knows your name. She says she has your answer."

The captain belched loudly and flicked his hand at her without even looking up. "Snake oil ands 'moke! I nee 'em —"

"Like I need a broken sword," Kyleigh finished.

His mouth fell open. He slung his head back and squinted at her. "Yous 'peak our lang'ed?"

She pulled her hood back and planted both of her hands on the table. "Hello, Lysander. I'd heard things weren't going well, but I must say that I didn't expect to find you in such a state."

Finally, realization seemed to dawn upon the befuddled captain. "Loo, Red!" He jabbed an unsteady finger in Kyleigh's direction, grinning like a fool. "Is the Draggurl! I'ms 'aved!"

Chapter 20
A Bargain

That time, even Thelred didn't catch what the captain gurgled. "The what, exactly?" he said with a frown.

Lysander slapped both of his hands on the desk top. "Th' Draggurl! Y'know." He curled his fingers and made a high-pitched noise. It sounded a bit like a cat stuck under a cartwheel.

When Thelred just shook his head, Lysander stood. He swayed and rocked dangerously back on his heels. "Abouf 'ace! To Wendegorim!" he barked. Then he spun, lost his balance, and fell headlong into the nearest bookshelf.

Several large tomes rained down upon him, including one on philosophy that conked him smartly on the head. He said a few words that made Aerilyn gasp before he hurled it across the room, demanding that it be locked up in the brig immediately.

"Sit tight, Captain," Thelred said as he hauled him up by the front of his shirt. "Try not to move —"

"Th' Draggurl!" He grabbed a fistful of Thelred's hair and wrenched his head to the side. "Drag — un — gurl."

That did it. When Thelred finally saw her without her hood up, his mouth dropped open. He lost his grip on Lysander — who flopped back on the ground with a moan.

Thelred stepped closer to Kyleigh, lightly, as if he was now suddenly afraid of her. He looked over her once before his mouth went tight. "My apologies, Dragongirl. I didn't recognize you. Had I known —"

"Things would have been a lot less interesting," she said with a smirk. "And stop with the titles, Red. You know my name."

Thelred shook her hand, and Noah rushed forward to be next in line.

Realization struck Kael like a blow to the shin. Good lord, her friends were pirates. *These* were the men who were mad enough to help them: this lot of drunken thieves with their magic fog. He could've kicked himself for trusting her.

"So she *was* the one those guards were after," Jonathan muttered to Kael. "I wonder what she could've done to get His Majesty's undergarments in a knot? Think I'll ask. Excuse me, gents — but what exactly is a Dragging-girl?"

Noah looked like he'd just uttered the foulest of all curses. "You've never heard of the Dragongirl?" He looked at Thelred. "Tide take us — they have no idea who they've been traveling with."

He sneered. "No lad, they don't. And that's because her name isn't known among thumbsuckers and softhands."

"Well instead of talking out your nose, how about you tell us?" Kael said. He was tired of Thelred — the cabin was so packed full of his airs that there was hardly room left to breathe.

"It's a name the King gave me when I served in Midlan," Kyleigh said before Thelred could retort. "My knight name. It was meant to be a secret, a way he could give us commands without our enemies finding out who we truly were. But then I left the army, did a few naughty things and," she shrugged, "my name got around."

Noah snorted. "*Naughty* is hardly the word for it. Last I checked, Lord Gilderick has had to rebuild his castle twice."

She smiled, as if she was looking back on a fond memory. "Ah, yes. One maniacal idiot, two very tragic fires."

"And then there was the stampede of elk at the Countess's birthday last year," Noah added.

Aerilyn clapped a hand over her mouth. "I remember that! We were there, presenting our gifts, when a great horde of beasts came tromping through. They slung their antlers about and ruined all of the lovely decorations —"

"And ole D'Mere hiked her skirts up and went screaming for the guards to do something!" Jonathan said with a grin. "I was laughing so hard I had tears rolling down my face."

"You know, it took me weeks to round those little blighters up. And I never got so much as a card for it," Kyleigh mused.

"That's probably because you nearly killed us all," Aerilyn said sharply.

A low, growling noise drew their attention back to the bookshelves. Sometime during their tales, Lysander had passed out. He was now snoring into the rug — his face resting gently in a puddle of his own drool.

"I should get the captain taken care of," Thelred said. "I'm sure he'll want to give you all a proper greeting. Why don't you show our guests to their quarters, Noah?"

****

Their quarters turned out to be quite a bit smaller than Captain Lysander's. The hallways beneath *Anchorgloam* were clean, but so tight that Kael actually had to turn sideways in some places just to squeeze through. He kept his head bent to avoid smacking it on one of the many low-hanging beams and watched the floor for stray coils of rope. Jonathan was hunched over ahead of him, and with every bend of his long legs, his knees nearly touched his chest.

Kyleigh and Aerilyn had a room to themselves at the front of the hallway, while Jonathan and Kael were packed into a tiny space with a dozen other men. Kael wondered how many times he could expect to fall out of the hammock thing the pirates called a bed.

"The days aboard *Anchorgloam* are no stroll in the woods," Noah assured them. "So by the time the watch bell sounds, you won't care where you're sleeping — just so long as you get to put your feet up. Now," he clapped his hands together and grinned, "do any of you scabs know how to play Brigand's Luck? No? Well I'll just have to teach it to you, then."

He led them back up on deck and found an empty barrel to use as a table. While the girls leaned against the railing and chatted, Noah taught the boys how to play Brigand's Luck.

It was a card game, but the pirate deck turned out to be completely different from the one Kael was used to. There were knaves instead of knights, brigands instead of lords, and in place of the dragon was a mischievous-looking imp.

Jonathan fanned his hand out and grinned. "Now *this* is the deck of a proper villain! I've got to get me one of these."

"Four coppers, and it's yours," Noah said with a smirk, and Jonathan immediately fished the coin out of his trousers.

The card the pirates used for the King was a man in a tricorn hat. It was tipped low over his eyes, revealing only his smirk, and in his hand he gripped a deadly cutlass.

"That's Sam Gravy," Noah explained. "He was the original scalawag — the first man to build a boat for plundering. We pirates consider him the father of our kind."

Aerilyn snorted. "The rest of the Kingdom considers your kind to be nothing more than a gang of sea thieves." She looked over the railing, down to where a group of pirates were lugging a treasure-laden crate up from the ruins of the merchant ship, and glared. "Does Captain Lysander spend all of his gold on drink, or does he save some to roll in?"

Noah frowned. "He doesn't spend any of his gold on drink. *Why pay for ale when you can steal it from a drunkard?* That's what he always says."

Aerilyn pursed her lips. "I'm sure he does."

"Yeah, you're not exactly what I thought a pirate would look like." And there was a considerable amount of disappointment in Jonathan's voice. "All the stories are about giant blokes with yellow eyes and black, rotten teeth —"

"And scars in the shape of their mothers?" Noah laughed. "Rubbish. The Duke's managers make those stories up. They can't cope with the fact that handsome, well-mannered gents like ourselves rob them blind. And the Duke would kill them all if he knew the truth."

"Well if anyone ever came across that captain of yours, there'd be no reason to doubt the stories," Aerilyn quipped. "I daresay he's the most ill-mannered man I've ever come across — and I've spent half of my life in taverns."

"The captain is a good man," Noah said, his eyes suddenly hard. "He does right by his men and right by the people of the High Seas. You ought not to talk about things you don't understand."

She raised an eyebrow. "Oh? Well, then by all means — enlighten me: the man reeks of liquor, swears profusely, expels his … humors, in the presence of a lady and looks as if he's tumbled straight out from between the pages of a dirty drinking song." She crossed her arms. "So what am I missing, exactly? Where's the *good* in Captain Lysander?"

Noah opened his mouth to respond, but instead leapt to his feet and touched his hand to his head in a smart salute.

Kael turned and saw Thelred making his way towards them, followed by a man he didn't recognize. He strode like a man with a purpose, whoever he was — swinging his arms in tight arcs and keeping his sharp chin level with the ground. A pair of stormy eyes looked out from beneath his crop of wavy hair, and a bit of scruff dusted the lines around his mouth, which was set in a frown.

As he climbed the stairs, Aerilyn whispered something to Kyleigh, and they both giggled. Kael stood a little straighter and made a conscious effort to stick his chest out. He didn't know who this man was, but he'd already decided that he didn't like him much. Besides, his nose was a little off-center.

The man stopped just in front of them and touched a hand to his chest. "Welcome aboard *Anchorgloam*," he said with a smile. "I can't tell you how excited I am to have visitors. I'm Captain Lysander."

Aerilyn gasped loudly and Kael couldn't have agreed more. The man standing before them now had no beard and no drool. Every button on his shirt was done smartly up, and not a wrinkle creased his trousers. He couldn't have been more different from the first captain.

Lysander's face turned slightly pink. "Yes, I've been told that I was a good deal less than civil," he said, fiddling with the cuff of his sleeve. "I was — ah — a bit down on my luck, I'm afraid, and that tends to drive a man to drink. Now," he clasped his hands behind his back and resumed his smile, "you've all met my cousin, Red. But I'm afraid I don't know any of you ... well, save for one."

His stormy eyes found Kyleigh and his smile widened into a grin, revealing two impressive rows of very straight, white teeth. He grabbed her by the arm and pulled her into a rather friendly embrace.

And much to Kael's annoyance, she didn't try to pull away.

"My dear, it's been far too long," Lysander said when he finally released her. "It's been leagues and years — and I didn't think I'd ever see you again. I don't think I ought to forgive you, either."

She returned his smile and took both of his hands in hers. "I told you I was looking for something, you silly pirate."

He rolled his eyes. "Oh yes, the *very important* something. How could I forget?" He lowered his voice, wisps of hair fell over his eyes. "And I hope this means you've found what you were searching for?"

She nodded. "It just took longer than I expected."

"Excellent." He kissed both her hands and then waved to the rest of them. "I'm very eager to meet your friends, Dragongirl. You always keep the most interesting company."

She gave their names while Lysander shook their hands. When it was Kael's turn, he squeezed a little harder than was probably necessary. But Lysander grinned on and didn't seem to notice.

Then he came to Aerilyn, and his smile faltered for half a second. "It's a true pleasure to meet a lady of the High Seas. I've long believed that our women are the fairest in the realm." He brought her hand to his lips, and Aerilyn's face turned the color of a ripe tomato.

All at once, a tremendous amount of heat and light flooded the deck. Kael looked up and saw the clouds were melting away — and in their place rose a burning sun. All across the deck, the pirates shielded their eyes and expressed their displeasure in swears.

Fortunately, the light didn't last long. By the time Lysander let go of Aerilyn's hand, the clouds were back.

"Ah, right." He cleared his throat and turned abruptly towards the stairs. "Follow me, all of you. We've much to discuss and very little time."

****

Back in Lysander's cabin, maps and books lay strewn all over the top of his desk and on the rug around it. Bits of wadded-up parchment made a trail from the door to the windows. "A dirty desk is a sign of progress," he declared as he got them lined up.

Kael wasn't sure he agreed with that. He thought there might have been a better way to make progress — one that didn't involve throwing books on the floor.

When Lysander had them all arranged, he clasped his hands behind his back and paced in front of them. For a few moments, that's all he did. Then he stopped and fixed them with a glare. "You're all criminals!" he barked, so loudly that it made Kael jump.

"I am *not* a criminal!" Aerilyn spat.

"Oh, but you are," Lysander said, his eyes glinting. "You've thrown your lot in with pirates — the sworn enemies of the Duke himself. Aye, from the very moment you set foot aboard *Anchorgloam* you turned your back on Puke Reginald, on His Maggotry, on tyranny —"

"On laws and other boring things!" Jonathan piped in.

"Aye, and especially on taxes." Lysander leaned back against his desk, smirking. "You gave up your petty lives for something more exciting. You've heard the siren's call, and you've followed it here — to the High Seas. It's the birthplace of the cutthroat, the threshold of adventure. And from here there can be no return. For that, my fellow seadogs, I commend you."

Aerilyn jabbed a finger at the center of his toothy grin. "I'm not a cutthroat, and I'm not a seadog! I'm an honest, decent merchant from a long line of honest, decent merchants. Last I checked, we didn't ask to be shipwrecked by pirates — we were kidnapped! And I refuse to stand here and listen to this — these — *accusations* any longer."

"I didn't know there was such a thing as an honest merchant," Thelred said from where he lurked in a corner of the room. "Maybe we ought send this one back to her father. That's where the dress-wearing sort of women belong, isn't it?"

The room hushed for half a second, the ominous silence before the storm. And then Aerilyn burst into tears. She fell into Kyleigh, who caught her and at the same moment said: "She's just lost her father, you idiot!" to Thelred.

Lysander's smile vanished. "I'm so sorry."

"I d — don't want your *ap — apologies* anymore than — than your accusations!" she wailed angrily into the front of Kyleigh's jerkin.

"No, you misunderstand me. I wasn't apologizing: I was sympathizing." Lysander took a cautious step forward. "I've lost my father, too. His name was Matteo, and he was killed fighting in the Whispering War when I was only a child. Sickness took my mother before I even had a chance to know her, so my father and I were very close. The man raised me — taught me everything he knew about living and fighting ... and I still miss him." He placed a hand on Aerilyn's shoulder. "So I think I might understand, at least a little, how you feel."

He couldn't have known how similar his story was to Aerilyn's, so he wasn't lying. But Kael still didn't trust him.

His confession silenced Aerilyn for a moment. She wiped her tears away and blinked. "Your father fought in the Whispering War?"

"He did, yes."

"So he wasn't a pirate?"

"Ah, he was, actually," Lysander admitted. "But in those days, King Banagher needed all the ships he could get. He couldn't exactly afford to be picky. What was your father's name, by the way? Perhaps my father robbed — ah, knew him."

She took a deep breath. "Garron," she said quietly.

He raised his eyebrows. "That wouldn't be Garron the Shrewd, would it?" When she nodded, he let out a bark of laughter. "Well then your papa was the one man on the High Seas that old Matteo never robbed."

She pulled away from Kyleigh, clearly intrigued. "Really? Why not?"

Lysander snorted. "Oh he made his excuses, but I knew it was because he was afraid of him. I don't know if you've heard this or not, but during the Whispering War, Garron captained the good ship *Avarice* — a vessel famed for her strength. He took everything but prisoners and would have made a blasted good pirate, if only we could have persuaded him." He grinned, shaking his head. "But Garron was a merchant, through and through. And he fought so well that the King gave him *Avarice* as a gift when the war was over."

She frowned. "But he never mentioned a ship. What did he do with it?"

"He gave it to an old friend," Lysander said simply. "But since you're the daughter of Garron the Shrewd, I'll make you a deal." He crossed his arms and leaned forward. "You don't have to be a seadog until you want to be one, all right? Until you change your mind, you'll just be an honest, decent merchant. But when you *do* change your mind — and you will — you have to give me a kiss before I'll turn you into a pirate."

Aerilyn glared through her blush as she shook his hand. "Fine, but that's never happening," she snapped, which only made him grin all the wider.

"Now, I'm afraid I can't offer the rest of you scabs the same out. Which means that you've got two choices: join my crew, or leave. You can leap right over the railings, and I promise no one is going to stop you." When a long moment passed and no one moved, Lysander grinned. "Well then, your worth has just increased threefold. That's right, lads —

you're pirates now! Wanted across the six regions and with a mountain of gold on your heads."

Jonathan punched his fist in the air and whooped. Kael wasn't sure how he felt about being a pirate, but he supposed there was no turning back. They were trapped on this floating pile of wood until Lysander was good and ready to take them ashore. So if swinging a cutlass and drinking too much ale would get him back to land, he'd do it.

They stood around while Lysander passed out their uniforms: a white shirt with tan breeches and a pair of knee-high boots. There was a red, upside down V painted on the front of every shirt.

"It's the symbol of our clan," Lysander explained. He mimicked the shape with his arms. "Our crossed swords are strengthened by the blood of our enemies and raised always in triumph."

"That's all well and good," Aerilyn cut in. "But I don't think I should have to wear one, seeing as how you've promised not to make me a pirate."

"Tie a man to an anchor, and he might wiggle free. Tie a man in a dress to an anchor, and you won't see him again till he rolls in with the tide," Lysander said. "I'd be sentencing you to death if I let you walk around in a dress. Everyone aboard my ship is required to wear this uniform. It's a rule."

She held the clothes away from her. "But I'm going to look awful in these! They've got absolutely no shape."

"Kyleigh has to wear them, too," Thelred muttered. "And she isn't complaining."

"Well *Kyleigh* would still look magnificent in a rucksack! Haven't you got anything more … feminine? Something like," she pulled at the hem of Kyleigh's mail skirt, "this — something flattering, but dangerous."

Lysander snorted. "Flattering but dangerous, eh? And let me give you a man's perspective: if I allowed women to walk around deck dressed like *that*," he nodded to Kyleigh, who rolled her eyes, "I don't think we'd ever get any work done."

"But what about lady pirate clothes?" she pressed. "Surely you have something that isn't so manly."

Lysander seemed to finally reach his wit's end. He threw up his hands and said: "Well it may come as a surprise to you, but in all my time as Captain I've never had the pleasure of having a woman aboard *Anchorgloam*. So I'm sorry, but I'm afraid I was ill-prepared."

Kael wasn't sure he believed that, but it made Aerilyn smile. "Never?"

"Never," Lysander assured her with a scowl. "Now, will you wear the uniform?"

She tossed her hair over her shoulder. "I suppose."

"Excellent." Lysander clapped his hands together. "*Anchorgloam* isn't a ferry, dogs — every man is expected to pull his weight. You'll rise at six bells, you'll have training, chores, and I'll be a merman's beard if I don't make decent sailors out of every one of you. Understood?"

They muttered a collective "Yes."

He raised his eyebrows. "When I ask you a question, you say *aye, Captain*! Understood?"

"Aye, Captain!" Jonathan's ear-bursting yell more than made up for Kael's half-hearted mumble.

Lysander cut his fist across his chest. "Well done. Now help the men finish loading up that treasure, seadogs!"

Aerilyn looked rather offended about being called a seadog, but she followed Jonathan out the door anyways. Kael made to leave when Kyleigh grabbed him by the arm. "You and I have things to discuss," she said quietly.

He didn't want to stay in Lysander's cabin a moment longer. He was hungry, exhausted, and had the beginning of what promised to be a nasty headache building at the base of his skull. "Can't it wait till morning?" he pleaded.

She shook her head. "The sooner we get this out, the better." Then she turned to Lysander — who was leaning over the desk, his nose inches from a map. "Might we have a word, Captain?"

"Yes, of course," he said, waving her to his side. "I was just thinking about our best route of attack. If we hit the south end — just there — do you think the cliffs might give us an advantage? Or would it be better to move west to east, through the woods?"

"I don't think we should be talking about this without Morris," Kyleigh said.

Thelred inhaled sharply, but Lysander didn't seem to hear him. "Yes, I suppose you're right. The helmsman ought to know, after all ..." He stood up straight and thrust an accusing finger at her. "You tricked me! I can't believe it, after all these years — and I thought we were friends."

"Oh please," she said with a roll of her eyes. "You already know my secret, it's only fair that I know yours."

Lysander pulled a dagger out of his boot and waved the blade in Kyleigh's face. "All I know is that *this* isn't an impetus, and *that*," he jerked his head at Kael, "isn't a mage."

That's when Kael realized that his hunting dagger wasn't in his belt — it was in Lysander's hand. "Hey —!"

"Oh, don't look so surprised," Lysander said over the top of him. "When you keep a dagger in your belt, you have to expect it to get nicked."

And Kyleigh inclined her head in agreement.

Kael caught the blade by its hilt. "I don't understand when you could have possibly had time to steal it."

"A thief doesn't need time — only opportunity," Lysander retorted. "And mine came while you were trying to crush my hand."

So he *had* noticed. Good. "Keep your hands away from my weapons, thief, and they won't get crushed," he said, with what he hoped was a convincing growl.

"A snappy little mountain mutt, aren't you?" Thelred sneered.

"You know, you might look good with an arrow between your eyes. And I'd be glad to make that happen —"

"Anyways," Kyleigh stepped between them, "I'm afraid we do need to see Morris. That's why we've come."

Lysander snorted. "Why do you need Morris? You're the Dragongirl! Lead us into battle, and I know we'll emerge victorious —"

"We need Morris because I'm not your answer, not this time."

He made a frustrated noise and sat heavily on top of the desk. "If you're not our answer then pray, who is?"

She nodded in Kael's direction and said, with all the confidence in the Kingdom: "Him."

Chapter 21
The Wright Arises

Kyleigh should have known how the pirates would react. She should have known that when she leaned back and said that the skinny, redheaded boy before them was the answer to all of their problems, that they would laugh. That Lysander would double over and Thelred would guffaw loudly from his corner.

She should have known better than to embarrass him like that.

"Oh Kyleigh, you've always been a merciless prankster," Lysander said as he wiped the tears from his eyes, still chuckling.

She didn't say anything: she just stared him down, a small smile on her face. Under the weight of her look, his grin faded away, slowly, until it was replaced by a frown.

"You're serious?" He glanced at Kael. "And why do you think he's the answer?"

"Because he's a whisperer."

And that dried up every stray giggle in the room. Lysander's mouth fell open and Thelred muttered: "Impossible."

"Is it?" She sauntered over to him. Her head barely came to Thelred's shoulder, yet he stepped to the side rather than allow her to pin him in the corner. "How else do you think he undid your little magic trick, hmm? If he isn't a mage, then he's got to be —"

"A whisperer," Lysander breathed. There was calm understanding on his face. "Red? Get Morris."

Thelred hurried out the door, no doubt eager to put as much distance between himself and Kyleigh as possible.

"What magic trick? And how did I undo it, exactly?" Kael asked as soon as he was gone.

"Whisperers are the natural enemies of the mages," Lysander explained. "Magic has no effect on a whisperer: he can tear spells apart with his bare hands. And it wasn't so much a trick as it was an ... unfortunate side effect." He smiled grimly. "I'm afraid that I'm a cursed man."

Annoying as Lysander was, Kael didn't doubt that someone had cursed him.

"Yes, I've heard about that," Kyleigh said. She'd kicked off her boots and was now sitting behind the desk, her bare feet propped on a thick tome entitled *Nautical Abnormalities*. "And what sort of mischief did you get yourself into, exactly?"

"Wendelgrimm," he sighed.

She grinned widely. "Oh you silly, silly pirate. You ought to have known better."

"What's in Wendelgrimm?" Kael said, intrigued.

Lysander groaned. "The *Witch* of Wendelgrimm. The old hag's been alive for at least a thousand years. She has her fortress perched on top of a cliff, overlooking the village of Copperdock." He tugged a wrinkled map of the Kingdom out from under Kyleigh's heel and pointed to a small peninsula. Tiny docks fanned out around it, and in the forest above lurked a dark, spindly castle. He tapped the castle and said: "That's Wendelgrimm. There used to be a family of whisperers who lived in Copperdock, and they kept her at bay for generations. But after the War ..."

They'd been sent to Midlan, Kael thought, *where they were never heard from again.* "So with the family gone, the Witch attacked the village?" he guessed.

Lysander nodded. "She cursed the villagers and keeps them still as her prisoners. I grew up hearing the tale of the Witch of Wendelgrimm, burning over it. So the day I was old enough to be Captain, I picked my crew and set out to free the good people of Copperdock."

"And I'm sure you gave no thought at all to the treasure," Kyleigh said sarcastically.

He shrugged, and a mischievous smile parted his lips. "Well ... I admit I was a *little* intrigued by the treasure. Legend has it that the dungeons of Wendelgrimm are bursting with history, plundered from all the ships that the Witch has ever sunk," he explained to Kael. "They say there's the crown of the first King, a ruby the size of a goat's head and an aquamarine chalice of immortality — all resting upon a mountain of gold."

"But none of those things actually interest you, do they?" Kyleigh said as she picked at her fingernails. "There's only one thing a fellow like you would risk going into Wendelgrimm for."

He placed a reverent hand over his heart. "The Lass of Sam Gravy."

"Wait — there's a woman locked in the dungeons?" Kael said, slightly alarmed.

Lysander snorted. "The Lass is a sword, whisperer — a blade said to give its wielder true and infinite luck. With the Lass in your hand, every lock falls away and every door swings open. You could stand in the presence of your greatest enemy, and he would never recognize you. In battle, you can't be beaten.

"That's what I went into Wendelgrimm for," he admitted with a sigh. "I thought if I had the Lass, that I could make a difference. That I could go to war with the Duke — with the Kingdom, even — and numbers wouldn't matter. But the Witch is strong ..." His eyes watched the distance, and his voice dropped to a growl. "My men and I marched on Wendelgrimm with our swords drawn, prepared to fight, and all it took was a single spell to defeat us. Her horrible voice burned our ears and the next thing we knew, our legs moved of their own accord. They marched us back to *Anchorgloam*, where our hands raised the sails and steered us away. We were a mile out to sea when her spell finally released us ... and then my curse began."

Outside, the sky had grown dark. Thunder rumbled and rain whipped the windows. The ship began to rock beneath them. Lysander grabbed two fistfuls of his hair and fell to his knees. He took several labored breaths, and as his breathing steadied, so did the ship. Slowly, the dark in the clouds faded away and the rain stopped falling. When the sky was a solid sheet of gray once again, he pulled himself to his feet.

His legs shook as he gripped the corner of the desk to steady himself. "I'm a cursed man. Everything I feel, every beat of my heart is reflected out there," he pointed to the windows, "in the weather around me. The first time it happened, I nearly wrecked us. We lost three — three good pirates — before I realized that the storm was all my doing."

Kyleigh got up and slung one of his arms across her shoulders. He leaned heavily on her as she helped him around the desk. He collapsed into the chair and pulled a green bottle out from one of the drawers.

With a quick, practiced motion, he popped the cork out between his teeth. "Somewhere between my anger and my sorrow, I found a grim resolve — a steely gray sky and a swift wind to sail by. But even at that, I have my moments of weakness. Sometimes a little fog is safer than what I truly feel," he muttered. Then he took a long swig and sat the bottle down. "I tried to get them to leave me, you know. I ordered them to maroon me on an island — someplace where I could never harm another soul again. But those stubborn dogs wouldn't do it."

"'Course we wouldn't — you're our captain!"

The outburst came from the man who'd just waddled into the room. He was short, stocky, and had a voice that sounded a bit like a frog's croak. Lysander raised his bottle in greeting. "Hello, Morris."

"Hello nothing," the man called Morris said. He walked past Kael without even glancing at him and pounded his arm on the desk top, knocking several precariously stacked books onto the floor. "Now put that bottle down, Captain. A young lad shouldn't drown himself in ale."

"And why not?" Lysander said, looking slightly amused.

"'Cause it'll make your liver swell up fatter than Duke Reggie's head, that's why," Morris grouched. He finally seemed to notice Kyleigh standing off to one side. "Dragongirl," he said with a nod. "I heard you were aboard. It's good to see you again — luck always seems to follow you. And what can I help you with, eh?"

"I need you to train someone," she said.

Morris was quiet for a moment. He squinted up his eyes and his mouth twitched beneath his bushy beard. "Train? But I don't ... there aren't none left, Dragongirl. Haven't you heard?"

"Yes, I wondered about that myself," Lysander said, leaning back in his chair. "But the boy's right here. And he's already proven himself against the fog."

Morris turned when he pointed and his eyes, sat back in their pouches, roved the length of Kael. Then they went to the top of his head, and his mouth broke into a wide grin. He was missing several teeth.

"Well my beard — you found one in the Unforgivable Mountains!" he said gleefully. "And what's your name, lad?"

"Kael."

"Pleasure to meet you."

Kael reached out to shake his hand and his fingers grasped at nothing. He looked down and realized that Morris's arm ended at the wrist. The nub of his severed hand was capped in a leather gauntlet.

"I got myself a matching set, I'm afraid," Morris said, holding up the missing end of his other arm. "Not everyone *died* in the Whispering War — some of us got souvenirs. Usually try to warn a man first, I do."

"Oh, um, it's not a problem." And he shook Morris's forearm instead.

"So what's your power, lad? Wait — don't tell me." Morris looked him over again. "You're real evenly balanced, got a long reach and big hands for a lad your size. I'll bet you've got a gift for war, don't you?"

He wondered if Morris might be losing his sight. "No, I'm a healer," he said. And he ignored Kyleigh's snort.

"A *healer*?" Morris burst out in a round of wheezing laughter. "You can't reel me in with that one. I've seen my share of whisperers, and I've got a real eye for talent."

"Well, maybe you need spectacles — because I've always been a healer."

Morris smirked. "I won't waste my time squabbling with you about it, why don't we settle this? Would you light a lantern for us, Captain?" Lysander took a lantern off the wall, struck a match and lit the candle. He slid it over the top of Morris's right arm and wedged it against his gauntlet. "Thankee, Captain. And would you happen to have a mirror?"

"Oh, he's got one," Kyleigh said. "A man doesn't get that sort of wave in his hair without a considerable amount of preening."

"I do not *preen*," Lysander said with a glare. He jerked open a drawer of his desk and handed Kael a silver hand mirror. "The wave is natural — and I only keep a mirror for signaling purposes."

Kyleigh waited until his back was turned before she rolled her eyes.

"There was an old trick they taught us before whispering became a crime," Morris said, holding the lantern up to his face.

The light hit his eye at a certain angle and a series of gold rings radiated out from his pupil, like ripples in a pond. They seemed to shimmer, and moved of their own accord in the candlelight.

"Do you see them?" When Kael nodded, he smiled. "Had the gift of craft, I did. I used to make weapons for King Banagher himself. But that was back before ..." He cleared his throat loudly and blinked. "All right, it's your turn. If you're a craftsman, you'll see rings like mine. A healer will be a diamond, and a warrior is a jagged cut straight across the middle. Got it?"

He nodded.

"Good. Now let me get this situated. The light's got to hit at just the exact right angle."

He looked straight ahead while Morris moved the lantern into position. The light touched his eyes and he could feel the warmth of the candle flame. Then he heard a loud *clang* as the lantern struck the floor.

"Tide take me!"

Lysander jumped to his feet. "What — what is it?"

Morris took several steps backwards. If his lids hadn't been so droopy, the white might have shown the whole way around his eyes. He jabbed one of his arms at Kael and sputtered: "See for yourself!"

Amazingly, the lantern managed to land upright. A little wax spilled out in its base, but the wick still burned brightly. "Don't move," Lysander said as he held it up.

"If there's something wrong, shouldn't I be the first to know?" Kael argued.

Lysander grabbed him under the chin and peered into his eye. After a moment, he grinned. "Hold the mirror up. You're going to want to see this."

Kael ignored the sharp lines of his face and his too-pale skin. He brought the glass close, until his illuminated brown eyes filled it. There was gold in the middle of his eyes, too. But it wasn't a diamond or a jagged cut, and there certainly weren't any rings.

A series of straight lines crisscrossed through the iris. They cut so close to the center of his eyes that it made his pupil look more triangular than round. "What is it?" he said without looking away. He was afraid that if he blinked, the pattern might disappear.

"It's this," Kyleigh said. She pulled a book off the shelf — a small tome entitled *Classifications of Whisperers*. She opened it and held it up so he could see.

A drawing filled the first page, a drawing of an eye with lines crisscrossing through it. He looked back and forth between the drawing and his eye, but there was no mistaking that what he saw were twin pictures.

Morris touched the end of his arm to the first set of triangles, the ones that fanned out from the point of the pupil. "Born of all," he moved his arm to the interlocking triangles beneath it, "lord of all," to black triangle in the middle, "behold — the Wright arises."

They could've heard a mouse chewing cheese in the silence his words left behind. Kael couldn't think of anything to say. He glanced around the room, but the others' expressions were far from useful. Kyleigh's face clearly said: *I told you so.* She was, no doubt, reveling in her triumph. Morris looked as if he'd just kicked open a chest of never-ending treasure. Lysander gazed out the window, a smile on his face.

Outside, the gray sky was churning.

"I'm not ..." Kael began, but couldn't quite get the words out.

"You are, lad." Morris's croak was surprisingly gentle. "Ever find that the things you make do exactly what they're meant to?"

Kael thought immediately about the traps, about how Kyleigh said it was so odd that he managed to snare something every time. He kept his mouth hard, but Morris read the answer in his eyes.

"I thought so. That'll be the craftsman in you. And ever taken a fall that would snap an average man's neck? Or made a shot that seemed impossible?" When Kael's face reddened, Morris smiled. "And that's the warrior. The eyes reflect the soul, lad. And the soul don't lie." Then he turned to Kyleigh. "So this is what you went looking for, eh?"

"I knew we'd be hopeless without him," she said. Her green eyes bored into his. Her expression betrayed nothing, yet he thought he could feel her excitement ... and her relief.

He didn't want that. He didn't care what the mirror said: he wasn't their answer. "Sorry, but you're going to have to find someone else. I'm just trying to save my grandfather," he said. He tossed the mirror onto the desk and turned to leave, but Morris blocked his path.

"The gift isn't easy, I understand that." He wedged his arm in the collar of his shirt and pulled it down. Through the tangled wires of black hair on his chest, Kael could see the whisperer's mark. "Do you know what this is?"

"It's a birthmark."

"No it isn't. See how red and raised it is, how it goes down in a straight line? You ever seen a birthmark like that? 'Course you haven't! 'Cause it's no birthmark, lad — it's a scar."

"Well whatever it is, it's not like I asked for it."

He laughed. "It isn't about what you asked for. You were *chosen* for this, long before you were even born. You were still in your mother's womb when the lady Fate split you wide open. She put her gift inside you and sewed you up tight — *that's* why every whisperer has a scar."

Amos never talked much about the history of their people, so he couldn't help but be interested in what Morris had to say. He just wished he hadn't brought Fate into it. "I won't let anyone tell me what I ought to do."

"No, you got it all wrong — Fate gives her gifts, but she lets us decide what to do with them. There's no reason why an ugly old seadog like me should have an eye for craft, or a redheaded, toothpick of a boy should have the gifts of a Wright." He grinned and touched his arm to the side of his head. "But we do. Now instead of jumping overboard, why don't you give it a shot, eh? Let me train you up a bit, teach you what I know about the gifts. *Then* you can decide what you ought to do with them."

He thought that sounded reasonable. Besides, whatever Morris had to show him might come in handy when he finally got to Titus. "All right —"

"One moment, please," Lysander interrupted. He slunk over from the window, arms behind his back and a sly smile on his face. "As Captain of this ship, I think I should be compensated for Morris's time."

Kael wasn't surprised. "Fine. I've got some silver in my pack —"

He raised his hand. "I don't want your coin. A man like me has little use for it."

"Then what *do* you want, Sandy?" Kyleigh said from where she lounged against the bookshelves.

He frowned at her. "Don't call me that."

243

"Don't behave like a pinch-fisted shop woman, and I won't name you like one."

"Fine." He turned back to Kael. "What I want is simple — freedom. Help me break my curse, and I'll consider it ample payment for your training."

Kael knew from his short time in the merchant's caravan that there was no such thing as a simple deal. "How do I break the curse?"

And just as he suspected, Lysander's smile wavered. "An obnoxiously clever little whisperer, aren't you? All right, I see no harm in telling you." His face turned serious. "In order to break the curse, you're going to have to slay the Witch of Wendelgrimm."

Kyleigh snorted. "That hardly seems fair."

"I'll bring him there myself," Lysander continued. "Thelred and I will go with him to the castle. But I can't ask my men to risk their lives again, not for my sake."

"And of course, I'll go as well," Kyleigh added.

"So there you have it." Lysander spread his arms wide. "That's every nook and cranny of our agreement, I've got nothing else to hide. What do you say?"

Kael knew he didn't exactly have a choice. So he took Lysander's hand and, glaring at the excited sparks of lightning behind his stormy eyes, said: "All right, we have a bargain."

Chapter 22
Galley-Scrubbing

"A Wright is born in times of trouble, when the Kingdom is near to killing itself," Morris said. "No one knows why, exactly, but that's always the way it is."

They stood on the steering deck — Morris glanced between the sun and the waves while Kael stared very pointedly at the deck below. He kept his arms crossed tightly and tried to ignore the fact that there wasn't a patch of land in sight. There were no landmarks, nothing to say where to turn or which path to follow. He felt as if they'd been swept out into another world, and he couldn't help but wonder if they would ever find their way back.

"Seems daunting, eh?" Morris said, as if he could read the worry on Kael's face. "Look here."

Next to the ship's massive wheel was a small wooden table. And upon that table sat an instrument Kael had only ever read about. It was a compass: capped in gold and with neatly drawn letters etched around it. Set in the middle of the compass was what looked like the arrow from a tiny bow.

"The head always faces north, no matter what. But we don't want to go north — we want to go south. So ..." Morris wedged his arms between the knobs of the ship's wheel and slid one limb over the other. The ship groaned as it turned, and Kael watched the arrow. When they were heading in the direction of the tail, Morris stopped. He grinned as *Anchorgloam* turned her nose, his eyes creased in their pouches. "See? Nothing to worry about."

Knowing which direction they were headed was useful, but Kael had to wonder why the only handless man aboard *Anchorgloam* was the one in charge of steering it. Then again, if he ever wondered about something strange aboard the ship, he only had to look as far as its captain for an explanation.

"How's that, Morris?" Lysander called from beneath them.

White clouds rolled by occasionally, but the sky had been clear most of the day: dominated by the merciless heat of the sun. Naturally, the pirates saw this as an excuse to strip off their shirts. Now they strutted back and forth across the deck, pretending to work — but all they really did was flex their muscles any time one the girls walked by.

Lysander had his hands propped up on his hips, sweat shining on every lithe muscle in his arms and chest. "Shouldn't we tilt the topsail just a hair? I feel a breeze coming from the east."

"No, it's coming from out your mouth," Morris muttered, which made Kael grin. "Move the mainsail to catch it, if speed's the thing you're after!"

Lysander jerked his head at the crew that worked the mainsail — which included Aerilyn. "You heard him. Now move, you mangy curs!"

"Aye, Captain!"

They hauled back on the ties, and Aerilyn struggled to keep her footing. When the wind caught the sails and jerked the line forward, she tumbled over with a squeak.

Lysander leapt to her side and took up her slack. "You've got to lean back on your heels, lady merchant," he said with a mocking grin. "Use your arms for an anchor and your legs for a tide."

Even from where he stood, Kael could see the muscles that bulged out from Lysander's arms. Aerilyn must have noticed too, because her face reddened and she turned quickly away.

"We've been stuck at sea for nearly five years, and in all that time I forgot what a show the captain likes to put on around the ladies," Morris grumbled.

Well, if Lysander wanted to keep his abnormally white teeth inside his mouth, Kael thought the only thing he needed to put on was a shirt.

"Anyways," Morris continued, "a Wright is always born in times of trouble. Think about all the ones you know — Charles the Wright was born during the rise of the mages, back when they tried to destroy the Kingdom. Setheran the Wright was born before the Whispering War, of course. And there are a lot of folks who believe Sir Gorigan was a Wright as well, but so much has been lost in the telling that I suppose we'll never know."

"Wait a moment — you believe in Sir Gorigan?"

"'Course I do! It's history, isn't it? Just because it wasn't written down at the time don't make it any less important. But the real question is," he squinched up his eyes, "what's Kael the Wright been born for?"

"To crush Earl Titus," he said darkly.

"Wrong!" Morris smacked him in the back of the head with the blunt of his arm. "You haven't been born for anything, not until you've been trained. And that's where I come in. Now, the bow's your weapon of choice, isn't it?"

"It's the only thing I know how to use," he admitted.

"Hmm, well we're going to have to fix that. But in the meantime," Morris gestured at the mainmast: the one Kael had to lean back to see the top of, "there's a knot in the wood near the crow's nest, do you see it?"

He followed the line down from the basket at the top of the mast and found the knot. It was darker than the rest and a bit raised — and probably about the size of his head. But from where he stood, it looked no bigger than the backside of a pin.

"I want you to shoot an arrow into that knot."

"Well, I can't do that." He knew that shot was well outside of his paltry range, and he didn't want to make a fool of himself.

But Morris wasn't going to let him off that easily. "Now see here," he said with a growl, pink rising through his scraggily beard. "If I'm going to train you, then you've got to do as I say, understand? I don't need your cheek — I just need you to shoot an arrow."

Kael was fine with that: the sooner Morris learned how weak he was, the better. He drew his bow and took aim at the knot, pulling back on the string until his arm shook. He released, and the arrow fell in a pitiful arc to the deck below — where it lodged itself in the wood a hair's breadth from Jonathan's boot.

"Be careful!" he shouted. "I've only got two of those, and I need them both to do the jig."

"Sorry," Kael called back. Then he turned to Morris. "See? I told you I couldn't do it."

"Wipe that smug look off of your face. Failing just to win isn't anything to be proud of." Then he leaned over the rails and said: "Noah, bring me an axe!"

A minute later, Noah jogged up the stairs carrying a small, two-headed axe. "Here you are," he said, handing it to Kael.

"Now don't think about it, don't worry over it and don't sass me!" Morris barked. "Just throw the axe. Throw it!"

He'd never thrown an axe in his life. But all Morris's screeching made him mad enough to rear back and fling it as hard as he could.

The weapon went sailing, spinning head over head. The pirates stopped their work on deck and watched, open mouthed, as it soared up and nearly out of sight. It disappeared behind the white light of the sun, and he thought he'd missed the mast entirely. Then it fell from the sky and — with a sharp *thud* — sunk into the exact center of the knot.

He heard Noah's jaw crack as it fell wide open. "How in Kingdom's name did you do that?"

"I have no idea." Kael said. He'd imagined the knot was Morris's head ... but he wasn't about to admit it aloud, not while he was within range of Morris's club-like arms.

"Contest!" Lysander declared, leaping to the top of the nearest barrel. "There's an extra round of grog in it for any man that can best that mark!"

The pirates cheered and jostled amongst themselves for a spot in line.

Every man aboard *Anchorgloam* gave it a shot — sometimes two or three. Big men stepped up to try their luck, men with burly arms and hairy chests, men who cracked their necks and roared when they made their throws ... men who grunted in frustration when their axes fell far short — when they missed the mast completely. Soon the pirates were scratching their heads in disappointment and muttering that the throw was impossible.

"Do you see it now?" Morris said quietly.

"See what?"

Kael hadn't exactly been listening. He watched as Thelred hurled an axe with all his might, and couldn't stop himself from grinning when it barely made it halfway up the mast. Thelred muttered darkly and kicked an empty bucket out to sea — and Kael had to turn away to keep from laughing outright.

Morris frowned at him. "It's all fun now, but know this: if a Wright doesn't doubt himself, there's not a thing he can't do."

Kael didn't believe him, not at first. Then dinnertime rolled around and not a single pirate had gotten anywhere close to besting his mark. When he followed the others down to the galley and Lysander gave him his extra round of grog, he looked out and saw the wide-eyed respect on the pirates' hardened faces.

Then he believed.

"To the throw that bested us all," Lysander said, raising his tankard high. "May the axe rest ever on its mark — as a monument to the pirate Kael!"

"Aye, to the throw!" the others bellowed, and they tossed back generous swigs of their drink in his honor.

"Yes, how *did* you manage to do that?" Aerilyn asked as he took his seat. She wrestled with a rubbery tentacle that poked out from her soup, trying to spear it with her fork.

"I'd like to know that myself, actually," Jonathan agreed. He plucked the tentacle out of her bowl with his fingers and stuffed the whole grayish wad into his mouth, earning himself a disgusted look.

Kael decided there was no point in trying to keep his gift a secret anymore. He was already an enemy of the Kingdom, and everyone around him was — quite literally — in the same boat. They'd have to be mad to try and turn him in.

"I'm a Wright," he said, watching as their eyebrows climbed. "I always knew I was a whisperer, but I just found out about the ... the other bit."

Jonathan let out a low whistle. "Well, we'd already guessed the whisperer part, but a Wright?" He grinned. "I bet the ladies would really go for that. If I were you, I'd have it stitched to the front of my tunic."

"Wait — how long have you known I was a whisperer?" Kael said.

"I guessed it after the first few hunting trips," Aerilyn replied with a shrug. "I've lived with the caravan my whole life, and I've never seen anyone come back with so much game. Only a whisperer could've managed it. I told Jonathan, and he agreed. And then we," she took a deep breath, "I'm sorry, but we went to Papa. We only did it because we didn't want to put the caravan in danger," she added, her voice imploring.

"But old Garron already knew. Turns out he'd known for awhile," Jonathan said. "He told us not to say a word. He said you were a good lad and danger or no, he wasn't going to leave you on your own." He smirked. "Not to mention the fact that those pelts you were bringing in made him a wealthy man."

"Yeah, but the gold on my head would have made him even wealthier," Kael said, fighting stubbornly against the sudden emotion that rose in his chest.

Aerilyn straightened her shoulders, as she did every time she talked about Garron. "*No worse bargain was ever made than the fool who traded friends for gold*. That was the first rule Papa ever taught me."

"Aye, and mates have got to stick together," Jonathan added with a playful punch in his arm. "So like it or not, you're stuck with us, mate."

Kael could only nod in reply. Then he mumbled some excuse about having a stomachache and ran up the stairs. He made it out into the solitude of the night and clutched his chest, pushing back against the waves that swelled in his heart — the ones that threatened to spill over and out his eyes at any moment.

******

According to Morris, every Wright had a leaning: an unbalance in his gifts that made him better at one thing than the other two. And he believed, rather unwisely, that Kael's leaning was in the direction of war.

"The mind is like any muscle, lad — you've got to use it till it gets sore, wake up, and use it again. That's the only way you're going to get any stronger."

"How exactly do I do that?" Kael asked.

Morris grinned. "Ever gotten a headache?"

"Yes, and they're horrible."

"That they may be. But then again, working yourself to a headache is the only way to build up the mind's strength. Each time you push yourself, it gets stronger. And the next time you'll be able to push even farther. Got it?"

Kael sighed. "I suppose. But how exactly do I get a headache? It's not like it's ever happened when I meant it to."

"There are several things that'll tucker you out: fighting off magic is one, and then of course using the skills you've got will always take a toll." Morris smirked. "But don't you worry — I think I've figured out a way to bruise your body *and* your head."

It didn't take long for Kael to discover Morris's plan: the next morning at six bells, Lysander called them all up on deck for sparring practice. Against the railings were crates full of different wooden weapons. They were ordered to take up the sword and wait in line while Thelred paired them up.

Kael was waiting his turn when Morris hooked him around the shoulders and pulled him aside. "I don't think so,

251

lad. None of those fellows will be near challenging enough. But I've found you someone I think'll give you a match."

As it turned out, his partner was the most experienced, ruthless, and mean-spirited fighter among them:

Kyleigh.

"No, no lad! You're not paying attention," Morris barked as Kael fell hard on his back. "You're just watching her swing."

"Well that's how I keep my skull from getting cracked open," he retorted, dragging himself to his feet. "I've got to watch after my head, don't I? Especially when my partner is doing everything she can to knock it off," he added.

She returned his glare with a smile.

Morris groaned loudly. "You can't waste time watching your head — you've got to *use* it! Every move she makes, you got to be asking yourself why she makes it. See there?" Kyleigh stepped to his left, her wooden practice sword hanging loosely in her hand. "Now tell me why she did that."

"Because that's her strongest side, and my weakest," he said automatically. He took several trips to the ground before Morris finally pointed out, with no small amount of exasperation, that Kyleigh was left-handed.

"Good. Now how are you going to keep her from slicing you across the back?"

She was being lazy: her sword hung low — nowhere near the proper guard position. It left her chest wide open for an attack. He lunged, and before he knew what happened, his sword was on the ground and Kyleigh was behind him.

"That was a *feint*," Morris said, trailing a slew of curses. "An experienced swordsman doesn't leave herself unguarded unless she has a plan. Now quit huffing around and pick up your sword!"

When he bent to retrieve his weapon, Kyleigh smacked him on the rump with the flat of her blade.

The world went red.

He spun around and swung at her with a roar, sending blow after blow wailing in her direction. He aimed for her head, her chest, her knees — anywhere he thought might teach her a lesson. But no matter how hard or fast he swung, she batted him away with ease. She spun gracefully out of his reach until he was gasping for breath, and he knew he only had one good blow left in him. He summoned what remained of his strength, swung his sword high over his head, and brought it down.

It was only after his blade broke, after it splintered and the two halves went sailing in opposite directions, that he realized he'd struck the unrelenting force of Kyleigh's upraised arm.

Now she had his sword wrist gripped in her hand, twisted painfully backwards, and the tip of her blade digging into his ribs. Her eyes blazed and her chest rose and fell quickly. The arm she held tingled strangely — and he realized she was probably cutting off the flow of his blood.

"All right, that's enough for today," Morris said with a frustrated wave of his arm. "I hope you see now why the angry man never walks away the winner — if he walks away at all, that is."

For an entire week, Morris subjected him to Kyleigh's torture. She beat him with every weapon in *Anchorgloam's* armory — maces, staves, swords, spears, and at least a dozen other things. Morris wouldn't stop the fight until Kael had developed a headache worthy of legend. Only when he was on his knees, swaying, trying to figure out which of the three lumps swimming in front of him was Morris's head, would the battle be over. Every night, he'd hobble down to the galley for dinner and afterwards collapse into his hammock, wondering if the beatings would ever end.

Then one morning, sparring practice was a little different. Lysander let them choose the weapon they wanted to work with, and Kael chose the stave: it gave him the longest reach and he could attack with both ends. After they'd chosen their weapons, Lysander had them clear out a space in the middle of the deck. The pirates were murmuring excitedly by this point, and Kael didn't understand why.

Then Lysander cupped his hands over his mouth and shouted: "Gauntlet!"

The pirates raised their weapons over their heads and let out a deafening roar. They stomped their feet and Kael stumbled backwards as they shoved each other into a large ring in the middle of the deck.

"The rules are simple — if a man is disarmed or knocked unconscious, the fight is over," Lysander yelled above the din. "If you win, you stay. The man who lasts the longest is our champion and will be rewarded with an extra share of the loot!"

This announcement brought another round of cheers, and Lysander had to wait nearly a full minute before he could continue.

"Every man can play, and must play at least *once*," he added, with a pointed look at Aerilyn. "The only exception is Kyleigh — who is not allowed to play because we all know she'd only rout us."

Several of the pirates murmured in agreement. A few glanced at the girl perched casually on the railings, but none seemed willing to challenge her.

"I'll keep the time," Lysander said, resting his hand on the oversized hourglass next to him. "Let the first brave soul step forward, and may the best pirate win!"

Kael was looking to see who would be the first to step out when he felt a pair of hands shove him hard in the back. He stumbled into the middle of the circle, spun around, and saw Jonathan give him an encouraging nod.

"I know you can do it, mate!" he said with a wave.

Kael would have cracked his skull — if it weren't for the big, tree-armed pirate that stepped between them. He raised the huge club he wielded high over his head, snarling through his tangled beard. And then he charged.

Fear sent all of Morris's lessons rushing to the front of his head. He'd harped for days about how speed was the only thing Kael had going for him — about how if he ever got caught between a big man and his weapon, he'd be cooked. So when the pirate swung down at his head, Kael spun away. He stepped behind him and jabbed his stave at the back of his knee.

It was a leaf straight out of Kyleigh's book, and it worked.

The pirate let out a surprised grunt and fell forward as his leg collapsed beneath him. His chin hit the ground and the club shot out of his grasp.

"That's it. You've been disarmed, dog," Lysander bellowed. "Next!"

Noah stepped out from the circle, grinning as he spun his sword effortlessly with a single hand. His first swing landed in the middle of Kael's stave, nearly jarring it from his grasp. Noah struck at mindboggling speeds: his blade would come whistling for Kael's neck and half a blink later, be at his shins. And for a while, all he could do was react. Noah had him pushed nearly to the edge of the circle when he let loose with a flurry of attacks — chest, head, knee, right, left, knee, gut, and then he spun.

His arm was cutting across, cocked back like a stone in a sling. When it landed, the blow would have enough force to knock Kael's stave into the ocean. There was just one problem: in all his movement, Noah left the full, broadside of his back unguarded.

Morris warned Kael never to turn his back on an opponent, especially on one within striking distance. And why was that again? Oh, yes.

Kael stuck his stave between Noah's ankles and the poor boy never saw it coming. His legs got tangled up and he fell hard on his back. Kael leapt forward and kicked the sword out of his hand before he could get to his feet.

"Disarmed," Lysander said cheerfully. "Next!"

One by one, his opponents fell. No sooner was one man disarmed than the next jumped in. Kael's feet didn't stop moving the whole morning — and yet he never tired. None of the pirates could wear him out the way Kyleigh did, and it was midday before he even broke a sweat. He stopped recognizing the faces before him and instead saw patterns: the movement of arms and legs, the angles of blows, the shift in height and weight.

At one point, he knew he was fighting Jonathan — and he was sure to land a few extra blows in his gut. When he knocked the club out of his hand, Jonathan grabbed him by the wrist and whispered: "See, what did I tell you? All those lessons with Morris the Handless Helmsman have done the trick — not a one of us can best you."

Kael didn't have time to respond: he heard the planks creak behind him and knew the next opponent was at his back.

The sky was red and the cool of evening was upon them when Lysander stopped the fighting. "We've only got light for one more round, and I said *everyone* had to play," he barked.

The break in the action jerked Kael out of his trance. He realized everyone was looking at Aerilyn — who had her hands twisted nervously about her stave. Her eyes flicked to Kael before they went back to Lysander.

"Can't we just say that he's beaten me and move on?" she pleaded.

"No, we can't," Lysander said firmly. "And if you even think about throwing your weapon down, I'll give you a week of galley-scrubbing as punishment."

There were only a few fates worse than death, but having to clean up after *Anchorgloam*'s notoriously bad cook would've been one of them. He used at least a dozen man-sized pots for every meal — which he only scraped out once a year. In fact, many believed the insides of the pots were actually made up of the charred-on remains of squid and crab shell.

When Aerilyn let out a squeal of terror, Lysander latched on. "Let's make this a little more interesting, shall we?" he said. "I declare that the loser of this duel will have a week of galley-scrubbing added to their duties!"

The pirates cheered, and while Lysander's decree was popular with the men, Aerilyn gave him a look that very clearly meant he'd just made it onto the list of people she'd like to see murdered.

"I won't hurt you," Kael promised as she stepped up to face him.

She nodded once, gratefully, and then they began.

Aerilyn was actually pretty good with the stave — her biggest problem was her lack of strength. Kael nearly knocked it out of her hand with his first blow, and he was only swinging half as hard as he usually did. Still, he did his best to give her a fair shot.

They danced around for a bit, and she let him do all the leading. He would swing, and she would block him. He grunted and made over-exaggerated movements, giving her plenty of time to react. The longer they went, the more excited the pirates got.

Maybe that skinny boy was finally getting tired. After all, he'd been fighting all day. What if little Aerilyn was the one to beat him? Wouldn't that be something?

The sharp clatter of a stave striking the ground brought their duel to an abrupt end. It took Kael a moment to realize that his hands were empty — *he* was the one who'd been disarmed. He'd gotten so into the play of it all that he didn't notice when Aerilyn had cut down over the top of him, knocking the weapon from his hands.

She seemed just as surprised as he did. She brushed the sweat-drenched hair out of her face and stared down at the stave like she wasn't sure how it got there. "Kael, I'm so sorry —"

"Don't be." He realized his voice was the only sound on the ship — everyone was watching him, waiting to see what he would do. And so he put a fist over his heart, mirroring the pictures of the defeated knights in the *Atlas*, and said: "I've been bested."

The deck erupted in cheers. Two burly pirates scooped Aerilyn up and balanced her on their shoulders while the others whooped and jumped around her. Lysander had a barrel of grog rolled out on deck — one so enormous that it took three burly pirates to lift it — and he poured Aerilyn the first tankard.

"To the lady merchant, for defending our pirate honor," he said, grinning. "We are forever in her debt!"

Celebrations went on long into the night. Though they were thrilled that he'd been beaten, the pirates still clapped Kael on the back and said they'd never seen a lad who could fight quite like him. Several asked if he might be willing to show them some of his tricks.

He'd just managed to escape the crowd when Lysander bumped into his shoulder, sloshing a good amount of his grog onto the deck. He wrenched Kael's head to the side by the roots of his hair. "You made history tonight, seadog!" he said, his words already a little slurred. "Twelve turns of the hourglass — only one other pirate has ever managed it."

Kael was going to ask him who else had managed to go twelve turns when Lysander jerked his head to the other side. "D'you think she'd dance with me?"

Through the crowd of swaying bodies, he saw that Aerilyn had started a jig. She was skipping to the tune of Jonathan's fiddle, her arm linked in Morris's. Whenever the notes picked up, she changed partners — spinning and latching onto the arm of the next pirate to jump in.

Her eyes were shining, her face flushed pink — and Kael knew it had nothing to do with the grog, because he'd watched her hurl it overboard the second Lysander's back was turned.

"What d'you think, dog?" he asked again. "Think I got a chance?" Before Kael could answer, he threw back the rest of his drink and dragged a sleeve across his mouth. "You're right — of course I got a chance. I'm a captain!" He saluted and stumbled purposefully towards Aerilyn, who was now spinning in an intricate pattern with Kyleigh.

Their antics earned them a fresh round of loud whistles and foot-stomping — so loud that Kael didn't hear Morris approach until he'd already run him over.

"I haven't danced like that since before I got fat," he said, slapping an arm to his ample belly. "Makes for a whole new jig, it does, having something so burdensome hanging off my chest. You ought to get in there and show them a thing or two."

Kael wanted to say that he thought dancing was for moonstruck idiots, but he held his tongue. "I think my legs have earned a rest."

Morris smiled and thumped him hard on the back. "They sure have, lad. I've not seen sparring like that in many tide turns."

Kael wanted to thank him for teaching him how to fight, for pushing him to the brink of death everyday, but he never got the chance. No sooner did Morris speak than the sky opened up and torrents of cold rain fell down upon them. Icy water soaked through their clothes and doused the lanterns — and sent the pirates rushing for their hammocks.

"All hands below deck!" Thelred said as he sprinted towards the captain's cabin. "Hands below deck — snuff your lanterns and get some shuteye, dogs!"

Kael would have loved nothing better than to snuff his lantern and go to sleep, but losing to Aerilyn meant that he had a week's worth of galley-scrubbing — starting immediately.

He jogged down the stairs to the kitchen, wringing water out of his shirt as he went, and nearly lost his footing when he saw the horrible task before him.

Every surface of the closet-sized galley was piled high in woefully grimy pots — some of which looked as if they hadn't been clean since the day they came out of the fire. They were stacked in teetering piles, held together by the greasy remnants of last week's dinner. Some of the stacks nearly reached the ceiling.

He would have thrown the whole lot out to sea if he didn't believe Lysander could come up with an even worse punishment for wasting dishes. So he rolled up his sleeves and went to work.

He was wrestling with a particularly stubborn patch of greasy black goo when he suddenly felt as if he wasn't alone. She hadn't made a sound, but he knew she was behind him. "Hello, Kyleigh. Have you come to scold me for letting my guard down?"

She leaned against the counter, an arm's reach from him. Her hair was dripping wet and little beads of water still clung to the skin of her face and neck. The smell of rain mixed with lavender was a nice reprieve from the stink of days-old food. "I haven't come to scold you, I've come to help you," she said, setting a tankard down by his elbow.

He saw the pale green foam before he smelled the sharp tang of pirate grog. "Thanks, but I don't think I could hold down another one."

She shook her head and took the filthy washrag out of his hand, her fingers brushing against his. She dipped the cloth into the tankard and wringed it out over the goo. Foam bubbled up and the greasy black chunks went sliding down — melted away by the sizzling grog.

"Well that's … useful," he said, though he was more than a little disturbed. "What's in that stuff?"

She gave him an amused smile. "Do you really want to know?"

No, he didn't. But if grog could peel off an ancient layer of grease, he could imagine what it might do to his stomach. He thanked her for the help and swore off drinking in the same breath.

She laughed and turned to leave. "That was kind of you to let Aerilyn win, by the way."

The tone of her voice startled him into looking up. The expression she wore confused him: she wasn't laughing, she wasn't angry or annoyed. He couldn't put his finger on why her mouth was set that certain way, or why her brows were bent in those particular arcs. He *did* notice the way she leaned against the door, and how having one arm propped over her head like that pulled against the soft material of her pirate's shirt, revealing a good deal of her figure.

"I didn't let her win," he said gruffly, because he thought being gruff might somehow hide the burn in his face. "I got distracted, and she beat me. That's all there is to it."

Her look didn't falter. "Only you know what you did or didn't do. But do you want to know what I think?"

He could only nod.

"I think, in a nobler realm, you would have made a terrific knight."

For a long moment, he couldn't respond. He scrubbed absently, trying to make sense of the sudden kindness in her words, trying to think of something to say in return, but he couldn't think of anything. She wasn't like Aerilyn — who flung out compliments like crumbs to the birds. So if she ever said anything at all, he knew it was because she meant it.

But when he finally thought to look up, the doorway was empty. Kyleigh was already gone.

Chapter 23
Dangerous Pets

Miles away from where *Anchorgloam* sailed, Duke Reginald was just finishing his evening swim. His arms glided through the water with ease. He came up for a quick breath, and the salty ocean ran off his short, wavy hair. When his lungs were full, he thrust his head back under. Above the waves, he could hear the sea beating against the jagged rocks behind him. But the world below was quiet.

He rather liked the solitude. And after having to deal with his squabbling managers all day long, he felt that he'd earned it. He took a few more strokes and, as he turned his head for a breath, he heard someone call his name.

" — inald! There's a — says he wants — "

Oh, what now? He stopped and flipped over on his back, letting the sea hold him in its bobbing embrace. A steward waved from the rocky shore. "What is it?" Reginald shouted.

"Manager to see you, Sir Duke!"

It was just like Chaucer to show up early and wreck his swim. "Let him know I'm on my way," he said, rather snappily.

"Very good, sir. Shall I send a boat to pick you up, sir?"

Reginald may not have been a young man, but he was not so desperate that he needed a boat to drag him in. "No, that won't be necessary. Be on about your business."

With a nod, the steward jogged away.

Reginald bowled through the waves without a problem and clambered up the iron ladder nailed into the stone beneath his castle. The fortress was built on an island of rocks, nothing but ocean surrounded it. Well, there was that bothersome bridge connecting the island to the shores of the Kingdom. But if it weren't for this ruler business, he'd have burned it up a long time ago.

Though the sun was setting, the air hadn't lost a bit of its stickiness. The water clinging to Reginald's skin cooled him for a few steps, but by the time he reached the wall where he'd tossed his shirt, the heat was back. Sweat beaded up on his face and trickled down his neck. He decided he'd rather not add a layer to his discomfort. So he ducked through the back gate of his castle wearing nothing but a pair of trousers rolled to the knee.

Not surprisingly, he caught the glances of several maids as he strode through the corridors. It was no secret that they hated him. That they loathed how he ruled ... and yet, they couldn't help but steal a look when he passed. To have that sort of power, the sort that forced admiration even in the midst of hate — well, Reginald couldn't have asked for better.

One maid stared too long, and he caught her with a grin. Red sprouted to her cheeks as she hurried away. "Run, little mouse," he said, and he could tell by the way her shoulders stiffened that she'd heard him.

He kept his office perched on the third floor. Most rulers had their chambers at the highest level, but for Reginald it wasn't about power or prestige: it was entirely about the view.

The captain of the guards droned on about how unsafe it was, but Reginald didn't care. The moment he was made Duke, he ordered that a large window be cut out of his westernmost wall. Now the first thing he saw when he entered was the sea, glittering in her shades of emotion. Tonight she was at peace. She welcomed the falling sun in her embrace and together they ignited the waves with the fiery passion of their love.

It would have been a magnificent scene, had he been able to see it properly. But unfortunately the broad shoulders of the man standing in front of the window all but eclipsed it, leaving him with only a sliver to look out of. When he closed the door, the man turned away, fixing him with solemn eyes.

Reginald sighed inwardly. Everything was always a matter of life or death with Chaucer. He couldn't even relax enough to let his beard grow out.

"So good of you to come. I trust your journey went well?" Reginald said as he took a seat behind his desk. It was made of dark oak, carved in one piece from a single tree — a gift from Countess D'Mere.

"Quite," Chaucer replied.

"Capital." Reginald made a show of rearranging some parchment on his desk while Chaucer waited in silence. When he looked up, he was shocked to find that they weren't alone.

How had he not seen him before? The man lurking next to the bookshelves was short and unremarkable to be sure, but still — he didn't see how he could've possibly missed a whole other body in the room.

"And who is this?" Reginald waved to the short man, who was staring vacantly at one of the many trinkets lined up along the shelves.

"My servant," Chaucer replied. "Shall I ask him to leave?"

Reginald normally wouldn't have allowed another person to sit in on their meeting. But the short fellow wore an expression of such incurable boredom that he doubted if he'd even bother listening in. "He can stay. Just make sure he doesn't touch anything."

"Very good," Chaucer said. He was waiting patiently, standing with his legs stuck together and his hands clasped firmly behind his back. He probably would have sat down, had there been another chair in the room. But Reginald preferred his managers never to get the idea that they were equal.

When he decided he'd kept Chaucer waiting long enough, he leaned back in his chair and propped his hands on his bare stomach. "The figures look good this season. Well done."

Chaucer inclined his head. "Much appreciated, Sir Duke."

"Yes ... there are, however, a few disturbing reports about pirates." Reginald held up a particularly angry letter. "Baron Sahar seems to think that you haven't been doing everything in your power to protect his goods. Just last week, another of his vessels went missing — disappeared shortly after it checked out of Harborville. He claims that he's losing money by the ton and sailors by the dozen. What have you to say to that?"

A muscle twitched at Chaucer's jaw line, but his expression didn't change. "Nothing, Sir Duke."

Though Reginald wanted very badly to throw a book at his head, he somehow managed to keep his voice even. "I put the desert in your charge because all the others failed so miserably. For years, there were only a few sightings here and there of pirates, but now," he smoothed the letter carefully on his desk top, "the ocean seems to be crawling with sea thieves. Can you think of any reason that might be?"

Chaucer might as well have been a stone gargoyle, for all he revealed. "There have been reports, Sir Duke, of an unfair advantage," he said. "The pirates' timing is too perfect — the conditions of the sea always seem to favor them. Time after time, it's the same."

Yes, Reginald knew all the stories. He knew the tales drunken sailors spewed around their fires when the chill of night settled in their bones. He knew the name they spoke with hushed voices and worried eyes. He also knew that men of the seas were born with lies upon their lips.

"You believe the Witch of Wendelgrimm is helping the pirates?" He let a large dose of disdain slide into his voice. "One of my managers — one of my *best* managers — is being scared off by a bedtime story?"

Chaucer's mouth bent in a smirk. "Forgive me, but I believe you know the Witch exists."

"Of course she exists. But do you know why she's called the Witch of Wendelgrimm? Because she never actually *leaves* Wendelgrimm. The Witch has claimed her prize, and she isn't at all interested in treasure ships. Try to use that head of yours. I know it must be difficult to be so irreversibly stupid, but do try."

Chaucer took his beating without a word. When Reginald was finished, he bent his head. "I yield to your knowledge, Sir Duke."

Reginald gripped the corner of his desk to keep the anger from his face. Try as he might, Chaucer just didn't intimidate. Someone could run him through, and he probably wouldn't even grimace. He'd likely die with the same serious expression he wore now.

"I think I've been more than understanding of your sailors' fears," Reginald said evenly. "I added a day to the route so the ships could avoid sailing too close to Wendelgrimm, didn't I?"

"You were very gracious, Sir Duke."

"Right I was. Now — I want this problem solved. I won't have anymore notes like this," he waved the letter in Chaucer's face, "coming across my desk. Tell the ships to travel in fleets, if you have to. At least if one gets attacked, the others can sail free. It's better than having them picked off one at a time. Blast it, Chaucer! This is why I hired you — to think *for* me! Do you have any idea how frustrating it is to be surrounded by incompetence?"

"Very, I would imagine."

"Insurmountably!" Reginald stormed. "Impossibly! I don't want to hear another word — not a single one — until you have the pirates under control. Send me their hearts in a crate, if you have to. Just don't make me kill you. I've lopped off the heads of enough bungling fools this season. My executioner has to sharpen his axe twice a week." He flicked at Chaucer with the back of his hand. "Now go. Leave me."

And with the smallest of bows, Chaucer strode from the room.

Reginald had completely forgotten about the bored servant, and jumped a little when he suddenly moved to follow Chaucer out. What an odd fellow. But at least he thought to close the door behind him.

When they were gone, Reginald slumped back into his chair. If he wasn't so blasted good at what he did, he thought he'd like to see Chaucer kicking at the end of a noose. His face might even turn a solemn shade of blue.

Well, his mood was nothing a glass of wine couldn't fix. He'd just finished filling a goblet to the brim when a soft knock sounded at the door. "Yes?" he growled.

The air crackled and the bright outline of a door appeared in the middle of the far wall. A man stepped through the portal and bowed. He wore long, red robes and had his thin lips pulled in a haughty pout. He kept the sides and back of his gray hair growing past his shoulders — though his top was bald.

"You couldn't use the normal door, Bartimus?" Reginald grouched.

Bartimus raised his brows. "And risk someone seeing our visitor? Not a chance."

The goblet nearly slipped out of Reginald's hand when he saw the creature that stalked in behind Bartimus. A wolfdevil, one that stood so tall that the tips of its furry ears nearly scraped the ceiling. He knew from its height and the thick black fur that covered its body who this devil belonged to. Though until now, he'd only heard rumors.

"What is that ... *thing*? Where did it come from?" he said, trying to sound surprised. He wasn't supposed to know about the devils — no one was. But his spies had ears all across the Kingdom, and especially in Midlan. It was amazing the amount of information a bit of gold could buy.

"He comes with a message from the King," Bartimus said carefully. "It is a most ... disturbing message."

Reginald took the leaf of parchment from his hand and read the scrolling words.

Reginald,

The Dragongirl is finally land-bound. Obviously, I cannot waste this opportunity. I had a spy tracking her movements, but he lost her in a fog on the High Seas.

*I have reason to believe that she is traveling south —
deep into your territory. She is not alone. I have sent
Bloodfang to your castle for protection, so keep him
close at all times. If she is nearby, he will be able to sniff
her out.*

*Be on your guard and look for every opportunity to
capture her. Alive, if possible. But I will settle for dead.
Do not disappoint me.*

*His Royal Highness,
King Crevan*

Reginald crushed the letter. This was bad. It was even
worse than Chaucer. "I refuse to have that mutt following me
everywhere I go," he fumed.

Bartimus spread his arms wide. "What would you
have me do, Sir Duke? The spell binding the devil is strong,
and the King's command will trump yours. You cannot send
him away."

Reginald thought about it for a moment. He snatched
the letter up, un-crumpled it and read it again. "Ah, see here?
The King sent him to my castle — not to me. I don't have to
tote him anywhere."

Bartimus cleared his throat. "The beast must be put
somewhere, Sir Duke. Somewhere we can keep an eye on
him."

He thought for a moment. "I'll leave him in your
charge, then."

It was an easy decision. Most of the mages welcomed
their new positions as servants of the Five. For centuries, the
whisperers had been the ones who licked the King's boots —
and under their authority, the mages were forced to live as
hunted refugees. Now the cards were in the other hand.

Bartimus wore the iron shackle around his arm like a
King wore a crown. To him, it was not a symbol of bondage,
but a token of power. He stepped forward and rolled back

one of his long sleeves. Reginald touched the shackle with the tip of his finger and gave the order.

"As Duke of the High Seas, I grant you command of the devil Bloodfang. Only my word will have power over yours."

At his touch, the iron grew hot and glowed. Bartimus flexed his fingers as Reginald's command resonated; Bloodfang uttered a low whine as the collar around his neck grew hot in turn.

It was a clever spell, really: the shackles worked on any being with magic flowing through its veins, tying it indefinitely to its master. Shortly after he disposed of the whisperers, Crevan invited the mages to study in Midlan — where he tricked them into coming up with a spell to control his devils. When he learned it would work on all magical creatures, he turned the mages' own spell against them. He bound them to his will and divided them up amongst the Five as gifts.

Reginald only wished that he'd thought of it first.

When the command was finished, he nodded to Bartimus. "I leave this situation in your capable hands. Keep him out of sight — I don't want any of my managers knowing he's here."

Bartimus bowed and shuffled out his door. Bloodfang followed, his deadly claws clicking against the stone floor as he went. When the door closed behind them, it evaporated with a *pop*.

Reginald took a long drag of his wine and steeled himself for the mountain of letters he was about to have to write. All of his managers would need to know about the Dragongirl ... though if she decided to attack them, it wouldn't do much good.

When he was finished with that, he would write to Countess D'Mere. He thought she might be interested to know that her suspicions were confirmed: she wasn't the only one in the Kingdom who kept dangerous pets.

Which would make things a bit more ... complicated.

Chapter 24
A Fancy

Reading turned out to be a large part of Kael's training. Morris claimed that the more a whisperer knew, the stronger his imagination — and the more powerful he became. He proved his point one day when he dropped a sword at Kael's feet and said: "I want you to tie this into a sailor's knot."

At first, Kael thought it was some sort of joke. But then he saw the firm set of Morris's bushy eyebrows and knew he was serious. "I can't do that."

"You can't *yet*," Morris corrected him. "And why's that?"

"Because I don't have arms the size of tree trunks." He anticipated the smack to the back of his head with gritted teeth.

"Wrong! It's because you don't know iron, you don't know what it's made of and you don't know how to treat it." Morris plopped his arm on the sizable tome next to him. "This here is *Blades and Bellows* — taught me everything I know about smithing. You've got an hour to read it. Then you'll show me what you've learned."

Kael didn't see how he was going to read a book in an hour. But he'd always wanted to learn how to smith, so he sat cross-legged on the ground and opened it in his lap.

There was plenty of information in *Blades and Bellows*: paintings of sweaty-faced men laboring over vats of open flame, diagrams on how to heat iron and how to cool it, drawings of a dozen different types of swords — and a missive on how to avoid a number of unfortunate injuries. It wasn't long before he was completely engrossed. So much so, that he was actually disappointed when he turned the last page and found it empty.

"So, what did you learn?" Morris asked.

He closed the book with a heavy sigh and looked up to respond. That's when he noticed that the sun had hardly moved: it was still high over their heads, drifting in and out of the clouds as it climbed towards noon. "How long have I been reading?" he said.

Morris chuckled. "Oh, about half an hour." He caught the surprised look on Kael's face and explained. "A Wright never really reads books — he absorbs them. He lives in the words, drifts into the world of the author and there becomes apprentice to his knowledge. And everything a Wright learns, he remembers. So now that you know a bit about smithing, how're you planning on tying that knot?"

Kael looked at the sword. Thanks to *Blades and Bellows*, he now knew that this wasn't just any sword: it was a broadsword with a double blood channel. It was designed for long, sweeping strikes and devastating thrusts. Such a blade was forged to be tested against even the most stalwart armor.

And he knew that bending it would be impossible.

When he told Morris as much, it earned him another smack to the head. "Blast it, you've fallen into the trap of doubt! I expected more out of you, I really did."

Kael rubbed the ever-present knot on his head, wondering vaguely if it would finally callus. "Well instead of beating me, why don't you tell me how to escape this *trap of doubt*?" he muttered, imitating Morris's croaky voice as best he could.

His joke wasn't lost on the helmsman. "No cheek," he growled. "Listen here — every time you learn something new, you've got a choice to make: you can let it hold you back, or you can feed it to your imagination. But no matter what you choose, your hands are always going to do exactly what you tell them to. Now, how're you going to tie that sword in a knot?" When Kael didn't say anything, he huffed. "Think about it, think about chapter twelve."

Chapter twelve was all about how to heat iron to prepare it for forging. Too hot, and the metal would melt. Too cool, and it wouldn't budge. There was an exact right temperature, a description Kael remembered as clearly as if he had it open in front of him. He thought about it, and as he let himself slip back between the pages of his memory, his hands began to tingle.

It was a strange power, like finding a muscle he never knew he had. He flexed it, feeling its strength course down from his mind and into the very tips of his fingers. He thought about the forge and the fires within it. He could see red flames rise up and wrap around his hands. Suddenly, he had an idea.

He grabbed the sword off the ground and held it by its blade. *My hands are the center of a blacksmith's fire*, he said to himself. *No metal can withstand them: they bend iron as the wind bends the grass.*

All at once, his hands turned white-hot. The sword groaned and red heat blossomed from the center of the blade. When it was just hot enough, he bent it easily into a U.

He was so shocked that his concentration nearly slipped, but he latched onto it again and pulled the hilt through, forming a simple knot. He let the sword fall out of his hand and the red retreated from the metal, cooling almost immediately.

"There it is," Morris said with a grin. "I knew you'd get the hang of it."

Kael grabbed hold of the railing, still clinging to his vision. The wood started to smoke under his hand.

"Watch what you're doing!" Morris barked, startling him out of his trance. "We aren't in the forest, lad. You burn this wood up, and we'll have to swim back to shore."

He quickly took his hand away, and it left a char mark in the shape of his palm on the rails. As he dragged himself back to reality, the fire in his hands went out completely — returning to their normal shade of pale.

"What else can I bend?"

Morris must have seen the excitement on his face, because he wasted no time quashing it. "I think just the sword for today. You don't want to push yourself too hard early on, or you might get a headache."

He was confused. "But I thought you said headaches were a good thing."

"They are," Morris allowed, "but only when they're used proper. The mind is tricky — you've got to start out small and then build up to the big things. But when you're lost in imagination, it's easy to get carried away. There's been many a young whisperer who tried something that was too big for him, and he didn't live to tell about it. So we'll stick to reading, for now. And don't you try anything without asking me first, all right?"

He reluctantly agreed.

****

Shortly after their gauntlet battle, Aerilyn asked him for a favor. "I know I'm not *very* strong," she admitted one afternoon over a lunch of slimy, colorless fish. "But I think I'm beginning to agree with Kyleigh — a woman ought to be deadly with something. And I thought, since our arms are about the same size, that I might make a decent archer. So if I *were* to try archery, would you be willing to ... teach me?"

Though she'd made a pretty painful comment about his arms, Kael found he couldn't douse the hope in her eyes. "All right," he said, and plugged his ears against her delighted squeal.

Morris didn't seem to mind that he'd added Aerilyn to his list of chores. "You can do as you please, lad. Just so long as you get your reading done," he said.

That was fine with Kael: he rather enjoyed his reading assignments. In Tinnark, he'd only had the same four or five dusty tomes to read. But the library aboard *Anchorgloam* had hundreds. The only bad thing about it was that getting the books required a trip to Lysander's cabin — which usually involved a lengthy conversation with Lysander.

He was beginning to wonder if it was worth the trade.

"And so I've been pouring over it day and night, and I just don't see what I've managed to do wrong," Lysander finished. His shoulders were sloped down and his head hung pathetically close to his chest. "What do you think I should do? How do I change, how do I prove to her that I'm not a horrible, drunken leech with all the depth of an inkwell?"

Apparently, when Lysander asked Aerilyn to dance, he hadn't got the answer he'd been expecting. Instead, he got a rather cold refusal that included several creative reasons as to why she wasn't interested in him. That was the gist of it. There were loads of other, more sentimental things in between, but Kael mostly ignored them.

"I don't know. Why are you asking me?" he said distractedly. He was looking for a tome on dragons, something fun that he could read in his very little spare time, and wasn't at all interested in whatever nonsense Lysander whined about.

"Because you're her friend."

"Well, then why don't you ask Kyleigh?"

It seemed like a reasonable enough solution, but Lysander just snorted. "Kyleigh is a *woman*. And ladies tend to give very flowery advice that makes a man feel good about himself, but doesn't actually solve the problem." He leaned back, propping both his hands on the desk behind him. "No, what I need is advice from a man — a fellow close to Aerilyn who can give me the honest truth."

Kael glanced up, and knew from the tilt in his chin that Lysander meant to get advice from him. "Uh —"

"No, don't think about it," he interrupted. "Lies need time to grow, and all I want is the truth. So out with it — what do I need to do to make Aerilyn think better of me?"

"Well, you could behave better," Kael said without thinking.

But Lysander wasn't at all offended. He leaned forward. "I see ... and how do I do that?"

The fact that he didn't know anything was wrong was a large part of the problem, in Kael's opinion. But if he explained it, Lysander might give him a moment's peace. So he reined himself in and tried to put it in words he thought the captain could understand. "Aerilyn is a lady."

"Yes, undeniably."

"No, she's a *real* lady. A gentle lady who likes to wear pretty things and doesn't enjoy having dirt under her fingernails."

"So?"

"So she isn't like Kyleigh — you can't scoop her up and spin her around in a circle, because it offends her."

"Ah ... I'm not sure I understand."

Kael wasn't surprised. He thought about it for a moment, tried to think of a way he could dumb it down even further. "She's like the treasures in your hallway: you can look at her, but you aren't allowed to touch her."

His handsome face became considerably befuddled. "But I *can* touch the treasures in my hallway."

"Because they're yours. Aerilyn isn't yours, she isn't anybody's. She's like ... a deer. She's wild and untamed and she won't go anywhere near you unless she trusts you."

"So I'm supposed to ... feed her?"

Kael wondered, briefly, if he might be able to kill himself with the corner of a book. "No, you're supposed to respect her, respect her territory —"

"And then lure her in and bring her down!"

"No!" Kael had reached the end of his very short rope, and could do nothing to keep the words from bursting out. "She's a lady, not a meal. And you aren't going to get anywhere near her if you think of her like that. You want to know how to get Aerilyn to like you? Stop behaving like a complete and total idiot. Stop swearing, stop calling her names, stop drinking, stop flirting with Kyleigh and — for mercy's sake — keep your shirt on!"

His voice seemed to ring off the walls for a good half-minute. He'd have been embarrassed about the way he acted if the good captain didn't so thoroughly need to be shouted at.

Lysander sat very rigidly in the aftermath, his mouth parted in a surprised O. "I see," he finally said. "If I want a lady to like me, then I've got to be a gentleman."

"Yes."

Lysander scratched his chin thoughtfully. "So I'm not allowed to flirt with Kyleigh anymore, eh?"

"No." The word came out a little sharper than he meant to.

Lysander smiled. "You were looking for a book on dragons, no? Well let me suggest this one." He crossed the room in three steps and pulled a bright red book off the middle shelf. "*Tales of Scales: The Complete Catalogue of Dragons*, there's not a more detailed book in all the realm. I should know — I nicked it from the fellow who wrote it, right out from under his quill."

Kael snatched it, muttered his thanks, and left before Lysander could trap him with another story. He was suddenly in a very bad mood.

******

Much to his surprise, Aerilyn turned out to be a pretty decent archer. More than decent, actually. She picked up on the form quickly and it wasn't long before she could hit the target nearly every time. They started out with Kael's bow, but it wound up being too much for her strength. That's when Morris suggested they try one of the longbows.

"But those are bigger," Kael said.

"Aye, but they're not as tough to pull back," Morris explained. "She'll get a stronger shot with little effort. You ought to consider giving them a try."

Kael wasn't about to give up his bow, even if it was more difficult to shoot. It was Roland's ... and the only thing he had left of Tinnark.

Aerilyn was a little intimidated by the larger bow at first, but it wasn't long before she figured it out. "This is *much* better," she said, as her arrow struck the center of the barrel lid they used for a target. "There's no grunting or swinging

276

clubs about — just careful aim and skill." Another of her arrows found its mark. "How's that?"

"Good," Kael said. "Just make sure you don't overshoot. I don't want to have to pull an arrow out of anyone's rump."

They'd weighed anchor next to a string of leafy green islands, and most of the pirates were out foraging. They swam in the crystal blue water beneath them, scouring the reefs for any unfortunate creature the cook might salt and turn into a deadly stew. Occasionally, a pirate would dive down and after a moment, bob back to the surface with a fish wriggling on the end of his harpoon.

As much as Kael wanted off the ship, he couldn't make himself put one leg in the ocean. He watched as Kyleigh climbed to the top of the rails and stood, harpoon in hand. She was wearing a shirt cut to the elbow and pants cut to the knee. Her feet were bare. At the goads from the pirates below her, she spread her arms wide and fell, headfirst, in a graceful arc.

He leaned forward and his toes curled when she struck the water. It was only after she came back up that he was able to breathe again.

"Yes, and speaking of rumps," Aerilyn said as she retrieved her arrows, "what's gotten into Captain Lysander? He seems ... well, he's been acting rather nice lately."

He pretended to watch Noah and Jonathan as they grappled on top of a reef, trying to fling the other into the water. He thought if he wasn't looking at her, he might be able to hide the guilt on his face. "I hadn't noticed him acting any differently."

She raised an eyebrow. "Really? You didn't notice that he hasn't taken a drink in nearly a week? Or that he managed to keep his shirt on all day yesterday? And he," she fidgeted with the hem of her shirt, "he's been sitting with me at every meal. It's almost as if ..."

"As if what?"

She shook her head. "Oh, never mind. I'm probably just being silly."

They shot for a few minutes in silence, and he hoped that was the end of it. But then she turned and said quite suddenly: "He hasn't mentioned anything about me, has he?"

He shrugged. "I don't know. How should I know?"

She made a frustrated sound. "Well don't boys talk about girls? Kyleigh and I talk about boys."

"Really? What boy does Kyleigh like?"

Red sprung to her cheeks. "It doesn't matter," she said quickly.

"But she *does* like someone?"

"No — which is why it doesn't matter."

Aerilyn's momentary weakness was over. Now she had her arms crossed and her chin set. He knew that even if he pried her mouth open with his bare hands, he wouldn't get another word out of her. Which was a shame, really, because he wondered what sort of boy Kyleigh might be interested in. He was probably some handsome, stone-fisted knight she met while in the King's army: a man who was just as deadly with a blade as she.

For some reason, that thought made his stomach hurt. "Lysander asked what your favorite color was yesterday," he admitted.

Aerilyn leaned forward, hands clasped in front of her. "And?"

"And what?"

She slapped him playfully on the arm. "And what did you tell him?"

"I told him I wasn't certain, but I thought it was blue."

She flung her arms about his neck with such surprising force that he nearly tumbled backwards. "Oh, you know me so well! But I wonder why ... do you think he might ...?"

Kael wondered if she actually expected him to be able to guess the ends of her sentences. "He might what?"

She screwed up her nose and tried to look severe, but in the end her smile broke free. "All right, you don't have to tell me. I know there's a code you gentlemen have to keep about these things. But I'm going to tell you something, and you can't tell Lysander I said it. Do you swear?"

"Sure, all the time."

She slapped him again, grinning at his feeble joke. "That's not what I meant. Promise you won't tell Lysander."

He sighed. "All right, I promise."

"Good." She leaned forward, her eyes shining mischievously. "I think, against every reasonable bone in my body, that Lysander is quite … handsome." She giggled and her face turned pink. "It's horrible isn't it, for a merchant to fancy a pirate? Did you ever hear of anything so completely scandalous?"

Kael tried to smile, but he thought there were worse things in the Kingdom than the fancy between a pirate and a merchant.

****

Every day, their list of backbreaking chores stretched on and into the evening. Only after they managed to choke down their last spoonfuls of a poisonous dinner were the pirates allowed to prop up their boots and relax. This they did on the main deck, out in the cool of the night and under the brilliant cover of the stars.

And because there was literally no end to his mischief, Lysander kept Jonathan's chores running through the evening. While everyone else talked or played at cards, he'd have to string up his fiddle and entertain them with a song. Lysander ordered that they be strictly historical tunes, and mainly verses chronicling their days aboard *Anchorgloam*.

But Jonathan managed to weave a good bit of his rudeness into every song. And it was so popular with the men that Lysander pretended not to hear. That particular evening, Jonathan seemed to have been inspired by the contents of the galley:

Ladles of soup with spindly legs
Of crab and gooey starfish eggs.

279

Barrel of scales and fishy eyes,
You're not quite like my mum's mince pies.

Shut my lids and serve a plate
Of heaping, steaming merman bait.
The cook tells me it's quite the catch,
So tip me spoon and down the hatch!

Oh, alas! My gut repels
The squirming, squiggling seahorse tails.
My stomach heaves, I turn a hue,
And out my mouth comes seafood spew!

The pirates whooped and clanged their tankards together as Jonathan took a deep, over-exaggerated bow. Only one man stomped off in a huff: and that was the cook.

Rumors flared up like bouts of scurvy aboard the ship, and it wasn't long before everyone knew about Kyleigh's secret. No sooner did Jonathan finish his song than the pirates were bellowing for her to sing their favorite tune.

"All right, *fine!*" she said, when it was clear they would never relent. She leapt to her feet and shouted: "Ahoy, rapscallions!"

They roared and raised their grog in greeting.

"Clean the seaweed out of your ears and listen up. I'm about to tell the saddest tale ever told." A forlorn note came off of Jonathan's fiddle as he joined her. "It's tale about a man. A man named Sam Gravy —"

Cheers rang out.

"— and how he lost his true love to the sea."

When Jonathan's notes pepped up into something the pirates could stomp their feet to, she started to sing.

There is a tale of courage and bold,
Of a lad who felled trees and built him a boat.
His name be Sam Gravy and this be his tale,
Of how he found love with a rudder and sails.

Across the High Seas, he sailed with his love,
Through forests of trees with tops high above.
O'er deserts that quelled with burning hot sand,
And never such love for a boat had a man!

Sam Gravy she sped
And he felt not a shred
Of doubt in his soul of her valor.
With him at her helm
They'd conquer the realm
And his heart would rest ever with she.

So it happened one day a serpent arose
Out of the sea and lunged at his boat.
Sam Gravy he turned on the wheel with a tug,
And threw his harpoon at the heart of the thug.

The serpent, he roared and with one final gasp
Drew up his tail and made such a splash,
That Gravy, his boat, his love and his pride
Were swept onto land by the force of the tide.

Sam Gravy she ran
Aground in the sand
Though he swore 'twould never be broken,
The ship he so loved
She never comes home
And his heart now belongs to the sea.

Yes his heart, it belongs to the sea.

It was a horribly sad tale, but Kael never got tired of listening to Kyleigh sing. She carried the notes so beautifully, so effortlessly, and it made him wish he could do the same. But all he had to do was think of singing and his ears would threaten to leap off his head and fling themselves into the ocean.

He left when the dancing started. There was no point in sitting around and watching everyone else do the jig. *Tales of Scales* sat under his hammock, still mostly unread. He always had every intention of reading it, but the moment he fell into bed, his eyes got heavy and the sentences drifted further apart:

Long have the race of men warred with the dragon, long have they envied him. Though the King bears his image upon his heart, he knows not the dragon's strength. He is Fate's first child and the most ancient of all beasts. His life stretches into the thousands of years, sword nor arrow can pierce his skin ... the fire that boils in his belly is more fearsome than the core of flame ... burns in his heart, sets fire to every drop of blood. The dragon loves most fiercely ... protects ... only once...

****

He woke with a start.

He dreamed of Amos again — only this time he'd been holding onto his arm, trying desperately to haul him back over the edge of a bottomless pit.

Let me go, Amos had said, his voice unusually resounding and deep. *Let me go, child. It's time to let go.*

He didn't want to let go. He tried to say as much, but his lips wouldn't move. Slowly, his strength failed and Amos slipped out of his grasp. He went plummeting, falling end over end for a thousand years, until the darkness finally swallowed him. Kael stood up and prepared to leap in after him when a strong hand gripped his shoulder.

A man held him back. His tunic and breeches were pure white and Kael thought he might have recognized his face. Just when he was about to ask the man who he was, a loud growl startled him out of his sleep.

Now there was a ring of cold sweat around his neck, and Jonathan was snoring too loudly for him to go back to sleep.

Long ago, Roland taught him how to see meanings in his dreams. And the meaning of his first dream was clear: Amos was still alive, but he thought the pit might have meant that worrying wouldn't help anything — that his fear would drag him down and under, if he let it.

The second dream was much more disturbing. Roland had warned him that Death often took the form of a man dressed all in white — and when he appeared, it meant danger was not far behind.

It was that worry that drove Kael to put on his boots and climb to the deck, just to make sure *Anchorgloam* wasn't about to run aground.

The night air was hot and sticky. He didn't think he'd ever get used to the weather: it was like wearing a cloak of steam everywhere he went. He'd intended to take a quick walk and go back to his hammock, but then he saw a cloaked someone standing at the mainmast, wielding a lantern.

He thought it might be Morris, so he made his way over. Then the person turned and he saw Lysander's teeth glinting in the lamplight. He tried to make a hasty escape.

"Kael, so good to see you," he said, beckoning him closer.

He realized that Lysander wasn't alone: there were three boatfuls of pirates bobbing on the waves, catching the sacks that two more pirates tossed down to them. Tiny lights blinked on the horizon and the dark, jagged edges of rooftops grew along the hills. He realized they were anchored less than a mile from a village.

"You're going to raid them?" he guessed.

But Lysander shook his head. "Not quite. Can you keep a secret?"

When he nodded, Lysander waved to one of the pirates, who tossed him a sack that he passed off to Kael.

When he opened it, he could hardly keep the surprise off his face. A loaf of bread, six apples and a handful of copper coins was not at all what he was expecting to find. "You mean there's real food somewhere on *Anchorgloam*?"

Lysander laughed. "Yes, but it isn't for us." He retied the sack and sent it down to the boats below. When they were full, the pirates rowed away, slipping into the dark quiet of the sea.

"You're sending it to the people," Kael said, even more shocked now than he'd been a moment before.

"Yes. No doubt you've noticed how the Duke keeps his subjects from earning their bread? It's wrong to try and keep us from the sea." Lysander's voice was dark, darker than Kael ever thought he could make it. "Saltwater flows in our veins, our hearts thump with the beat of the surf. We live by the turns of the tide ... it's as sickening as trying to keep two lovers apart."

Kael knew how the people of the High Seas felt. Those few weeks when he wasn't allowed to go into the forest were torture. To be able to see the trees and not walk among them made him want to drive a dagger through his heart. He thought death might have been a kinder sentence.

"We do what we can," Lysander continued. "We sneak in rations and coins small enough that the guards aren't likely to notice, but I wish we could do more." He took a deep breath and when he turned around, his smile was back. "Look here — there's something I want to show you."

He held the lantern up to the mainmast. The light chased the shadows away, bending them backwards until he could see the fresh words carved into the wood. *Kael the Wright — twelve turns*, they read.

"I had Noah cut this in yesterday. I told him to put your name just below our previous champion," Lysander said.

He raised the lantern a little higher, so that he could see the name carved above his: *Kyleigh — twelve turns*.

Kael was more than a little shocked. He thought the number next to her name would have been much more ... infinite. "Wait, does that mean someone actually beat her?"

Lysander smiled. "It does, clever lad."

"Who was it?"

The light climbed higher, stretching into the shadows above Kyleigh's name. Another carving came into view, so faded that he had to squint to read it. But when he did, his heart nearly stopped beating.

"Who else?"

Chapter 25
The Tempest

Setheran the Wright.

There was no number carved next to his name, no explanation at all. And it wasn't needed. For the one thing every historian seemed able to agree on was that Setheran the Wright was the greatest warrior who ever lived. So of course he'd been able to defeat Kyleigh ...

Hold on a moment. "That isn't possible." Kael did the sum quickly. "Setheran died seventeen years ago, which means Kyleigh would have been an infant."

He thought it was some sort of joke: that the pirates were saying the only one who could ever have a hope against her would have been Setheran.

But Lysander just smirked. "Kyleigh is no ordinary woman. She hides her powers well: there are few who know her for what she truly is, and none who know her story. But believe me when I say that she's not at all what she seems." He stepped back and gestured around him. "I was only eight years old when Kyleigh and Setheran fought on this very deck. I wasn't there, but my father told me all about it. He said it was the greatest battle he'd ever seen."

Kael wasn't sure he believed him. He couldn't imagine Kyleigh being twice his age. She didn't look older, and she certainly didn't act like it. "That isn't possible," he said again. He searched Lysander's face for any hint of a joke, any whisper of a lie. But there was only calm assurance.

"She's a powerful woman," he said quietly. "Perhaps one day she'll let you see her other side."

"Why can't you tell me?"

"And betray the trust of a dear friend? I think not."

"Only a dear friend?" Kael didn't know why he asked that question. He could have kicked himself for changing the subject.

At any rate, it seemed to amuse Lysander. "Yes. Does that surprise you?"

He made his face serious. He had to know for sure — for Aerilyn's sake. "It does, actually. The two of you seemed very ... close."

Lysander laughed, and the light bounced with the movement. "You flatter me, but no — Kyleigh and I were never more than friends. It would take a better man than me to *tame* her, as you put it," he added with a grin that made Kael want to punch him. "Any man who chased after Kyleigh would have to charge in fully-armed. He'd have to be her match in every way: strong, cunning, and dangerous."

"And handsome," Kael muttered.

Lysander looked at him curiously. "Do you think so? Perhaps, but then again she's never been much interested in treasure — which is why I've often said that she makes a horrible pirate." He touched two fingers to his forehead. "I'm afraid I must take my leave. I've got to make sure the weather doesn't stay too clear. If anyone were to spot my good deeds, it might tarnish my ruthless reputation. Ah, don't worry — it'll be rain, not fog." He clapped him on the shoulder. "Sleep well, for danger lurks on the 'morrow."

He glanced at the mast, and the lantern barely caught the curved edge of his grin. Then he disappeared in the direction of his cabin, leaving Kael alone and baffled in the darkness.

****

A few hours later, he'd stumbled back downstairs and fallen into his hammock. He knew from the forlorn cry of the watchman's bell that it was three o'clock when he finally drifted back to sleep.

Two bells later, Morris jostled him awake.

"No, it's too early," he groaned. He tried to roll over and temporarily forgot that he was in a hammock. The result was that he wound up on the floor, his nose inches from

Jonathan's boots. He didn't know if it was the fall or the stench that cleared the sleep from his eyes.

"Come along, lad. We've got a lot to do today," Morris whispered, which made his voice even more croaky and broken.

"What could we possibly have to do that I need to get up an hour early for?" Kael muttered as he crammed on his boots.

"Not we," Morris jabbed an arm at him, "*you*. You're the one who's got to steer us through the tempest. I would, but," he held up his nubs, "I can't make the turns so sharp anymore."

An icy feeling twisted in the pit of his stomach. "What tempest? Are we in a storm?"

"Nah, not yet. Now quit your fussing and let's go!"

An hour, a stale biscuit and cup of warm water later, Kael stood alone at the ship's wheel. It only took him a few minutes to understand how to turn it, and a few minutes more to order the sails into position. He found he'd absorbed most of what he knew through watching Morris.

"There you are, now you've got the hang of it," Morris said approvingly. "Keep her on course. I'll be back in a while."

"Where are you going?" Kael said after him.

He turned and grinned through the gaps in his teeth. "To catch a little shuteye, of course."

He was lucky Kael needed both hands to steer.

The sea was calm and the weather was fairly pleasant: the sun wasn't high enough for things to get too hot. He was actually enjoying the peace when Lysander skipped up and ruined it all.

"Are you ready?" he said.

Kael glared at Thelred, who sneered back from over Lysander's shoulder. "Ready for what?"

"To pay off your debt, of course. We're leagues and a bit from Wendelgrimm. I think it's time to give the Witch a knife in the ribs. Or two."

In all of the excitement of the past few weeks, Kael had nearly forgotten about his debt. But now that he was reminded of it, he wanted nothing more than to settle it. "All right, I'm ready."

Lysander nodded. "Good." He made to turn, and then turned back. "Ah, I may have forgotten to mention this earlier, but there's a bit of an obstacle we're going to have to get through *before* we can actually sail into Wendelgrimm."

"What is it?" Kael said warily.

Lysander combed a hand through his hair, making it stand on end for a moment before it fell back in waves. "Oh, nothing much. Just a bit of rain and wind — nothing a Wright can't handle."

"It's a tempest," Thelred said, his sneer growing wider. "A spell that the Witch of Wendelgrimm cast to keep trespassers out of her realm. It's a fury the likes of which few sailors have ever seen ... and even fewer live to tell about."

Lysander gave him an annoyed look. "It isn't all that. Stop trying to make an ocean out of a raindrop."

"I don't understand. If you can control the weather, why can't you just make it sunny?" Kael said.

Lysander's smile faltered. "Because, my dear boy, the Witch gives my curse no power in her realm. Ironically, it's the one place in the Kingdom I can go without putting anyone in danger. Now," he clapped him on the shoulder, "let's meet this thing head on, eh? No hesitation — not like the last time, when we let Morris steer. I don't mind saying that we all very nearly perished. But I'm sure a fellow of your talents and, ah, appendages won't have a problem."

He slipped off before Kael could question him further, pretending to correct the way Jonathan mopped the deck. Thelred gave him one last smirk before he followed.

He figured the truth was somewhere between the two stories, but only one person knew for sure: and he'd decided that now was the perfect time to take a nap. Perhaps Kyleigh might have known something, if only he could get her attention. There were several times that he waved to her as she passed, but she never looked up. It was almost as if she was trying to avoid him.

He blamed Lysander. He probably let slip that he mentioned something about her being much older than she looked, and now she knew Kael was going to question her about it.

Blast.

The day passed uneventfully. The pirates went about their usual chores and the clouds stayed the same boring shade of gray. It was only when the sun began to set that he noticed something amiss: the sky wasn't red or orange or any of the normal sunset colors. It was turning ... green.

They sailed closer, and he realized that it wasn't the sky after all. No, it was a wall of sickly green clouds.

They rested squarely on top of the ocean, billowing up from the waves and stretching skywards. *Anchorgloam* drifted towards them and they reached out with mile-long tendrils, wrapping them neatly in a cold embrace. It wasn't long before they were surrounded on all sides. Ahead, fog yawned to swallow them.

"It's the tempest," Morris said loudly, nearly scaring Kael out of his skin. He hadn't even heard him waddle up.

"*This* is the tempest?" So far, all he could see was a lot of fog.

There weren't any storm clouds or even an ominous rumble of thunder. In fact, it was eerily silent. The pirates lined up at the railings, whispering anxiously to each other as the green clouds sealed them in.

"Every man to his station, every man in a lash!" Lysander barked, and they scrambled to get ropes knotted around their waists. "Fall overboard in a lash, and we might be able to reel you in. But fall untied, and you might as well — Aerilyn!"

She'd been in the process of tying her lash when Lysander ripped it out of her hands. "Just what do you think you're doing?" she said angrily.

"Get below deck this instant! A tempest is no place for a lady."

"I thought you said this was only a raindrop," Kael called, and he was rewarded with a glare.

"I think I've earned the right to sail through anything," Aerilyn said indignantly. "I've kept up, haven't I? I'm just as much a part of this crew as anybody else."

Lysander wasn't use to being argued with, and he didn't take her mutiny well. "It isn't about rights, it's about survival. Now get below —"

"Or what?"

"Or I'll haul you down myself."

She gasped. "You wouldn't dare."

"Oh, I would," he brought his face down to hers, "and I will."

She didn't back away. She stuck her nose to his and jabbed a finger in the middle of his chest. "If you even *think* about throwing me over your shoulders and carrying me around like a sack of potatoes, I'll make sure you limp for the rest of your life."

That was Kyleigh's doing. She was the one who'd taken Aerilyn aside and taught her everything she knew about inflicting pain. Under her careful instruction, Aerilyn had become less like a dainty merchant's daughter and more like a force to be reckoned with. She could bring tears to any grown man's eyes — and Lysander knew it.

So rather than risk a life-altering injury, he turned his anger on Jonathan. "Make sure she's tied!" he roared, flinging the lash at him. "If I have to dive in and save her, I'm coming after you. Do you hear me, scallop skull? My ghost will haunt every foul note you ever play!"

Jonathan stumbled over himself in his rush to get her tied to the nearest mast.

It wasn't long before the fog closed in on them. It swept up, covering everything in a cloud of green. The deck disappeared and voices bounced around in every direction. Lysander's orders drifted in and out of Kael's ears. Three words would come from in front of him, and three more words from behind. He itched madly where the fog touched his skin and had to keep taking his hands off the wheel to scratch.

"Steady, lad. I know the magic is tickling you, but this

is the tricky part," Morris said. Kael could just make out the side of his stout arm. "Hold your course, listen to the waves."

He focused every ounce of his concentration on the sounds of the ocean. He closed his eyes so the fog wouldn't distract him, blocked out the panicked whispers that swam through his ears from the deck below. The steady, rhythmic slap of waves striking *Anchorgloam* was his heartbeat, his breath. And then it suddenly wasn't right.

He spun the wheel to the left and the ship groaned under his command. Pirates cursed and stumbled sideways, holding onto whatever piece of rigging they could grab. Kael heard something whoosh by, and turned in time to see the object they'd so narrowly missed: it was the full half of a wrecked ship. Its nose stuck up out of the water and its tail was hung on a jagged cluster of rocks. He blinked, and the fog swallowed it back up without a sound.

Morris's breath came out in a hiss. "That was a good turn, lad. I nearly lost my britches, but it was a good turn."

"Veer right."

Kyleigh's voice startled him. He didn't know how she'd managed to find the wheel when he could hardly see it himself, but he felt the ship turn as she leaned around and pulled down on it.

On their left, a mast stuck out of the water. The sails that clung to it were tattered and filthy. Their ragged ends swayed a little in the breeze, reaching feebly upwards like a wounded soldier begging for mercy.

Then the air started to rumble.

It began as a low growl — the start of a snarl deep inside a wolf's throat. It grew and grew, until it filled their ears with an awful, guttural roar. Kael thought the world was ending: he thought the sea was being sucked downwards as the clouds caved in. Morris leaned over the rails and bellowed to the pirates on deck, who shouted back.

Kael couldn't hear what they said. All he knew was that the cold feeling in his stomach was back. It reared up and though he fought with it, his hands still shook. He turned the ship to avoid another wreck, and the rumbling faded back —

which only worried him further. Now he didn't know if the danger was behind or before them.

"Kyleigh?"

"Yes?" She was right at his ear.

He cleared his throat. "You *do* think we'll make it out alive, don't you? You don't think we're going to … wreck, or anything?"

He could almost hear the smirk in her voice. "When you've seen as much as I've seen, you stop worrying about death." Then after a moment: "A friend of mine had a chant he used to say before every battle — something that steeled him for the fight, I suppose. Would you like me to teach it to you?"

"Yes." He thought learning something new would keep him distracted, at the very least.

"All right." She took a deep breath. *"There are times when death seems certain, and hope is dim. But in those times, I forget my fears. I do not see the storm that rages, or the battle that looms ahead. I close my eyes to the dangers — and in the quiet of the darkness, I see only what must be done."*

Her words coursed the length of his every vein, filling him with something like molten iron — something that burned furiously enough to beat back the icy monster of his fear. His hands stopped shaking and he gripped the wheel tighter, prepared to face whatever awaited them on the other side.

After a few moments, he was calm enough to ask her something else. "How old are you, by the way?"

But Kyleigh didn't answer. She'd either wandered off or, more likely, was ignoring him.

Shouts rang out from the bow. He heard a message being passed along, the same sounds hollered by different voices. A wave of panic washed over the crew and set their boots pounding in a frenzy of motion. Morris nearly knocked him over in his rush to get back to the wheel.

"Hold on tight, lad!" he cried.

Kael barely had time to breathe before the fog disappeared. It brushed passed his face, taking the cold itch

293

with it, and left behind something much more terrifying.

A mountain of black storm clouds hovered above them. They churned and bubbled up, swelling against the fierce beast trapped within them: a storm that belched thunder and spat jagged lines of lightning into the sea. But that wasn't the worst part, not by far.

He could almost hear Morris's jaw drop as he said: "Well, this is new."

A few yards ahead, the ocean dropped away. It fell from all sides and into a bowl the size of a village. Green-blue, foamy waterfalls poured down in straight lines, and the roar of crashing water drowned out everything else. They already had *Anchorgloam* swept up in their current, pulling her in, and Kael could do nothing to stop it. All he could do was make sure they didn't wind up in splinters at the bottom.

The bow slipped over the edge and he pulled hard on the wheel, turning the rudder until the ship was nearly parallel with the lip of the bowl. Then the wood groaned as the whole thing toppled forward.

He held the wheel and at the same time, fought to keep his feet on the ground as they fell. He knew if they went straight down, it would smash them to bits, so he made the ship turn and take the fall at an angle: just like how Roland taught him to climb down tricky slopes.

It worked. *Anchorgloam* skirted the wall and reached the bottom of the bowl with a splash and no splinters. But the tempest wasn't done with them yet.

At this bottom of the world, the waves climbed to three or four times the height of their tallest mast. They were monsters of the deep — leviathans with jaws the size of Tinnark. As the waves stalked them, the wind and the rain worked together: one whipping while the other stung. The cold seeped through their skin and froze the marrow in their bones. Lightning toyed with them, striking a fingernail away from their sails and illuminating each terrified line on their faces.

The ocean scooped *Anchorgloam* up and tossed her from one wave to the next, she rocked dangerously as the wind beat her sails. Kael's arms were shaking from the force of trying to hold the wheel steady. He could feel his strength fading; his mind began to lose its sharpness.

"Hold fast, men! With all that you are — hold fast!"

The cry came from Lysander. He and a dozen others were wrestling with the sails, trying to get them tied down. But the wind swirled from every direction. It cut back and forth in painter's strokes, ripping through the sails and making the ropes scream in agony.

Kael realized they wouldn't be able to tie them down. There must be another way. The library was chalk full of books on storms and sailing, and he was grateful now that Morris insisted he read them. He combed through his memory, searching frantically as the words and pictures flashed before his eyes. Then he had an idea.

"Free the sails, track the wind!" he shouted, and he heard Morris echo him.

Lysander passed the order on, and soon all the men had stumbled over to a tie — wading through icy water and fighting against the gales. They latched onto the ropes and hauled back, tilting them until they were full.

Anchorgloam lunged forward, narrowly escaping a towering wave as it crashed behind them. The force of the wind and the wave shot them across the bowl. He could see the other side rising up ahead of them. It was every bit as steep and swift as its brother.

"I'm sorry, lad!" Morris said, his eyes wide with terror as they took in the wall. "I've doomed us, there's no way —"

"Yes there is!" Kael said. A wave crashed over him. It burned his eyes and he spat out a mouthful of water so cold that it made his teeth hurt. "Tell the men to keep tracking. We've got to get every last gust of wind."

"Aye, aye!"

Morris passed the order along while Kael spun the wheel. They would climb just as they fell: at an angle.

The bow hit the wall and the rushing water tried to shove it back down, but the power of the wind was greater. *Anchorgloam* began to climb, propelled by her full sails. The pirates moved back and forth, shouting to each other as the wind changed directions, and sprinting to catch it. They climbed fast; soon they were nearly halfway up the wall. And then the tempest struck back.

Shadows crossed Kael's hands, and he felt something enormous eclipse the sky above him. When he turned around, he saw a wave so monstrous that it was worthy of legend. Foam gathered at its top. It groaned, leaned forward, and Kael cried out in warning. Then it fell.

He'd never been crushed by a boulder, but he imagined it couldn't have felt worse than being crushed by a wave. A giant's arm slapped into the middle of his back, knocking him off his feet. The water took his breath and his legs. It tried to rip his arms off the wheel, but he held it stubbornly in place. He refused to let the tempest win.

When the wave finally fell back into the ocean, his knees struck the ground as the earth reclaimed him and his face smacked into the wheel. He was so numb with cold that it wasn't until he wiped the hair out of his face that he saw bright red blood staining his sleeve.

"The sails, to the sails!" Morris bellowed.

Kael looked up and saw that all of the pirates had been washed off their posts. They were stuck in a tangled mass of bodies and ropes at the back of the ship and while they struggled, the sail ties flapped freely.

Without her full sails, *Anchorgloam* began to slip backwards as the water reclaimed her. It pulled her down slowly, like a spider dragging in its paralyzed prey. He knew if the sails stayed empty much longer, they'd all be smashed to bits.

He wasn't about to let that happen.

"Hold the wheel!" he said, and Morris wedged his arms obediently between the knobs.

"Wait — where are you going? No, put that back on! You'll drown!"

But Kael ignored him. He ripped off his lash and sprinted down the stairs.

Kyleigh managed to break free of the tangle and was

holding down one side by herself, using her impossible strength to drag the sail back into position. Kael grabbed the other side. He didn't think about the fact that he was about to do something a dozen men had just been struggling to do: he just knew it needed to be done.

"Starboard!" he said, and Kyleigh nodded. They moved back and forth, catching the wind and pulling *Anchorgloam* out of her fall. One by one, pirates broke free and lined up behind him. Kael could feel a headache pulsing at the top of his skull, but he ignored the pain and kept pulling.

They were nearly there, he could see the lip of the bowl. They were almost over it. They just needed one final push. "Pull down, men, down!" he said, and he heard the pirates grunt as they obeyed.

The sails tipped back and caught a jump of wind, just enough of a gust to pop them over the wall and onto the solid ocean once again. The bow tipped forward and pulled the hull over. It struck the water with a splash — a splash that he hadn't exactly been counting on.

He felt every drop of his momentary elation get sucked right back down to his stomach as he watched the terrifying, blue-green beast rush towards him. The wave hit him in the gut and knocked him off his feet. The sea rushed over his mouth, nose and eyes as his body was thrown backwards. Then the water was gone ... and he was falling.

He plummeted over the side of the wall, watching as *Anchorgloam*'s rudder slipped over the top to safety. He shut his eyes tight and let the roar of wind whipping past his ears deafen him. He knew how far he fell by how much time he had to regret.

Why hadn't he listened to Morris? Why hadn't he held the rope a little tighter? Why hadn't he been expecting that blasted wave?

He wasn't surprised when he finally struck the bottom of the bowl and felt all the air get punched out of his lungs. The icy monster in the pit of his stomach rose up as the waves dragged him under. It seized his heart, gripped his limbs in madness. He fought against the ocean's hold; he kicked and squirmed.

Slowly, he lost track of where the surface was. His lungs screamed for air, but the briny water rushed in and silenced them. He became part of the ocean: a drifting, aimless being with a body and little else.

He couldn't hear the tempest rage, couldn't hear the bubbles that slipped out from between his lips — though he imagined that when they reached the surface and popped, the whole realm would be able to hear his screams.

But here, the world was quiet. So endlessly, blissfully quiet ...

Chapter 26
Secrets

Kael knew he was dreaming again. He knew this because people did not rise up out of the ocean and go flying through the clouds. So if he was flying, if he'd somehow managed to escape the icy clutches of the tempest, he knew it was because he was dreaming. Or perhaps he was dead.

The clouds still belted out rain by the river-full. He passed them, moving through a dark tunnel of gray and ice, but he couldn't feel a thing. The cold didn't burn his nose and the wind didn't lash his cheeks.

Then he wasn't in the sky. He knew this because the sky was above him, and the hard earth was under his back. The rain that struck his face sounded hollow, distant: more like it was striking some roof high above him.

His lungs tightened under a sudden pressure on his chest. Then he felt another pressure, strange and foreign, upon his lips. It happened again, this time sharper and more insistent. He thought he could almost hear the desperation behind the pressure, the far-off cries of someone begging him to come back. He fought against the numbness. He stretched out, reached for the cries —

Air rushed into his lungs. It broke the seal and his chest convulsed as water spurted up and out his mouth.

It all came rushing back: the cold, the stinging rain, the rough earth beneath him, his screaming headache. Someone was pounding him on the back, jarring his aching head with every stroke. He recognized her voice as she cried:

"Breathe, Kael! Breathe!"

And he did. He sucked in a full breath of the biting cold air and swore that nothing had ever tasted sweeter. It burned his lungs, but he didn't care. He rolled over and tried to pull himself up, but his arms collapsed beneath him. His chin hit the ground and he could feel the pain in his head radiating down his spine. He groaned as his body turned over onto his back, urged forward by a pair of impossibly strong hands.

A streak of lightning flicked across the sky, illuminating the worry on her face as she leaned over him. "Kael? Are you all right? For mercy's sake, talk to me!"

"I'm fine, Kyleigh. I'm fine," he said, and the effort nearly cost him his supper. "Ugh ... my head's about to explode."

He closed his eyes against the bright flashes of lightning and felt her hands on either side of his face. She lifted him gently, and he gasped as fire glanced his forehead.

It was a burn the likes of which he'd never felt. Heat blossomed in his cheeks, his stomach — it rushed down and warmed the frozen tips of his toes. The pain in his head was driven back by it, burned away by the flames. He opened his eyes.

Kyleigh was gone, but the warmth in his body lingered. He rolled over on his side and put his arm over his head, trying to block the rain. Soon, the heat was back — and this time it was familiar. Orange light danced behind his eyelids and the smell of burning wood filled the air. Somehow, Kyleigh had managed to get a fire started.

He felt her lay down beside him, felt her arm drape across his chest. He was too exhausted to try and push her away, too cold to mind how her closeness burned him. Sleep was coming fast. "How did you do it?" he muttered. "How did you save me?" He didn't see how it was possible. For all he knew, they were both dead.

Her arm tightened around his chest and she whispered: "A knight never reveals her secrets."

Her breath tickled the back of his neck — sending another wave of heat that picked him up and carried him gently into the realm of dreams.

****

When morning came, Kael had to peel his eyes open. Salt, capped off with a light dusting of gritty sand, crusted over every inch of him. His throat was so dry that he could hardly swallow. He opened his eyes and had to blink several times before the world came back into focus.

A small fire was the first thing he saw. Three rabbits cooked over it, filling the air with the smell of roasting meat. Though the sky was gray, no rain fell. The trees around him were pines — so spiky and tall that for one mad second, he thought he was in the Unforgivable Mountains.

But then he remembered where he was, and all the events of the night came groggily back to him. His face burned to think of how he nearly drowned. Morris would never let him hear the end of it — provided he ever saw Morris again.

A bent strip of bark lay on the ground in front of him. He stretched for it, grimacing as his muscles stung and wincing when his grimace pulled at the tender skin above his left brow. A shallow pool of water glistened in the crook of the bark, and he wasted no time gulping down a mouthful. It was cool and sweet.

He studied his reflection in the water's surface. Even the leviathan would lose its appetite if it saw how bruised his face was. There was a narrow gash that ran through his left eyebrow, and it twinged every time he blinked.

He was trying to decide if he had enough energy to heal it when he saw something move in the reflection behind him. He'd nearly forgotten about Kyleigh. "Are you as covered in salt —?"

Everything: his breath, his question, his heart, caught in his throat. For the enormous beast he was tucked in next to was not Kyleigh at all.

Fear gave him wings. He leapt up and tried to dart away, but his mind moved faster than his legs. He tripped over a log and fell hard on his elbow, cursing as he rolled over and got back on his feet. He was going to sprint into the woods, put as much distance between himself and the monster as possible, when a noise made him stop.

It was low and light. A growl, but not ferocious. And for some reason, it embarrassed him.

He turned slowly to face the beast that lay beside the fire. Its head was a little larger than a horse's, topped with a pair of curved horns. Its body was easily the size of two horses. Long, crooked claws stretched out from each of its four legs. The front two were crossed and digging lazily into the dirt. A spiked tail coiled around its body, and the barbs that stuck out from it looked more than a match for any suit of armor. Enormous wings furled from its back. One was slightly bent over the spot where Kael had been sleeping.

All fear left him, replaced swiftly by a feeling he could only describe as shock: it was a dragon — a *real* dragon.

From the tip of its long snout to the last barb on its tail, the dragon was covered in snow-white scales. The only part that wasn't white was its eyes: they were green ...

No, it couldn't be. But then the dragon turned its enormous head to look at a dagger sticking out of the ground, inches from its front claw. Kael checked his belt to be sure, but there was no denying the knife in the ground was his.

"Kyleigh?"

The dragon — *she*, Kyleigh — inclined her horned head, and her snout bent in what he could only describe as a smirk.

"But ... how?" He closed the space between them quickly. He couldn't help it: he wanted a closer look. "Did the Witch curse you, too?" he guessed, but she shook her head.

He was about to ask another question when she touched her snout to his hand. A picture flashed before his eyes, so sharp and fast that he jerked away.

"What in Kingdom's name was that?" he gasped.

She looked highly annoyed with him. *Give it a moment, and you'll see what it is*, her face clearly said.

In the end, curiosity won out over his worry. He put his hands on either side of her scaly face and braced himself for what he was about to see.

An image rose out of the darkness. He recognized the rocky canyon as Bartholomew's Pass. A wolf monster leapt in front of him — its black eyes boring into his. A flash of white, hot blood spurted up into his face, and the monster lay dead. Then the scene changed: he saw himself leaning over a half-buried wolf, helping to lay the stones.

He was so excited that he took his hands away, breaking their connection. "You're like them. You're a shapechanger, aren't you?"

She inclined her head, her eyes shining warmly. She was pleased that he'd guessed it so quickly.

"Well, I'm not a total idiot." But he was too thrilled to be angry with her.

So *this* was Kyleigh's great secret — the source of her power. And it all made sense: her ability to travel so quickly, her impossible strength ... and her age. Roland told him once that shapechangers lived two lifetimes: their human years, and those of the animal whose shape they took. So if Kyleigh's life was entwined with her dragon life, she could live for thousands of years ...

Mercy's sake, she must be ancient.

"I've never heard of a shapechanger who could take a dragon's form. Are there others like you?"

She shrugged. Then she saw the grin on his face and cocked her head at him.

"Oh, nothing," he said, still smiling. "But I think I might have figured out why we never ran into any bandits in the Valley. You didn't, um, eat them, did you?"

She shook her head. The deep tones of her growl rumbled in his chest and probably would have been terrifying, if he didn't know it for what it was: she was laughing.

Then he thought of something else. It seemed like ages ago that Roland had burst into the hospital, worried over the fact that the monster of Tinnark hadn't taken his sacrifice. And now Kael realized why. "So it was you all along — *you* were the beast that tormented us!" he said accusingly.

She showed her pointed teeth and her rumbling laughter sounded deep inside her chest.

"I used to sleep with the covers over my head because of you. Amos said that if I didn't behave, you'd carry me off in the middle of the night — it isn't funny!" he snapped, as her shoulders shook with the force of her laughter. "I thought you were a bloodthirsty monster from the summit. You might have told us you were just some great silly girl."

She wasn't sorry, not in the least bit. He imagined she must have giggled every time Roland left an offering for her — and eaten it just to humor him.

"Lysander told me you once fought Setheran the Wright. Is that true?"

This staunched her laughter. She nodded once, and it was all he could do to keep from squealing like Aerilyn.

"Will you show me your memories of him? That's what I'm looking at, isn't it?"

She nodded, her face crossed between surprise and annoyance, then bent her head down so he could reach.

This time when the picture flashed, they were back aboard *Anchorgloam*. The waves glistened warmly in the fading light, he could hear cry of gulls in the distance. A man bent over the rails directly in front of him. His thin face was shadowed by his hair — hair that burned as red as the setting sun.

"What have you got there, Seth?" Kyleigh's voice rang inside his head, as if he was speaking her words.

A smile creased his face, lines creased his eyes. He held up the bit of wood he'd been carving and Kael saw it was a deer. The creature was so full of life, so intricately detailed with every tuft of hair and every point of its horns standing tall, that he almost expected it to leap out of Setheran's hand and go galloping across the deck.

"Do you think he'll like it?" Setheran asked. He had a deep, rumbling voice — one that didn't quite match his lithe frame.

"I can't imagine any child not liking that," Kyleigh replied.

This made him smile again. "I hope you're right." Then he held the deer out to her. "Take this for a moment, will you?

I've got to clean up the shavings before Matteo sees."

"Yes, we wouldn't want that. He'd likely get his breeches in such a knot —"

Black. A burst of light. Rain struck his face, wind ripped at his wings. He crashed through the ocean's surface and it hurt, but he didn't care. He saw his own body lying cold and lifeless in the mud. A terrible fear tore at his throat and choked him with un-fallen tears. His lips were blue and parted, his chest didn't rise.

Then breath came back to him. He watched himself double over and cough up the ocean, and relief struck him like a wave. It welled up and spilt out his eyes — just as another feeling burst from the very center of his chest.

It engulfed him, consumed him. It raged like a tunnel of fire: burning deeper and more dangerous than the sea. Though it threatened to drag him down and under, he found he didn't care. Let the waves come! Let the rain fall! He would lose himself to this storm, purge his soul in the flames. Let it take him —

Kael ripped his hands away and fell onto his back. He struck the ground and gasped as tears poured down his face. Where on earth had they come from? He dashed them away with his sleeve. "What *was* that?"

She said nothing. She wouldn't even look at him.

Whatever lurked inside her head had grabbed him and wrung him out like a wet cloth. His legs shook as he got to his feet. "Were those your ... *feelings* —?"

"Kael! Kyleigh!"

A chorus of three voices rang out from the trees, followed by three people. Thelred popped out first, turned around and bellowed: "Found them! They're over here." He didn't seem at all surprised by the fact that Kyleigh was now a large white dragon.

Lysander was next to appear. His right eye was swollen almost shut and ringed by a nasty, purplish bruise. He walked stiffly — his back arched away from the blade Aerilyn had digging into it.

"There, we've found them," he grouched. "Now will

you kindly release me?"

But Aerilyn wasn't paying any attention to him. Her eyes found Kael and she gasped in relief. She dropped the sword and flung herself into his arms, smacking him in the back with the bag she had clutched in her hand. "Oh Kael! I'm so happy you're alive. So very, *very* happy!" she said, her tears wetting his neck. "I thought you were gone for good. And then Kyleigh leapt in after you, and I thought I'd lost you both — where is she, by the way? I've got her armor."

Kael turned her by the shoulders and she froze when she saw the white dragon smirking at her. She clamped a hand down on Kael's wrist, looked the dragon over once, and finally squeaked: "Kyleigh?"

She barely had a chance to nod before Aerilyn grabbed her around her long neck.

"Why didn't you tell me you were a, um ...?"

"A shapechanger, more generally. And a halfdragon, specifically," Lysander said. He tried to smirk, but ended up wincing instead.

Aerilyn's arms fell limply back to her side. "A shapechanger?" She cleared her throat. "Well, it doesn't matter. All that matters is that you're my friend. And on that note — how *dare* you." She jabbed a finger in Kyleigh's face — a gesture made much less threatening by the fact that she had to point so far upwards. "How could you just go leaping off the ship like that? You might have told me you could sprout wings and fly! But no, you disappeared without a word and left us with naught but a pile of clothes, all slashed to ribbons—"

"Your clothes?" Kael sputtered. His face burned when he realized what that meant, and Kyleigh's laughter started up again.

"It's not funny," Aerilyn scolded. "It isn't ladylike to go frolicking naked in the woods."

"Would you stop squawking and help her get dressed?" Thelred grumbled. "We've got too little time as it is."

Aerilyn shot him an icy look. "Come along, Kyleigh,"

she said haughtily. And they disappeared into the trees.

Thelred carried Kael's bow and quiver across his back. He pulled them off, thrust them impatiently into Kael's hands, and went to carve up the rabbits.

While Thelred got their breakfast ready, Lysander fussed over his eye. He touched it gingerly, wincing. Then he muttered a string of curses and snatched the discarded cutlass off the ground. "Women," he said, thrusting the weapon into the sheath at his belt. "You can't hold a man hostage with his own sword. It's completely against the rules."

Kael was sure he deserved whatever he got. "What did you do?"

Though he made a great show of scowling, a reluctant smile pulled at Lysander's lips. "When we anchored in Copperdock, I promised to search for you the best I could. But your forest friends were determined to come ashore. For some reason, I don't think they trusted me," he mused. "Anyways, I told them they couldn't come. And then Jonathan tried to mutiny, so I had to throw him in the brig."

"You did *what?*" His words came out in a growl that made Lysander take a hasty step back.

"Don't worry: he'll have plenty of food. And I've told Morris to keep an eye on him," he said quickly. "Jonathan made a scene, but Aerilyn was smarter. I was heading to the deck when she ambushed me — socked me in the eye, disarmed me and threatened me with my own sword." At this point, Lysander was grinning to either ear. "She paraded me in front of my men and straight down to the docks. I can't imagine the sort of ridicule I'll have to endure when I get back ... but," he touched a finger to his swollen eye, "I think this means she likes me."

Kael was about to tell him how very wrong he was when Kyleigh returned. She strode into the clearing, fully armed in black and with Aerilyn close behind. "Let me see." She took Lysander under the chin and turned his head to the side. "Nicely done," she said approvingly. "Though in the future, try to aim for the nose. It's a great deal more painful."

"Don't encourage her," Lysander said, batting her hand away. When the girls left to get their share of the rabbits, he leaned towards Kael and whispered: "What did I tell you, eh? If she didn't like me, she would've swung for my nose!"

Chapter 27
Battlemage Jake

Shortly after breakfast, Lysander informed them that he'd given the crew permission to sail off at sunset. "If we haven't returned by then, they'll just assume we're dead. So obviously, time is of the essence."

Obviously, Lysander had no concept of geography. Because by the time they made it into Copperdock, it was almost noon. They could see the spindly towers of Wendelgrimm perched high on a cliff above town, leering over the rough stone houses like a vulture over corpses. Kael wagered it would take them at least another hour to make the climb, and then they'd still have to face the Witch.

And he had no idea how long that would take.

Copperdock turned out to be an awful lot like Crow's Cross — with its winding streets and houses crammed end to end. The only real difference he could see was the complete lack of people. Small gardens stood overgrown and abandoned in front of their houses. Wagons stopped in the street, almost in mid-roll. Tattered laundry hung dirty and forgotten on sagging lines.

He imagined the people must have fled in quite a hurry. Once they lost their protectors, there would have been no one to stop the Witch from swooping down and gobbling them up.

He was trying to peer through the dusty windows of an old shop when he tripped over something lying in the road. A glass bowl rolled out from under his feet, sloshing half of its water and a small fish onto the cobblestone. The poor thing flopped helplessly until Kael managed to scoop it up and drop it back into the bowl.

"Watch where you're going," Thelred said.

Kael glared at him. "How could I know there'd be a fish bowl out in the middle of the road?"

"It's not like they had a choice," Lysander said. "The villagers are stuck exactly where they were when the Witch cursed them."

Aerilyn looked horrified. She glanced at two bowls perched on a wagon seat. "You mean these fish are ... people?"

Lysander nodded grimly. "It's awful, I know. But that's precisely why it's so important that the Witch be stopped. Her death would not only free me, but the good people of Copperdock, as well."

Kael couldn't believe the fish were really people. He knelt down next to the bowl and stuck his nose to the glass. The fish swam up to him and stared back with watery eyes. It turned to the side, and that's when he noticed how very strange its markings were. The coloring of its scales made the fish look as if it was wearing trousers with suspenders, and sporting a set of thick sideburns on either side of its face. Perhaps it really *was* a man trapped in a fish's body.

"Don't worry, I'm going to kill the Witch," Kael said quietly.

The fish blinked in reply.

"And sorry for ... knocking you over like that," he added as he got to his feet, just in case the fish could understand him.

The others had moved on down the road, but Kyleigh stayed back. She must have heard his conversation with the fish, because she smiled and said: "That was kind of you."

He couldn't tell if she was heckling him or not, but to be safe he grumbled: "Leave off." And stomped past her.

****

The climb to Wendelgrimm was steeper than they'd been expecting. The winding dirt road was long overgrown. Years of neglect invited thorns, which snaked out from the stone and latched onto their breeches whenever they could.

Some parts of the path were nearly crumbled away, leaving only a thin ledge between them and a dizzying drop into the violent ocean below.

Kael was used to steep climbing. The most annoying thing about it all was the fact that the road twisted so much. With every bend they came to, he could feel another handful of minutes slip away. He tried not to worry about the time and instead listened to the belabored breathing of his companions.

It gave him some satisfaction to see how Lysander and Thelred struggled with the climb. He thought it was good for them to get a little sweat on their brows. Aerilyn panted like a dog, but kept her chin stubbornly in the air. And then there was Kyleigh.

He thought, if he tilted his head just right, that he might be able to see a drop of sweat glistening on her brow. Other than that, her face was calm. Pleasant, even. Just to look at her, he might have thought they were going for a stroll through the woods — not climbing to what might very well be their deaths.

They'd made it a little more than halfway up when Lysander suddenly came to a halt. He drew his cutlass and held his hand taut, signaling for them to stop.

"What is it?" Aerilyn asked. She had an arrow drawn and ready to fire. Kael was proud of how steady her hands were.

He leaned around Thelred and saw someone standing out in the middle of the road. He wore plainclothes and had a staff gripped in one hand. From such a distance, he couldn't tell if the man was facing them, or had his back turned.

"A spy," Lysander said out the side of his mouth. "The Witch has posted a guard to thwart us. We'd better kill him quickly."

Kyleigh stepped up behind him and peered over his shoulder. "That's a statue, Sandy."

"What?"

311

She picked a rock up off the ground and hurled it at the figure. It ricocheted off his head with a sharp *thwap* and sailed into the ocean.

Lysander cleared his throat. "Well how was I supposed to see that? Not all of us can have dragon's eyes," he mumbled. "All right, pressing on."

They were nearly to the statue when a breeze swept in from the ocean. It blew past the figure and directly into Kael's face, carrying with it a stench that burned his nose ... and made him itch.

"Magic!" he said, but not soon enough.

The statue cracked down the middle and blasted into a thousand pieces. Kael put his arm over his head, trying to shield his eyes from the sharp bits of rock that stung his body. As the stone fell away, a man stepped out from the rubble.

He had a thin face and a long nose — hardly the look of a killer. And yet the eyes behind his round spectacles were cold and unfeeling. He raised his staff over his head and shouted sômething unintelligible, then brought it down with a roar.

It struck the ground, and the road in front of them cracked. It split from the cliff side and broke away, tumbling down into the waves below. Thelred managed to leap to the other side while the rest of them dove back the way they came. Kael heard Aerilyn scream and spun around in time to see her lose her footing. She was falling backwards, arms waving frantically as she tried to regain her balance, and he couldn't get there fast enough to save her.

But Lysander could.

He dove and landed on his belly, grabbing Aerilyn's hands just before the fall could take her. They froze like that for a moment, with his arms shaking as he held her over thin air. Then the weight of her body began to drag him over.

He dug the toes of his boots into the ground, sliding helplessly towards certain death as he tried to find something to latch onto. "Don't worry — I won't let go!" he said.

"Well you should!" Aerilyn's voice shrilled from over the edge. "If you don't let go, we'll both die!"

"Never!"

He was almost halfway off the cliff when Kael grabbed him by the legs. It wasn't the best plan: the rocks were slippery and when he tried to get his feet situated, he lost his concentration. In that split second of distraction, he lost his mind's strength — and the weight of two bodies dragged him to the edge.

He was preparing himself for the fall when Kyleigh's arms wrapped around his waist in an iron hold. With one mighty step backwards, she dragged them all a foot towards safety.

Across the rift, Thelred stepped in front of the mage and raised his cutlass to strike. A spell hit him in the chest and he fell over with a grunt. Kael thought he was dead at first, then he moved. He got back on his feet, but couldn't seem to lift his sword off the ground. He jerked madly, trying to wrench it free.

"Just let go!" Lysander snapped at him, his voice a little strained from being stretched out so far between Kael and Aerilyn.

"I can't," he shouted back. "My hand's glued to the hilt!"

Lysander's cry caught the mage's attention. He looked up at them, saw the plight they were in, and sneered.

"Kael, you have to shoot him," Kyleigh said in his ear. "You have to shoot him now!"

"I can't! If I let go, the others will fall."

"Let me take care of them," she said quickly as the mage raised his staff. "Take your shot! Move!"

The staff was pointed in their direction, aimed for Kyleigh. Strange, muffled words were already on the mage's lips. In a second, the spell would come whistling for them. It would strike Kyleigh in the chest and send them all to their deaths.

Kael decided quickly. He let go of Lysander's legs, leapt to the side, whipped out an arrow and drew it to his

313

chin. Blue light had gathered at the end of the mage's staff when Kael's arrow struck his shoulder. The blow knocked his aim to the side and his spell struck the cliff beneath them. Dirt and pebbles exploded out as huge slabs of rock crumbled off the cliff and crashed into the ocean with a spew of foam.

Dark red blood spurted out from the mage's wound. He collapsed on the ground and clutched the arrow with a shaking hand. The stench coming from his blood was incredible. It burned Kael's nose and made anger pulse at the backs of his eyes. Rage billowed up from the soles of his feet, climbing higher and higher until it consumed him.

He forgot about his friends, forgot about the Witch and all the danger they were in. He must stop that blood. He must rip the mage's heart out of his chest and hurl it into the deepest part of the sea!

"Stop it!" Kyleigh's voice was in his head, warring with his anger. He hardly felt it when she pinned him on the ground. "Stop hitting him! Can't you see the man's begging for his life?"

It was the shock behind her words that brought him back. The second he stopped fighting, the full weight of Kyleigh's body nearly crushed him. She had to roll away to keep from breaking his every bone.

"Were you trying to kill me?" he shouted when he had air in his lungs again. "Why would you do that?"

"I'm sorry, but it was the only way I could get you to stop."

"Stop *what*?"

She pointed behind him, and he couldn't help but notice the slight tremble in her hand. "That."

He wrenched his head around and saw the mage lying in the dirt, spread-eagle and unmoving. His face was covered in blood. He coughed, and red drops went spraying everywhere. "Couldn't help ... couldn't stop," he moaned, his head lolling from side to side.

Kael looked up and saw Thelred, still hunched over and bound by his sword, staring at him in shock. Across the rift, Lysander and Aerilyn sat safely in the middle of the road. Their eyes were on him and their mouths hung open.

That's when he looked down and saw the blood on his knuckles … and he realized what he'd done.

"They say the whisperers hunt mages like the shark hunts blood," Thelred said, his eyes still wide. "But I never believed it … until now."

"It's in your nature," Kyleigh said to Kael, placing a steady hand on his shoulder. "Whisperers hate magic, and the blood of a mage is magic in its rawest form." Her grip on his shoulder tightened. "You controlled your anger well."

Kael heard himself make a sound that was halfway between scorn and disgust. "I pummeled a man for no reason."

She smiled softly. "I've seen full-grown whisperers, men much older who should know better, fly into a rage and tear mages limb from bloody limb. For as young and powerful as you are, believe me when I say that you controlled yourself well."

He still didn't think she was right. But then the mage groaned again, and he forgot about arguing with her. He crawled over and tried not to breathe as he inspected the damage. The arrow needed to come out, that much was certain. The rest of his wounds were mainly on his face: a busted lip, broken nose and an eyebrow split neatly down the middle.

He grabbed onto the arrow and was preparing to break it in half when the mage's hand clamped down on his. "Please," he said thickly. He held his arm up to Kael's face and he saw a rusty iron shackle clasped around his wrist. "I know our people are enemies, whisperer. But I beg you — free me."

Kael was going to ask him what he was talking about when he noticed something odd: a thin, milky white film covered the shackle's surface. He touched it, and it felt sticky.

"A spell?" he asked, and the mage nodded. "If I release you, how do I know you won't just attack us again?"

The mage turned his wrist in reply, so that Kael could see the symbol stamped into the metal. It was a sea serpent being pierced in the tail by a harpoon — the symbol of the High Seas.

"I've never been my own man. The Duke captured me when I was a child and had his court wizard bind me by this spell. You might say I was raised in captivity." He tried to take a breath and coughed as blood ran into his mouth. "Gah ... I served unwillingly as a battlemage on one of the Duke's trade ships until we ran aground here. Then the Witch, she's kept me in that stone prison for three years." He brushed an impatient sleeve across his mouth and gripped Kael's arm. "Please, the pain clears my head for a moment, but I can already feel the madness creeping back in. The voices are trying to take me. Break the spell, whisperer, and I'll be forever in your debt."

Kael didn't want that, not at all. He already had a halfdragon following him around because he'd saved her life. But when he met the mage's eyes, he saw the cold edge was gone from them. They were clear blue and intelligent, even kind. Though he still smelled horrible, it was obvious the mage meant them no harm.

Kael turned his head to the side to get another breath of fresh air before he went to work. He dug his fingernail into the white film, and it broke. After that, it was simply a matter of peeling the spell off — one milky strip at a time. When the film was gone, he put his fingers between the shackle and the mage's skin and thought:

It isn't iron — it's only a piece of parchment. The iron changed to paper in his hands. He tore the shackle clean in two and tossed it aside.

The mage gasped in relief. "Thank you —"

"Yeah, all right," Kael said quickly. "Just hold still while I patch you up."

The mage picked up his now slightly-bent spectacles and placed them gingerly on the end of his long nose. "Do you mind if I watch? I've never seen a whisperer at work before, but I hear from the older mages that it's quite a sight."

"Sure," Kael said. "Just as long as you hold still."

It didn't take him long to close the mage's wounds or set his nose straight. After everything Morris made him do, healing came back to him easily. The worst part about it was how horribly his blood itched: Kael had to rub dirt on his hands to keep from scratching his palms off. The mage went on about how amazing it was to see a whisperer heal until Thelred very grumpily said:

"Yes, we're all excited for you. But if I have to stay bent over like this for another second, I might rip my own arm off — and then I'm coming after you with the other one, mage."

"Ah, yes. Sorry about that," he said, getting quickly to his feet. He picked his staff up and cleared his throat. "I know what you're thinking: it's embarrassing for a full-grown mage to still be carrying around a child's impetus. But I was never allowed to make my own."

Kael didn't understand three words of that. But Kyleigh explained. "An impetus is the object a mage uses to channel his magic. And I'm no expert, but I think a smaller impetus is a sign of a more powerful mage."

"Yes, because it takes a great deal of skill to link spells tight enough to fit into something as small as, say, a ring," the mage said. He touched his staff to Thelred — who went toppling backwards as the spell suddenly released them. "A long time ago, a wizard made the mistake of toying with Fate. So great was her ire that she separated our souls from our magic. Now we must be content with scribbling them onto things and casting like that."

Kael had never heard that story before, but he wouldn't let the mage think he was interested in it. He moved behind Kyleigh — just incase. If the anger took him again, she was the only one who could stop him.

Lysander and Aerilyn were making their way over the rift, edging across the narrow ledge left by the mage's spell. Lysander kept trying to take her hand, and she kept batting him away. "I'm quite capable of walking on my own," she snapped.

"I'm only trying to help, my dear. Let me be a steady hand to you."

"I'm not your *dear*. And you'd do well to keep your steady hand away from my rump," she said, smacking him away again.

"Don't be preposterous." Lysander sounded hurt. But when he looked up, Kael saw he was trying to hide a grin.

The mage offered his staff to Aerilyn, and pulled her over the last bit. Then he helped Lysander. "Thank you," Aerilyn said to him. She pushed by Lysander, tossing her hair rather primly as she went.

He ignored her, and held out his hand to the mage. "Thank you ... uh?"

"Jacob," the mage supplied.

"Well I thank you, Battlemage Jake," Lysander said with a toothy smile, and shook his hand so hard that the poor man's spectacles nearly slid off his nose. "We'd love to stay and chat, but I'm afraid we've got some Witch-slaying to do." He stepped to the side and clapped his hands together sharply. "Come along, lords and ladies. We don't have time to waste —"

"Wait a moment," Jake said.

Lysander stopped. He turned around, eyebrows raised. "Yes?"

Jake pushed his spectacles back up his nose and clutched his staff nervously. "I was just — I was wondering if I might come with you, seeing as how it was the Witch who held me prisoner for so long. I'd like to help."

"You want revenge?"

"Yes," Jake said firmly. The knuckles clamped around his staff went white.

Lysander sauntered over to him, tapping his chin. "Interesting ... but I'm afraid I run a tight ship. I can't let just anyone join."

"But I'm a mage," Jake said. "I'll bet you don't have one like me in your crew."

Lysander looked surprised, like he hadn't thought of it before. "True. I suppose you could be useful. But you should also know that we're all pirates."

"Not all of us," Aerilyn interjected.

"Right. Some of us are stubborn-arsed merchants," Lysander said, and grinned when she gasped indignantly. "The point is that we aren't exactly on good terms with the Kingdom. Sail with us, and you might never see decent society again."

Jake didn't seem at all put off. In fact, he stood a little straighter. "That's well with me, Captain. I've got no love for the Kingdom."

Lysander held out his hand again, and this time when Jake took it, he said: "Welcome to the crew, dog."

Chapter 28
The Witch of Wendelgrimm

At long last, they reached the top of the cliff. Up close, Wendelgrimm castle looked like little more than a crumbling pile of rocks. Three of its towers reeled like they'd been hit by a strong wind and never quite recovered. The fourth tower stood tall, but had a hole in its roof large enough for a dragon to land in. Vines took over what was left of it.

Blood-red flowers sprouted up from their stems and nearly covered the outer walls. The sharp tang of magic seeping off their petals was enough to make Kael take a step back.

"Don't let those vines touch you," Jake warned. "If you get too close, they'll reach out and strangle you."

"How enchanting," Aerilyn muttered.

The only part of the castle that wasn't covered in vines was the entrance. A pair of wooden doors filled the archway of the castle's outer wall, and they didn't look particularly sturdy: large patches were simply rotted through.

"Well, this shouldn't be difficult," Lysander said. Then, with a glance at Aerilyn, he marched straight for the doors. "There's not a plank on this whole thing that could withstand a blow from my boot."

He was preparing to kick it in when Jake said: "I wouldn't —"

Lysander's boot struck the wall and his whole leg bounced off of it. His knee snapped back and hit him squarely in the chin, knocking him onto his rump. It was easily the most ridiculous injury Kael had ever witnessed.

"You could've warned us sooner, mage," Thelred snapped as he bent over his cousin.

"Am I missing a tooth?" Lysander said, pulling his lip down in a panic.

"No, they're all there," Thelred assured him.

"It's nothing dangerous, just a simple warding spell — one designed to keep would-be intruders out," Jake said. He walked up to the doors and studied them for a moment. "All right, maybe it isn't a *simple* one."

"How are we going to get through?" Aerilyn said. She glanced over her shoulder in the direction of the falling sun. "Kyleigh, can't you fly back and tell the others to wait?"

She snorted. "And leave you lot here to fend for yourselves? I think not. Besides, most of the crew isn't exactly aware of my, ah, less attractive half. I wouldn't want to start a panic by soaring around in broad daylight."

Jake looked at them curiously, but seemed to think better of asking Kyleigh to explain. Instead, he turned back to the doors. "I could try to figure out a counterspell. I'm sure it would be quite simple ... if only I knew the language it was written in."

"Perfect. I've found the Kingdom's one illiterate mage," Lysander grumbled as he got to his feet. "Can't you read your own language?"

Jake smiled wryly. "It's more complicated than that. There are several dialects, depending on what material you use for your impetus. Wood," he held up his staff, "is the most basic. Silver is the most temperamental but gold, by far, gives you the most power. Unfortunately, few have discovered how to make spells stick to gold — and of course they guard the secret jealously." He frowned, and his lip curled slightly. "Only the slimiest mages use leather ... they're naught but common warlocks, if you want my opinion. Iron and steel are the choice of necromancers and rogue practitioners: people like the Witch of Wendelgrimm."

"Yes, I see ... so what you're saying is you can't get through it," Lysander said.

Aerilyn made a frustrated sound. "No, that isn't what he said at all — he *could* figure it out, but because the Witch

321

uses steel instead of wood, he's having a hard time reading it. Honestly, don't you listen?"

"Ah ... wait a moment." Lysander's eyes went suddenly wide. "What sort of steel does she use? Have you seen it?"

Jake shrugged. "Sure, but it just looked like a rusty old cutlass to me."

Lysander hung his head. "That's it, then. We're done. We might as well head back the way we came —"

"Why?" Kael said. He wasn't about to come this far just to turn around and march back empty-handed.

"Because, my dear boy," he said with over-exaggerated patience, "the Witch is in possession of Gravy's Lass, which means she can't be beaten. If we face her now, we might as well just slit our own throats —"

"No, she can definitely be beaten," Kael insisted, which made Lysander stop.

"Oh? And how do you figure that?"

He thought quickly. "Because Sam Gravy was the father of all pirates, wasn't he?"

Lysander put a reverent hand over his heart. "Aye, he was."

"And you wouldn't want anybody but a pirate to use your ship, would you?"

"I daresay I wouldn't. And he better be a blasted good pirate, at that."

"Well, I don't think the Lass would work for anyone who wasn't a pirate."

Lysander was beginning to realize, slowly, where all this was headed. Understanding crept across his face. "Go on."

Kael sighed and tried to keep the impatience out of his voice. "Sam Gravy wouldn't want his Lass falling into the hands of just anyone — he'd want a pirate to inherit it, a blasted good one. And he'd have been powerful enough to make sure of it."

It was an outright lie, but a necessary one. He didn't believe there was any sword that could grant its wielder the ability to win every battle, and he wasn't going to let a myth scare Lysander off. The people of Copperdock deserved to be fought for ... even if it was a losing battle.

"You're right, of course. You're absolutely right," Lysander said, now thoroughly convinced. "The Witch doesn't deserve Gravy's sword — the Lass will be on *our* side! We can't possibly lose. Now all we have to do is find a way into the castle."

"I have an idea," Kael said. He stepped up to the doors, and this time he knew what he was looking for. Yes, if he squinted a bit, he could see the milky white spell that covered them. He dug into it with the nails of both hands and wrenched a large, slimy chunk of it off, just enough for them to get through.

"Well done," Kyleigh said. And with one powerful kick, she broke through the planks.

They walked into a courtyard that looked as if it had been the stage for many battles. The ground was beaten and craggy, the grass was brown and dry. Huge boulders jutted out of the yard in odd places. Kael realized it was because they'd been flung over by catapults. In fact, he could match the chinks in the wall to the shapes of some of the boulders.

"We aren't the only ones to try and defeat the Witch," Thelred murmured. "Whole armies have marched on Wendelgrimm ... never to be seen or heard from again."

Oddly enough, his story didn't do much to steady Kael's nerves. Though it *did* convince him to get an arrow drawn and ready.

They were in the precise middle of the courtyard when the castle doors flung open. They slammed against the wall, and a wrinkly old crone hobbled out from between them. "What's the meaning of this?" she shrieked. "I'll not have a ragtag bunch of travelers tromping through me courtyard — *you!*" She stabbed a boney finger at Jake. "Why ain't you where I left you?"

"Because he's been freed, Witch," Lysander said.

Kael groaned aloud. *This* was the dreaded Witch of Wendelgrimm? This hag with more wrinkles than the backside of his trousers? He wanted to kick Lysander for dragging him through the tempest to fight an old woman. It was a waste of a perfectly good arrow.

The Witch's dark eyes locked onto Lysander. Then her mouth cracked open and she bared all three of her yellow teeth in a snarling grin. "Why hello, Captain. Come to keep an old witch company?"

He made a face. "Not hardly. My friends and I are here to kill you — to free the good people of Copperdock and reclaim stolen property!"

"Stolen property?" Her snarl widened. "You wouldn't mean this, now would you?" She drew a cutlass from the folds of her tattered robes. The blade was plain steel with chinks all along the edge of it. The hilt looked as if it had been whittled by a child and set by a blind man.

But Lysander gasped at the sight of it. "That belongs in the hands of a proper pirate! Hand it over —"

"Or what?" she hissed. She spun the sword by its hilt — an impressive move for someone so ancient. "Sorry, Captain, but the Lass belongs to me. And now, so do you."

She cut the blade across her chest and black chains shot out of the ground in front of them. They wrapped around their limbs, pinning them where they stood. Kael watched his companions grunt and struggle, but even Kyleigh couldn't wiggle free. When Jake tried to mutter a spell, a length of chain shot up and slapped him across the face, knocking his spectacles askew.

"Now, then," the Witch said lazily. "The twiggy battlemage will go back to guarding me path, and I think I'll keep the handsome captain for company."

"Nev — mpft!" A chain stuffed itself in Lysander's mouth, silencing him mid-protest.

"As for the rest of you ... fish!" She cackled evilly, throwing her head back and whipping her tattered robes about her.

Kael chose that moment to step out of his chains. He pulled them off, cringing as the slimy bits stuck to his palms. By the time the Witch stopped cackling, he had an arrow trained on her heart.

"No!" she shrieked, her eyes wide with fear. "It ain't possible, your kind are all dead!"

Lysander laughed through the chains in his mouth and said something to the effect of: "Meet your doom!"

But the Witch wasn't going to give up so easily. Kael was a breath from loosing his arrow when she jabbed her sword at Kyleigh — who grunted as her neck bent involuntarily backwards. "Let go of that string, and I swear I'll slit her throat," the Witch hissed. "I'll do it, even if it's the last spell I ever cast."

"Don't —" Chains wrapped around Kyleigh's mouth, snuffing out whatever she'd been about to say. She redoubled her efforts, squirming and railing on through the gag.

"Go ahead — shoot me. At least I'll get to watch the blood drain out of her pretty little face before I go," the Witch taunted. She was studying him, her bottomless eyes digging into every line of his features, trying to find a weakness.

And she found it in abundance.

He couldn't hide the cold that suddenly sunk into his limbs and made them tremble. He tore his eyes away from his mark and focused them on Kyleigh's neck. He could see the vein throbbing below her chin. It made him weak to think that vein might stop throbbing, that her heart might stop beating. It terrified him.

But the Witch never intended to kill her: it was a feint. The second Kael lost his concentration, she sent a spell screaming for him. It struck his bow and he felt the weapon tremble, shudder, just before it burst into a thousand pieces. He was left holding only a jagged remnant of the grip: the wind swept the rest of it out to sea, taking everything left of Tinnark with it.

"Kael, you have to free us!" Aerilyn screamed at him.

He looked up in time to see the Witch drive the Lass into the ground. Green fire spurted up from the earth and covered her in a protective ball. It raced around the courtyard, catching onto the walls and trapping them in a circle of flames. Then the ground began to shake. It tossed and rolled so violently that he had to dive to make it to Jake.

He stuffed the splintered remnant of Roland's bow into his pocket and then ripped the chains off of Jake. Together, they freed the others.

"What were you thinking?" Kyleigh said when he tore the bindings from her mouth. "Why didn't you shoot her? You could have killed her before she even had a chance to cast!"

He glared and ripped the rest of the chains off. "I don't know — I got distracted, I suppose! It was more than a little nerve —"

She clamped a hand over his mouth. "Do you hear that?"

No, he didn't hear anything. The fire still burned around them, but the ground had stopped shaking. It was eerily quiet.

"Circle! Form a circle!" Lysander bellowed, and they leapt to obey.

They stood in silence for a long moment, their weapons facing out into the courtyard and their breath coming in quick gasps. Every hair on the back of Kael's neck stood on end. He gripped his hunting dagger and steeled himself for whatever trick the Witch had in store. Then a loud noise in the center of their circle made him spin around.

Dust and bits of earth flew skywards as a skeletal arm burst out of the ground. It clawed itself free by the sharp tips of its fingers and Aerilyn screamed when it reared its horrible, grinning head.

Kyleigh stepped forward and kicked the skull off its shoulders. It went sailing to the other side of the courtyard, but the body kept moving.

"Let's see how you fair against the cold edge of steel, whisperer!" the Witch cackled.

At her words, the courtyard erupted. Bony limbs sprouted from the ground, clawing for fresh air as they pulled their bodies out of the earth. Skeletons climbed out of the rubble. They wielded rusty swords and wore ancient suits of armor that screeched when they moved. And Kael thought he might have figured out where all of those lost armies wound up.

Kyleigh hacked the skeleton in the middle of the circle to bits, then thrust Harbinger into his hands. "Treat him well!" she said.

He watched her charge headlong towards the first wave of skeletons and held his breath. She leapt up and kicked off one of the boulders, launching herself above the fray. Wings sprouted from her back, her arms grew long and dagger-like claws curved out from her hands. By the time she landed — crushing a good number of skeletons beneath her — she was the white dragon once again.

She opened her mouth, and a river of yellow flame spewed out. The fire struck a line of soldiers, reducing them to a charred, twisted pile of bones and steel. Even from where he stood, Kael could feel the heat rising up from the smoldering earth.

"No!" the Witch cried. Kyleigh shot up into the clouds, narrowly missing the Witch's spell. It struck a group of skeletons behind her, and they crumbled to ash.

"It's no good, my arrows aren't doing anything!" Aerilyn wailed. She fired a shot that rattled harmlessly inside a skeleton's ribcage before falling out onto the ground.

"Here!" Jake tapped her quiver with his staff, and the fletching of her arrows turned a bright, dangerous red. "That should do the trick."

The next shot she fired hit a pack of soldiers and exploded. Kael's ears rang with the noise and it knocked the rest of his companions off their feet. Lysander clamped his hands over his ears and glared as bits of charred bone bounced off his head. "Try aiming further away, will you?" he shouted at Aerilyn. "If I must die today, I'd rather be buried in something a little larger than a stocking!"

Between Aerilyn's explosions and Jake's spells, they were able to keep the skeletons at bay. When Aerilyn ran out of arrows, Kael gave her his. The second they hit the bottom of her quiver, their fletching turned red.

Any stray soldiers that managed to make it to their circle they had to fight off with swords. Lysander and Thelred worked together, hacking skeletons to bits. The first time he

327

swung Harbinger, Kael thought he'd missed. The blade was so sharp that it cleaved through bone and armor with hardly any force. As the sword shrilled in delight, he felt a wave of fresh energy wash over him. He felt like he could have chopped skeletons for a fortnight without breaking a sweat.

Kyleigh dipped down when she could: spewing fire for a couple of seconds before she had to dart back into the clouds. The Witch sent spell after spell in her direction, but none found their mark.

They held their ground for several long minutes before the battle took a turn against them. "I've run out of arrows!" Aerilyn said. And without her explosions keeping them back, a great horde of soldiers swarmed to fill the gap.

Sweat lathered Jake's brow. His teeth were gritted down and he had to push his spectacles up his nose more and more often. Kael didn't know how much longer he would last.

He knew he must do something, because if he didn't, the Witch's grisly army would overtake them. They would chop them into tiny bits with their rusty swords and grin the whole way back to their graves. Something must be done, and quickly.

"Here!" He shoved Harbinger into Aerilyn's hands and found a likely looking boulder. It was only a few yards away, and he wagered it stood tall enough to buy him some time. "Jake, clear me a path to that rock!"

He didn't ask why, he just turned and sent a ball of wind blasting through the soldiers. Kael sprinted down the path it made and scrambled arm over leg to the top of the boulder. He raised his fist high over his head and yelled: "Kyleigh!"

The Witch heard him. He saw her horribly wrinkled face go white behind her ball of flame. "Stop him! Stop the whisperer!"

The courtyard went silent — then came the sound of a thousand skulls as they ground against their bony necks, fixing him with the dark of their empty sockets. Kael stood with his arm raised high even as the first skeleton climbed the boulder. His friends fought to get to him, slashing frantically through the wall of bones, but he knew they wouldn't reach him in time.

There was only one hope for him now.

"Kyleigh!" he said again as the first soldier reached him. It stood on its wobbly legs and the plates of its filthy armor screeched as it raised its sword. Kael imagined death by a dull blade would hurt much more than death by a sharp one. It might take several swipes to cleave his head. He closed his eyes as the skeleton's arm dropped, preparing for the pain.

Claws wrapped around his arm and he tensed as Kyleigh jerked him upwards. They left the courtyard behind, left the skeletons clawing over one another and left the Witch cursing. He watched until the clouds swept under his boots, hiding the world from view.

"It's about time!" he shouted at Kyleigh, who roared in reply.

Her voice made his lungs rattle inside their cage. She squeezed his arm tightly and an image of the Witch struck him, hard and fast. He realized what she was trying to say.

"Right, I have a plan." He sent her a very detailed picture of what he wanted her to do, playing it out for her exactly as he imagined it. Then she sent him a reply, one in which she showed what would happen — in gruesome detail — if she missed. "I don't want to think about that," he said quickly. "We have to save the others, and we haven't got time to waste. Now fly!"

She turned sharply and the next thing he knew, they were falling.

He left his stomach far behind — somewhere safely above the clouds. He curled his toes and gripped his hunting dagger so tightly that he thought he might break his own hand. They dove into the courtyard and she jerked to the side as the Witch hurled a spell. Red, blue, black flashes of light whooshed past them as Kyleigh dodged spell after spell, careening dangerously for the ball of fire. He could hear the Witch's screams rising in panic. They were so close that he could almost see the terror on her wrinkly face.

Then, at the very last moment, Kyleigh shot up. His arm slipped out from her claw and he fell through the fire, hot blood pulsing in his every vein. The flames lapped at him, but could not burn. His legs kicked out and he held the dagger high over his head, waiting for the blink of time when he'd break through the fire and have a clear shot. When that moment came and he saw the look on the Witch's face, he knew he'd won.

Fear ringed her eyes — so sharp and white that it couldn't have been anything else. Her mouth gaped open and the folds of skin hanging off her neck trembled from a scream he couldn't hear. She was a rabbit stuck in a trap; a beast so clever and quick that she thought this day would never come. But now it had, and she was letting out a scream she'd been holding back for centuries:

Her last.

Kael's dagger struck her heart, sinking into her flesh and stopping at the hilt. He let go, and it took every ounce of his remaining strength to fall correctly. He hit the stone and rolled until he hit the wall. Sharp pain pounded mercilessly in his ears, and he knew he'd pushed himself too far. He watched the Witch squirm for a moment, writhing in her death throes before she finally lay still. A loud *crack* ripped through the air and a blast of wind knocked his body aside.

He'd survived the tempest, he'd killed the Witch, and now he was finished. He knew, even as he heard his companions rushing to his side, that it was too late. He couldn't fight against this pain: so blinding he could hardly feel it.

He was dying.

****

Light — light powerful enough to cut through his torment struck the gathering darkness and pushed it back. The world swam before his eyes and breath caught in his lungs again. He could smell the grass, hear footsteps grind to a halt — feel Kyleigh's hand clutched in his.

Her dark brows were bent in concentration, red brushed her cheeks. "This is horrible," she groaned, half-laughing. "How do you whisperers stand it?"

"Are you healing me?" he heard himself ask.

She grimaced. "No, it's a ... a dragon thing. We can sometimes share pain."

He heard Jake gasp. "But I thought that could only happen if —"

"*Shhhh!*" Aerilyn and Lysander said in unison.

Kael didn't hear what they argued over. He suddenly realized why his pain was fading back, and why Kyleigh's hand was starting to shake. "No, don't take it." He could barely push the words past his lips. With the anguish fading, a new darkness was creeping in — one that would carry him into sleep. "Don't ... I can manage ..."

She snorted, and winced. "Don't fight me, you stubborn mountain child."

She moved her arm to his chest, and he noticed she was still wearing her armor. He gripped her wrist in his other hand and mumbled: "How ...?"

"It can hold both of my forms," she said quietly. "I can't tell you how, though — it's a very great secret."

He thought he knew. For some reason, he thought he knew immediately why. But then the darkness made him forget.

Chapter 29
Witchslayer

What Kael woke up to definitely wasn't what he fell asleep to. When he managed to clear his vision enough to see Jonathan's clownish face, he jumped.

"A*ha*!" the fiddler said, much too loudly. "See? I told you he was awake."

"That's just because your breath knocked him right out of his dreams," Noah retorted. He shoved Jonathan aside and frowned at Kael. "Are you really awake?"

"I am now," Kael muttered. He was still weak from his headache. His limbs felt like the mush at the bottom of a stew kettle. But at least he was alive. Jonathan and Noah helped him sit up and as he blinked, his surroundings came slowly into focus.

It was dark: he could see the stars twinkling above him. Firelight danced merrily all along the street — illuminating cut stone walls and darkened house windows. Laughter floated in and out of his ears. Shadowed forms of people sat hunched around the fires, sipping from tankards and chatting while slabs of meat roasted between them. Rough cobblestone made up the ground under his bedroll — which explained why his back ached so fiercely.

"We're in Copperdock," he said, and they nodded. "Good to see you've made it out of the brig, Jonathan."

He grinned widely. "That's not all. Look at this!" He turned to the side so that Kael could see the cutlass at his hip. "When Captain Lysander got back to the ship, he gave me my very own fish-sticker."

Kael was more than a little shocked. "Well that's a far cry from mutiny."

"Yeah, he blathered on about how he wasn't often wrong, but wound up thinking I was a brave chap for wanting to come search for you," Jonathan said, his dark eyes glinting. "A sword's better than a noose, don't get me wrong. But I thought a bit of coin might've had a sweeter ring to it. There's rats down in that brig, mate! Buck-toothed villains with a horrible appetite for toes."

Noah rolled his eyes. "It's not all that bad. I've been in loads of times. The worst part is Morris boring you to tears with all of his stories. Sometimes I think I would have preferred the noose."

"Is Morris around?" Kael asked.

Jonathan shook his head. "Nope. He stayed with the rest of the men to watch the ship. You'll see him tomorrow, though. And speaking of romance," he grinned mischievously, "how *was* the kiss of life?"

Noah leaned in expectantly, but Kael had no idea what they were talking about. "The what?"

"Come on, mate." Jonathan edged closer and put a hand to the side of his mouth. "You nearly drowned, right?"

"Yes ..."

"And Kyleigh said she had to bring you back."

"And?"

"And we all know there's only one way to breathe life back into a drowned sailor," Jonathan said with a wink.

Mercy, now he remembered. The illustrations in *A Sailor's Guide to Staying Alive* hadn't exactly been romantic, but just the thought of Kyleigh putting her lips on his, even to get him to cough up water, made his stomach flip.

Jonathan pointed at his burning cheeks and cackled. "Ha! He *does* remember. So how was it?"

Kael shoved his hand away. "I don't know, I wasn't exactly conscious," he snapped. But that didn't stop Jonathan from whistling loudly and making kissing sounds.

Noah punched him in the arm. "Leave off. He nearly died — it's nothing to joke about."

"Even Kyleigh thought it was funny," Jonathan said. "She and Aerilyn haven't stopped giggling since sundown."

That makes perfect sense, Kael thought darkly. A girl like Kyleigh was much more likely to giggle than swoon over kissing a boy like him. He could see why she would laugh, and he knew he shouldn't be hurt over it. But that didn't stop it from hurting.

"Anyways," Noah said, with a sharp look at Jonathan, "the captain says he wants to see you, Kael. He sent us to make sure you were awake."

There weren't too many things worse than having to talk to Lysander, but brooding was one of them. So he got to his feet.

They weaved through the narrow streets, careful not to step on anybody's toes. The villagers, freed from their glass prisons at last, were crowded together in lumps. Husbands held their wives, and children were fast asleep in their parents' laps. Whole clans had their bedrolls stuck side by side, with hardly any space between. Though Kael was happy for them, seeing the families together made him homesick.

"Hail, Witchslayer!" someone said, and he turned to see a burly man leaning against a wagon. He raised his tankard, the thanks in his eyes meant clearly for Kael. And he was just the first.

At every fire he passed, men and women got to their feet. They seemed shaken and wobbly. If he couldn't see the steadiness in their eyes, he might have thought they were drunk. But no matter how they struggled to stand, stand they did. They raised tankards and fists to him. "Witchslayer!" they said.

"They're talking about you," Noah whispered out the side of his mouth.

Kael wasn't used to having so many eyes on him — and he certainly wasn't used to the gratitude in them. So he kept his head bent low and answered their cries with a nod.

Eventually, they found Lysander sitting with his back against the wall of a house. He spoke quietly with a man on his left, and when he saw them approaching, he stuck a finger to his lips.

The excitement of the day seemed to have been too much for Thelred and Aerilyn. He was curled up on the other side of the fire, his arms crossed over his chest and the hood of his cloak pulled over his eyes. Aerilyn, on the other hand, had her face buried in Lysander's arm. She looked peaceful enough, but as they got closer, Kael could hear her snoring.

"Isn't she lovely?" Lysander said. He was sitting like a human statue, fighting to keep her head balanced on his shoulder.

"Like a baby bear with a cold," Jonathan cooed.

Lysander glared at him. "Don't you have a song to write, fiddler? Today is destined for history! I can't believe you aren't jumping to be the first bard to sing about it."

Jonathan scratched his scruffy cheek. "Nah, I usually leave the jumping to the frogs."

"How about the flogging?" Lysander growled.

That seemed to change Jonathan's tune. He saluted quickly. "Point taken, Captain! I'll just get right on that." And he hurried away.

Lysander nodded to Noah. "Follow him, will you? Make sure he stays on task." When they were gone, he gestured to the man sitting beside him. "Kael, this is Shamus — master shipbuilder of Copperock."

The man looked about the same age as Morris. He saluted with his tankard and his smile spread to either end of his bushy sideburns — which was precisely how Kael recognized him.

"Hail, Witchslayer," Shamus said. "I'd rise to greet you like a proper man, but I've not used my legs in nearly twenty years — and they're a bit wobbly, yet. Why don't you have a seat and help yourself to the vittles?"

Kael needed little encouragement. After weeks of nothing but fish, he was prepared to eat his weight in game. Shamus served him a generous slab of venison, and he stuffed the first bite in his mouth — nearly swallowing it without chewing.

"There you are, lad. You eat, and I'll talk. The one good thing about the curse is that I haven't aged a day — my arms are still strong." Shamus poured him a tankard, and he was glad it was only water. "I know you probably think it's odd that we aren't serving ocean fare at our tables. We're proud children of the seas, I'll have you know. But when you've been a fish for so long, it just don't feel right to be eating them."

"No, I imagine it doesn't," Lysander agreed.

Kael nearly choked when Shamus clapped him on the back. "But we're fish no more, and it's all thanks to you," he said, smiling. "You kept your word — you told me you were going to kill the Witch and lo, she lies dead. The good people of Copperdock owe you their freedom."

So he'd been right: the fish he accidentally kicked over on the way to Wendelgrimm was Shamus. He didn't know where the villagers were getting their information, but he thought he should set the tale straight. "I didn't fight alone — I couldn't have done it without my friends."

"And they all said they couldn't have done it without *you*. Now I know it's hard for you great men to take the credit," Shamus said, placing a firm hand on his shoulder, "but the villagers are already calling you their champion. There's naught you can do now but bow to the cheers, Sir Wright."

He leaned back, as if that settled it, and Kael leaned around him to glare at Lysander — who'd suddenly become very occupied with sharpening his dagger on the side of his boot. "You told?" he said angrily.

Lysander was the picture of innocence. "My dear boy, a whole village witnessed you flying through the air with a dragon. What could I tell them?"

"It wasn't your secret," Kael snapped back. He was livid. His next bite of venison stuck to his tongue like sand.

"Don't worry about Copperdock — we're friends of the whisperers," Shamus said quickly. "And after Miss Kyleigh helped us catch dinner, we've become friends of halfdragons as well."

Kael slammed his tankard on the ground. "And you told about Kyleigh? I thought you were supposed to be her friend —"

"Ah, actually we figured that one out on our own," Shamus said. He pointed to a dark corner of the street, where Kyleigh was sleeping soundly — in full dragon form.

She had her tail curled up to her nose and her chin propped on her forearms. Kael was surprised to see that a small mob of children had taken up residence in the crook of her legs, using her tail for a giant pillow. Their faces were pink and smooth with sleep.

"The young ones don't know fear like the rest of us," Shamus said quietly. "Nor prejudice. They've never seen a dragon before, so what do they do? Walk up and make friends with her. I tell you — if all men had a child's courage, the Kingdom would be a better place."

"Speaking of that," Lysander cut in, "what do you plan to do, now that you've got your legs back?"

Shamus smiled and spread his arms wide. "What all shipbuilders do — rebuild. I'll imagine the Duke's fleet has gotten a little worn down over the past decades, and we'll be happy to take the gold off him."

"Aren't you afraid he'll swindle you?" Kael asked.

He shook his head. "You can't pilfer skill, lad. We work when we're paid. And speaking of coin," he leaned forward, "the Witch had a fair bit of treasure stored up in her dungeons. You can have whatever you want in payment."

Kael shook his head. "I don't want anything, thanks. It'd just be something else to lug around."

Shamus raised his brows. Then he laughed outright.

Lysander looked appalled. "Well that's not very pirate-like at all. Everyone chose something."

Shamus pursed his lips. "Yeah, but I'm still not sure why you wanted that old broken sword."

"Broken?" Kael said.

Lysander nodded. "Jake explained it all. Because the Witch was using the L — ah, the sword — for an impetus, it was tied to her soul. So it shattered when she died. It's all right, though. I happen to know an excellent blacksmith."

Shamus raised his eyebrows. "I didn't know it was her impetus. That *would* be a prize, if you could stomach having it around."

"Yes, that's the difficult part," Lysander said carefully.

He didn't know why Lysander was keeping the Lass a secret, but after all the telling he'd done, Kael had a good mind to give Shamus the complete history of it.

Lysander must have seen the storm brewing on his face because he quickly changed the subject. "And what'll you do, Master Kael, now that you've paid in full for your training?"

That question caught him off guard. He had no idea what his next step ought to be. "I suppose I'll just continue on," he said with a shrug.

Lysander leaned slightly forward, careful not to jostle Aerilyn — though he had to raise his voice to be heard over her snores. "Really? Well I only asked because Morris mentioned something about a quest for vengeance. A certain, ah, *rebellion* against Earl Titus."

"Did he?" For such a highly secretive lot, pirates were proving to be horrible confidants. But Kael had been around Lysander long enough to know what that tilt in his chin meant, what his overly casual airs were sure to carry with them: a bargain. And this time, he was ready for it. "Maybe that's true. But I don't see why it ought to matter to you."

Lysander's mask slipped, and he grinned. He was obviously very pleased that Kael was playing his game. "It doesn't *matter*, per se. And I know you aren't a fellow who's interested in gold, but it seems to me that you're nevertheless a man in need of an army."

Kael broke a twig and tossed it into the fire. "Oh? And I suppose you think you can find me one?"

"Perhaps. But even if I do help you raise a force, we'll have no way to transport it. We can't move men and horses across the Kingdom if the seas are crawling with the Duke's managers."

He tried to play the game, he really did. But Amos was right: he simply had no patience. "Fine, what do you want? Out with it."

His barking startled Aerilyn, briefly interrupting her string of noises. Lysander waited like a man before a snake until she went back to snoring. "The solution is simple," he continued at a whisper. "I know a couple of fellows who might be able to help us — men on the inside. With their knowledge and your skill, we just might be able to make the ocean a little ... freer."

Shamus whistled. "You aren't planning to sack the Duke, are you?"

Lysander made a face. "No, I'm planning to throw him *in* a sack, preferably with some rather large rocks, and toss him off the bow of my ship." He turned back to Kael. "It's very dangerous, I won't lie to you. And even if we do succeed, we'll have made some very dangerous enemies. But I already sleep with a dagger under my pillow, so it makes me no difference. What I need to know is: are you willing to trade safety for infamy?"

Kael thought about it — or rather, he pretended to. All he had to do was think of the children of Harborville and the ache in his gut told him exactly what must be done. "If I help you sack the Duke, will I have *your* help, when the time comes?"

There was no trick in the glint of his eye. "I'll follow wherever the gales take you, friend," he said, and held out his hand.

Kael took it. "Then the Duke had better start digging, because he's as good as dead."

"Excellent," Lysander said with a grin.

There was just one other person Kael felt ought to know about the plan. He left Lysander and Shamus to their chatting and walked over to where Kyleigh slept. Though he swore his boots didn't make a sound, she cracked one of her green eyes open before he even got close to her.

"You weren't asleep at all, were you?" And he could tell by her smirk that he'd guessed correctly. "So I suppose you heard about our plan, then?"

She nodded, ever so slightly. She was being careful not to wake the children who slept next to her.

He knelt down so that his face was even with hers and said: "You don't have to come along, you know. You pulled me out of the ocean. You saved me from certain death, and I know the debt between us is settled. But if you *were* to come with me, I certainly wouldn't complain. I've never sacked a Duke before. I might need your help."

He didn't know what made him say it. He knew she could hear and understand him perfectly. But for some reason, being honest with a dragon was much easier than being honest with a girl.

And her answer shone clearly in her eyes: she would follow him anywhere, he didn't have to ask.

****

They rose with the first wink of sunlight and headed straight for the docks. Jake begged to come along and after Lysander made him swear not to cast any spells, he agreed. "You're a useful fellow and we're happy to have you," he said. "Just don't burn my ship!"

Shamus and a few of the village men came to see them off. He leaned heavily on a homemade crutch and when they stopped, he had to hold onto a dock post for balance. Or at least Kael thought it was for balance. But by the look on his face, Shamus could have been fighting to stay conscious. Because when he saw *Anchorgloam* he very nearly fainted.

"Tide take me. Is that who I think it is?"

Lysander smirked. "The one and only — the terror of the High Seas."

Shamus hobbled to the gangplank and craned his neck up. "That's her, all right. The good ship *Avarice!*"

Aerilyn gasped so loudly that everyone turned to look at her. Her eyes went to Lysander and got dangerously teary.

Then she fled up the ramp and onto the ship — where they heard her burst into sobs.

"I said you should've mentioned it," Kyleigh growled as she followed her.

"How was I to know that a ship she'd only just heard of would drive her to tears?" Lysander called after her. She made a frustrated sound and batted her hand at him, but didn't turn around. "She's the daughter of Garron the Shrewd," he explained to Shamus, who nodded.

"I thought I recognized the stubborn set of her mouth. Poor lass. Garron was a blasted good merchant and an even better sailor. It broke my heart when you told me he'd passed." Shamus cleared his throat and turned his head to the bow. "You've renamed her."

"*Anchorgloam* is a better pirate name, don't you think?" Lysander said with a wry smile. "I've kept her in order. Would you like to come aboard and have a look around?"

Shamus took a step back. "I think not. It's bad luck to board a ship you had a hand in building. And I've only just got out from under the last curse. Good journey to you, Captain." He clasped hands with Lysander, and then Kael. "You're welcome back here anytime," he said with a smile. "There's a home for you in Copperdock — whenever you should want it."

Kael didn't know what to say to that, and anything he might have said got caught up in his chest. So he nodded once and then walked very quickly up the ramp. He went straight for the wheel — where Morris was waiting for him.

"You done it, lad! You done it!" he croaked, grinning through the wiry tangles of his beard. He pulled his arms out from between the knobs and used them to smack Kael on either shoulder. "The sun was real close to setting, but when we saw the clouds break and the tempest get sucked back into the sea, we knew you'd done it. Now steer us home!"

Kael was only too glad to take the wheel. Pretending like he was concentrating on something would keep him from having to wave goodbye to the villagers. "Which direction are we headed?"

Morris grinned. "South."

As they pulled away from the docks, Shamus got smaller and smaller. He waved cheerily and shouted his thanks until they could no longer hear him. Kael was sorry to leave Copperdock, but he was even sorrier to leave land. He didn't realize what a breath of fresh air their adventure had been until he found himself surrounded by ocean once again.

"Cheer up, lad," Morris said. "We'll sail into Gravy Bay at noon tomorrow."

"Is that your home?"

Morris nodded. "My home, and the home of every proper hooligan of the High Seas. Pirates have always lived there. But its location is an absolute secret, understand? Not even the Duke knows where it is."

Kael had a hard time believing that. He figured there must've been someone, some disgruntled mutineer, who would have sold the location to the crown. But when he said as much, Morris's face got serious.

"Sure, there've been a few who tried to give it away," he said quietly. "But if you even think about telling, Gravy's curse will strike you dead."

Kael believed in the curse even less than he believed in the secret location. But he was too tired to argue with Morris about it. Besides, he had other things on his mind. "So ... Kyleigh's a dragon."

"Halfdragon," Morris corrected him, and Kael felt like punching something. Had *everyone* known about her powers but him? "I figured you must have seen when she dove in after you. She prefers to keep it a secret, but sometimes it can't be helped. That's how Lysander and Thelred found out about her."

Now he was interested. "Did she have to save them, too?"

Morris nodded. "When they were young lads, they used to go sailing on their own little boat. Matteo ordered them to stay inside the Bay, but of course Lysander didn't listen. One day, they got caught up in a riptide and swept out to sea. We searched for hours, but then the sun fell ..."

"And it was too dangerous?"

"Aye. We were more likely to run over than rescue them at that point," he grunted, squinting his eyes against the bright sun. "Kyleigh happened to be staying in the Bay, and when we got back, she disappeared. But at sunrise we found all three of them sitting at the breakfast table — the two boys tired and burnt red as crabs, and Kyleigh splitting a glare between them." Morris broke out a smile that quickly turned into a chuckle. "Old Matteo — oh, he was so mad! He spent a good half hour ranting before he thought to ask Kyleigh how she'd done it. Setheran made her tell, of course. She never would have oth —"

"Wait, *Setheran* was there?" Kael interjected, and Morris nodded. "You knew Setheran the Wright?"

"Of course I did," Morris said, scoffing at his incredulity. "Setheran and Kyleigh fought through the Whispering War together. Now I don't know where he found her, originally. I can't tell you that. But," he glanced over his shoulder and dropped his voice, "I *can* tell you they were the reason we won the war. They'd go off on missions for weeks at a time, and then we'd hear the news that one rebel army or another had mysteriously disappeared. I can't prove it, of course. But," he tapped a nub to the side of his head, "I knew it was them."

And Kael thought he knew, without a shadow of a doubt, what Lysander meant when he said that any man who chased after Kyleigh would have to be her match in every way. He'd have to be strong, cunning, and dangerous.

He'd have to be Setheran the Wright.

Chapter 30
Gravy Bay

"Stop trying to avoid the question, lad! Just answer me straight."

Kael hadn't heard the question. His mouth was dry and his tongue was stuck somewhere in the back of his throat. The burn in his stomach made his arms go numb. He didn't know if he was angry, or about to be sick. All he knew for certain was that Kyleigh and Setheran had been lovers — it all made sudden, horrible sense.

"What did you ask?" he said, barely getting the words through his swollen throat.

Morris made a frustrated noise. "I asked if you and Kyleigh were able to talk. Could you speak to her in her dragon form?"

Kael nodded.

"I see, and what did it look like?"

He explained the pictures the best he could, describing what he saw. He didn't mention anything about his glimpse of Setheran. But he thought he knew what the thing was inside Kyleigh's head — the thing that wrenched his heart and brought her tears to his eyes: she was still heartbroken over Setheran.

When he was finished, Morris nodded, as if he'd been expecting to hear it all. "Yeah, that's how Setheran used to talk to her, too. But he was an accomplished Wright. Mind-walking is dangerous if you don't know what you're doing."

Kael was just glad to have an excuse to turn the conversation away from Setheran. "Mind-walking?"

"It's a branch of healing," Morris explained. "You can enter a person's mind through touch, and share things like memories or even imaginings. It's quite useful for dealing with mental plagues and the like. You can go through the eyes, too — but you shouldn't. It's real dangerous."

"How so?"

"Well, I've obviously never done it myself, but I've heard it explained before ... and I've seen what happens when it goes wrong. The mind is a house with many rooms." He set his arms out, like he was explaining how to build it. "Someone powerful in healing — a Wright, for example — is actually able to *enter* the mind, to walk around in it like you would a house."

"Hold on," Kael interrupted. "So if I were to enter someone's mind —"

"But you won't, because it's too dangerous."

"I know," he said, slightly annoyed. "But say I did — would my whole body get sucked up inside their head, or what?"

Morris chuckled. "No, but that'd be a sight. It's just your soul that goes — your body stays behind, completely vulnerable. If it's not left in the proper care, you may not have a body to come back to."

Kael thought for a moment. "But it seems like mind-walking *could* be useful, particularly if you needed to find something out."

Morris narrowed his eyes. "Sure, it can be useful. It can also be abused, too. If you know what you're doing, you could easily turn someone into a mindless slave. Now what you did with Kyleigh was more like looking through a window: you saw only what she allowed you to." He screwed up his eyes and poked an arm in the middle of Kael's chest. "And that's just as far as I want you to go, all right? You can talk to Kyleigh because she knows what she's doing, but I don't want to hear about you tampering with anyone else."

"Fine, I won't."

But it was more to appease Morris than anything. He wondered what it looked like inside Aerilyn or Lysander's mind, even Jake's ... though he was afraid to think about what he might find in Jonathan's. The whole idea of mind-walking fascinated him. And promise or no, he decided that if he ever found anyone to teach him, he would learn.

****

The sun was a hand's breadth from noon on the following day when *Anchorgloam* erupted in cheers. Kael had been so lost in thought that the sudden burst of noise made him jump.

"All hands to the rails," Lysander said as he jogged towards the bow. "Just think, dogs — today we'll lunch with the ones we love!"

More deafening cheers followed his cry as the pirates crowded around on deck. They had their belongings hoisted over their shoulders, every one talking as loudly as he could.

"After five long years, I'm looking forward to sleeping in my own bed tonight," Morris said, turning the ship. When they got close to Gravy Bay he'd insisted on taking the wheel. Apparently, the entrance required a fair bit of skill to get through. But so far, Kael hadn't seen anything that looked remotely like a village.

On one side was the open ocean, and on the other they passed a huge island of rock. It was remarkable: like a mountain rising up out of the sea. The rock was bleached white from the sun and if he tilted his head back, he could see trees perched on top of it.

"Are you ready, lad?" Morris said. "We're about to make a sharp turn."

Kael glanced around. "Into where?" Then Morris nodded in the direction of the island and he blanched. "You can't be serious."

"Of course I'm serious! There's a crack in the wall. You'll be able to see it when we turn. Granted, it ain't a big crack, but I wouldn't hold your breath — I've only ever wrecked one ship trying to get through."

Kael didn't know if he was joking or not. But he grabbed onto the nearest rail, just in case.

"Here we go!" Morris spun the wheel hard and the ship groaned under his command. She moved quickly, turning until they faced the rocks head-on.

A slight shadow cut down the middle of the high cliffs, hardly wider than a crack. And Kael realized, as they barreled down upon it, that Morris meant to squeeze them through it. He gripped the rails and bit his lip as the current swept them up, sucking them helplessly towards the crack. As the bow slid into the gap, he waited breathlessly for the noise of splintering wood ... but it never came.

The current pushed them through, and before Aerilyn had a chance to scream, they popped out on the other side and floated into Gravy Bay.

It was a large plot of land, a little world of its own, hemmed in on all sides by cliffs. There was a lake-sized pool of ocean between the entrance and the first sliver of beach. A mound of houses squatted behind that, and then a forest, acres of it, stretched back against the gray opposite mountain in the distance.

Kael felt emptiness when he saw the trees. He tried not to dwell on the fact that his bow had been destroyed, but seeing the woods made it hard to forget. Perhaps he would try his hand at the longbow. There was bound to be game lurking among the trees — and no doubt it'd been left at peace far too long.

The rounded front lip of the Bay was covered in rock, upon which numerous houses sat. Some were short and fat, others were tall and thin. They were built strangely — as if the pirates made their homes with whatever materials they happened to pillage. He counted at least four different types of stone, none the shade of the cliffs around them, and a dozen different lumbers. One house had a garden wall that was made entirely from slabs of purple, glittering rock.

Trinkets of all sorts littered the stone yards around the village. There were statues perched in odd places, some arranged in hilarious scenes. In one yard, a gargoyle that looked as if it had been pilfered off the side of a castle crouched in the garden. Lodged between its open jaws was the golden head of King Crevan that, judging by the ragged edges of his neck, had been hewed from the larger statue that stood next door.

His Highness was not without a crown, however, as someone had the good sense to weld the brazen, laughing head of a donkey upon his shoulders.

"You think that's something?" Morris said when he pointed it out. "Take a glance up the hill, lad, and you'll see the mansion of Gravy himself!"

The mansion was most enormous house he'd ever seen. It perched high on a cliff above the village, and more wings grew from it than from an army of butterflies — each with its own particular character. There was one section out to the side that he immediately liked the look of: its walls were made of dark red brick and the arches of its windows were shuttered in steel.

He imagined it would be a good place to find some peace and quiet.

As they sailed closer to the docks, the sharp *clang* of a bell rang out, drawing the villagers from their houses with its song. They stood along the beach, shielded their eyes from the sun and strained to see which ship was heading for the harbor.

When they recognized *Anchorgloam*, Kael thought it was lucky he was still several yards away, or he might have gone deaf from the cries that exploded from the shore. No sooner did he think this than the pirates answered with a roar of their own. They jumped up and down like children and pounded their fists onto the rails. Even Jonathan hollered along, so contagious was the excitement.

They barely had a chance to get the ramp lowered before the pirates flooded off the boat. They ran down the docks as the crowd ran down the sand — and the two groups collided somewhere in the middle.

Wives cried and didn't seem to be able to stop kissing their pirates. Children leapt off the dunes and unabashedly into their fathers' arms. Sons shook hands and tried to keep their faces stern while daughters held on tightly and cried.

There was one little girl who seemed more unsure than excited. She was young, so young that Kael doubted if she'd ever met her father. She watched with big blue eyes from safely behind her mother's skirts, staring bashfully at the pirate who knelt and tried to coax her out. At her mother's urging, she took a hesitant step forward, then raised her little arms to the man whose eyes matched hers.

She screamed in delight as her father hoisted her off the ground and held her high in the air. He spun once, tightly, just before he brought her back to his chest for an embrace.

"C'mon, Kael! I'm famished," Jonathan shouted.

He tore his eyes away from the crowd and saw all of his companions lined up on the dock, watching him curiously. "Coming," he said, then he turned to Morris. "Well, I suppose you're going home?"

"Aye. But I'll be right down the path, should you need anything," he said with a smack on the arm. "Mine's the one with the bronze octopus out front."

He bid Morris farewell and then hurried down the ramp. As he followed his companions down the road, he took one last glance at the happy scene behind him. He could only imagine how the pirates felt, to have lost the ones they loved only to find them once again. But he hoped that he would know the feeling for himself, one day.

****

It was no surprise that the great house on the cliff belonged to Lysander, and yet when they stopped at the huge front door, it still shocked him.

A horde of servants must have been waiting eagerly behind it, because no sooner did they stop than the door swung open and the whole mob came rushing out. They swooped in, distracted them with curtsies and bows, then made off with their luggage.

"Where are they? Are they here?" An old man's voice bounced out of the front door, followed closely by the old man himself. He was dressed very smartly in pressed

349

trousers and a pressed shirt. A carefully-groomed mustache topped his wide swindler's grin. "Well, well, you've finally come back, have you?" he said as he hobbled towards them, leaning heavily on a polished oak cane. "And what have you done with my favorite ship?"

"She's tucked safely in the harbor, Uncle Martin," Lysander said.

"Good ... because now I'm going to give you a piece of my mind!" His face went dangerously stern. "Do you see what comes from stealing off in the dead of night? From chasing after wild tales and fancies?"

"It wasn't a fancy, Uncle. The Witch was —"

"I *know* she's real, that isn't the point." And Uncle Martin reiterated this with a none-too-gentle tap of his cane. "The point is that you absconded with my ship, threw caution to the wind and convinced a good number of impressionable pirates to sail straight into the heart of folly — and for what? A few sparkly trinkets?"

"The Lass isn't a trink — ow!" Lysander took another furious tap to the chest. He massaged his bruise while Uncle Martin ranted on.

"You've got charisma, boy, and you always have. Your father had it too: he charmed his way out of more executions than any man in history. But," he raised his cane, and Lysander crossed his arms defensively over his chest, "charm is something you use on your enemies, not your brothers. And certainly not on my favorite son!"

"I'm your only son," Thelred reminded him.

Uncle Martin inclined his head. "True, but my favorite nonetheless." Then he turned back to Lysander. "I have a mind to brand your arse with something ridiculous for every year you wasted, but I won't — provided you swear to never chase folly again."

"Fine, I swear," Lysander said. He stood straight when they shook hands on it, obviously trying to regain some shred of his dignity. But all he did was give Uncle Martin the opening he needed for one final cane-thrust to the gut.

While Lysander was doubled over, groaning in pain, he leaned down and whispered: "By the way, did you find it?"

He nodded stiffly, and Uncle Martin ruffled his hair.

"Good lad," he said, his wide grin returning immediately. He straightened up and took a quick glance at the rest of them. "My, my, picked up some interesting cargo on your journey, eh? Well I — Gravy save me, it's the Dragongirl!"

He squeezed between Jonathan and Jake and snatched both of Kyleigh's hands. "How very lovely to see you again, my dear," he said, planting a lingering kiss on the backs of them. "Though I'm a bit peeved that you didn't return sooner. Seventeen years ago, I was a younger man ... and my eyes were a bit sharper."

Kael thought Uncle Martin must have gotten his fair share of charisma. There weren't many men in the Kingdom who could wink at Kyleigh and live — much less make her laugh. But that's precisely what he did.

"I had work to do, Martin," she said when he released her. "Not all of us can spend our days smoking pipes and harassing the cook."

"Don't even get me started on the cook. That woman will be the death of me, I guarantee it. But," he wagged his eyebrows at her, "with all that's wrong in the Kingdom, I don't mind saying that the sight of you certainly puts the wind back in my sails."

Jonathan hastily turned his laugh into a cough when Thelred glared at him. Kael even pounded him on the back to make it look more convincing.

"Shall I introduce you to the rest of the crew?" Lysander said, tactfully interrupting whatever string of nonsense Uncle Martin had been whispering in Kyleigh's ear.

It turned out that Uncle Martin had an entertaining opinion of every one of them, and he didn't mind sharing. He said all sorts of things to Aerilyn that would have earned anyone else a slap in the face. But coming from Uncle Martin, it was just hard not to laugh. "My late wife kept a whole wardrobe of dresses upstairs, and I'll bet we can find one that fits," he said, after he'd ranted about how her garb was *an obstruction of a perfectly good view.*

Aerilyn's face lit up immediately. "Oh thank you, Uncle Martin! I can't tell you how exhausting it is to wear men's clothes day in and day out. In fact, it's nothing short of torture," she added, with a glare at Lysander.

"No problem, no problem at all. My wife always used to say that there was absolutely no point in being a woman if she couldn't show off her figure. Of course, I didn't argue with that. And *I* always say that Lysander's no-dress-on-deck rule is the seventh worse thing to ever happen to this Kingdom!" he declared, shooting a glare at his nephew — who rolled his eyes in retort.

When Uncle Martin shook Kael's hand, his glance went immediately to his hair. "Poor boy, we'll have to find you a sharper razor."

Kael tried to flatten his curls, but felt them spring stubbornly back into place. "There's nothing I can do about it."

"You could try essence of sea urchin. I hear that's what a certain fussy captain uses to get his characteristic wave," Uncle Martin said loudly.

"That's not true," Lysander cut in. "I don't fuss over my hair — it simply falls this way."

"Sure it does," Uncle Martin teased. "And when I wake up, my mustache looks exactly like this." He twirled one end into a perfect loop.

When it was Jake's turn, Uncle Martin had to fish him out from the back of the group — where he'd been hiding. "A mage, eh?" he said with an inscrutable look. "You know, we've got a whole room in the house that's completely spell proof. You could summon a rainstorm in there and it wouldn't wet the curtains."

Jake's glasses slid down his nose as his eyebrows shot up. "Really? Where is it?"

"Ha!" Uncle Martin barked. "Not so fast. I know your lot — you'll disappear into your studies and we won't hear another peep until you venture out for food. I'm not going to miss your story. Sit through one meal, and then I'll tell you where it is. Fair?"

Jake nodded, though a bit reluctantly.

Finally, it was Jonathan's turn. As they shook hands, Kael could feel the rest of the party hold its breath. No doubt they were all thinking the same thing: if anyone could offend their host, it would be Jonathan.

"And what do you do?" Uncle Martin asked, crossing his arms.

Jonathan mirrored him. "I'm a rogue, by trade. Though occasionally I like to do a little string-twiddling. Here lately I've done naught but follow orders. Putting a cramp in my fingers, it is."

"I see. And what music do you play when the old Captain isn't cracking a whip?"

Jonathan leaned in, like it was a very great secret. "The sort that makes you want to call up a chord and kick it in the shin!"

Uncle Martin laughed. "Strictly indecent, eh? I knew I liked you! You'll have to fiddle for us after dinner — I enjoy having a bit of rude music when I take my pipe."

Jonathan looked absolutely delighted, but everyone else groaned aloud. Kael was just shocked that all of his strange ramblings actually meant something to someone.

When the introductions had been made, Uncle Martin stepped back and waved his cane at them. "Enough chatter, let's go get our bellies full!"

And they followed him eagerly through the door.

Chapter 31
Dark Things

The inside of the mansion was even more spectacular than the outside. Uncle Martin chattered excitedly as he led them through the main hall: a room shaped in a perfect circle. It was so large that Kael thought the whole of Tinnark could have lived in it quite comfortably.

"These are all the pirate captains who've made Gravy's mansion their home," Uncle Martin said, gesturing at the white statues that stood guard around the room. "They're all here — from Gravy to Matteo."

"What about Lysander?" Jake asked.

"Ah, I shouldn't hope to join them for quite some time. You see, it's only *after* a captain's died that his likeness is made into a statue. Did you notice the objects they have with them? Every one is either wearing or wielding the cause of his death."

And he was right. Most of the captains, including Sam Gravy, held a cutlass. But there were some whose deaths were a little less conventional. The man a few slots down from Gravy had a sea serpent latched onto his upraised arm by the fangs. Another held a goblet in one hand, and a bottle of poison in the other. Some were missing limbs, had arrows in their hearts or axes at their necks, but each one of the captain's faces was surprisingly fixed and noble. Matteo was the only exception.

Kael was drawn immediately to the sheer detail of his statue. His hands were bound behind him and a noose hung around his neck. His head was bent slightly, every wave of his hair flowed as if brushed by the wind. But it was the expression on his face that truly made him come alive.

354

His eyes bored into Kael's, and though empty behind the white, they seemed to say everything. Or perhaps it was the arch of his brows, or the ever-so-slight lines on his forehead that told his story. No, it was definitely and without a doubt his smirk: the bend in his mouth and the unspoken mischief behind it.

But when Kael took it all in, Matteo's face said one thing very clearly: *I have won.*

"Remarkable, isn't it?" Lysander said from at his shoulder — so suddenly that it made him jump. "Morris was at his execution. He saw my father's face just before they kicked the barrel out from under him ... and this was his final taunt."

Kael could hardly grasp it. "*Morris* carved this?"

Lysander smirked, and looked so much like his father. "It was the last thing he did before ... well, you know."

No, Kael didn't know what had happened to Morris; he'd never felt like it was his place to bring it up. But now that he knew what Morris had been capable of, it angered him. Fate angered him. He thought of how it must burn to have such an eye, to be able to see the potential beauty hidden in a slab of stone ... and yet have no means of giving it life.

He imagined it felt horrible — worse than breaking a thousand bows.

"I thought your pap died in the Whispering War," Jonathan said, interrupting the long silence left by Lysander's words.

"He did," Uncle Martin replied. He grinned at Jonathan's confusion. "Is this not what you expected, Sir Fiddler? Perhaps you imagined him dying with sword in hand, hmm? Well, the War didn't end in the final battle, I can tell you that. Thanks to our worm of a King ..." Fury glanced his face for half a moment, searing his cheeks before he managed to mask it with a smile. "But I digress. The important thing is that Matteo died fighting for what he believed in. He may not have been on the battlefield, but he still died a warrior's death."

A heavy silence followed his words. It hung in the air like a raincloud until Aerilyn said: "Were there any lady pirate captains?"

Uncle Martin seemed relived that the conversation had roamed to something a little lighter. "I'm afraid not, at least not officially. Though I've often wondered about Slayn the Faceless."

He nodded to one statue that was a little more slender than the others. A cowl covered his head and a piece of cloth was tied around his face, revealing only his eyes. Tongues of flame lapped his legs and touched the palms of his noticeably dainty outstretched hands.

"There's a lot about Slayn that makes me think he was actually a woman in disguise," Uncle Martin mused.

"Like what?" Aerilyn said, stepping up to get a closer look.

"The story goes that after Captain Crux perished, his daughter went out into the woods to mourn … and never returned. Not three days later, this Slayn character appeared and said he wanted a chance to duel for the captaincy."

"And he won?"

"Aye, but there after he always used a bow — a weapon more suited to a woman's strength."

Kyleigh stifled a bout of laughter, and Kael elbowed her.

"Whatever happened to Slayn?" Aerilyn said over the top of them.

Uncle Martin laughed. "Well, he claimed that he wore a scarf over his face because he'd been badly maimed by a witch's spell. And do you know how he perished? In a fiery blast from the Witch of Wendelgrimm! Blew him to dust." He touched a finger to the side of his nose. "They say that Fate doesn't like to be cheated, and in this case Slayn — if she was indeed the daughter of Crux — cheated when she refused to give up her identity. So if you ask me, I think the explosion was Fate's way of laughing last."

Jonathan strode over, rolling up his sleeves as he went. "Seems to me that there's only one way to solve this mystery!" He shooed Aerilyn out of his way and stretched his arms forward, his fingers curled and his eyebrows bent in intense concentration. Then he lunged ... and grabbed Slayn's marble chest.

Uncle Martin and Lysander both burst out laughing. Jake turned red. Kyleigh clapped a hand over her mouth to hide her grin, and Thelred just raised an eyebrow.

"Get your hands off of her!" Aerilyn shrieked, smacking him upside the head.

Jonathan had to take his hands away to protect himself from her blows. "All right, all *right*! Turkey legs, we're not even sure she was actually a woman." Then he turned his back to her, found Uncle Martin and mouthed: *She was.*

"Ah, well let's just let it be," Lysander said, before Aerilyn could work herself into a proper fit.

"Quite right," Uncle Martin agreed, still chuckling. He pointed his cane up at the ceiling, where an elaborate spiral staircase drifted down from a large hole and touched bottom gracefully in the center of the room. "Up there's where you'll be staying. There's no bedtime here — you can come and go as you please. Now move along, we've got a lot of ground to cover!"

And he wasn't joking. Fortunately for Kael's rumbling stomach, Uncle Martin didn't give them a full tour, but led them quickly through the many winding hallways. Any comments he made were brief and on the move.

"There're seven doors in this hallway," he said as they walked through a passage with walls painted entirely red. "Don't ask me why there's an odd number. Our friend the battlemage will be interested to know that behind one of these doors is the spell room. But I'm not telling which one!"

Jake glanced at a door so badly charred that there was a permanent line of black soot on the floor from where it'd been opened. "I can hardly bear the mystery," he said dryly.

At long last, they reached a set of doors at the end of the hallway and Uncle Martin stopped. "This is my second favorite room in the whole place — the dining room!" He pushed the doors open.

A table long enough to be a small boat awaited them, laden with food. The seasoned fumes of pork rose up from the tight skin of a roasted hog and made Kael's mouth water. And that was before he even saw the rest of it: mountains of fruit, fresh vegetables, the golden tops of bread, and cheese — a dozen different wheels just waiting to be eaten.

"It's beautiful," Aerilyn said, and Kael was about to agree when he saw that she wasn't even looking at the feast.

Had he not been so blinded by hunger, he might have noticed that the far wall of the room was made up entirely of glass: a huge sheet of it that stretched from the ceiling down to the floor. Outside, the ocean glittered beneath the white cliffs. Small fishing boats rode the waves and hauled in nets teeming with sea life.

"Yes, I always thought so," Uncle Martin said as he joined her. "This particular sheet of glass was meant to grace King Banagher's great hall, but sadly the shipment never quite made it there."

"Because you looted it," Aerilyn said, trying to look severe.

Uncle Martin snorted. "I'd resent the implication if it wasn't true. Yes — I stole it. And much to my brother's dismay, I knocked out this wall and had it put in here."

"Why was Matteo against it?" she asked.

"Oh, some rubbish about it not being safe," he said, with a wave of his hand.

"Well it isn't." Jake's face reddened when all eyes turned to him. "I only mean it could break easily. Something like, say, a rock could bust it. And then of course you could always fall out and," he glanced down at the jagged rocks below, "I believe you'd die."

Uncle Martin crossed his arms. "Oh? Why don't you fix it, then?"

Jake looked taken aback. "Sir?"

"Yes, you mages are a smart lot — make it unbreakable, if it's so dangerous."

"But I'm a battlemage. Home protection spells aren't exactly in my staff."

"Well, get them there. No, my mind's made up," Uncle Martin said before Jake could refuse. "I want you to enchant this window, *and* you can start immediately."

Jake clamped his mouth on whatever argument he'd had ready, grabbed a handful of provisions off the table and practically jogged out the door.

"Do you need me to tell you where the spell room is?" Uncle Martin called after him.

"No, I think I've got a pretty good idea. Thanks."

"Strange folk, the mages," Uncle Martin said when he was gone. "I swear they're happiest when buried under a mountain of spell books. Now," he clapped his hands together, "let's tuck in!"

Uncle Martin handled the seating arrangements — not surprisingly, he managed to situate himself between Aerilyn and Kyleigh. No sooner did they sit than the kitchen doors swung open, and a herd of maids bustled in. They filled glasses with water and goblets with wine, supplied white squares of cloth and poured sauce wherever it was needed.

Kael was already well into his second round of pork when Kyleigh reached over and tucked one of the cloth squares into the front of his shirt. She seemed torn between laughing and groaning at the sheer amount of grease on his confused face. "It's a napkin," she explained.

"What in Kingdom's name is a napkin?"

"It's like a shield for your shirt — in case that hog decides to fight back."

He thought napkins were a ridiculous idea. But she could have tied a scarf around his eyes and he wouldn't have cared — just so long as it didn't get in the way of his mouth. "Why aren't you eating?" he asked when he noticed her empty plate.

"I've got the cook working on her favorite dish," Uncle Martin said while batting the breadcrumbs out of his mustache. "It should be — ah, here it comes!"

A maid edged through the kitchen door, her arms shaking from the weight of the platter she carried. Kyleigh took it from her before she had to go too far and set it down in her place. Five slabs of meat were stacked upon it. When she cut into them, the seared outside gave way to the raw, marbled pink flesh underneath.

"What is that?" Kael asked. It certainly didn't smell like any game he knew.

"Bcef," she admitted. "I know it's not very sportsmanlike of me to eat a fence animal, but I can't help myself. Here." She cut off a chunk and sat it on his plate.

Aerilyn looked alarmed. "You aren't going to eat that, are you?"

He'd been planning on it. In fact, the beef was already halfway to his mouth. "Why, is something wrong with it?"

She wrinkled her nose in disgust. "It's not even *cooked*! Only barbarians eat raw meat."

Lysander's fork clattered onto his plate, and that was very suddenly the only sound in the room. "How dare you," he snapped.

"I didn't mean it like that," Aerilyn said defensively. "I only meant —"

"There's enough ignorance in the Kingdom without you adding to it," he continued, half out of his chair. "And here I thought you understood —"

"I *do* understand!" Aerilyn shouted, rising up to meet him. "She knows I didn't mean it like that, I didn't mean *her* —!"

"Just her kind, eh? Just the rest of them?"

"Enough. Sit down," Kyleigh barked.

They sat stiffly, still glaring daggers at one another.

Kyleigh jabbed her knife at Aerilyn. "Stop arguing. You know what you meant. And you," she turned the blade on Lysander, "there's no reason to make every slight into a battle. I've got thick skin. I promise I'm not going to run off crying to my room every time I'm called a name — unlike some of our number."

Aerilyn looked on the verge of being indignant before she inclined her head. "I suppose I deserved that."

"You certainly did, you filthy merchant," Kyleigh said with a grin. Then she elbowed Kael. "Just try it."

And he did. And he decided that he liked beef very much, even raw.

"I confess I don't know what's wrong with women these days," Uncle Martin grumbled. "I suppose it's all this war and unrest — but it's making them too ... agreeable. When Matteo and I were lads, there was little to do besides sneak into the nobles' parties and get the girls to fight." He laughed and dabbed his napkin at the corner of his mouth. "That was always the best distraction. Two dignified ladies rolling around, clawing each other's faces off would stop any ball dead in its tracks. Then while the gentlemen tried to separate them, Matteo and I would make off with the silver ..."

They spent the rest of the day trading stories. Uncle Martin relived his glory days while Lysander gave him a very drawn-out and over dramatized version of their battle with the Witch. "And then Kael tore the chains off like they were naught but seaweed —"

"Hold on a moment." Uncle Martin leaned around and fixed him with a serious look. "Tore the spells apart, did you? Is there something you aren't telling me?"

"Don't play coy, Martin," Kyleigh said, taking a sip from her glass. "You know very well what the man is."

He never took his gleaming eyes off of Kael. "So it's true, then? I'll admit I *did* wonder," he said, and his eyes flicked involuntarily to the top of Kael's head. "Well, it's been years since I've had a whisperer to grace my table." He raised his goblet high in the air. "To your health!"

Every few minutes or so, they'd have to put down their forks long enough for Uncle Martin to give a toast. He toasted good friends, interesting conversation, heroism, and warm bread. Then when the sun began to set, he toasted the evening.

"Where'd you find all of this loot?" Jonathan asked. He was in the process of groaning his way through a fourth helping of potatoes.

"To Lord Gilderick's gullibility," Uncle Martin declared, raising his glass. "Had he not made the very serious mistake of transporting his goods overseas, we wouldn't have such a feast set before us!"

Even Kael would drink to that.

When the sun dipped low and took the light with it, maids slipped in and lit the many candles spread out across the table. Lysander waited until they'd gone before he said: "Why don't I recognize any of the servants? Have things changed so much?"

Uncle Martin screwed up his nose and folded his napkin very neatly onto the center of his empty plate. "Most of the girls you knew are married, now. They've got homes and children to tend to. And then we've had to take most of the lads on as pirates."

"But he's right: I don't recognize a single face," Thelred said. "And when we left, there were only a few servants. Now it seems like you've got one for every room."

Uncle Martin's face turned serious, a worry plagued his voice. "There are dark things happening in the Kingdom, dark things indeed."

"What sorts of things?" Thelred pressed.

"Dark things." Against the pale candlelight, Uncle Martin's face suddenly looked a hundred years old. "A year ago, we raided one of the Duke's personal vessels. It was a bitter fight, and after we'd tipped the last of the bodies overboard, we went to inspect our loot. I went below with some of the lads and saw cargo marked as livestock, heading for the Endless Plains ... only it wasn't cows or sheep we found. It was people — clapped in irons and stamped for sale. We've found three others since." He nodded towards the kitchen. "That's where most of the new ones came from. They've been split up from their families, and I haven't the heart to throw them out. The least I can do is give them work, teach them a trade and put a roof over their heads until things get better."

A long, impossibly heavy silence trailed his words. Then Thelred's voice came out of the shadows, hissing like a man with no air: "*Slaves?*"

Uncle Martin nodded. "Dark things, I tell you."

Lysander said nothing. His face was so contorted with rage that Kael imagined there would have been a hurricane lambasting the window, had he still been cursed.

"But we have a plan," Kael reminded him, firmly. "We'll put an end to this."

"You're right," Lysander said after a moment. He took a deep breath and snatched his goblet up. "To freedom!" And he downed the whole thing.

"Absolutely," Uncle Martin agreed with a swig of his own. "And I think we could all do with a slice of cake. Bimply!"

The way he said it, Kael thought it was a swear. But then a plump woman stepped out from the kitchen and bustled over to their table. "You called?" she said.

Lysander sprang to his feet and nearly crushed her in his embrace. "Dear Mrs. Bimply, how I've missed your cooking! I wish you'd join the pirates. A good galley makes the journey that much shorter."

She blushed and pushed him away. "I've told you a thousand times, Captain — a ship is no place for an old woman like me."

"Quite right, quite right," Uncle Martin interrupted. "But after all this dark talk, we've agreed that we could do with some cake. How about a chocolate one with extra sugar?"

Mrs. Bimply frowned, planting her hands on her stout hips. "You know you aren't supposed to have any cake, Mr. Martin. It's not good for your heart."

"Not good for my —? I tell you, Lysander, I've been living in a dungeon. Everyday, she finds a new way to torture me." He shot a glare at Mrs. Bimply, who gasped.

"I never —"

"Denying me cake," Uncle Martin said loudly, rapping his cane on the table. "Plundering my secret stashes of cookies — all twelve of them! And," he narrowed his eyes at her, "she trims the fat off my roast. How's a man to keep up his strength, I ask you, if he's got no fat on his roast? Abomination!"

"Well forgive me for wanting to keep your health," Mrs. Bimply said through pursed lips. "You'll eat yourself into an early grave if you don't take care of your heart, just like your father did."

Uncle Martin leveled his cane at her. "Don't bring Papa into this. The war is between you and me, Bimply, and I intend to win. Cake!"

She opened her mouth to retort, but Lysander stopped her. "It's not worth the bloodbath," he said quietly. "He's likely to have an attack just screaming over dessert."

Mrs. Bimply threw up her hands and disappeared into the kitchen. A few moments later she returned — carrying a tray nearly bent under the weight of a sprawling chocolate cake.

Uncle Martin cackled in triumph and tucked his napkin under his chin. "Ah, my very favorite. Kyleigh likes the edge pieces, if I recall. And I'll take one from the middle. I want as much sugar as possible on the top!"

Kael thought if he tried to stuff anything else down his throat, his stomach would toss it right back. The pork was sitting heavy and the warmth made his eyelids droop. So while the others argued over cake, he slipped away and headed for his room.

He climbed the spiral staircase and nearly tumbled straight back down when a maid leapt out from the shadows and said: "Your room's right this way, Master Kael."

"Thanks," he muttered, and followed her down the hall.

A large bed that squatted next to the window took over a good portion of his room. The hearth nearly covered one entire wall. A small dresser sat off to the side, and in the opposite corner crouched a bath. Steam rose up off the water in lazy tendrils, and he suddenly realized how very filthy he was.

"There's spare clothes in the dresser, should you need them," the maid said, with a quick glance at his wretchedly stained shirt. "Do let me know if you need anything else."

"All right." He turned to the bath again, but he could feel the maid staring at him. "What?"

She was young, barely his own age, and when he spoke, her cheeks turned pink. "Begging your pardon, sir. But is it true what the kitchen maids are saying? That *you* were the one to slay the Witch of Wendelgrimm?"

Something about the way she stared made him uneasy. He ran a hand through his hair. "I suppose so. It was my dagger that found her heart, but I had plenty of help," he added quickly when she gasped.

"You're a true hero, then." She clasped her hands tightly in front of her and smiled in a way that made him take a step back. "I've never met a hero before."

"I'm not a hero," he snapped, hoping his temper would scare her off. But it didn't.

She giggled, and gave him a long look. "Well ... do let me know if you need anything, Master Kael. Anything at all."

"All right, fine."

When she finally left, he breathed a sigh of relief. He'd stripped off his shirt and boots when a knock came at the door. "Yes?" he said, and hoped to mercy it wasn't that odd maid again.

"It's me. Why on earth is your door locked? Are you expecting an attack?"

"Something like that," he muttered as he let Kyleigh in. She had her hands behind her back and raised an eyebrow when she saw him. "Good lord *what*?"

"You're testier than usual," she said with a frown. "I've only come to say I have something for you." She brought her hands out and showed him what she'd been hiding.

It was a bow, though unlike any bow he'd ever seen. The wood was rough and gray with age. Where the string attached, three short branches stuck out of it — like the maker hadn't even bothered to fully shape it. The grip was made of simple leather and cracked from years of rough use. Strange, swirling patterns covered the length of it. He imagined the previous owner had carved them in: perhaps a soldier trying to steady his hands before battle, or a knight counting his victories.

He held it, and marveled at how light it was. He pulled back and nearly gasped when the string went straight to his chin without a fuss. It may not have looked like a King's bow, but whoever made it certainly knew what he was doing.

"Where did you find this?" he said, pulling the string back again.

She shrugged. "In Wendelgrimm, of course. I knew you wouldn't choose anything for yourself, so I dug through the treasure and found something I thought you might like."

She'd given him a gift that he had no way of repaying. He'd just settled his debt with Lysander and had no intention of gaining a new one. "I can't accept this," he said, thrusting it back at her. But she wouldn't take it.

"Don't be ridiculous — I can't use it. Besides, Harbinger gets jealous if I keep another weapon around," she said with a grin. "Just keep it. Now, I've got to get back down there and make sure Martin hasn't nicked my cake —"

"Hold on a moment." Kael narrowed his eyes at her. "You won't eat vegetables because they're *prey food*, and yet you'll have dessert?"

"Is that a problem?"

"Not really. I just wonder who we're going to have to bury first — you, or Uncle Martin."

"Clever." Though her look was more amused than annoyed. "But I think I've got a few years on him. Go back to your bath, whisperer."

"How did you know I was about to take a bath?"

She raised an eyebrow again, and this time her gaze went to his chest. That's when he remembered how very horribly bare it was.

"Don't cover up," she said with a laugh, prying his arms away. "It's not like you've got anything to be embarrassed about."

"Yes I have! I've got skin the color of paste, ribs poking out every which way, and what else? Oh, yes," with a heave, he pulled her forward, "a great bloody mark that puts me at the very top of His Majesty's execution list," he hissed, though for some reason it only made her laugh harder. "Let me go!"

She did, and he stumbled backwards. "All right, *Master* Kael," she said with a curtsy. "And I want you to know that you don't owe me anything — I consider our score more than settled."

"What? Why?"

She stopped in the doorway, turned, and with an impish grin looked very pointedly at his chest.

He hurled his shirt at her, but she ducked and disappeared into the hallway. After a few moments, he thought she was gone. Then he went to close the door and heard her whistle loudly from somewhere in the shadows. "Get out of here! I had no idea dragons were such pests!" He slammed the door on her giggling, locked it, and climbed into the tub.

She could be such a fool sometimes, and he didn't understand it. Why did she get so much joy out of embarrassing him? Why did she tease and otherwise torment him to no end? Why ... *why*?

As he scrubbed the filth away, he twisted everything he felt into anger, because anger was easier to deal with.

Chapter 32
The Unraveling Plan

For one entire week, Kael could wake when he wished and face the day however he chose. Most of his time he spent exploring the mansion, looking through every strange quarter and passageway.

He found a training room the first morning, complete with several body-shaped targets, and spent hours riddling them with arrows. It was amazing how well his new bow responded, how easily it bent to his every command. He supposed it was because the wood was so broken-in by its previous owner that he didn't have any trouble pulling it back. He would narrow his eyes at whatever point he chose: eye, hand, even a single fiber of the burlap skin — and no sooner did he imagine it than his arrow would strike its mark.

When the targets were so badly maimed that their stuffing leaked out, he moved on to another room.

The enormous library was easily his favorite refuge. It was two levels tall — breached by a grand staircase that spilled from the upper level and fanned out onto the ornate rug beneath it. He'd spend hours in one of the many wide, cushioned chairs, reading armfuls of whatever tomes struck his fancy. Though he was interested in ancient civilizations, mining and the history of giants, he never found anything on the topic he was most interested in: dragons.

Before they arrived in Gravy Bay, he'd gone to gather up his belongings and noticed that *Tales of Scales* was missing. At first, he thought Jonathan had hidden it as a joke. But when he adamantly denied it, Kael had been forced to consider other options. Lysander swore he hadn't reclaimed it and even let him tear his cabin apart looking for it. Noah had no interest at all in books. As far as anyone knew, the only things he ever read were the fronts of cards.

"Just ask Kyleigh," Lysander had said as he watched Kael dig through the shelves for the third time. "I'm sure she can tell you whatever you'd like to know."

He'd already thought of that, and he'd already tried. The problem was that Kyleigh wouldn't tell him anything.

"Just read about it, if you're so interested," she'd snapped over dinner.

"I've lost my book," he'd said through gritted teeth. "If you could just answer one thing —"

"No, because one thing will lead to another, and soon I'll have wasted my whole evening talking about it," she retorted. "Do you think you're the first to ask to hear my story? Great skies, there's no end to the people who've asked!"

"Well, why don't you just tell them?"

She squared her shoulders. "Because I don't like their look, that's why."

"Their look?"

"Yes. They all look at me like I'm some sort of creature behind the glass. And I don't like being treated like a ... specimen." Then she'd stood up and marched off, taking her plate with her.

Oh, the whole thing peeved him to no end.

But then he'd discovered the mansion's library, and renewed hope along with it. Surely, somewhere among the countless thousands, there was a book about dragons.

He combed through every shelf, climbing ladders to reach the tallest and crawling on his hands and knees to scan the very bottom. It was a maddening task, but he refused to give up. Sometimes he would reach a section and his heart would begin to hammer. He would run his hands across the spines, reading their topics in a frenzied rush.

Dice games, dogma, dormice ... druids.

And there, right where *dragons* ought to have been would be an empty space and a trail of dust — left behind from where someone had snatched a book from its shelf. And

369

he knew exactly who that someone was, who it must have been:

Kyleigh.

But by trying to stop him from learning, she only made the fires burn hotter. Now he was certain she was hiding something. And whatever it was, he was determined to find out. She couldn't have possibly taken all the books. There must have been one she missed and by mercy, he was going to find it.

He was high atop a ladder, squinting to read some far off titles when Lysander wandered in. "I thought I might find you here."

He jumped, and the ladder jerked sideways on its mechanism, nearly bucking him off. "You can't just bust out yelling at people!" he raged as he very shakily made his way down.

"I'm terribly sorry," Lysander said, though the amused look on his face said quite the opposite. "I'll try to remember to scuff my shoes on the rug, next time. Do you have a moment?"

"Sure," Kael grunted.

"Excellent." Lysander met him at the foot of the stairs and lowered his voice. "My informants have arrived — remember the men I told you about?"

"The ones from the Duke's circle? Sure."

"Well," and he lowered his voice even further, "we aren't exactly friends, and I can't say I really trust them enough to tell them about your ... gifts. So I think I'll introduce you as strategist. What do you think about that?"

Kael didn't get a chance to say what he thought before Lysander cut his fist across his chest and declared:

"On to the meeting room!"

****

There were no windows in the meeting room and hardly any decoration. The only light came from the lanterns hung across the wall. They'd been set so crookedly that the flames ate the candles at sharp inclines, leaving the wax to pool and drip out the bottom. The only smells were burning wick and old parchment. A few high-backed chairs ringed an ancient table — and they looked stern enough to be a punishment.

It took Kael a moment to adjust to the dimmer light, but after he blinked a couple of times, he noticed a man standing next to the hearth. He was tall, with broad shoulders and a neatly-trimmed beard. His face looked like a perfect match to those chairs.

"This is Chaucer, one of the Duke's most prominent managers," Lysander said. When Kael shook his hand, he couldn't tell if Chaucer was pleased or put off to meet him. "And this is Geist."

He turned in the direction of Lysander's nod and very nearly bumped into the man called Geist. He was short and ... well, Kael had a hard time trying to find anything unusual to remember him by.

"Charmed," Geist said. Only he didn't look charmed. He looked bored.

"Geist is a man of many, ah, talents," Lysander said lamely, as if he was grasping to find some way to set him apart from the curtains. Then he introduced Kael as a strategist — about which neither man seemed to have any opinion — and invited them all to sit.

"I admit I was surprised when you finally answered my letter," Chaucer said as he pulled out a seat. For such a big man, he moved very lightly. His chair didn't even groan when he sat.

"Yes, well, I've been busy," Lysander said offhandedly.

Chaucer smirked. "I heard some interesting news the other day. Apparently, Copperdock is up and running again. It seems the Witch of Wendelgrimm has finally been defeated — and by a ragtag band of pirates, no less."

Lysander snorted. "I doubt they were ragtag — or pirates at all, for that matter. Wherever did you hear such a wild tale?"

"I have my sources," Chaucer said. And he watched Lysander like a hawk eyeing its prey.

Their staring match had the potential to drag on for hours, but Kael had no desire to spend the rest of his day locked in a windowless room with the three of them. He tried to get things moving. "I have a question: what's in it for you? I know what Lysander and I hope to gain, but why would a manager and a ... whatever, want to sack Duke Reginald?"

"I have absolutely no interest in the matter," Geist said dully, and Kael believed him.

"*Why?*" Chaucer made it sound like it was easily the stupidest question he'd ever heard. "I'll tell you why: because there's no sport in it anymore. I'm a merchant, bred from a long line of merchants, and I'm not being allowed to trade. It was thrilling at first, the idea of buying up all of the ships on the High Seas and driving prices skyward. But now we've got all the gold and all the bread. What's there left to do?" He propped one elbow up on the table and kept his fist clenched at his head. "The Duke calls us his managers because that's what we are — we herd his ships across the Seas, *delivering* whatever cargo he tells us to. We aren't merchants anymore — we're couriers. Overthrowing the Duke would allow us all to reclaim our dignity and our trade. That's *why*."

Not once, not even for a breath, did Chaucer mention how his conquest had enslaved the people of the High Seas. He had all the gold in the region, and now he was simply *bored*. Kael wanted to reach across the table and knock every last tooth out of his pompous mouth.

"Regardless of the reason, we're grateful for your support," Lysander said, shooting a warning look at Kael. "I trust the other managers have come around?"

Chaucer nodded, ever so slightly. "Most feel the same way I do about it. There are a few who don't ... but I'll take care of them."

"Right." Lysander turned quickly to Geist. "Do you have the map?"

He produced a large roll of paper from somewhere in the folds of his coat and handed it over.

"He's been working on this for months," Lysander said as he spread the parchment out on the table.

Kael found it hard to believe that the man staring aimlessly at the wall had rallied his interest long enough to draw something so detailed. And yet, the plans were exactly that: every room was drawn to scale, down to the arrangement of the furniture inside of them. Windows were marked by width and height, entrances labeled by the tumblers in their locks. Out to the side, he'd even written in cramped letters when they might expect the guards to change their shifts.

"Excellent." Lysander clapped his hands together so loudly that Chaucer flinched. "Now all we have to do is figure out someway inside ..."

****

Hours later, half of every candle was burned away and they still hadn't figured out how to crack the Duke's fortress. It was on an island of stone with nothing but ocean for miles around. They thought about attacking by sea — but quickly realized that if they were spotted, the Duke's battlemages would have no trouble blowing them to pieces. And, as Chaucer so bluntly pointed out: "Waves aren't usually tall enough to hide behind."

They very briefly entertained the idea of coming by land and charging across the mile-long bridge on foot. But when Chaucer mentioned it was rigged to burn, they dropped the idea entirely.

"He'll wait until you're out in the middle before he lights it. I don't think even the pirates can outrun fire."

Lysander looked up from where he'd been massaging his forehead and glared. "Just what do you mean by that?"

Chaucer shrugged. "Perhaps charging in isn't your best option. Aren't thieves usually better at throat-slitting and backstabbing?"

"You tell me," Lysander retorted, and he went back to the map. "There's got to be a way … some method of attack we've overlooked."

"We could always sprout wings and fly," Chaucer muttered, propping his boots up on the table.

"That's a grand idea, I'll hire a catapult," Lysander said sarcastically. "And if you don't get your feet off my table, I'll let you be the first to try it out."

Chaucer smirked and put his hands behind his head, but didn't move his feet. "Just come up with something quick, will you? I've got the Duke's party in a fortnight and I don't want to be late."

"Wait — the Duke is having a party?" Kael said, interrupting whatever retort Lysander had at the ready. "What for?"

"Power," Chaucer drawled. "He likes to force his managers out of hiding every now and again for a ball. Makes us prance around like idiots while he sits on his throne and lords it over us."

Kael felt an end pop loose in the back of his head. The tangled mass of information he'd absorbed suddenly came undone, and the mystery of how to get into the castle began to unravel. "What are the parties like?"

"Like?" Chaucer snorted. "Have you ever had a red-hot poker rammed up your —?"

"Be serious," Geist said — the first words he'd spoken all afternoon.

Chaucer raised his eyebrows, but strangely enough, he didn't argue. "All right. They're nightlong affairs with plenty of food and drink —"

"And dancing?"

"Yes —"

"Is anyone else invited, or is it only the managers?"

Chaucer made a face. "You ask a lot of questions, whelp."

"Answer him," Geist droned, and Chaucer waved his hand impatiently.

"I will, great seas! If there's going to be dancing, there has to be ladies. So the Duke requires us to bring our wives and daughters of age. I've got neither. Do you know what that means? I've got to dance with all the ugly ones —"

"What about guards?"

"Well of course there are guards! Are you daft?" Chaucer dropped his boots off the table and leaned dangerously inward. "The Duke's got them everywhere, on every level. They swarm all over the walls and buzz through the hallways. And if they catch you poking around anywhere you shouldn't, you get to spend the rest of the party in the dungeons with the castle torturer. Does that sound like fun to you, whelp? Want me to get you an invitation?"

"Actually, yes."

It was all unraveled, lying open and obvious before his eyes. He couldn't believe he hadn't thought of it before. He played it over again, just to make sure he got it exactly right. As he watched his plan unfold, he found he couldn't hear anything — not a sound. Not even Chaucer as he roared or Lysander as he bellowed back. Nothing.

The scenarios consumed him, the possibilities clogged his ears. When he was finally certain, he stepped back into the chaos of reality. "I have an idea."

After a long moment of stunned silence, Geist was the first to speak. He intertwined his fingers and said: "I knew you did. And I'm very interested to hear it."

Chapter 33
Madness

When Kael was finished explaining his plan, Lysander let out an astonished gasp of air. "Madness, pure madness," he muttered. But as he pulled thoughtfully at the hair on his chin, his smile grew wider. "Madness."

"Ridiculous, is what it is," Chaucer huffed, and he spun on Kael. "What if the Duke leaves the ballroom? What if he wanders upstairs during your little escapade and catches you haunting his hallways?"

Kael had an answer for that — and for every other question he asked. Nothing said was anything he hadn't already thought of, and with each calm rebuff, Chaucer grew more agitated.

"But what if it simply *fails*?" he finally blurted out, the stern lines of his face tinged with furious red. "What if Fate herself comes waltzing in and says it's not to be?"

"Snake oil and smoke," Lysander said with a wave of his hand. "If anything, Fate's on *our* side. And if she isn't, then it simply isn't meant to be. Either way," he continued before Chaucer could sputter on, "your part doesn't come until the very end. The Duke won't know you've gutted him until we've already got him clapped in irons. Don't worry, merchant — your hide is safe."

The red in Chaucer's face slowly retreated. "Fine," he said after a moment. He stood and jerked his coat over his shoulders. "I'm ready to do my part. Quickly, now — I've got mounds of letters to write."

Lysander rapped on the door and two brawny pirates entered. One of them wielded a rough-looking burlap sack. Both wore menacing grins.

Chaucer rolled his eyes at them. "Really, Captain. How much longer must I endure this humiliation? Won't you ever trust me?"

Lysander smiled wryly. "Sure I will. When my beard starts growing in purple, I'll tell you exactly where you are. But until then ..." He gestured to the pirates, and the one with the burlap shook it at Chaucer.

"I still don't understand why *I* have to be blindfolded," he whined on. "Why don't you ever —?"

He gestured in Geist's direction, but all that remained of the short, unremarkable fellow was his empty seat. Sometime during their conversation, Geist had simply ... vanished.

"That's why," Lysander said triumphantly. "Now, let's get your blindfold on."

The pirate stepped forward and crammed the sack over Chaucer's head while he cursed. They had him nearly through the door when he turned and thrust a finger in Kael's direction. "I want you to know, whelp —"

"He's to your left," Lysander said, and Chaucer turned until he was facing the empty room.

"If this plan falls through, I won't shed a tear at your execution," he continued, shaking his finger threateningly at the table and chairs. "In fact, I'll gladly bring the axe." Then he turned ... and ran smartly into the doorframe.

"Ah yes, watch out for that. Lead him away, dogs. And do *not* throw him off the boat again!" Lysander added with a glare.

When they'd gone, Kael gathered the map off the table and walked out into the hallway, his head spinning with all he had to do.

Lysander caught up at a jog. "What's next? Naval strategies? Traps? Archery practice —?"

"We have to talk to Aerilyn," he muttered, hoping that might halt him for a breath. And it did.

"Aerilyn?" he said, and Kael could hear the worry in his voice from down the hall. "*Our* Aerilyn? Whatever for?"

"Just come on, and I'll explain when we get there."

****

After a fair bit of searching, they found her. She was tucked away in one of the mansion's highest wings, abusing a large canvas with a brush and a smear of atrocious colors.

"What do you think?" she said, her excitement showing clearly through the splatters of blue across her face. "Uncle Martin says I have quite a gift."

A gift for turning a beautiful view into a nightmare, perhaps. Under Aerilyn's strokes, the brave white cliffs of Gravy Bay had melted into the sea, crumbling as they bled with long drips into waves that awaited them with too-sharp peaks. Her treetops were solid blobs of green and her clouds looked as if they'd eaten something that didn't quite agree with them.

"It's lovely," Lysander said as he stepped up for a closer look. "Simply amazing. We ought to have the window knocked out and hang this in its place."

Aerilyn turned pink and crammed her brush roughly into a nearby basin. "Don't be ridiculous. A canvas won't keep the rain out."

"But perhaps on sunny days —"

"We need your help," Kael said quickly, before the conversation could spin entirely out of hand. "We've finally come up with a plan to sack the Duke."

Aerilyn gasped, and that's when Kael remembered no one had actually told her about it. "Are you mad?" she hissed.

"You don't *have* to do anything. But we could use your —"

"We'll all be executed, or locked away forever!" she wailed, clutching at her apron. "I don't think I could bear to be so far from the sun."

"You don't have to help," Lysander gently reminded her.

She looked at him like he'd just stomped on her foot. "Oh no, I'm *certainly* going to help. Reginald has completely destroyed my region. He's starved my countrymen and driven respectable families into poverty. I'll not stand by and let him rule a moment longer!"

"All right," Kael said, before her tirade could take off. "If you want to help, here's what you've got to do ..."

When he was finished explaining, Aerilyn's fears were all but banished. She clapped her hands and declared: "Brilliant! Reginald's vanity will be his undoing. It's positively poetic."

"So you'll do it?"

"With pride."

Only Lysander seemed to have any reservations: he stared fixedly out the window and had grown strangely quiet. But when Aerilyn agreed, he suddenly had plenty to say. "Why her?" he demanded. "Why not Kyleigh, or — anybody else?"

Aerilyn laughed. "Kyleigh? Oh please. If a man laid a hand on Kyleigh, she'd break it. No, it's got to be me. Don't worry, Captain," she added with a smirk, "this isn't my first turn about the harbor."

"Not your first —? And what's that supposed to mean? Have you lured a man to his ruin before?"

"Perhaps not to his *ruin*, but I've certainly gotten more than a fair price on several occasions. How do you think lady merchants get on? We have to rely on our own talents."

"Talents?" Lysander bellowed. "*Talents?*"

Her brows snapped down as she crossed her arms. "Yes, *talents*. Men have muscles to do the persuading for them, is that any different? Why should a woman not be allowed to use her looks —?"

"Oh, I'll tell you why — because men are monsters, *that's* why!"

Kael didn't have the energy — or the time — to try and separate them. A fortnight would come and go if he let himself get distracted. So he left the pair to their argument and slipped out to find Jake.

****

379

"Are you sure it's set in right? If this shatters my window, I'll be a very cranky old pirate!" It was Uncle Martin's squawking that led Kael to the dining room. He opened the door and found him bent over, his face inches from the enormous window.

Kael only had to breathe in to know that the room was rank with magic.

"Mage glass is a halfway-useful invention," Uncle Martin went on. "You can see the spells, but I'll be blasted if I know what any of the squiggly little blighters mean. Are you sure it's set?"

"I think so," Jake said. He waved his staff at the window and the whole thing glowed for half a moment. "Yes, it's definitely covered."

"Well, then." Uncle Martin straightened up and turned on his cane. He grinned when he caught sight of Kael, blinking out through a monocle that made his eye thrice its normal size. "You're just in time for the demonstration, lad! Jonathan's about to put the spell to the test. Are you ready?"

Jonathan held up the metal saltshaker he had gripped in his hand. "C'mon mate, this isn't nearly big enough. Let's throw a chair or something."

"We'll start out small," Uncle Martin said as he joined their line. "Then if nothing too disastrous happens, we'll go a little bigger. Ready when you are! Arm the catapults!"

All Kael could think, as the saltshaker went sailing through the air, was how marvelously bad of an idea this was.

It struck the window and at first, he thought it'd gone straight through the glass. But then sunlight winked off the hole and he realized that the glass wasn't broken — somehow it was bending backwards, stretching against the force of the throw. It cradled the shaker like a stone in a sling.

"Duck!" Uncle Martin cried, and they fell to the ground just as the window snapped back into place.

The saltshaker shot over their heads, faster than an arrow, and struck the wall behind them. It ripped through a portrait of a mermaid — taking all of her teeth out with it.

The gaping hole in her mouth left her looking as shocked as Uncle Martin.

"Gravy save us, what was that?" he said as Jonathan helped him to his feet.

Jake rushed over to the window "I don't — oh, no." His thin shoulders slumped and he turned back to face them. "I accidentally linked the spell of indestructibility to one for ballistics when I etched it on my staff."

"What? I just need to know if it's safe to eat my breakfast in here."

"It should be. But just know that anything that hits the window is going to get catapulted right back out."

"Anything?" Jonathan asked.

"Yes ... wait — don't!"

But it was too late. Jonathan sprinted for the window, left his feet with a *whoop* and collided with the glass. It bent, screeching to hold his weight until it finally belched him back out. He crashed into the table — taking napkins, plates and several large candlesticks down with him — before he tumbled to the floor.

"What are you doing to my dining room?" Mrs. Bimply shrilled. She stuck her head out from the kitchen, and when she saw the carnage, the rose in her plump cheeks turned scarlet. "Those were my good dishes, Mr. Martin!"

"They were the Baron's good dishes, actually. And I'll make sure the boys steal you another set. Now back to your lair, harpy!"

With a rather indignant huff, Mrs. Bimply slammed the door on them.

Uncle Martin twirled his mustache like a man up to no good. "Now that we've got all the spoilsports taken care of, lets nick some mattresses and drag them down here — then we'll all have a go!"

Jonathan was certainly up for that. They left in a rush — giving Kael a moment to talk to Jake.

"Obviously, I won't ask you to risk your freedom — not when you've only just got it back," Kael said, when he'd finished explaining. "But I don't see how we can do this without your help."

Jake hadn't said anything: he'd been staring out the window, and only moved every now and then to push his spectacles back up the bridge of his nose. Kael had no idea what he was thinking until he said: "You mean ... you figured me into your plan?"

He thought that was an odd thing to say. "Of course I did. Having a mage on your side is pretty useful — especially if you think you can help us stay hidden."

Jake nodded, slowly. "I'm sure I can ... it shouldn't be too difficult." Then his mouth bent in the tiniest of smiles. "Of all the things a whisperer's ever called me, *useful* certainly isn't among them."

Kael could understand that. He liked Jake all right, but mercy — the man stank. He had to turn his head every now and then just to get a breath of fresh air.

"Speaking of mages," he said, changing the subject. "Do you think there might be any more in the castle worth saving? Any that might join our side?"

Jake's smile went hard. "The Duke is many things, but unfortunately *stupid* isn't one of them. He only keeps his most loyal mages inside his fortress. The rest — like me — are posted on cargo ships. The one you've really got to worry about is Bartimus."

"Who's Bartimus?"

"The court mage," Jake said, rather darkly. "He's got a gold impetus: a ring he wears on his middle finger. He's the one who cast the spell that bound me to the Duke." He leaned back in his chair and propped his hands where an average man's belly might've been. "It's smart of you to attack on a party night. The Duke doesn't like to have the mages around his guests, so he keeps them locked up in their tower. Which should make things easier."

True. Grisly as it was, having the mages pinned in and defenseless made things *much* easier. Kael thought for a moment. "In that case, if I were to mix a basic sleeping compound, do you think you might be able to make it a little more ... potent?"

"Certainly," Jake said, his smile hard. "Death is a battlemage's trade, after all."

****

When all the others were informed, there was only one person left that Kael needed to talk to. Unfortunately, he couldn't find her anywhere. After he'd scoured the mansion twice over — a task that took him several days — he still had no idea where Kyleigh was hiding. He didn't even know where she slept. And everyone else seemed to know about as much as he did.

"No, I haven't seen her since yesterday —"

"Yesterday? Where was she?" Kael interrupted.

Aerilyn frowned. "In the spell room with Jake. They were pouring over books and muttering about all sorts of boring things."

He'd already looked in the spell room — twice. And he had no desire to go back in. He'd hardly gotten the door open before the tang of magic washed over him and made the bile rise in his throat. He fought his way through the teetering shelves and piles of yellowed parchment for as long as he could hold his breath, and then he'd slammed the door.

"You haven't seen her since?"

Aerilyn shook her head. "No, but I wish I had. Everything's so ..." She twirled at her hair for a moment. "Perhaps you can help me."

Kael took a step back. "I'm actually sort of —"

"It's about Lysander. I know he cares for me — after he went off the other day about my part in the plan, I knew he cared. I can tell by the way he looks at me, how he compliments my horrible artwork. And Papa obviously trusted Matteo ... he must have. Why else would he have given the pirates his ship?" She smiled for a moment, then slipped back into a frown. "But Lysander's still a *pirate*! A

383

horrible, grog-gulping pirate! Oh, I don't know what I should do. What *should* I do?"

She leaned forward, as if he had all the answers and all she had to do was listen. He realized there was only one path of escape. No promise to Lysander was worth sitting through one of Aerilyn's crying spells.

"I'm going to tell you something, but you can't tell a soul, all right?"

When she nodded, he told her about Lysander's secret. He told her what he did for the people of the High Seas under the cover of darkness. He told her everything, and while he spoke, her eyes grew wider.

"He's a rogue only in costume," she said when he was finished. "He pretends to be a bad man in order to hide the fact that he's not." She grabbed the front of Kael's shirt, so roughly that it put him on his toes. "He's not really a pirate at all — he's a good man, isn't he? I knew it! Oh!" She flung her arms around his neck and very nearly choked him. "Thank you, Kael! Thank you for telling me."

"You're welcome," he gasped.

As soon as he broke free from Aerilyn, he headed straight for the library. If she'd been looking over books with Jake, then she must have gone to the library to find them. All he had to do was set up camp and wait for her to return.

But when he opened the doors, it wasn't Kyleigh he found: it was Lysander.

"Fancy meeting you here," he said with a grin. "What luck!"

Kael doubted very seriously that luck had anything to do with it, especially since the book Lysander was pretending to read was upside down. He'd been waiting.

"I think I forgot my —"

"Actually, I was hoping you'd be here. Do you have a moment?" He set the book on the table behind him and began to pace, hands clasped smartly behind his back. "I confess I have something to ask you. It's about Aerilyn."

"What about her?" Kael said, discreetly positioning himself next to the door.

"I can't stop thinking about her," Lysander replied after a moment. He quickened his pace and his words came pouring out. "No, that isn't entirely true — I *ache* for her. I can't sleep, I can hardly eat anything, and anything I do eat just tastes like sand. It's maddening!" He crossed his arms and glared stoically through the waves of his hair. "I need to know, once and for all, if I have a chance. Do I have a chance?"

"Uh —"

"And even if I do, I *don't*," he exclaimed, thrusting his hands in the air. "I can't love her — she's a *merchant*, by Gravy. We are the sea and the sky! The sea may love the sky, but can he ever reach her? Can he ever hold her in his arms? Must they be forever doomed to live apart?" Lysander slumped into one of the chairs and buried his face in his hand.

Only when he stopped talking did Kael realize how he truly felt. It was the fall of his shoulders, the ragged defeat in his breath that finally convinced him: Captain Lysander was heartbroken.

He told himself he wouldn't get distracted, but as much as he wanted to sprint from the room, he couldn't leave Lysander in torment. "What if the sky became the sea? If Aerilyn became a pirate, could you love her?"

"Of course," he said, rather spitefully. "But however will I convince her? She's so good and I'm so ... well, I try my hardest not to be good."

"And yet you are," Kael said, playing on the words Aerilyn had spoken only moments before. "Someone always has to be good. If the Duke is bad, and if merchants like Chaucer serve the Duke ..."

"They're bad too?" Lysander guessed. He thought intensely for a moment, the lights behind his stormy eyes pulsed as they worked to generate a conclusion. "If those who write the laws are bad, and *someone* has to be good, then it's got to be us — it must be the outlaws, the pirates! Ha!" He slapped his knee and sprang to his feet. "Aerilyn is so good that it's only a matter of time: she'll come around to being a pirate, and then we can be together!"

385

Kael was glad he hadn't been the one to say it. He didn't want to get Lysander's hopes up.

"Hold on a moment," Lysander called when he tried to make a hasty exit. "If you're heading out, would you be so kind as to take this down to the basement for me?" He pulled a vial of dark liquid out of his breeches pocket. When he held it to the light, it turned red.

"I didn't know there was a basement," Kael said as he took the vial. It was strangely warm.

Lysander cleared his throat. "Yes, well, it's sort of out-of-the-way. There's a trapdoor under the main staircase that'll lead you to it. I'd take it myself, but I'm already running behind. I was supposed to meet Jake an hour ago — we're practicing the attack formation," he added with a grin.

He strode from the room before Kael could object, leaving him with yet another unwanted task. At the rate things were going, he thought it might be a full year before they were ready to face the Duke.

Chapter 34
Foolishness

Beneath the spiral staircase was a battered trapdoor — right where Lysander said it would be. At least the basement didn't look as dark and damp as Kael imagined it: a dim light glowed out from the depths, illuminating the narrow ladder leading into the room below.

He tucked the vial of dark liquid into his pocket and tried not to step too heavily as he made his way down. The ladder creaked under his feeble weight. He thought it might collapse at any moment and fling him into the bowels of the mansion. But miraculously enough, it held.

As his boots touched the packed earth floor, he realized he was sweating. He thought it was his nerves at first, but then he breathed in and his lungs nearly shriveled under the heat. His collar began to cling to the back of his neck as he made his way towards the light.

Clang! Clang! Clang!

The noise ricocheted off the walls, tore through the hot air and made his heart leap directly into his throat. It was sharp, and stabbed mercilessly at the insides of his ears. He had to clamp his hands over them just to keep moving.

He hurried around the corner and nearly tripped when he saw what awaited him on the other side: a trough of fire, filled to the brim with low-burning tongues of yellow flame.

He thought he couldn't have found anything odder in a basement. The trough had been set into the wall; it produced enough light to fill the whole wide-open room around it, and enough heat to melt the snow from a dozen winters. To the right of the trough were an anvil and a small shelf.

And leaning over the anvil, thrashing at a red-hot piece of metal, was Kyleigh.

Her eyes glowed in the fire of her work. Sparks flew up as her hammer came down. A wisp of flame rose, hissed, and she beat it back into the iron. Then she turned and thrust it into the trough, where the flames lapped hungrily at it. She dragged an arm across her forehead and her eyes widened when she noticed Kael haunting her doorway.

"Hold on a moment," she said. Then she reached up and with a sharp tug, pulled a metal lid down on the flames, leaving only a thin sliver of light.

By the time his eyes adjusted, she was standing next to him. She wore a loose-fitting tunic and breeches with a thick leather apron tied over the top. Her gloves were cracked and covered with singe marks. Her feet were bare — which Kael didn't think was a particularly good idea, considering the condition of the gloves.

"I was wondering how long it would take you to find me," she said, her lips bent in a smirk. "I'll admit I was expecting you much sooner."

"You're a blacksmith?"

She shrugged. "Not really. It's a hobby more than anything. But I do find it intriguing."

"Smithing?"

"Fire." She smiled, and light glanced her eyes. "Perhaps it's the dragon in me, but I've always enjoyed watching the flames do their work." She held out her hand. "You have something for me, don't you? From Lysander? I thought so. I can smell it on you."

"What do you mean?" he said as he handed the vial over.

She pulled the cork out with her teeth and spat it away. "Nothing reeks quite as grandly as fresh blood," she said, waving the vial at him.

His stomach twisted to think that he'd been carrying blood around in his pocket. "Whose is it?"

"Lysander's, of course. I'm going to use it to mend the Lass," she said, in answer to the question on his lips. "Come along and I'll show you."

He stood to the side as she pulled the Lass out of the flames. "What's left to be done?"

"I've fixed the blade, but now I've got to wake her up," Kyleigh said. "Normal swords are one thing, but the Lass has magic in her. In order to bring her back to her former glory I need two things: blood of a pirate, and dragon flames. Lucky for me, I already use dragon fire to light my forge."

So *that's* what she'd been doing in the spell room with Jake. "How does it work?"

"I'm about to show you."

She held the Lass over the forge and with a quick swipe, drizzled a line of blood on either side of the blade. It met the steel with a hiss, it bubbled and popped as she turned it, letting the blood run down to the very tip. Then she thrust it deep into the coals.

A blast of hot air erupted from the trough, knocking Kael a step backwards. The flames rose and fell onto the Lass, batting it in angry waves. They made a strange, high-pitched shrilling as they danced. His toes curled at the sound of it.

When Kyleigh pulled the Lass free, she turned and immediately drove it into a barrel of water. The blade sighed and steam billowed up in a giant puff.

"What *was* that?"

"I told you — I had to wake her up." She pulled off her gloves and waved him over to the shelf. "While we wait for her to cool, I've got something for you."

Not again. How many debts must he owe her? Amos would be ashamed if he knew. "Well I can't accept it, whatever it is. I just needed to talk to you about —"

"The grand sacking of His Dukeness? Lysander told me all about it this morning. You know I'll do my part."

He was slightly peeved. Had she appeared to everyone in the Kingdom but him? "Where were you?"

"In the library, of course."

"Oh, so I suppose you were nicking books again. That's really clever of you, by the way."

"I don't know what you're talking about," she said lightly. "I hate reading."

His astonishment knocked whatever he'd been about to say right out of him. "How can you hate reading? How can *anybody* hate reading?"

"I don't know. I suppose I'd rather be killing things than reading about it," she said, with an impatient wave of her hand. Then she snatched something off the shelf and handed it to him. "Here. These are for you."

It was a pair of gauntlets — so odd and remarkably made that he couldn't stop himself from staring. They were black as night and forged of what appeared to be iron. He stood quietly while she pulled them over his hands, admiring how strangely light they were. They stretched halfway up his forearm, their tops ridged and slightly sharp. He imagined he could do a fair bit of damage just punching someone.

The gloves were the oddest part: they were cut off at his second knuckle on all fingers and a circle had been cut out the bottom, leaving his entire palm exposed.

"That's how Setheran always wore his," Kyleigh explained as she snapped the buckles into place. "He said he couldn't whisper properly if he couldn't feel what he touched."

"I suppose you made him some gauntlets too, huh?"

His tone was not lost on Kyleigh. She stopped what she was doing and pulled back from him, the corners of her open mouth bent in a smile. "Ah, so *that's* the problem."

"What's the problem?"

"You think I was in love with Setheran, don't you?"

"What? No —"

"You do!" she said with a laugh. "You thought we were lovers! That's why you've been so particularly cranky, isn't it? You think I'm so sad and brokenhearted, and now you don't know what to do with me."

"I do not," he said, even though it wasn't true. He shoved her hand away and fumbled with the buckles on the gauntlets. He refused to stand down in that insufferably hot basement and be made a fool of. "Here, keep your dodgy gloves."

She grabbed his arm, covering the buckles so he couldn't pull them loose. "They're gauntlets, not gloves. I'm not a seamstress," her brows dropped into a dangerous glare, "and nothing I make is the least bit dodgy. He was married, Kael," she said as she released him. "He was madly in love with his wife and they were expecting their first child. So if you'll kindly get your knickers out of a twist —"

"They aren't in a twist," he said impatiently. "Setheran had a child? Why have I never read about that?"

A strange look crossed her face. She went back to cinching up his gauntlets, undoing all the work he'd just done to pull them loose. "The historians didn't mention it because it didn't matter. Setheran only got to hold him once before Fate took the child and mother away."

He knew his mouth was hanging open, but he didn't care. Now he knew why Setheran the Wright sacrificed himself in the final battle against the rebel whisperers. He must have looked just as the songs described him:

Like heroes of old before, he knew what must be done:
With sword in hand and eyes alight,
The cry he loosed shook the mountains down,
And buried foes with Seth the Wright.

He'd called the mountains down upon himself because he had nothing left to live for. What the Kingdom thought was a sacrifice was actually Setheran's great relief ...

"Do they fit well?"

Kyleigh's voice brought him back from the battlefield, where he'd been watching Setheran meet his end in a whole new light. "They fit perfectly," he said, and it was no exaggeration. The gauntlets molded to his skin. He felt as if they belonged there. He reached up and ran his fingers across the material: it was smooth, impossibly hard. Certainly not iron and yet ... familiar. He grasped at a memory. "It's made of dragon scales, isn't it? That's why your armor doesn't tear when you change form —"

She clamped a hand over his mouth. It was an involuntary movement; the shock in her eyes gave her away. "Blast you whisperers and your memory for things," she muttered. "Yes, they're made of dragon scales — *my* scales, actually. And no, before you ask, I won't tell you how it's done."

"Why're they black?" he said from around her hand.

She pursed her lips. "I blacken them to attempt to hide the obvious. But now that you know, you have to swear not to tell a solitary person. Do you understand? This has to stay between you and I."

He had no idea why she should be so defensive about it. But he thought if he didn't agree she might very well kill him and bury his body under the floor, so he nodded.

She studied him for a long moment, her eyes hard, before she released him. "You can take the Lass up to Lysander and leave me be. I've got a lot of work to do."

The Lass was whole once again, but he could see very clearly where she'd patched the pieces back together. The crisscrossing lines looked like the mends in a traveler's cloak.

"It suits her," Kyleigh said as she handed the sword over. "It reminds her of the urchins and thieves she loves to protect."

"You ... talk to it?"

He meant to hide his skepticism, but didn't do a very good job of it. She spun him around by his shoulders and shoved him towards the door. "Off with you," she snapped.

As he left, he couldn't help but think that the strokes of her hammer were coming down a little more maliciously than before.

****

It was a full week before Geist returned, and he didn't even bother to announce himself. Kael simply came out of his room one morning and nearly tripped over what he thought was a poorly placed chair. Then he looked down and realized it wasn't furniture at all: just Geist holding a traveler's chest.

"I thought we might practice your disguise, if you have a moment," he droned.

"All right," Kael said, still a little taken aback. "Oh — hold on a moment." He ducked into his room and returned with the potion Jake had finished mixing the day before.

"Ah, thank you," Geist said, slipping it into his coat pocket. "Shall we?"

Kael didn't even bother to ask whether Geist thought he would be able to sneak into the mages' tower unnoticed. He just nodded and followed him to the meeting room.

Geist plopped his chest down in the middle of the table, stirring up a cloud of ancient dust. "The first thing we've got to do is get you properly dressed," he said, with all the same energy of the dust settling around their shoulders.

He popped the chest open: first at its lid and then sideways, revealing a number of tiny shelves. There were several jars of paint, labeled by color and arranged by hue. Canisters of powder sat next to the paint, and a number of wigs hung on hooks beneath them. But the most exciting thing by far was the vast collection of fake mustaches.

Kael picked up the bushiest one he could find and stuck it under his nose. He laughed when he saw himself in the chest's tiny mirror.

Geist plucked it off and set it back in its place. Then he picked up another — one that was slightly gray and shaped like an upside-down comb. He popped the cork out of a small, green glass bottle and selected the tiniest of his many brushes, which he dipped into the bottle. He swiped a bit of clear, sticky liquid onto the back of the mustache without explanation.

"Why do you have all of these things?" Kael said, partly to break the deafening silence. He wasn't even certain Geist was breathing.

"Why does the mason carry a chisel, or the bard his lute? These are the tools of my trade, whisperer."

While he was still in the process of being shocked, Geist stuck the mustache under his nose. The paste was cold and dried quickly to his upper lip. "How did you know I was a —?"

"It's my business to know," Geist replied, as if it was easily the most boring business in the Kingdom. "Let's set all the questions aside for now and try to focus our limited attention on the task at hand, shall we? Splendid. Am I right to assume that you've never taken a character before?"

"What?"

"Hmm, I thought so." Geist sat up straight: a movement that seemed almost as laborious as it was bothersome. "The manager you'll be impersonating is a man called Colderoy. He's very fat, and most people find him annoying."

Kael wasn't exactly sure what he should say in the long space Geist left him to respond. "All right ... so, how do I do this?"

"Every character has his prop — the feature or mannerism he abuses to no end. Colderoy's," he traced his upper lip with thumb and forefinger, "is his mustache. In fact, ninety percent of his personality is in what grows under his nose."

Kael suddenly felt unsure. "Isn't there someone easier I could impersonate? Someone less of a character?"

Geist shook his head. "I can hide your face and your body, but I can do nothing to hide your eyes. Though he married a seas woman, Colderoy is originally from the forest. He is the only one of the Duke's managers whose eyes are brown."

Kael scratched at his nose, where the little hairs of his mustache were starting to tickle. "But what about Aerilyn?"

"What about her? Colderoy's daughter is just now of age: this was to be her first official ball. No one will know if she is the real Margaret or not — she's a stranger either way. Now, Colderoy has a very particular way of speaking. He thrusts his words out through his mustache. Observe." Geist closed his eyes and cleared his throat. "Good ephening."

He sounded like a completely different person. His words were obnoxiously drawn-out: inhaled through his mouth and breathed half out his nose.

Kael spent a whole hour just trying to master the voice. Geist would ask questions that he thought the Duke might ask, and he would have to answer as Colderoy. He struggled to remember everything Geist told him about the tax collecting business — Colderoy's particular area of expertise — all while trying to mimic the gestures Geist showed him.

"Bounce your belly when you walk," Geist said. He stood and took a step forward with his stomach stuck out. "See how my shoulders are sloped down, how my neck juts out like a condescending vulture? That's how Colderoy walks. Give it a try."

Kael's attempt didn't seem to particularly impress him.

"I suspect it'll look better when you've actually got a belly. Things to remember when pretending to be Colderoy," Geist listed them off with his fingers, "chew with your mouth open, talk with your mouth full, and get as many crumbs lodged in your mustache as possible. Crumbs are useful projectiles — should anyone begin to ask questions, spraying them with bits of pastry usually scares them off. In fact, when you aren't dancing, you should be eating —"

"Dancing?" Kael said, slightly alarmed.

Geist frowned. "Yes, you'll have to dance. It's tradition for a father to dance with his daughter on the night of her first ball. You'll have to take the first turn with Aerilyn." When he saw how much blood had gone from Kael's face, he sighed. "Another rut in the path, is it? Well, I suppose we've still got time to teach you."

****

On their way down to dinner, Geist vanished. Kael had no idea how long he carried on a conversation with the tapestries before he finally noticed the man was gone. Then something equally extraordinary happened shortly after dinner: Thelred emerged.

"I need the merchant and the whisperer," he snapped over the top of their chatting.

Uncle Martin looked up from where he'd been admiring Aerilyn's latest disastrous work of art — a pair of white-socked kittens with their furry faces melted together — and frowned. "Whatever for?"

"Geist said I'm to teach them how to dance. Lysander's already waiting, and the sooner we get this over with, the sooner I can get back to my work."

"Oh, your old woman can wait," Uncle Martin said with a laugh. "That's the beauty of being in love with something that weighs nearly a thousand pounds — it's not like she's going anywhere!"

Thelred glared at him. "You've only got an hour of my time. So if you want to learn, I suggest you get off your rumps and follow me."

"To the ballroom!" Uncle Martin declared.

"Dancing, eh? Good thing I just happen to have my fiddle," Jonathan said with a wink. And he pulled the instrument out from under his napkin.

Thelred swore loudly.

****

The ballroom was nearly as big as the library, but it was completely empty. Uncle Martin had to drag in a chair from another part of the house in order to have a place to critique them from. "Tickle her for me, will you?" he called as Thelred took his place.

The mystery girl turned out to be an enormous piano. Kael had only ever read about them, and he knew only the wealthiest nobles could afford to keep them. "Where did you find that?" he asked.

"Wendelgrimm," Thelred said from over his shoulder.

"It's more bulk than worth, if you want my opinion," Aerilyn muttered to Kael, rather haughtily. "I do believe it was the most impractical trinket in the entire castle."

"What did you choose, then?"

"This," she said, waving to her dress. It was powder blue and looked elaborate enough for a queen.

She fanned out her skirts and twirled, revealing the intricate white lace beneath it. And Kael thought she might have found the one thing more impractical than a piano among the Witch's treasures.

A sudden string of noise drew his eyes to the opposite end of the room. For all his stomping and cursing under breath, the second Thelred touched the piano, the whole room filled with music. He played only a few quick notes, but they rang out so sweetly that Kael had to stop to listen.

Aerilyn ran into him from behind. "I hope this isn't a sign of your skills," she said wryly.

But unfortunately for both of them, it was.

Lysander spun her around the room a few times, just to show Kael the steps. They moved through a waltz like fish through water, laughing and carrying on as they went. Every now and then, Aerilyn had to jerk Lysander's hand back up her waist — from where it'd been wandering dangerously close to her rump.

The dance ended when she slapped him full across the face and stomped away.

"And that's how it's done!" Lysander said. He took a deep bow while Jonathan and Uncle Martin applauded.

"Horrible rogue," Aerilyn muttered as Kael got his feet into position. But for all her fussing, he didn't think she looked particularly upset. "At least I can count on you to be a perfect gentleman."

Gentleman he was, but dancer he most certainly was not. The whole idea of prancing around to music was ridiculous to him. He didn't understand how anyone could enjoy looking so completely foolish. He tried to make the steps as quick and un-flourished as possible — which didn't turn out well.

"Ow!" Aerilyn hopped away from him as the music ground to a halt. "Kael, that's the twelfth time this dance!"

"I'm sorry —"

"I don't know if my toes can take it any longer. At this rate, you'll have me peg legged before sunrise!"

"Can you not just step to the beat, man?" Thelred grumped, dragging his hands down his face in exasperation. "Or are mountain children born idiots?"

"There's no call for that," Uncle Martin said before Kael could retort. "I, for one, would like to see him take the lead every now and then. It doesn't do to keep a woman at the helm."

"Agreed," Lysander said. "Try holding her tightly, Kael. There should be inches between you, not leagues."

He was absolutely not going to do that. "I don't see why it matters if I'm any good or not. Everyone looks like a fool dancing."

"Though some more than others," Thelred muttered.

Kael had a very inventive reply at the ready, but at that moment Geist walked through the door. "I was wondering if I might borrow Aerilyn," he said, and his voice had the snuffing effect of a damp towel on their argument.

"Yes, you may. We'll just pick up here tomorrow," Aerilyn said as she hurried to follow Geist out the door. Kael had every intention of going right behind them when Lysander leapt in his path.

"Just where do you think you're headed?"

"I had a very slim shot at freedom, and I was planning to take it."

Lysander spun him around and shoved him back into the room. "No, you aren't going anywhere. Not until we get this dancing mess sorted out."

"But my partner's just run off, in case you haven't noticed."

"We'll just have to find you a new one."

"I don't want —"

"Either we find you a new girl, or you're dancing with Jonathan. It's entirely your choice."

Kael glanced at the fiddler, who made a very pronounced kissing face at him, and decided on the lesser of two tortures. "Fine. Get another girl."

Lysander stuck his head into the hallway and glanced around for a likely victim. "Ahoy there, Kyleigh. Would you help me with something?"

Jonathan and Uncle Martin let out simultaneous *Ooooos* as she said she would. Kael was so humiliated he thought he was in danger of burning through his clothes.

When Kyleigh saw him, she raised an eyebrow. "Why do you look as if you've just taken an arrow to the rump?"

This made the others burst out laughing, while Kael burned all the redder.

"I was hoping you might help us teach him to dance," Lysander said when he managed to catch his breath.

Kael was fed up with their teasing, and thought if he stayed another moment he might be forced to put a rather large dent in the side of Jonathan's head. "This is ridiculous. I'm turning in," he said, before he could hear Kyleigh's refusal.

He tried to leave, but she grabbed him by the arm and held him like a vise. "I'll be glad to help. Which dance?"

"Oh, I don't know ..." Lysander's mouth bent in a mischievous grin, "how about *Moonlit Lovers*?"

Kael would have given him an exceptionally rude gesture, had his hand been free: Lysander knew very well how much he hated that dance. But nothing, not even his swears could keep the music from playing. Though he fought with all his might, Kyleigh pulled him into her.

"I don't want to do this," he said, but she ignored him. She laced her fingers in his and stuck his other hand to her waist. Fire rose in his stomach again and he wrestled it back as she began the steps.

He glared down at her feet to avoid having to look her in the eyes. "You should probably put some shoes on. Aerilyn left because I squashed her toes flat."

"You'll have to do worse than that to get rid of me." He could hear the smile in her voice, and the flames swelled up. "Why do you look as if you're in pain?"

Because I am *in pain*, he thought. "It's nothing. Let's just get through this."

"All right."

She took a step that caught him off guard, a turn he wasn't expecting. He had to rush to catch up with her. "That's not one of the steps."

She laughed. "Oh? Says who?"

"Says everyone! It's not the way it was written."

"We aren't mixing potions — we're dancing. I can almost promise that we won't explode if we add in a few things."

"Still, if I'm to learn this, I ought to learn it properly."

"I think you're scared."

He met her eyes. "I most certainly am not."

"Just try to keep up," she said, grinning.

He accepted her challenge. He refused to let her beat him at something so ridiculous. Whatever steps she came up with, he matched. She turned, and he anticipated. She spun, and he was there to catch her. They moved with the music: stepping in, touching, pulling away. Intertwined for some notes, tangled limb for limb. Then separated, yearning, and finally pulled back in.

He could feel the sweat on his brow and feel his lungs burning for air. The fiddle thrummed the chords of his heart and the piano told him where to put his feet. He sparred with his partner, locked in a desperate battle. He watched the bend of her arms and the arch of her neck, waiting hungrily for the thrill of her next move. And when it came, he was ready.

Then the music stopped.

Their bodies locked in the final motion. Feeling came back to his limbs. He was first aware of the hand clenched in his, how their forearms were latched together just as tightly as their fingers. Then he felt his other arm, strong and confident, wrapped around her waist. She clung to the wrist of that arm. In the lingering fervor of the dance, he knew she wasn't trying to pull him away: it was desperation that sewed her to him. In the throb of her fingertips, she begged him to stay.

He drew breath, and so did she. They breathed together, every contour of their bodies mashed into one. His breath moved the wisps of hair on the back of her neck, the ones that must've pulled free as they spun.

And then fire.

He tore himself loose and staggered backwards. Lysander called after him, asked him where he was going, but Kael didn't stop. He couldn't explain the ache in his chest. He'd never known a pain like this. There was no salve for this wound, there was no way he could mend it.

He staggered back to his room and slammed the door. He turned the key so hard that it snapped in the lock. He let the broken half fall to the floor and tried to wrestle his pain away, but he couldn't. It was too powerful, too relentless. His whole body convulsed with the torment of it. He knew that if he didn't do something, he would die. So he turned and brought both of his fists down on the top of the dresser — as hard as he could.

The wood split in half and showered splinters into the top drawer. He sat down hard on the edge of the bed, his hands still shaking from the effort. He'd tried so hard to bury it, to hide it in the deepest, darkest part of his soul. And then that stupid dance ...

Slowly, he calmed. His chest was sore, but the worst of the pain was gone. "Don't be a fool," he said to himself between every ragged breath. He glared at the shattered drawer, and his nails dug into his palms as he clenched his fists. "Don't be a fool."

Chapter 35
Liquid Courage

The morning before the Duke's party, Kael's nerves finally caught up with him. He was so worried over his plan, so lost in scenarios that he could hardly stay in the present for more than a few moments at a time.

"I said to raise your glass, lad!"

Uncle Martin's bark startled him back into the dining room. He muttered an apology and grabbed the small crystal glass in front of him. It was filled to the brim with a dangerous-looking green liquid. He wasn't sure, but he thought it might actually be smoking.

"Gravy grog — a pirate's liquid courage," Uncle Martin said, grinning around the table. "A swig on the morn of any adventure, and you're guaranteed not to regret it until you're too far out to turn back."

Jake took an apprehensive whiff of his glass and made a face. "What's in it?"

Uncle Martin frowned. "I can't tell you."

"Because it's a secret?"

"No — because my great grandfather lost the recipe! Every batch is different: we just sort of add things in the mix as we find them. Now," he tipped his glass higher, "may the winds be fair, and the maids even fairer. Gravy's luck go with you!"

At his lead, they took a deep breath and threw their grog back.

It was at least a thousand times more potent than ale. Kael didn't let it touch his tongue, but it still torched his throat as it slid down. Then it hit his gut and exploded. He fell on the ground, coughing madly. He tried desperately to keep his lungs from burning up. He blinked through the tears in his eyes and saw that he was not alone: everyone but Kyleigh had collapsed under the table.

"I'm dying!" Jonathan gasped as he clutched at his throat.

Jake's nose and eyes leaked freely, his face was covered in sweat. Aerilyn and had her arms around her gut and groaned as she lay on her side. Thelred and Lysander swore magnificently between coughs.

"I think this may have been the batch with the serpent venom — the one Matteo and I mixed as a joke," Uncle Martin wheezed from where he lay spread-eagle under his chair. "I think he'd be pleased to know that the only one of us who can stand it breathes fire half the time!"

****

The grog did its work well. When the burning faded from his lungs, the rest of the afternoon became a distant memory — albeit one that was slightly blurred around the edges. It was only after they were well out to sea that Kael realized what he'd done.

The fog cleared from his eyes and he started to see the faces around him more clearly. He recognized many of the pirates from his original voyage on *Anchorgloam*: men who'd been separated from their loved ones for years before. And now they were back at sea, hoisting sails, climbing through the rigging, sharpening their blades — preparing for battle.

A battle Kael was leading them into. One that, if things went wrong, might cause many of them to never see their families again. Guilt slid between his ribs like a knife.

"What have I done?"

"Done? Nothing, yet," Morris answered him. He'd taken the helm for the trip south. It was only a day's journey to the Duke's castle, but in order to avoid being spotted by his fleet, they had to stay close to land. Which made the water a great deal more treacherous.

Kael nerves started to push back into his limbs. "I can't ask the men to do this. I can't ask them to risk their lives again."

Morris snorted. "Aye, 'cause asking wouldn't do you a splinter of good. Every man here volunteered for the fight. In fact, I hear there were so many volunteers that the captain had to cast lots just to keep it fair."

Kael didn't believe him. "Why?"

"Because they want freedom for their region! They put their names on this list in particular because they believe in your plan," he poked a nub in the center of his chest, "because they believe in *you.*"

Kael suddenly felt a mix of emotions that he blamed entirely on the grog. "Well, they shouldn't. I didn't ask them to."

Morris smiled just widely enough to reveal the gaps in his teeth. "Belief is a burden, lad. It's something put on you, not something you put on. Speaking of," he propped one flap of his coat open, "I've got something for you — it's tucked right in that inner pocket. Took me half an afternoon to pull it out of the drawer, and another half to wedge it in my coat. So if you want it sometime today, you'll have to get it yourself."

Kael reached into the pocket and pulled out what looked to be a small leather wallet. But when he opened it, it wasn't coin he found: there were rows of knives lining either flap.

They were small, only about the length of his palm and made out of single pieces of steel. He could tell by the many hairline scratches that covered their surface that they were well used. Yet the points still looked sharp enough to split stubble.

"Those were from a friend of mine," Morris said. He tugged gently on the wheel, steering them around a sharp clump of rocks. "It was right after the War ended. He gave these to me and said it was because a Seer told him to, said his warring days were over. Ha!" He shook his head, his smile etched in sorrow.

"Morris, I couldn't —"

404

"Sure you can." He waved his arm impatiently. "I think he'd be proud to know a Wright was using them. They're perfectly balanced, see — won't cost you hardly anything to throw them straight. And that wallet folds over, too. You can strap it to your arm and no one would even know you had it."

Kael worked the buckles around his upper left arm and showed it to Morris.

"There you are, lad," he said with a grin. "Now you look the part."

****

Surprisingly enough, Geist seemed pleased by his new weapons. When Kael went down to the brig to change into his disguise, he glanced at his arm and mumbled: "Those will be much more effective than a hunting dagger, I'm sure. Now — let's get you into your belly."

It took an hour to apply all the paste, stuffing, paint and false hair to Kael's body. When Geist was finished, he held up a small hand mirror for approval.

A fat, sallow old merchant blinked back at him. Kael could hardly believe it. "Geist ... it's amazing."

"You approve?"

He nodded, and grimaced when he saw how his chins wobbled with the motion. "I'm disgusting myself."

"Perfect. That should keep anyone from wanting to talk to you."

His work was astonishing, no doubt about it. But Kael did have one final concern: "What about the real Colderoy? How are you going to keep him from showing up?"

"There is a particular inn he likes to dine at before he attends these parties," Geist said, packing up his trunk with sloth-like grace as he spoke. "Apparently, he's fond of the keeper's mince pies. Tonight, however, he and Margaret will contract a rather disturbing stomach condition shortly after their meals — one that I suspect will keep them busy well into the following day. Colderoy will write to the Duke, explaining his absence. But unfortunately, his letter will never arrive."

"Because you're going to lose it?"

Geist shook his head. "Not me, dear boy. A rather bungle-headed courier with a b — bit of a st — stutter will be to blame."

****

It was sundown when *Anchorgloam* stopped at a certain bend in the shoreline — one with a large boulder shaped like an eagle's crown sticking out from the water. Lysander arranged for a rowboat to be let down and accompanied them to shore.

Aerilyn's disguise was as beautiful as his was revolting. Geist had labored over her curls, twirling each one into a perfect golden-brown ring. He'd painted her lips and the tops of her eyes to give her smile near insurmountable allure — not that it was really necessary. The red dress she wore was more than inviting.

Lysander seemed unable to keep his eyes off of her. They pulled onto the beach and he nearly tripped over his own boots in his rush to be the one to help her out of the boat.

Since he was obviously so preoccupied, Kael let out a low whistle into the tree line, signaling for Chaucer and his men to come on.

Three carriages rolled promptly out to meet them, pulled along by horses that looked to be the clean-cut, stern image of their master. "It's about time," Chaucer snapped as he burst from the door of the first cart. "You had me waiting out in this heat for a good half-hour. I was about to have to lead us around in circles just to get some air ..." His lip curled at the sight of Kael. "Excellent work, Geist. I can hardly stand the look of him." Then he settled his gaze on Aerilyn. "Very lovely. Lovely, indeed."

"Take those appraising eyes off of her," Lysander growled, which drew a smirk from Chaucer.

"Just make sure your toy boat is ready to do battle, *Captain*." He straightened his already-straight coat hems and marched back towards his carriage. "Move, all of you!" he barked from his window. "We haven't got time for weak knees — the hands are turning."

Lysander hurled a clump of wet sand at his carriage as he rolled away. It stuck to the back window with a *thwap*. "For all his talk of weak knees, you'd think he'd actually be doing something," he muttered.

Kael turned to bid Geist farewell, and saw that the third carriage was already rolling away. His traveler's chest was secured to the back of it.

"Promise me you'll be safe," Lysander begged as he helped Aerilyn in after Kael. "Don't go anywhere alone with him —"

"I'm not an idiot. I'm well aware of Reginald's reputation," she said haughtily.

"Just promise, will you?"

"Why?"

He looked up at her from under the waves of his hair. "Because it would set my heart at ease."

Something strange passed between them — and it made Kael slightly uncomfortable.

"Very well," Aerilyn said after a moment. "I promise not to leave the ballroom."

"Thank you. Gravy guard your path, my friends. Fate willing, we'll meet again." He slammed the door shut — hard — and marched back to the rowboat without a backwards glance.

The carriage ride was bumpy and insufferably hot. Geist had packed his clothes in with so many layers of stuffing that Kael thought he was in real danger of boiling alive. They kept the curtains drawn over their windows, just in case. It wouldn't do for the same villagers who witnessed Colderoy arriving earlier that day to witness him again.

At first, the dirt of the road muffled the movement of the wheels. Then they struck cobblestone, and the horses clattered smartly across it. When the road sounded hollow, broken every now and then by a rhythmic *thump*, Aerilyn began twisting her hands nervously.

"We must be on the bridge," she whispered.

Which meant they had less than a mile left to go. "Don't chew on your lip," he said, and she stopped immediately.

"You're right — no one wants to dance with a girl who already has bite marks," she said with a nervous laugh. Then quite suddenly, she reached across and grabbed both of his hands. "Tell me it's going to be all right, Kael. Tell me it's all going to work out."

He wasn't a Seer: he couldn't know for sure. Their bodies might adorn the castle walls by morning. But that was his burden, not hers. So he took her hands and squeezed them tightly. "Everything's going to be fine, Aerilyn. I promise."

To see the relief on her face made his stomach sink down to his knees. Now the plan had to work, they *had* to succeed. So many people were depending on it. As the carriage stopped and the doors swung open, he steeled himself for what must be done.

****

"Charmed, Jefferies," Reginald said through his grin, though it was no great secret to either of them that he wasn't charmed — he was actually rather peeved. And he made that abundantly clear.

"So — ah — good to see you," Jefferies gasped, as Reginald crushed his fingers. "Always a delight."

"Isn't it?" Reginald didn't let go. In fact, he squeezed harder. "Though I think it might have been a great deal more delightful if my chairs weren't in such dismal shape. If only that shipment from D'Mere had come through, you all might have had something a little nicer to plant your rumps in."

Sweat beaded up on Jefferies' brow, his smile slipped ever closer to a grimace. "Yes, bloody pirates and all that. I'll see to it that you have a new set in three — ah, *two* weeks!"

"See to it that you do," Reginald said. He turned his smile to the woman standing behind Jefferies and extended his hand. "Accidents happen everyday, I'm well aware of that." He kissed the back of her silk glove and released her.

Jefferies, thick as he was, was no fool. He caught Reginald's threat and his face went white. "It will be done, Sir Duke. I'll double the guard and I won't lose another shipment this quarter, you'll see." Then he hurried off, dragging his wife behind him.

Chaucer was next to step up. He bowed, made some drab remark about the décor and stomped inside. Reginald ignored his rudeness. He might host twice as many parties next year, simply for the pleasure of making Chaucer furious.

At the sight of his next guest, Reginald's grin fell away, replaced immediately by a snarl:

Colderoy.

That fat waste had no business at such a grand event. From his stubby legs to that hideous, food-stained mustache — he clashed horrifically with the golden grace of the ball. If he hadn't had such a brilliant mind for numbers, Reginald would have sent him to the gallows long ago.

Well that, and the fact that he had yet to find a rope thick enough to support a man of Colderoy's girth.

"Good to see you," Reginald said halfheartedly as Colderoy bounced towards him. "I was beginning to wonder —"

"Good ephening, Sir Duke," Colderoy interrupted. He wore a bright yellow tunic that made him look more like a bread roll than a man. "Lophly night, is it not?"

Reginald glanced up at the stars — anything to spare his eyes from the atrocity before him. "I suppose —"

"You haphen't met my daughter, haph you?"

"No, I don't think —"

"May I present Miss Margaret Colderoy?"

It was the strangest twist of fortune Reginald had ever seen, that Colderoy should have fathered such a flawless creature. He kissed Margaret's hand, never once taking his eyes off her face. "My dear, I'm truly charmed. The sun pales in comparison."

She blushed, which he liked very much. "Please, Sir Duke, I'm unworthy of such a compliment."

"On the contrary — though words are hardly enough to celebrate it. I hope you'll save me a dance." He flashed a grin, and her blush deepened.

"I'm sure she will," Colderoy butted in. "Now mophe along, Margaret. The Duke is a busy man."

Reginald didn't say anything to the next manager; he didn't even look at him. He was far too busy admiring Margaret's figure as she climbed the steps into the castle. Oh yes, tonight the dancing would be especially good.

He rushed through the last few greetings and then ordered the guards to close the front gates, locking the managers and their carriages inside. No one left until the party ended — which would happen the minute he got bored.

"There's a fog creeping in from the west," one of the guards called down.

Reginald couldn't see the ocean from where he stood, and he wasn't interested in climbing all the way up the stairs to look. "Tell the patrol to weigh anchor until it clears. There's no point in trying to hold their routes — they're more likely to run into each other than catch any intruders."

The guard took a pair of torches off the wall and used them to relay the message. When he was finished, a chorus of bells rang out from across the sea. The patrol understood.

Reginald closed the front doors himself, locking them tightly with his personal key. Then he strode purposefully towards the music that floated out from his ballroom.

It didn't take him long to find Margaret — even in an ocean of beauty, she would have stood out. He watched her first waltz, and her grace astounded him. Her dress swept along behind her as Colderoy guided her through the steps. He didn't know which was more astonishing: Margaret, or the fact that her father could actually dance.

"I'm ready when you are, Sir Duke." Bartimus stepped in front of him, blocking his view.

"Ah … very good. Stand by your post and wait for me," Reginald said, craning his head over Bartimus's shoulder.

"But Sir Duke, your safety is —"

"Almost assured. The guards are posted along the walls, through the hallways, and now there's a fog rolling in — so I seriously doubt anyone's going to risk attacking us. I assume the extra, ah, security is in place?"

"Right where you wanted him."

"Excellent." Reginald watched the first dance end and sneered as Chaucer took Margaret for the next one. "Enjoy the party, Bartimus. Kingdom knows I will."

And with that, he strode confidently towards the ballroom floor.

****

The sweat pooling on Kael's face was a collective effort: the heat, his nerves, and the sheer amount of pastry he stuffed down his gullet all contributed to it — not to mention the stress of dealing with talkative managers. For such an annoying man, Colderoy had a never-ending line of people eager to speak with him.

In several cases, he'd had to turn to his last resort. He sprayed two gossipy ladies and half a dozen prodding gentlemen with bits of pie before they would leave him alone. One man walked up with his hand outstretched, and Kael staged a very convincing sneeze. The damage was so severe that a servant had to lead him away to find a fresh change of clothes.

Other than the unwelcome visitors, everything else seemed to go according to plan. Chaucer stepped in after the first dance, and paraded Aerilyn in front of the Duke several times before he finally took the bait: shoving his middle-aged partner aside and cutting in without so much as asking Chaucer's permission. Now Aerilyn had Reginald tied securely around her smallest finger, giggling and blushing her way into his good graces. They'd danced three times without stopping to breathe.

411

A flash of movement caught his eye, and Kael watched over his biscuit as an old man dressed in robes took his place by the Duke's throne. He realized it must be Bartimus — the mage Jake said could travel through air. Bartimus scratched at the top of his bald head and Kael thought he saw something gold glint on his finger.

Unfortunately, Chaucer was right: the Duke was no fool. Wherever the dance took them, he kept close to the throne.

The ballroom ceiling extended to the second floor, where a company of guards kept watch from the banisters. Their hands stayed on the hilts of their swords as they watched the revelers twirling beneath them. Kael swore they never blinked.

"Wine, Mr. Colderoy?"

"Yeah, phanks," he said around a mouthful of tart. He took a goblet off the tray without even glancing at the man who served him.

"Of course. I'd be happy to show you to the facilities, Mr. Colderoy."

Kael looked down and the pastry nearly fell out of his mouth. This servant looked just like all the others: his face was painted white, his lips painted red, he wore a ridiculous powder wig and balanced a silver tray on the pads of his white glove. And yet, he looked so decidedly bored that Kael recognized him at once.

"Um, yes. Right then — lead the way," he said, loudly enough for passersby to hear. Then he followed Geist up the stairs — knowing full well that he would return a villain.

Chapter 36
A Warrior's Boon

"You have fifteen minutes until the next watch shows up," Geist said as he helped Kael out of his disguise. His other clothes were underneath. They were badly wrinkled and a little wet, but Geist said it would only add to his character. "No one commented on your shoes, I presume?"

Kael shook his head. It was amazing that no one noticed Colderoy showing up in scuffed hunter's boots. But he supposed Geist was right: people rarely glanced at anything below the knee.

When he'd shed the rest of Colderoy, they stuffed him into a chest in a corner of the room. It was one of the guest rooms, and because the wardrobe was empty Geist presumed it wasn't being used. But he'd picked the chest's lock and replaced it with one of his own, just in case.

"Fifteen minutes," Geist repeated as he stepped out into the hall. He glanced left and right, then gave a slight nod. He walked back towards the ballroom as Kael jogged in the opposite direction.

Several tapestries lined the wall, and he counted them as he went. When he reached the third one, he ducked into the next alcove and found a small wooden door. One hand he placed on the knob and with the other, he touched the hinges. He quickly imagined that they were well-greased, and the door opened silently.

He stepped onto a narrow landing and took a deep breath as he shut the door behind him. This was the part he was most dreading.

The top of the stairs opened to the night sky. He was now on the castle's western wall, the one facing the open sea.

Carefully, he stuck his head around the corner to get his bearings — and nearly swore aloud.

Apparently, the guards had decided that the thick fog settling over the ocean was going to do their jobs for them, and now they were taking a break. Three soldiers drank wine and played cards directly in front of him, where there was only supposed to be one.

Blast. How was he going to do this? If he struck the first man, the other two would sound the alarm. The message would pass down the wall and into the ballroom, where the Duke would hear. He and Bartimus would vanish — leaving his formidable army to take care of the guests.

Kael could almost hear the sand slipping through the glass and sweeping minutes away with it. There was no time to think, he had to act quickly. He drew two knives and raised a third slightly out of its pocket. He held them by their blades and waited for his targets.

The middle soldier laid his hand down and the one on the left leaned forward to swear. That's when Kael's knife found his throat. It struck just as the right soldier tilted his head back to laugh. He fell backwards, gurgling in shock as the second knife cut him short. Before his companion's body could hit the ground, the middle soldier looked up and his jaw dropped open in shock. The surprised O of his mouth made for a good target.

Whatever he'd been about to yell never came out. Instead, he stumbled backwards, grappling with the knife between his teeth until he tipped off the wall with a moan.

For a long moment, Kael didn't move. He didn't want to get anywhere near the bodies. As long as the shadows covered their faces, he wouldn't have to see the lives he'd just ended. He knew any man who served the Five had blood of kin and friend on his hands, but he didn't relish the killing.

A soft *click* drew his attention to the ledge. If he hadn't been looking for it, he never would have seen the hook that lodged itself into the stone, or the trembling of the rope as Kyleigh climbed it. She popped over the edge of the wall; her armor hid her perfectly in the thin sliver of shadow untouched by the corner braziers. She plucked the knives from the soldiers' throats in quick, practiced movements. He crouched and went to meet her.

"That third fellow nearly crushed me," she said quietly as she cleaned the blades on one of their tunics. "If I hadn't heard the wind whistling off his helmet, I think the Kingdom might've been short one halfdragon."

She handed him the blades. When he took them, they stuck to his hands. He pulled them off and a thin string of goo trailed behind. "What in Kingdom's name?"

"Jake's fog spell went slightly awry. He accidentally put a word for evaporation too close to one for binding, and now we all look like the top side of a pastry." She clapped her hands together and pulled them apart. Threads of goo breached the space between them. "The sails are all stuck together and Lysander's fit to be tied. They're having to row *Anchorgloam* by hand just to get her here."

Terrific, Kael thought. Never once in his planning did he account for a scenario in which the pirates would have to sail their way through slime. "How long do you think that will take?"

"Not long. They'll be a few minutes behind, but they were rowing hard."

"All right."

A long, weighted silence hung between them. He kept his eyes away from her as much as possible, and she returned the favor.

"So, I'll get the walls and you'll get the upper stories," she said as she slung a pack off her shoulders. Inside was his bow, a quiver of arrows and his gauntlets.

He got equipped as quickly as possible and took the grappling hook from her. "I'll see you in a bit. And Kyleigh?" She stopped and turned to face him. "Check on the mages, if you have time. I want to make sure Jake's potion worked."

A disappointed look crossed her face — so quickly that he wasn't sure he actually saw it. "Very well. And do be careful."

Then she disappeared into the shadows, leaving him to his task.

****

The guard barracks sat on top of the stairs leading to the third floor. Kael would have to face them eventually, but he knew popping up in the middle of their living quarters wouldn't exactly give him an advantage. Fortunately, there was a less conventional way of reaching the upper floors.

Moonlight glinted off the large window above him, one that — according to the map — would open directly into the Duke's office. He spun the grappling hook in his hand, holding on to the image of it lodging firmly into the narrow ledge. Then he made his throw.

It landed perfectly. He tugged a few times to be sure, and when he was convinced it would hold his weight, he began to climb. At the top, he had to stand sideways to fit his boots on the ledge. He tried not to think about what might happen if he lost his balance. With a quick jab, he punched through the glass and reached in to pop the latch open.

Inside, the darkness was unsettling. One lantern glowed feebly next to the window, but the moon put out more light than it did. He tried not to fret over it. Geist had done so well with his details that he knew exactly how many paces it would take to reach the door. All he had to do was move.

He reeled the rope in and set it next to the wall, out of sight. Then he began his steps. *One, two, three, f —*

Something wasn't right.

He had an eerie feeling in his gut. The animal in him was wide-awake, stirred by a presence he couldn't see. Yet he knew it was there. He reached out and his hand touched something coarse. It felt like a rug ... no, the threads were far too small, too fine to be a rug. Perhaps it was the back of an animal skin chair. Yes, that was probably it. He just felt odd about it because he hadn't expected it to be th —

416

Then the chair let out a low, rumbling growl, and Kael didn't even have time to swear before something struck his gut and sent him flying into the opposite wall.

His back hit the stone and he felt his joints pop. He reached out to slow his fall and grabbed a fistful of tapestry, which he ripped off its hangings. As boy and decoration fell forward, they managed to knock the lantern loose. It shattered and the flames escaped, feeding eagerly on the worn threads of the rug beneath it.

A huge monster rose out of the darkness. He recognized it immediately from Bartholomew's Pass: it was the King of halfwolves, the one that had managed to escape. It must have tracked him down, patiently followed his scent — and now it was here to settle the score.

The cut Harbinger left across its chest was now a thin, shining scar. Its thick black fur bristled in the flames. Its lips pulled back in a snarl and its knifelike teeth glistened wetly. The eyes beneath its furry brow locked onto Kael's and dilated. Its nostrils flared to catch his scent, and it reached up with one dagger claw to touch the missing tip of its pointed ear — just to remind him.

Then it howled.

He dove to the side, narrowly missing the claw that swung out to rake his throat. Instead, he took a blow to the back of his knee. There was nothing to grab onto, and the wolf dragged him across the floor by his leg. It reared to bite him, but caught a boot in the teeth.

With a roar, it grabbed the front of his shirt and hoisted him off the ground. He kicked madly, but the wolf held him at the end of its long reach, well out of range. Its head snapped forward with lightning quickness and Kael swung blindly for its face.

The ridged backs of his gauntlets connected with wolf's jaw, and he was rewarded with a high-pitched cry as it lost its grip. He fell hard on his ankle but forced himself to roll away. He caught his feet and had an arrow drawn just as the wolf leapt.

This would be it: either his arrow would find its mark or he'd be snapped like a dry twig. He exhaled sharply and released.

The wolf yelped and fell backwards, striking its head against the wall. It wrapped one claw around the arrow sticking out of its chest and ripped it free. It clamped a paw over the wound, but blood spurted out twice as fast. The wolf panted heavily and glared at Kael, but didn't try to rise.

He knew then that the fight was over.

The wolf seemed to know it, too. Though its body was a monster, its eyes were clearly human. They reminded him of what Kyleigh said before, about how Crevan had enslaved the shapechangers and twisted them into his minions. He didn't know if there was still a man trapped inside the monster or not, but he decided to give it the respect of dying in peace.

"Mountain … child …"

A rough voice stopped him cold. He spun around.

"Time," the wolf said. His voice was decidedly male, though his words were clumsily spoken around his sharp teeth. "Please," he pushed down on his wound, "time."

He was shocked to hear the wolf speak, and leery of getting close to him. Then he remembered what Jake said about the slaving spell: pain could sometimes clear a man's head and give him back his mind. He looked in the wolf's eyes and saw that the monster was gone from them. He was looking into the eyes of a man, not a beast.

And he wouldn't let a man die without hearing what he had to say. It was the least he could do.

He put his hand over his heart and willed it to keep beating. "I can't heal you," he admitted. Amos could have — he could heal just about every organ in the body. But Kael had been too busy being rebellious to learn anything other than skin, bone and the first few layers of muscle. Now he regretted it deeply.

"I want … death," the wolf said. Then he touched his chest. "Bloodfang."

It took Kael a moment to realize *Bloodfang* was the wolf's name. "Kael," he said in return.

"Kael ... of the mountains." Bloodfang's eyes rolled back and he closed them. It was a long moment before he spoke again. "My pack is gone, all gone. Only two ... remain." His snout bent in what could have been a pained smile. "Soon ... only one. I ask a warrior's boon."

Kael had no idea what that was, but he nodded.

"As my ... defeater, I ask that you guard ... guard my kin. My last sister."

Somewhere in the back of his head, Kael knew time was running out. He only had a few more minutes left to clear the upper floors before the shifts changed and someone found those guards dead around their card table. "All right, where do I find her?"

Bloodfang's laugh turned into a gurgle as he fought to stay alive. "You wear her scent ... her very skin. Do you not ... know?"

In his sheer and utter disbelief, Kael's concentration slipped. Blood leaked out from under his fingers as he tried desperately to regain his grip. "Kyleigh? Do you mean Kyleigh?"

But Bloodfang didn't answer him. The light in his eyes was fading fast; they rolled aimlessly in his skull. "Until the last ... sun ... rises," he whispered. Then he lay still.

Kael sat back and his hands hung limp before him. The lantern flames had consumed the rug and were making their way down the tapestry. He beat them out before they could set the whole room ablaze. As he sat in the darkness, a horrible feeling tore at his heart.

A voice suddenly came from the other side of the door: "I ain't going in there — I've seen what that thing is capable of. He's probably just irked about being locked up, anyhow."

"But what if that ain't it?" another man said. "What if there's been a real intruder?"

The first man snorted. "Then I'm sure he's been taken care of."

"Yeah, and if he ain't been, it's *our* necks in the noose."

The first man considered this for a moment, then grunted in defeat. They opened the door just a crack, just wide enough to stick their heads in, and that was all Kael needed. Two well-placed arrows ended their argument forever.

He moved through the halls numbly, killing every guard he came across without a second thought. All he could think about was the horrible thing he'd just done and how Kyleigh would never forgive him. Now he understood why she hadn't killed Bloodfang when she had the chance: she'd been trying to save him.

The guards were shocked when he kicked in the barrack doors. The first few to rush him got knives in the chest. While the rest struggled to climb over the bodies of their companions, he had time to get his bow drawn. After that, things went quickly.

A few sprinted down the stairs and away from him, no doubt heading for the wall. Kael retrieved his knives and followed them at a walk. He heard Harbinger's shrilling cry and a few startled gasps. Only one man escaped Kyleigh. He dashed up the stairs, heaving under the weight of his armor, and skidded to a halt when Kael's shadow crossed over him. He looked up, and fear ringed his eyes.

Kael put an arrow through the left one.

"Is that all of them?" Kyleigh peered through the doorway at the foot of the stairs. She held Harbinger loosely. Blood trickled off its blade and sank into the mortar.

"Yes," he said without looking at her. "What about the mages?"

"They're all dead. Looks like none of them survived their dinner."

"Good." His steps were heavy as he made his way towards her. When they were only a stair apart, he stopped.

He didn't look at her, but he could feel her eyes on him — moving from the top of his head and down. If she could smell Lysander's blood inside a corked bottle, there was no doubt she could smell the deed that stained his hands.

After a moment, she stepped back. Her boot scraped the ground and he knew the full, heavy weight of what he'd done finally hit her. When she spoke, her voice was the smallest he'd ever heard:

"So he's ...?"

"Yes," Kael heard himself say. "I killed your brother."

Chapter 37
Fire

She turned away. Her whole body shuddered as she clamped a hand over her face. He wished she would've broken his jaw, slit his throat, run him through. If only she would take blood for blood, then he wouldn't have to stand there while she cried — while he wasted away under her tears.

Then she grabbed him by the shoulders, and he braced himself for the moment when she would fling him into the sea.

"Thank you."

Astonishment drove his eyes to hers. He'd been expecting the tears on her face, but never the gratitude. It didn't make any sense. "Don't thank me, kill me! Kingdom knows I deserve it —"

She put a hand over his mouth, gently. "No you don't. You did what I should have done — what I couldn't do. He begged me to kill him in the Pass, but I ..." She ducked her head and came back with a glare. "I refused him. I thought there might be a way to save him, but I realized too late that he never wanted to be saved."

"He said he was your brother."

She nodded. "Not by blood, of course. Bloodfang's thrice great grandsire found me wandering through the forest four hundred years ago. I don't remember who I was before ... the pack is all the family I've ever known."

Kael was silent. He was afraid to breathe. He let everything she said sink into him and tried to understand it. He was afraid if he asked her anything that she would stop talking, and then he'd never get to hear her story. So for once, he kept his mouth shut.

"There are few who know this," she continued, her voice gaining strength, "but King Banagher captured many of the shapechangers at the start of the Whispering War. He thought he might be able to use us as weapons against the rebel army — but he could find no way to control us. And so he locked us in his dungeons for safekeeping. My pack was among those captured ... I thought I could free us, but Bloodfang made me swear not to show my other shape to our captors, and I couldn't ignore the alpha's command.

"Because I didn't look like the others, Banagher never suspected my powers. He released me to his most trusted advisor, Setheran, who taught me the way of the sword. My fighting prowess earned me knighthood at the end of the War. Finally, I thought I had enough power in the King's court to free my pack." She smiled hard. "I was knight for a day — and then Crevan took the throne. He bound my brothers in magic ... and I realized I could never free them — not unless I killed Crevan. I tried, and though I very nearly succeeded, I failed. And I've been on the run ever since.

"I realize now that Bloodfang saved my life when he told me to hide my shape ... though he always blamed himself for what happened to us." She took a deep breath and wiped her tears away. "But that's a story for another time. Thank you for giving him the peace he longed for. I know that he's in the eternal woods now, hunting with the pack mates who've been waiting so long for his return. You've put my heart at ease."

Kael realized that he'd been holding his breath. He couldn't believe how selfish he'd been. Had he stopped worrying about his own quest for half a moment, he might've realized that he wasn't the only one who'd lost something dear to him — that his wasn't the only cause in the Kingdom worth fighting for.

She may have been relieved that Bloodfang was at peace, but that wasn't good enough for Kael. Now that he knew her story, and knew how much she'd sacrificed to try to free her family, he felt Kyleigh deserved more than relief. And there was no putting aside the fact that he'd just murdered a man who didn't deserve to die.

The debt between them was great ... and there was only one way to settle it.

He stepped past Kyleigh and grabbed a torch out of its sconce. All across the sea, the waves were covered in deathly white fog. The air was quiet. Then he waved the torch in a series of arcs and all at once, a dozen rowboats crept out of the mist, drawn to his signal. They made their berth on the rocky shore and dark fingers scrambled up the iron ladder that jutted out from the waves. Moonlight caught the glint of the cutlasses strapped to their hips.

"Come on," he said to Kyleigh. "Let's finish this — for Bloodfang."

She smiled through the tears that still wet her cheeks. "Agreed. I wouldn't let you clap me in irons for anyone else."

****

Margaret's resolve was crumbling, he was sure of it. "The ballroom's getting rather stuffy. Why don't we go for a stroll? I could give you a tour of the castle," Reginald said in her ear. He could feel the heat coming off her blush.

"But Sir Duke, what would the others think of us?"

He tightened his grip around her waist, pulled her closer. "My dear, what could they think? I'm their ruler — their very lives depend upon me. Anyone who speaks ill of me has his tongue cut out ... and anyone I favor will have power unimaginable." He dropped his voice to a growl. "Come with me, Margaret."

She was teetering on the edge, he could see the struggle behind her clear blue eyes. But he already knew what her answer would be. In just a few moments, she would be his.

BANG!

The ballroom doors burst open and the music screeched to a halt. Reginald spun around. If it was some guard coming in to complain about the fog, he'd have his head lopped off. But as the crowds parted, murmuring to one another, he saw something he'd never expected.

A young man strode across the floor like he owned it. He wore rough spun peasant's clothes and a bow across his back. The candlelight from the gold branches of the chandelier touched his hair, revealing deep red hidden within his curls. His face was smooth, thin, and not particularly handsome. He tugged roughly on the chains gripped in his hand, and his prisoner stumbled out of the crowd behind him.

Reginald may not have recognized the man, but he certainly recognized the prisoner. He saw her eyes, his blood turned to ice. He shoved Margaret aside and she toppled into the crowd with a squeal. "Bartimus!"

"Hold on a minute, Sir Duke!" the young man called after him. "She's no harm to anyone: I've got her in enchanted bindings."

"Do not be deceived," Bartimus countered. He stood by the throne with one leg already through his magic door. He held out his hand and glared at the young man from over Reginald's shoulder. "The boy could be her agent — sent here to trap and kill you."

The young man snorted. "Her agent? She's a barbarian, mage. She thinks of nothing but red meat."

"And who are you?" Reginald said, half-turning.

"A hunter, Sir Duke," the young man bowed, "from the Unforgivable Mountains."

The room lit up with the frenzied buzz of voices. Men and women whispered over their shoulders, leaned across their circles. Barbarian? Surely not. The Unforgivable Mountains? Impossible!

But Reginald ignored them. His eyes were on the irons clamped to the Dragongirl's wrists. He squinted and thought he saw the symbol of Midlan etched into them. "Where did you come across those shackles, boy?"

The room fell silent.

"I picked them up out of a shipwreck," the young man replied with a shrug, his thin face untroubled. "Surely you wouldn't begrudge a man the right to reclaim lost goods?"

A hundred heads swiveled to Reginald for an answer.

"No, of course not," he said through pursed lips.

Behind him, Bartimus grunted. "Be quick, Sire. My strength fades fast. I'm not sure how long I can keep the door open."

"Close it," Reginald said, his mind made up.

"But Sir Duke —"

"Just do it."

Bartimus gave him a hard look, then reluctantly stepped out of the portal as Reginald took a step towards the young man. "Do you have some proof that she is truly bound?"

He smiled wryly. "I think if she weren't, I'd already be dead."

There were a few patches of nervous laughter, but Reginald silenced them with an upraised hand. The longer the Dragongirl snarled at him, the more confident he became. Surely, if she were free to do as she wished, the curtains would already be ablaze. He decided to have a little fun.

"Ladies and managers, this young woman who stands before you is not what she seems," he said, thrusting a finger at her. "She's a monster of the woods — a shapechanging barbarian!"

Gasps rang out. People stood on their tiptoes, craning around each other's wigs for a better look.

"But she is more than that — in fact, you may know her as the Dragongirl."

This news gave him the reaction he was looking for. The tittering grew to a rumble and every eye in the room went wide. Several people took backwards steps towards the door, but most surged forward for a better look.

Oh yes, he had them *precisely* where he wanted them. The news of his victory would reach Midlan by tomorrow morning, and Crevan would have no choice but to set him up above all the other rulers. He might even strip the mountains from that dog, Titus, and hand them over as a gift.

But Reginald wasn't finished. News was good, but spectacle would be even better. A little intrigue might keep the tale fresh for months. "So, hunter," he turned back to the young man, "if what you say is true and the Dragongirl really *is* under your control, you'll have no problem proving it."

Amid the next wave of whispers, the young man raised his brows. "Prove it how, Sir Duke?"

"Strike her."

Women gasped, men murmured — but the young man didn't seem at all concerned. "Considering all the trouble she caused, don't you think the King would rather do the bruising himself?"

The crowd laughed. That mountain boy had a good point.

Reginald forced himself to smile and thought quickly. "I see ... well if you won't hit her, I suppose there is another way you might win us over. I think the good people of the seas want some proof." They cheered, and Reginald raised a fist to quiet them. "So if you won't strike her ... then I suppose you'll have to kiss her."

****

The word echoed in Kael's ear. Heat singed his face as the ladies in the crowd started to giggle. He could feel their eyes on him, feel them craning and leaning forward for a better look. He could hear the clink of armor as the guards on the second floor shifted their weight. He could feel their eyes boring into the top of his skull.

"Go on, give her a kiss!" someone — a very drunk someone, by the sound of it — shouted. Nevertheless, his cry brought on a murmur of agreement from the rest of the crowd. They wanted to see some proof.

But Kael's limbs seized up under the pressure. All he could feel were the tips of his fingers, and they flexed involuntarily for the knives at his arm. He could do it, he knew he could. The Duke was pacing right in front of him, grinning as he egged the crowd on. If he wanted to, he could throw the knife and end it all right now.

They'd probably even make it out alive.

Then a movement caught the corner of his eye. A short, pale-faced servant squeezed his way to the front of the crowd. The people he pushed through looked annoyed at first, but soon seemed to forget he was even there. Geist had a tray balanced on his palm and one hand clamped smartly behind his back. He met Kael's eyes, and his face was about as encouraging as stone.

Yet, he was a firm reminder of all the people who were depending on him. If he killed the Duke, war would ensue. There would be a mad dash for his empty throne and oceans of innocent blood would be shed. Nothing would stop the army of Midlan from marching through the seas, burning and killing to punish in the name of the King.

And though he knew it would ruin him, Kael could not trade his feelings for lives. He would do what must be done.

"All right," he declared, and the room broke out in cheers. He turned to Kyleigh, careful to avoid her eyes. "Come here, girl." He tugged sharply on her chains and she stumbled forward. He caught her with an arm around her waist and quickly stuck his lips to hers.

His whole body ignited. Fire raced through his veins and filled his ears. He wrestled with it, tried to pull himself out of the flames ... but in the end, it consumed him.

He was helpless, like a child caught in the flow of a savage river. Heat washed over him and dragged him down into a place where he thought he couldn't breathe. There was no air, no beating of his heart — there was only the feel of her lips on his. She was holding him by a thread. He was completely at her mercy. And when she pushed back against him, he very nearly drowned.

At long last, she set him free. He was relieved — and then the second she pulled away, pain ripped at his chest. There was nothing but a bloody hole left: a raw gap of torn muscles and shattered bone. He could feel the agony stabbing in his teeth. It made him want to scream. He grabbed his chest, expecting his hand to slip through and touch his spine ... but it didn't. He met the rough threads of his shirt and gripped them in disbelief.

Remarkably, he was whole.

"Bravo!"

Duke Reginald led the round of applause that snuffed the last smoldering embers in his blood. He took a very shaky bow and while his head was bent, he wiped the cold beads of sweat off his face with the back of his sleeve.

"Excellent work, hunter. I'm thoroughly convinced." Reginald clapped his hands together sharply and a steward pushed his way out of the crowd. He handed Reginald a large sack, which he proceeded to toss at Kael's feet. "There's your reward. Now leave."

Kael bowed and stepped to the side as Reginald snatched the chains out of his hand.

"Ladies and managers, I give you the Dragongirl," he said, jerking Kyleigh forward. "What a grand victory for the High Seas! Where all the other regions failed, *we* have triumphed."

The people cheered and raised their goblets to the Duke: as if he was the one who'd singlehandedly captured the King's most hated enemy. And more than likely, that's how the story would have been told. But Kael's plan told it a little differently.

He looked at Kyleigh, and she nodded slightly. Her face was calm — no remnant of his kiss lingered behind her eyes. *And why would it have?* he reminded himself. To her, it had all been an act.

The shriek of metal froze Reginald mid-celebration. Kyleigh wrenched her shackles apart, and he must have read the open-mouthed shock on his guests' faces because he tried to run. But Kyleigh had him pinned to the ground, her knee driven into his back, before he could even finish screaming:

"Bartimus!"

A burst of red lightning erupted from Bartimus's outstretched hand, aimed right for Kyleigh. It would have struck her and likely killed her, had Kael not been in the way. In the midst of their triumph, everyone seemed to have forgotten about the boy from the mountains. And while they'd been occupied, he put himself between the Duke and his mage.

Now it was *his* chest the lightning struck. The magic washed óver him and tickled horribly, but could not hurt him. He saw the realization dawn on Bartimus's face just as the knife left his hand.

"Whis — gah!" He toppled over, his robes flailing out beside him. He wriggled for a few moments as he tried to wrench the knife from his chest. Then he lay still.

"Guards!" Reginald squealed.

Kyleigh put her elbow on his throat.

Screams rang out across the ballroom, and several ladies fainted, when they saw the rogues that encircled the banister in place of the Duke's guards. The pirates had done well: not a soldier was left alive. They slumped over at their posts, their heads lolling in pools of their own blood. Every cutlass was stained red.

"People of the High Seas, do not be alarmed!" Chaucer stepped out of the crowd, followed by a handful of stony-faced managers, and held up a sealed roll of parchment. "In my hand is a contract — a writ of resignation. Tonight, I will ask the Duke to sign his title and his land back over to the people. We have lived under this tyrant for far too long, and it's high time that we start making the gold for ourselves. By morning, we'll be managers no more — but free merchants once again!"

Applause started slowly, nervously, but soon grew to a roar. Managers ripped off their wigs and stomped on them. Servants dragged their arms over their faces and let the silver trays fall out of their hands. A few people tucked the gold cutlery into their pockets and slipped out the door. Lace and frilly coats went flying, goblets smashed on the floor. All across the room, people shook hands and grinned to either ear.

It made Kael sick. Not a moment before, these people had been congratulating the Duke on his victory. And now they seemed to have completely changed their minds.

A familiar, high-pitched screech drew Kael's glare from the revelers and to the musicians' stage — where Jonathan had somehow managed to weasel his way in. Fiddle in hand, his bloodied sword hung forgotten at his hip. "I call this *The Duke's Dirty Underpants!*" he declared.

The other musicians hurried to keep up, thrumming their gold-crusted instruments in time with Jonathan's fiddle. The guests clapped to the tune and then began a jig. Several people kicked Reginald in the rump as they skipped by.

Lysander tore down the stairs right after Jonathan, his hair a wild, gooey mess. He shoved his way through the crowd and seemed to see no one but Aerilyn. "Are you well?" he said as he reached her. "He didn't hurt you, did he? Because by tempest if he did, I swear I'll —"

"What?" she said, hands propped on her hips. "Roast him alive? Hang him from the mast?"

"I was thinking more along the lines of using him as a figurehead, but I'm certainly open to suggestions."

"Oh? Well in that case, I suggest you kiss me."

The fury on his face vanished, replaced very suddenly by shock. "Wait — does this mean you want to become a pirate?"

She rolled her eyes, a smile pulling at her lips. "That was the deal, wasn't it?"

"Well it was, yes. But I certainly don't want to force you into anything. I'd still love you no matter what. I'm sure Uncle Martin would come around to the idea —"

She slapped him straight across the face. Then she grabbed two fistfuls of his tunic and pulled him forward. "Shut your mouth and kiss me, you impossible pirate."

And he did. And soon the kissing grew so robust that people began to cheer and Kael had to look away. As he retrieved his knife from Bartimus's corpse, he noticed a pool of gold under his hand. Apparently, his impetus melted off when he died. Kael picked it up and found that it had already hardened into a disk. He tucked it into his pocket.

"You made a good decision — nothing breeds war quite like an assassination."

The statement came from Geist, who'd somehow materialized at his side. He was the only servant in the room with his wig still intact.

"Thanks," Kael said, and shook the hand he offered.

"What will you do now?"

He was growing tired of hearing that question. "Lysander and his men have promised to help me. I've got some ... unfinished business, in the mountains."

Geist's face was inscrutable. "Interesting. I actually have a friend who's headed for the mountains."

"Really? Who is he?"

"That isn't important. I only mention it because he seemed rather intent on hiking to the top of it — where he hoped to meet an enemy who'd stolen something very dear to him. And I told him it was folly."

Kael thought he knew who Geist's friend was. What he didn't know was how on earth he could've possibly found out. "Oh? And why is it folly? He's got an army at his back."

Geist inclined his head. "True, though not one nearly large enough. And when I told him as much, he asked for my advice. Do you know what I said?"

"No. What?"

"I said that what he was looking for could be found in the Endless Plains," Geist finished with a smirk.

Kael was about to ask for details when Chaucer cut over the top of him. "Come on, boy!" he barked from halfway up the stairs. He was following Kyleigh as she shoved Reginald along — with one arm twisted painfully behind his back.

Kael didn't even bother bidding Geist farewell. He knew without looking that the man was already gone.

"You're a fool, Chaucer. A bloody, pig-brained fool!"
Reginald spat. They had him tied to one of the guest room
chairs, pulled up close to a small desk. The only limb he was
free to move was his right arm.

Chaucer spread the contract out on the desk and
dipped a quill in a fresh well of ink. "I'm fairly certain anyone
who walked in might be inclined to think that the man
strapped to the chair was the fool among us. But what do I
know?"

"Nothing," Reginald said vehemently, his goatee
trembling. "The King is going to destroy you — all of you! His
army will impale your bodies down the coast, he'll feed your
flesh to his dogs —"

"How?" Chaucer interrupted. He seemed to be fighting
back a smile. "Every man with any ounce of power saw you
sacked tonight. Your resignation will not be sealed in blood,"
he held up the quill, "but in ink. Our business will continue
just as it did before the Five, just as it has for centuries. The
King may send his armies but unless he drains the ocean dry,
there's no way he can catch us without a ship."

The blood drained from Reginald's face, he licked his
lips as his eyes flicked nervously about the room. They
roamed from where Chaucer and his fellow merchants stood,
to Kyleigh and Kael. "What will happen to me if I sign your
contract?" he said, not taking his eyes off them. "How do I
know you won't feed me to the whisperer and his pet once
you have my signature? Yes, I know what you are."

Kael flinched involuntarily when Reginald spoke. It
was stupid: he knew anyone who wasn't blind saw the spell
strike him and do no harm. Anyone who wasn't deaf

would've heard what Bartimus said with his dying gasp. Even now, he could feel the merchants shifting their weight, moving from boot to boot as a long moment passed and he said nothing to deny it.

His secret was out.

"You'll be allowed to live the remainder of your days in peace," Chaucer said. He pointed to the neat words a few lines above the space for a signature. "The details are all right here. No one is going to be eaten. We're businessmen after all, not barbarians."

Kael gave Chaucer a glare that he hoped might melt the man's face off, but he only smirked.

"Fine." Reginald snatched the quill and scribbled on the line. "There. Now what?"

"Your pendant."

Reginald pulled the solid gold medal over his head and slapped it into Chaucer's palm. "You're probably going to melt it into coin the second you get the chance."

Chaucer smirked, but said nothing. He passed the medal off to one of his cronies, and it disappeared among his coat pockets.

"I've signed your bloody contract, now set me free!" Reginald snapped.

"One moment, please." Lysander strolled into the room. His hair was even more tangled than it had been before and a good amount of Aerilyn's lip paint stained his neck. "I have a some questions for the former Duke. It's about the slave trade."

Chaucer made a disgusted sound. "Slavery? Don't be ridiculous."

"Yes," Reginald said, his eyes hard. "There hasn't been a slave in the Kingdom for three centuries. Everyone knows that."

"The young people taking refuge in my hold would say otherwise," Lysander countered.

Reginald sneered. "Well I'm sorry, but I don't know what you're talking about."

All at once, Kyleigh broke from the shadows. She grabbed the back of Reginald's chair and dragged him across the room, only stopping when she had him against the wardrobe.

"What are you doing?" he said as she walked away. He squirmed against his bonds but couldn't wriggle free. "You swore I'd have my life, Chaucer! You swore!"

"I'm not going to kill you," she said. She stood next to Kael, their shoulders touching. "My friend here is fairly good at sniffing out falsehoods. So I'm going to ask you a question. And if he thinks you're lying ... he's going to throw a knife."

Reginald's jaw locked down. The whites showed around his eyes.

"Tell us about the slave trade."

"I know nothing about any slaves!"

Kael threw a knife. It whistled through the air and thudded into the wardrobe — a hair from the top of Reginald's head. He moaned, and his face shone with sweat.

"Why are you selling the people of the High Seas to Lord Gilderick?"

Reginald licked his lips. His eyes were wild, but still defiant. "I'm not." He shuddered when the next blade landed beside his throat. "I know you won't kill me!" he screamed through gritted teeth. "That whelp is a whisperer — he can't miss!"

Kyleigh inclined her head. "True." She nudged Kael with her elbow. "What does a man with no title need with two ears?"

"You know, I can't think of a reason —"

"Stop!" Reginald cried, just as he was preparing to make his throw. Sweat dripped off his chin and stained the gold threads of his shirt. "I admit it — I was selling slaves to Gilderick."

Chaucer snarled and the other merchants broke out in heated whispers. They glared a hole through Reginald as he stammered on.

"I don't know what he wanted them for, probably to tend his blasted fields. All I know is that he paid me well. The logbook is in my office, in the top drawer of my desk. It has everything recorded: how many males and females I traded, the dates they were traded on, the dates of future trades — it's all there!" he finished. His eyes went back to Chaucer. "So now you know. I've told you everything. I demand that you honor the terms of the contract and set me free!"

After a long, icy silence, Chaucer nodded to two merchants at his side. They untied Reginald's bonds, but kept him held between them.

"Set me free!" he demanded again.

Chaucer's face was unreadable. "The terms of the contract said only that you would be allowed to live out your days in peace — it mentioned nothing about freedom. Take him to the dungeon."

They could hear Reginald's boots scraping the floor the whole way down the hall. He screamed and threatened them with brutal deaths until a heavy door slammed shut, cutting him off mid-rant.

"Let's go find that book," Lysander said quietly, while the merchants were occupied. And they followed him out the door.

****

When they made it up to the Duke's office, one of the merchants was already rummaging through the desk. He pulled out a rough, leather bound book and stuffed it hastily into his coat pocket.

"Now see here," Lysander said as he marched up to him. "If we're going to stop the trade, we're going to have to read —"

"That book is the property of the merchants," Chaucer said from behind them. He pushed past Lysander, took the logbook and planted it inside his own coat.

While they argued about who had the right to read what, Kael watched Kyleigh. She'd discovered Bloodfang's body next to the window. She knelt down in front of him and

436

closed his eyes with her fingertips. Her head was bent, strands of dark hair hid her face.

"No, I'm going to destroy it," Chaucer barked. He was standing chest to chest with Lysander. They looked like a pair of bucks sparring over territory. "We'll hold the vote for high chancellor within the month — and I can't let nasty rumors like slavery affect my bid!"

"Blast your bid!" Lysander snapped back. "These are innocent people we're talking about, *our* people!"

Chaucer snorted. "Your people are murderers and thieves. Mine are the masons of society — and I'll not risk their lives to attack the Endless Plains. You *do* know that's what it would take, don't you? A full-fledged war with Gilderick and his army of giants. No," he held up a firm hand, "I'll not risk it. The seas have only just got the wind back in her sails. We haven't the army to face Gilderick, not while we're nearly rotted out the bottoms, ourselves." He held out his hand. "Your services are no longer required, Captain. Take your rats back to their nest."

Lysander seemed on the verge of cracking him across the face. But at the last moment, he relented. With a heavy sigh, he took Chaucer's hand. "So that's it, then?"

"Most definitely. If I see your face again, I'll be sure and put a dagger through it."

"I trust you'll give me two days peace?"

Chaucer smirked. "One. And that's entirely too generous."

He gestured for his men to leave the room and shooed Lysander out behind them. Kael brought up the rear. Chaucer stopped in the doorway and glared over his shoulder at Kyleigh, who was still crouched in front of Bloodfang.

"What's she doing?" he said with narrowed eyes.

At this point, Kael was so fed up with Chaucer that he could no longer control himself. He shoved him hard in the back and sent him stumbling out into the hallway. Then he slammed the door, barring it with crossed arms.

"Just what do you think you're —?"

"Move," Kael snapped.

437

Chaucer blinked, then frowned. In the end, he seemed to think better of challenging a whisperer. He turned and stomped down the hall instead, swearing under his breath at every step.

Kael waited until he was gone before he opened the door. The window was shattered — Kyleigh and Bloodfang were gone. He closed the door quietly and left to rejoin the pirates.

****

"You done it, lad!" Morris was waiting for him at the helm. The minute Kael got within range, he slapped him across the back. His arm was so covered in goo that it stuck to his shirt. "Sorry about that," he said as he pulled free. "That blasted mage took us all for a trip."

"At least I managed to get it fanned back," Jake muttered. He nodded to the west, where the fog was slowly drifting out to sea.

"What will happen when it strikes land?" Kael wondered.

Morris shrugged. "There isn't a thing in the Westlands but monsters and barren ground. That's where the Kings used to send the worst villains in the realm. They'd pack them up and ship them off with a doomed captain and his crew."

Kael waited until Morris went to tend to other things before he slipped the remnants of Bartimus's impetus to Jake.

"What's — oh." He turned the gold disk over in his hand, his eyes narrowed. "You killed him, then?"

"Yes."

"Good. I was hoping he wouldn't manage to crawl away." He slipped the disk into his pocket and held out his hand. "Thank you. I don't know how I'll ever repay your kindness."

"It was a gift," Kael said, which made Jake smile.

Not surprisingly, Jonathan managed to pilfer several bottles of wine from the ballroom. He drank from one as if it was a flask. "Slayer of witches, toppler of thrones," he said as he stumbled into Kael. "Here, have a nip of His Former Dukeness's finest wine!" And proceeded to pour it down his collar.

Every pirate aboard *Anchorgloam* stepped up to congratulate him. They shook his hands and ruffled his hair, offered him tankards of grog and plates of whatever delicacies they'd nicked from the ball. By the time he made it through the crowd, his ears were rattling from all the good-natured pats on the back.

Lysander and Aerilyn stood at the front of the ship, dancing to no music whatsoever. Her hair was loose and her face paint was divided between them in equal smears.

When she saw Kael, she threw her arms about his neck. "You were brilliant!" she said into his hair. "I don't know what I would've done, had the pair of you not arrived when you did. Reginald was getting very pushy," she added, wrinkling her nose.

"Yes, and what's happened to our favorite halfdragon?" Lysander said, craning his neck above the revelers. "Has she run off?" When he caught Kael's nod, his face softened. "Don't worry your head over it — to leave is in her nature. But she always comes back."

He didn't want to talk about Kyleigh. The wound in his chest was still too fresh. He wanted to shove his worry aside and find something else to occupy him. "What will we do now?"

Lysander took Aerilyn back in his arms and smiled hard. "That's for you to decide, Wright. You've done me — and all the people of the seas — a great service. My ship is at your command."

Kael was impatient to get back to his quest. He wanted to see Amos rescued and his village avenged. But the thing Geist said haunted him. It plagued the back of his mind and made him worry.

What if his army wasn't big enough to face Titus? What if he marched off right away and led the pirates straight to their deaths? As much as his heart ached for home, he couldn't risk their lives — not when there was a large chance they might not succeed.

He decided quickly. "If we're going to storm the mountains, I think we'll need more swords."

Lysander raised an eyebrow. "I see. And where do you plan to find them?"

"I hear the giants are good to have in a fight."

Lysander smiled in relief, then threw his head back and laughed. "Aye, I've heard that, too. So it's off to the Endless Plains. And I suppose you have a plan of attack?"

That was the frustrating part. "I wish we had that logbook. It'd make things a great deal easier."

Lysander grinned mischievously and reached inside his vest. "You mean *this*?"

Kael caught the book he threw at him and could scarcely hide his astonishment. "When —?"

"Ah, not when — *how*," Lysander cut in. "A thief doesn't need time, remember? Only opportunity. And I'll bet Chaucer's wishing he would have done up his buttons, right about now. The nerve of that blighter," he said darkly. "*Chancellor* Chaucer — can you imagine? I'll have to make sure the votes get tampered with."

"But won't he follow us and try to take it back?"

Lysander snorted. "He'll have a rough time catching us without his sails."

That's when Kael looked up and noticed *Anchorgloam* was outfitted with new billowing blue sails, stamped with the emblem of the High Seas. Aerilyn gasped and smacked Lysander in the shoulder.

"What? Mine were all gooey," he said.

She crossed her arms and tried to look severe. "You're a bad man, do you know that? An absolute villain."

He silenced her accusations with a kiss.

440

Chapter 39
Until the Last Sun Rises

The evening sun was falling, washing Gravy Bay in orange light. It fell behind the cliffs and bled out onto the sea. *Anchorgloam* was a toy boat in the distance — a shadow bobbing gently on the waves. Kael watched her rock, watched the gulls circling hopefully about her sails and for a moment, felt at peace.

And then a great head of wiry hair blocked his view. "Is it sunset, yet?" the man the hair belonged to said. And the planks of the dock creaked as he stood on his tiptoes to see over the woman in front of him.

Kael clenched his fists tightly as more bodies shifted to look at the sun. He tried not to think about the fact that there were naught but a few planks between his boots and the ocean — or how the sheer number of people packed onto the docks must be buckling them.

But he thought he could hear the wood grunting under their weight.

He turned back around and nearly got clipped by Lysander — who was pacing nervously in the space between Kael and Thelred.

He wore a clean white shirt and his customary tanned breeches. His hands twisted behind his back and Thelred watched him carefully — as if he might fling himself into the ocean the first chance he got.

"How much longer?" Lysander snapped, and this time it was Thelred who replied patiently:

"Hardly another minute."

"Good. I don't think I could wait much longer." He reached up to fuss at his collar, but Thelred grabbed his wrist

441

and gave him a stern look. "You're right — I shouldn't get all wrinkly."

A bell rang out across the harbor, and it might as well have been an arrow that found its painful mark: Lysander leapt back into position so zealously that he nearly fell off the dock. Thelred had to pull him back over the edge by his shirt, wrinkling it fantastically in the process.

"The lady arrives!" a man at the back of the crowd called out, and the docks groaned as they all stood on tiptoes.

A long procession lined either side of the road, waiting to be the first to greet Aerilyn. She walked among them, dressed in a beautiful blue, flowing gown that Uncle Martin had especially made for the occasion. She wore no paint, but her face burned with a glow Kael had never seen before. She caught sight of Lysander — standing tangle-haired and disheveled at the end of the docks — and her smile warmed them all.

For once, Kael was glad that Lysander had been right: Kyleigh *did* return, and not an hour too soon.

Now she walked beside Aerilyn, their arms looped together. She smiled at the crowd and nodded in thanks to their well-wishing, but never once stopped talking to Aerilyn — who looked closer to fainting with every step.

They reached the foot of the docks and Kael realized, in one heart-stopping moment, that all of Aerilyn's begging had finally paid off: Kyleigh was wearing a dress.

It was the same ridiculous, frilly gown she'd once climbed a tree to get away from. And Kael couldn't help but notice how completely *un*-ridiculous it looked on her. The emerald skirts flowed down and brushed the tops of her slippers with every graceful step; the gold-trimmed waist held her figure like a frame held a painting — capturing, drawing the eye, and at the same time taking nothing away from the wonder. The sunlight struck the waves of her hair and her eyes ignited ... and Kael very nearly stopped breathing.

He thought he could've gone on staring for ages, if the sight of her didn't make him so miserable.

When Aerilyn finally let go of Kyleigh, it was to take Lysander's hand. The two of them looked each other over, laughed and whispered nervously until Uncle Martin shouted: "Oh, get on with it!"

This brought a roar of laughter and loud agreement from the other onlookers.

"All right, *fine*," Lysander said, waving his arm at them. Then he turned to Aerilyn and began the vow of pirate marriage. "Will you sail with me through the storms, hold my hand in the gales? Will you stand by my side in battle? Will you take me as your love?"

She took a deep breath, and said with a smile the words she'd been fighting to memorize for days on end. "I'll sail with you through the storms, cleave to you in gales. In battle, you will be my cry. Though the weather may change, my heart will never wane. Yes, I'll take you as my love."

The last word was hardly out of her mouth before Lysander scooped her up and kissed her — much to the thrill of the pirates.

"Enough of that," Uncle Martin hollered, using his cane to wedge them apart. "You've got the rest of your lives to be foolish. Let's get through with the ceremony and on to the party!"

He shoved Thelred towards the nearest rowboat. And while he undid the ties, Aerilyn bid them all farewell. She hugged Jake tightly, punched Jonathan in the arm for whatever rudeness he whispered in her ear, and then fell into Kael. "It feels strange to be leaving you all here," she said, her chin resting on his shoulder. "After all the adventures we've had —"

"It's only a short journey," he reminded her, before she could work herself up into tears. "We'll be right here on shore."

"And you won't leave me?"

"Of course not. You know I can't swim."

She laughed.

Uncle Martin hugged Aerilyn once, tightly, and though he didn't cry he certainly *harrumphed* and blinked an awful lot. Then Kyleigh kissed her on the cheek and helped her into the boat.

"Row quickly," Lysander barked.

"Aye, Captain," Thelred muttered as he took her out to sea. *Anchorgloam* waited in the distance, perched in the middle of the Bay. They propped their hands over their eyes and watched as Thelred helped her climb aboard. When she was safely on deck, he made his way back towards the docks.

"Steady, lad," Uncle Martin said as Lysander resumed his pacing.

"He's taking too blasted long."

"He's rowing as fast as he can. I smell the sweat coming off him from here. Just take a deep breath and —"

But Lysander must have been tired of waiting, because he charged past Uncle Martin, leapt off the docks and into the sea. He popped up a few moments later — having swum out of the reach of Uncle Martin's cane.

The docks groaned again as a hundred bodies leaned forward to watch him paddle away. He swam past Thelred — who tried, and failed, to wrangle him into the boat with an oar — and clambered onto *Anchorgloam* by her rigging. He turned and raised a fist at the crowd, just a small figurine in the distance. The pirates cheered as he disappeared over the railings.

"That girl is going to make him bake on deck till he dries," Uncle Martin muttered as he took Kyleigh's arm.

"I very seriously doubt that," she said with a smile.

****

The wedding party stretched from one end of the village to the other. Lanterns hung from every house and shop, filling the streets with merry light. Tables piled high with food sat on all corners — every man, woman and child could have as much as they wished. And of course, the grog flowed freely.

Uncle Martin even had Jake enchant the fountain in the middle of town. Now the twisting serpents spat red wine into the giant basin instead of water. The wine smelled good, but anyone who drank it could expect his skin to turn an alarming shade of purple — and Jake wasn't sure if the color was permanent.

But that didn't stop Jonathan from filling several goblets to the brim and passing them out to unsuspecting guests. It wasn't long before an army of angry purple pirates marched through the revelry with Jonathan hoisted high above them, and tossed him straight into the fountain.

A small group of musicians gathered together in the square. They played on a matched set of very fine, gold-crusted instruments that looked suspiciously like the ones from the Duke's ball.

Kael found a quiet porch to sit under at the edge of the party, and leaned his back against the wall of a fletcher's shop. Though he tried to smile and nod to everyone who greeted him, the plate of food in his lap sat uneaten; the goblet beside him went untouched. He watched the villagers dance without really seeing them. The music never quite reached his ears.

"Won't you dance with me?"

It wasn't so much the question as the voice that carried it — she seemed to be the only one who could give the world around him any life. He looked up and felt his stomach twist when he saw she was still wearing that emerald-green dress. He figured she would have ripped it off by now. Why was she still wearing it?

"I'm not feeling well," he muttered, after he remembered that she'd asked him a question. "What are you doing? You're going to get your skirts filthy."

"They'll wash," she said as she sat beside him.

They watched the party in silence. The space between them felt like a chasm to Kael — a chasm ringed in daggers with only a very narrow safe space down the middle. He felt as if any word he might have said would be the wrong one, and that one wrong word would send him scraping down the wall of daggers for all eternity. So as much as he wanted to speak, he didn't.

Occasionally, the silence would be broken by a man who would step up to Kyleigh and very nervously ask her for a dance. Her answer was always the same: she was flattered, but still exhausted from her journey. Surely he understood.

"You ought to dance with someone," Kael said as the last defeated man walked away.

"I know I ought to, but I can't. You so impressed me that I think any other partner would be a disappointment." She brushed the hair out of her eyes. Free from the bonds of her customary pony's tail, it hung in waves across her shoulders. When she ran her fingers through it, he thought he smelled roses.

But he bristled against her words. "Well, we all have to be disappointed about something. That's the pattern of life."

She was quiet for a moment. "Do you really believe that?"

"Of course I do. There are some things we can't change." He felt his anger rising, felt the hopelessness in his chest grip his heart — and the dark thoughts he'd fought so hard to keep locked up shoved their way out through his words. "A weak man has to get used to being weak, because he'll never be strong. Just like an ugly man has to get used to being ugly, and a poor man to being poor."

"Surely it's not all so immovable —"

"But it is, Kyleigh! As much as we may want to change our lot, we can't. Fate's rolled the die and stuck us with something, and now it's our burden to carry. It's like the ocean and the sky," he muttered, remembering what Lysander had said before. "A fool may think they're close, but any wise man knows they are worlds apart."

She stared at the cobblestone. "Wisdom is your burden, not mine."

"No, *this* is my burden." He thrust his hand at the revelers, at all the people who were dancing and eating and drinking entirely too much grog. She would understand the weight on his shoulders, and she would assume it was the responsibility that dragged him down and under. He thought she would never guess what truly haunted him.

446

But he was wrong.

"You're not alone, you know. You'll always have me." And their eyes met for one searing moment before he looked away.

"No, I won't. I can't drag you into this and ask you to risk your life —"

"You never have to ask —"

"I won't!" he snapped, so loudly that it made her jump. "Don't you understand? I want to be alone." He saw the hurt on her face, and for a fleeting moment, he wished he had the courage to say what his heart begged him to. But even as the words pressed against his lips, he knew his hope was doomed. And so he said nothing.

He stood, because he thought if he sat beside her for another moment he might crumble to the ground. He hiked back to the mansion, ignoring the cries of his companions to come back and join the party. His legs shook under the weight of his heart, and they simply weren't strong enough for dancing.

****

In the morning, he was sorry. He wished he wouldn't have let his anger get the best of him. By night, his words seemed true. But by the dawn of day, he knew they were false. He couldn't go on without Kyleigh: she was the light that kept the darkness away. Without her, he didn't know if he would have the strength to press on. He'd rather let the ache in his heart burn him alive than find himself lost in a world without any light.

And so he had every intention of apologizing to her over breakfast.

When he arrived in the dining room, Jonathan and Uncle Martin were already there. They had dark circles under their eyes and looked as if every bite they took was agony. Kael was just glad to see that Jonathan was no longer purple.

"I should have never let you convince me to ride that goat," Uncle Martin groaned. Someone dropped a pot in the kitchen, and the noise made him wince. "Good Gravy, that beast must've crawled out of the bowels of the under-realm."

"Speak for yourself." Jonathan switched the raw chunk of meat he held from one eye to the other. "I had no idea those things could kick with both feet at once."

Uncle Martin sat up straight. "Did I kiss a mermaid last night?"

"No, you're thinking of the octopus statue outside of Morris's place."

"Ah, right. Nice chap — but he *did* have wandering tentacles."

Their laughter very quickly fizzled into moans. When Jonathan left to be sick, Uncle Martin spotted Kael. "Hello there, lad! I didn't expect to see you this morning. I figured she would have taken you with her."

"Who?" Kael said as he sat.

"The Dragongirl, of course! Who else?"

His heart actually stopped beating. "Wait — what do you mean? Where's she gone?"

"Calm down, now. Everyone knows she does this from time to time. She's not in any danger —"

"Where is she?"

The hard edge in his voice wiped the smile off of Uncle Martin's face. "I'm sorry, lad, I thought you knew she'd gone. I'm not sure where to, but she left this note for Lysander —"

Kael snatched the parchment out of his hand and nearly ripped it in his rush to get it open. Neat handwriting covered a paltry fourth of the page.

Captain Lysander,

I'm writing to let you know that I'm carrying our cause to new lands. If we plan to take the fight to Titus, we'll need all the help we can get. There are a few rumors I'd like to follow. I hope they'll bring us the numbers we need.

Give my love to our companions,

Kyleigh

- Also, you should know that I've stolen the battlemage. So sorry for that.

He read her note three times before he crumpled it and hurled it across the room. So she'd write to Lysander, she'd take Jake with her, but she couldn't be bothered to tell him goodbye?

"I'm sorry —"

"Don't be." Kael cut Uncle Martin short because he didn't want to hear it. He didn't care if he was being rude. "I'm not hurt by it. She has her task, and I have mine." He grabbed a plate of food off the table and headed for the door.

"Where are you going?"

"To work," Kael said bluntly. "If we're going to take on Gilderick, we're going to need a plan."

Uncle Martin tipped his glass. "Absolutely. Our fate is in your hands, Sir Wright!"

Kael was well aware of that. And yet all he could think about as he marched purposefully down the hall, was that Lord Gilderick had better be prepared to do battle. He'd better shore up his walls and sharpen his swords — because he would get no mercy, come spring.

There was simply no room left in Kael's heart for it.

****

Shamus thought the repairs were coming along nicely. Already, the outer wall of Wendelgrimm was rebuilt and the great hall restored. There was still a good deal of work to be done before it could be deemed livable, but he thought he could actually see daylight.

About a month ago, ships began pouring into Copperdock for repairs — sailing in from every end of the High Seas. They hobbled up to the docks, carrying in all manner of goods, and of course — all manner of rumors. Shamus had heard about a dozen different versions of how it

449

was the Duke came to lose his throne, and none of them came close to the truth. But he supposed it was probably for the best.

Since the treasures of Wendelgrimm left them with a fair amount of gold, Shamus had begun trading repairs for building materials, instead. There was one fellow from the desert who thought he might be able to procure new glass for the windows, but Shamus was far from convinced.

"I know they got molds for the smaller windows, but what I want to know is: have they got a mold for *that*?"

He pointed to the highest tower of the castle, the one that teetered so badly he'd had the men build scaffolding around it just to keep it from tipping over. Below the roof was a large window with eight sides. The little glass left in it hung on in jagged pieces.

The captain narrowed his eyes at it. "Well, it'll certainly have to be replaced."

"I know that, Captain. Have you got the glass to fix it?"

"I meant the tower." When Shamus didn't laugh, he cleared his throat. "It's difficult to get special items like this without paying the Baron's craftsmen an exorbitant fee to make them. But I think I can find you something for, say, twenty-five percent off my repairs?"

"Ten," Shamus countered. "And another five once you've got it."

"Deal."

With the captain taken care of, he turned his attention to the men working on the front gates. They'd managed to trade for a good bit of hard oak from the Grandforest. With any luck, they'd have the new doors up by week's end.

"Seal her tight, lads. We don't want the rain to abuse her too badly," he said, and the men raised their hammers to show that they'd heard.

He was helping unload a fresh shipment of stone when the sound of hurried footsteps made him turn. A young lad sprinted towards the castle, kicking dirt up behind him. When he got within shouting distance, he gasped: "It's — the Dragongirl!"

Shamus couldn't stop himself from grinning. He made sure the lad got a cup of cool water before he jogged down the path. It only took a handful of days to find his legs, but he still hadn't quite gotten used to the feeling of having them beneath him. He didn't know if he would ever get used to it, but he knew one thing for certain: he'd never take the ache of a hard day's work for granted again.

He met Kyleigh about halfway down. She had that white sword at her hip and she looked well enough. He was surprised to see Jake following behind her.

"I thought you might be making your way back to us," Shamus said as he took her hand. "And to what do we owe this great honor?"

She smiled, and he saw it: the heaviness in those strange eyes of hers, the almost certain sadness hidden behind her grin. It was a haunting look he knew all too well.

"I thought we might stay with you for the winter. Though it's really too hot to call it winter, isn't it?" She propped her hands on her hips, squinting up at the sun. "The truth is that I've got some mischief to prepare for — and Jake thought he might be useful."

Shamus clapped him on the shoulder, and thought he might have bruised his palms on Jake's bones. "Sure you can. We've got a lot of work going on at the top of the hill. The lads might need a little magic to make the building easier."

"All right, I can do that," Jake said. And he walked on ahead of them.

Shamus followed next to Kyleigh at a much slower pace. She still moved gracefully, yet she dragged her heels — as if all the sunshine had been soaked right out of her sky. He knew that walk.

When Jake was out of earshot, he bent his head and whispered: "He's a nice lad, don't get me wrong. But he's not the one I thought you'd be bringing back with you."

She sighed heavily. "How long have you known?"

"Since the day I saw you carrying him down from Wendelgrimm. He was out cold, and you were so fussed over him I thought we might get our arms lopped off if we tried to take him from you."

She smiled slightly. "You very well might have."

They walked the rest of the way in silence. Then at the top of the hill, she gasped. "It looks so different," she said, her eyes wandering the length of the castle. "Good to see you've got those nasty vines taken care of."

Shamus chuckled. "Aye. When the Witch died, they shriveled up. After that, it was just a matter of setting the tinder and striking the flint." He watched her stare for a moment more. "You see the possibility, don't you?"

She nodded. "I imagine it was a very grand place, once."

"Aye, that it was. And it will be again."

"Though it seems like the stones might be worth more than the actual structure, in places." She glanced at the teetering tower. "Why are you bothering to fix it?"

Shamus tried to bring it up casually. "Well, about a month ago, a fellow sailed in and said he was running his own trade. I told him that was illegal, and he said no it weren't because the Duke had been sacked. You hear anything about that?"

She smirked. "I hear lots of things, Shamus. Most of it isn't true."

"Hmm. Well this certainly is, because now I've got all sorts of captains from different trades packing up my harbor. They've snagged whatever ships the Duke's army left behind and brought them here for work. It seems like the old ways are coming back — people are organizing, towns are appointing their lords and ladies. I hear they've even got a new high chancellor. What was his name again?"

"Colderoy." She seemed to be fighting back laughter as she said it. "Apparently, it was quite the upset. Not a soul will admit to voting for him."

"I'll bet not," Shamus muttered. He squared his shoulders at her and took a deep breath. "All this talk of the towns picking back up has got me thinking: Copperdock used to have a noble family —"

"Of whisperers. Yes, I've heard."

"Well," Shamus put a hand on her shoulder, "it's got me thinking that we could use a lady here in Copperdock."

It took her a moment to catch the look on his face. But when she did, she took an involuntary step backwards. "I don't think —"

"Good, don't think — just say you'll do it. We're real easy people, we mostly govern ourselves. It'd just be nice to have an official protector." He lowered his face to hers. "So will you stay here with us? Be our lady?"

She seemed resigned to her fate. "What do I get for it?"

"All of this," he said, with a sweeping gesture at Wendelgrimm.

She laughed.

"And I'll even let you give it a new name."

"I'm not very good at naming things."

"You're a dragon, aren't you?" He spread his arms wide. "And this is your roost. So why don't you call it —"

"Roost," she said, grinning to either ear. "Castle Roost. It's brilliant."

They both laughed. But in the end, the name stuck. As they walked around and he showed her all the work to be done, that's how they referred to things. Roost had mold growing on her ceilings; Roost had a colony of mice living in her cellars; Roost needed more support on the upper levels, or she was likely to cave in. And the more they talked about it, the more Shamus came to like it.

They watched Jake use a spell to cut lengths of wood into planks. He could get the same number done in half the time of an axe. The men had to run to keep his workspace full of logs. Shamus couldn't be sure — it was hard to tell with magefolk — but he thought Jake looked pretty happy.

"I've got a question for you," he said, and Kyleigh raised her eyebrows. "What sort of mischief are we going to be getting ourselves into, come spring?"

"The main party's heading to the plains. I know," she said when Shamus whistled, "it'll be no stroll in the woods. As for me … well, I was thinking I'd search somewhere a little hotter."

"And drier, and exceptionally sandy? Yeah, I think I know the place you're talking about," Shamus said, returning her smirk. "And while I don't fancy the desert, I certainly don't envy the poor fellows treading on Gilderick's soil. There're some pretty salty rumors wafting up from that place. I hope they know what they're getting into."

She wrinkled her nose. "I doubt it. But they're in good hands."

He watched her stare vacantly at Roost: looking, but not really seeing. There was no end to the emptiness behind her eyes. He couldn't stand it any longer: he had to ask. "Will we ever see young Master Kael again?"

Her shoulders rose and fell. "That's entirely up to him."

"Haven't you got a choice?"

"No, I haven't." Her eyes hardened, she seemed to be fighting against a great swell of emotion. "It's a strange feeling … and here I thought I'd been wounded in every possible way. I'm not sure how to go on. How *does* one go on?" She turned to Shamus, the steel in her eyes replaced by hurt. "How can anybody stand it?"

Poor lass. Shamus put a hand on her shoulder, squeezed until his fingers hurt and doubted if she ever felt a thing. "You can't stand it," he said, and tried to say it gently. "It bites us all, Lady Dragon — no matter how thick the armor. And you can't heal it, not really. You just got to bury it under your work and let time do the rest."

She smiled, then, though it was a sad smile. She crossed her arms and looked out at the sea, and still smiling, she said: "Well, time is something I've got plenty of. I suppose I'll just wait for him, then. And I'll wait forever … until the last sun rises."

Made in the USA
Lexington, KY
13 January 2015